I live in the Jungle, in the twenty-block rectangle of Township 25 that recognizes me as its authority figure. They call me by my digger name, Bander Snatch. Outsiders call me a Jungle Lord.

So begins a young man's odyssey into time, space and the infinite reaches of the human psyche, set in a future far closer than we may know.

BANDER SNATCH

BANDER SNATCH

By

KEVIN O'DONNELL, JR.

BANDER SNATCH
A Bantam Book / June 1979

ISBN 0-553-12620-2

Published simultaneously in the United States and Canada

Bantam Books are published by Bantam Books, Inc. Its trade-
mark, consisting of the words "Bantam Books" and the por-
trayal of a bantam, is Registered in U.S. Patent and Trademark
Office and in other countries. Marca Registrada. Bantam
Books, Inc., 666 Fifth Avenue, New York, New York 10019.

PRINTED IN THE UNITED STATES OF AMERICA

To Kim, who supported me in every way while I wrote this, and who patiently read it again and again until it was right, I dedicate this book with gratitude, and with all my love.

ACKNOWLEDGEMENTS

I'd like to thank Deborah Atherton, L. Kathryn Jackson, Al Sirois, and Bob White. The comments they made and the insights they offered helped this be a better book.

BANDER
SNATCH

BOOK ONE

1

An artificial peninsula juts into Lake Erie. A 100-square-kilometer spit of landfill that steams in summer and ices over in winter, it is drab and crowded all year round. In the least run-down of its 25,000 three-story apartment buildings live some one and a half million people who, for whatever reason, haven't quite figured out how to survive in a free enterprise society.

To the government, aka Big Unk, this is the Federal Dependents' Resettlement Area Number Three, and its residents are those who most need society's compassion.

To the wealthy, industrious citizens of Ashtabula and the other northeast Ohio ho-coms, this is the Jungle. According to these kindly folk, who are still flamed off that they lost ten kilometers of swampfront 130 years ago, the Jungle is full of murderers, robbers, welfare wasters, arsonists, sanders, and other assorted losers. Their road maps portray nothing north of Boulevard A, FDRA#3's southern boundary. They content themselves with the legend that "Here There Be Monsters."

Many occupants of FDRA#3 resent that, and maintain that the Jungle is limited to Townships 19, 20, 24, and 25—the sixteen square kilometers in the southeast corner that were bombed, burned, and otherwise broken during the Food Riots of 2128. According to them, most people in Fedra Three are very nice sorts who simply have problems earning a living, while it's the 150,000 in the Jungle who are the psychopathic felons who give poverty a bad name.

They might be right.

I live down there, in the twenty-block rectangle of Township 25 that recognizes me as its authority figure. They call me by my digger name, Bander Snatch. Outsiders call me a Jungle Lord. Among other things.

One of them, an HEW Necessities Distribution Center Director by the name of Jenkins, was going to call me an astonishing variety of other, mostly vulgar things. He'd have reason to. I was about to have him coughed.

Jenkins had directed the Center in Township 25 for nearly thirty years, and had been trying to magic our food for almost as long, often successfully. His first gimmick had been to insist that each individual collect his own rations in person, on his assigned ration day, regardless of how old, sick, or unavailable he was. That worked well for the good director, up until 2124, because some people just never got around to collecting their due. While they did without, the cans and bags and sacks cluttered the warehouse, driving Jenkins into a mania of neatening. He knew he couldn't leave HEW property in a mess, so he didn't. He loaded all leftovers onto a truck, and disposed of them.

When the rations were generous, nobody went hungry. Irritating as it was to have to share with somebody who hadn't picked up his own food, hell, what were friends for? But then, six years ago, Big Unk halved the rations.

As it turned out, Jenkins' truck had been heading for the Ashtabula market web, which was so avid for low-priced groceries that it would overlook their source. After paying off the clerks who'd abetted or ignored him, he'd pocketed the rest. He'd been well on his way to an L5 retirement bubble.

That did not please us, so we organized a system that got everybody to the warehouse on the designated day. I mean *everybody*. Clever-handed kids converted grocery store carts into strollers, wheelchairs, pallet beds, what-have-you. From sunrise to sundown, the sidewalks'd rumble with the rasp of composition wheels; the streets'd swarm with people going to and fro. The atmosphere was almost festive. And damned if everybody didn't eat . . . for about three years.

Jenkins' expensive habits apparently began to diminish his old-age fund. Starting in 2127, he slowly, warily, cut back on the allotments—a distributor of flour to 75,000 people can amass more than a little by subtracting an ounce from each five-pound ration.

All too soon, his truck was groaning under its old accustomed loads, and we were wondering why that gnawing had returned to our bellies. We accused him of shorting us, of course, but that's an accusation you always make, without thought and without malice. It's almost a form of humor.

And he denied it with weary detachment. He told us he was just following orders, and that we could check with HEW if we didn't believe him.

Ever call Big Unk on the viphone and ask for the facts about something?

I have visions of entire government office buildings staffed with series of secretaries, each series devoted to fast-stepping one caller into oblivion. "Yes, sir," says the first, while she winks to the second, who nudges the third to wake up the fourth. "Let me transfer you to the appropriate department," she says, and her fingers dance on the buttons. One after another, until the last loosens your grip and shakes you off the line. Then they grin at each other, and wait for the next sucker.

We couldn't find the truth, but the tongues didn't care. They wagged all over that chunk of Fedra Three: not accurately, but very, very quickly.

Crowds gathered. Tempers flared. Within hours, the Food Riots were on. The frogs (out of leapfrogs out of LEAP'ers out of Law Enforcement Agency Personnel; in their typically tangled way, the bureaucrats made LEA part of the Ohio State Police) fell back before the flames, abandoning control of Township 25. 24, 19, and 20 followed in rapid succession. The firemen gave up, too; they drove off in what was left of their equipment and haven't come back since. Neither have the leapers.

The next morning, elements of the Fifth Army rolled in. Their commander, Major George Patton Dourscheid, was cagy enough to demand that he be given the HEW ration schedules, and then to invite every community "leader" to talk with him. I was a semi-nobody—fifth in command of my particular street gang—but I took him up on his offer, and got all the facts I wanted. Jenkins was guilty as hell.

While the riot turned into a firefight, I bargained with Dourscheid. Pointing out that he was confronted by four rival gangs, in addition to ten or twenty thousand unaffiliated gasheads who got their kicks from torching buildings and blowing away other gasheads, I guaranteed to neutralize one gang and as much territory as possible:

If he would arm my Zulus. (That, by the way, is a generic term for a gun-wielding ganger; its etymology is

5

hazy, but it has been applied panracially since Fedra Three was completed in 2022.)

If he would overlook my coughing three or four influential obstacles.

If he would double-goddam warranty that we got our food, or Jenkins if we didn't.

He hemmed long enough to flame off a sewing machine, hawed a little on the side, and finally agreed.

My Zulus got their assault rifles that afternoon, and by nightfall we held all of Township 25. Of the 1,252 buildings in it, we managed to protect 713. The rest had already burned.

The four people who used to give me orders objected to my coup. Three got pine coffins, and I became Jungle Lord. (The fourth, Catkiller, escaped to strike a similar deal with Dourscheid, who was growing desperate as his casualty list lengthened. Catkiller counterattacked that night, after my Zulus had endured nine hours of constant fire, and by morning we had lost seventy-six of the Township's hundred blocks. We dug in, in the twenty I still hold. The four blocks comprising the Township Center remain no-man's land.)

We got our food, from 2128 to the present, under an agreement which specified that the Fifth Army would deliver it to the HEW Warehouse in the Township Center, sign it over to Jenkins, and then ignore his outrage when we magicked it. Dourscheid had insisted that he couldn't present it to us directly because of red tape, but that he had no obligation to interfere in the distribution program. If representatives of the impact community chose to assume the onerous burden of necessities' distribution, why, he and all his men would testify that they reflected prevailing community sentiment.

Love the way that man's face stays so rushmore when he slings around his bureaucratese . . . "prevailing community sentiment" means forty Zulus with M-33's . . . though I can talk the same way (I use six or eight different kinds of speech every day, depending on who's listening to me), I just can't take myself that seriously. . . .

But he keeps his word. That morning, after tipping me off, he led a thirty-truck convoy to the HEW NDC. We were entering the warehouse to collect it when a shot rang out, sending seven of us diving to the dusty, oil-spotted cement floor. A determined little clerk had barricaded himself behind his desk, apparently to deny us the shipment. I felt like a damn fool lying there, and hearing somebody laugh didn't improve my mood. Slow Squeeze recouped some dignity for us—his first shot broke the comperkid's wrist—but too many of the HEW people had seen us lose face.

They can't think of me as a buffoonish ganger. I can't stop them from realizing that I'm human, but damned if I'll let them think I'm humane. I can't afford to. Success depends on convincing them that if they cross me, they die. I'm an interface between Big Unk and the man on the street, and the only lubricant that keeps me from being torn apart by conflicting forces is fear.

So while Ralphie was bandaging the clerk with a strip torn from the guy's shirt, I sent No-nose, my oldest friend and most trusted aide, to find out what had happened. Then I strolled off a bit, perched on a desk, and rested my feet on an overturned wastebasket. Scattered all around it were crumpled sheets of memo paper covered with three-digit numbers; comping randoms—betting on which random number a computer will generate next—passes time almost as well as tic-tac-toe.

No-nose returned in about two minutes. A scowl on his ebony face, he said, "Jenkins's dealing with Catkiller, Ban. He told that comperkid to cough us."

God only knows why. I don't think that skinny little fellow had ever fired a gun before his one, startling flash of almost-glory.

"Yeah," I sighed. I didn't like any of the immediate futures, but I had to settle on one of them quickly. A Jungle Lord has to make snap judgments—and correct ones—because time is one luxury he can't command. He can't postpone his decisions; that just backs up all the rest. He passes his days in a haze of insufficiency: not enough time, not enough data, not enough assistance. The price he pays for being on top is that he cartwheels through his life, never stopping long enough to grasp the totality of anything . . . or anyone.

So I sighed again, shook my head, and told No-nose: "Take Jenkins to the burned-out building; it's got a nice wall. I'll be along in a minute or two."

Over my shoulder came a strong, familiar voice: "Why the wall, Bander Snatch?"

I used my lazy pivot to redefine a relationship. It told my questioner that he'd been allowed to make his stealthy approach because I didn't fear him. It let him know that I was turning because *I* wanted to look at him, not because *he* wanted me to. I didn't rush it. It was my Jungle, not his. Down there, people waited for me.

"It's for melodramatic effect, Major. You ought to appreciate that. I need an authority figure, and a firing squad will do nicely. You scan?"

"Melodrama and symbolism, yes." He glared down at me from his 195 centimeters. The wrinkles around his eyes gave extra emphasis to his frown. "Executions, no."

I resent being contradicted by tall people. Maybe it's a hangover from a bullied childhood, but I keep expecting them to say, "I'm righter 'cause I'm bigger." So I waved Dourscheid into the chair that belonged to the warped plastic desk beneath me. "You asking me to ignore those shots?"

"Why not?" Blue eyes steady in a lean, impassive face, he shrugged. "You're the Jungle Lord. You can afford a little magnanimity."

"Toward my own, sure. Toward these pocket-picking bureaucrats? Hah!"

"What have you got to lose?"

"Their respect."

He started to argue, saw what I meant, and subsided. "So what?" he said at last. "How can that hurt you?"

"I'm not sure," I admitted. I like to be honest: it keeps people off balance. "Seems to me, though, that they could do me in a thousand ways . . . if they weren't afraid to."

He nodded thoughtfully, as though my logic's destination were inevitable but undesirable. "I suppose," he said slowly, "that you do have to preserve discipline."

"You're scanning true."

"And I suppose I have no business butting into this."

"Again I say, you scan realfine."

He thumbed his steel helmet backwards, exposing his bare scalp. There was no malice in his voice as he continued, "And I suppose you'd be in a real spot if I told my men to protect Jenkins."

"Hey!" I slid off the desk, and thrust my face into his. His breath smelled of cigars, and of real coffee. "You wouldn't!"

"Why not?" The gambler spun an ace across the table. "It'd save the fool's life, and keep your image intact."

"Uh-uh." Dourscheid was the closest thing I had to a friend from the outside, but I could not let him push me around. His superiors itched to clean out the Jungle, and only his insistence that we were all wild-eyed maniacs was holding them in check. For his stories to be convincing, though, he had to stay just a little bit frustrated with me. "This Jungle is mine. I don't take orders from *nobody*. You guard that guy, we fire. And I would like to point out that you are out-numbered." I bellied up to his brass buttons and hoped that he'd blink first.

Impasse city. Neither of us was going to budge. It'd escalate until the goddam Fifth Army was dropping mortars on Maple and Aster.

Luckily, No-nose tapped me on the shoulder and drew me away. That was okay. You don't lose points if a subordinate's got something urgent.

"Yeah?"

"The clerk—I asked him, were there witnesses?" That desire to get all the facts straight had always been one of No-nose' strengths. He'd be a worthy successor when something happened to me. "He says a couple, maybe three."

"They talk?"

He made a disgusted sound. "Like holo-hosts."

The Jungle Lord in me smiled. It was my bloodthirsty smile, the one that splits my cheeks when I'm planning to put it up somebody really good. "Major?" A hush had fallen over the cavernous room, and my voice echoed hollowly. I wasn't completely satisfied with the decision I'd just made, but since I didn't have hours to weigh the pros and cons . . .

"Yes?"

"Two years ago you promised we'd get Jenkins if he relapsed into light-fingeredness—and now he has—and now I'm calling you to keep your word. But to make it easier on you, we'll give Jenkins a fair trial."

He chewed on that one like it was a cigar butt, then nodded. "Deal." Hoisting himself to his feet, he patted his helmet down to cover his receding hairline. "Got to have some honest jurors, though."

"Oh, we will," I vowed, grinning like a fiend. "We always do."

Out on the cracked cement of the warehouse parking lot, we assembled a jury—six of the major's men and six of mine, none of whom had been fired upon—and then we brought out the witnesses. Jenkins protested so whiningly that we had to stuff a burlap bag into his wide, toothy mouth.

The wounded clerk, a scrawny guy with a big jaw and

9

pop eyes, spoke first. Teeth chattering with fright, he swore that Jenkins had handed him the gun and ordered him to do us. He was new, he said, and didn't know we came by regularly; he lived in the same ho-com as the rest, but he'd never heard anybody mention our system. Several other clerks, two typists, and a maintenance man who'd been going to the john all vouched for his story. The jury huddled for a minute, then broke.

Sergeant O'Rourke, the major's burly point man, spoke for them all. "It's unanimous, sir," he told me, the presiding judge. "Jenkins is guilty of inciting a riot and suborning a felony, to wit, homicide."

"Thank you, gentlemen," I said, wishing for cool marble chambers instead of sun-bleached concrete. "That'll be all, I think."

The knot of Zulus untangled itself and cleared a pathway to Jenkins. I stood above him, nudging his layers of lard with my boot. "Jenkins," I said, loudly enough for those on the loading dock to hear, "you've been found guilty of two felonies, by a jury of men who're too good to be your peers. You got anything to say before I pass sentence?"

At my signal, No-nose knelt and eased the gag out of Jenkins' mouth. A waste of time. Most of what spewed from between his thick lips was incoherent; the rest was obscene.

"All right." No-nose cinched up the burlap again. "I've thought it over, Jenkins. You're a smog-faced bad-ass and you been making magic as long as you been here. Nobody's going to miss you. I sentence you to be executed by firing squad."

The men gave a cheer that was chillingly feral. Jenkins shit his pants. Billie and Pete the Prick caught him up under the armpits and dragged him to the burned-out building. Five stories, originally of reinforced concrete, it was taller than anything else in the vicinity. Its tenants had been Big Unk's boys, who were all paper addicts. They'd stored half of Canada's forests inside. The night of the Food Riots, while my Zulus were guarding apartment houses, some idiot—probably charged into a nervous frenzy by go-gas—had incendiary-grenaded it. Flared like a house of cards. The fire trucks had already vanished. Its flames had lit the Township Center till dawn had relieved them.

Now it was an abandoned shell, with soot marks above the windows like black tongues licking cement lips. The

10

shattering of the solar collectors had saw-toothed the roof-line. Staring at it through half-closed eyes, you could imagine distant mountains against the robin's egg blue of the sky. Up close, though, you couldn't miss the bullet holes.

Jenkins was trying to get away from Billie and Pete the Prick. Tied up though he was, his kicking and jerking gave them a hard time. Billie had to clout him over the ear with the butt of her rifle.

I picked half a dozen cold faces out of the crowd. "Ralphie, Slow Squeeze, you soldier—is it okay, Major? Thanks—Hairless, you with the sharpshooter's ribbon, and Tomtom. Along this line. Do the ready, aim, fire bit. I want those guns to go off at exactly the same time, give the man's widow a break and aim for the chest. All right? Ready. Aim. Fire!"

Just before the gunbursts startled the pigeons off the baking square, Jenkins gave a strangled grunt and a wild flop. Didn't do him any good.

"Okay," I said, walking down the line and patting each shoulder, "you shot good. Major? You take custody of the body?"

"Sure, Bander Snatch." He blew air out through his nose. "What am I supposed to call this one?"

"Say you heard shots as you were about to make your delivery—"

"He signed for it already."

"So much the better. You made it, heard shots, came back to find him dead and the warehouse empty. Besides, you think the frogs'll care? Jenkins was Federal, not State. And none of the HEW people here is going to talk, right?"

They nodded, trying not to look too green around the gills. They'd known their neighbor for what he was, but his execution still upset them. Nova. They'd be less likely to emulate him. At my wave, they filed back into the empty building, to sit at empty desks, and compose empty memos. At least their paychecks were full.

Eight-fifteen already, and the day hadn't even begun. I could tell it was going to be a frantically bad one.

"Hey!" I called over No-nose's aide, a drippy-nosed twelve-year-old who had the invoices clamped to his clipboard. His greenish eyes were shielded by the thick lenses of his glasses; on a level with my own, their anxiety made them seem much closer to the ground. "You done the papers?"

"Yes, sir, it's all figured out." He swiveled the clipboard and offered it to me as though it were gold.

11

I brushed it away. "I trust you, kid. What's your name?"

"Ronnie, sir."

"That your real name?"

Paling at the attention, he nodded.

"Listen, Ronnie, that's a nice name, but you shouldn't ought to use it around here. See, if the frogs look close at us, well, you don't want them to know your real name because they might take away your welfare rights. So get yourself a digger name, huh?"

That's why I'm called Bander Snatch. I'd needed a *nom de guerre* before my guardaddy would let me run with a gang, and I'd picked it out of a book. I'd almost used "Jabberwock," because I didn't want to identify with a secondary character from a minor poem, but the Jabberwock got itself killed, and I'd rather be secondary than dead.

Ronnie's logical mind was so intrigued that it began to supersede his nerves. "But, Bander," he said in his high, squeaky voice, "if they arrest me, I won't be able to collect my benefits anyway."

"Yeah, that's true, *you* won't—but if the leapers only know your digger name, then they can't stop the benefits 'cause those go to your real name. Which means other people can collect on 'em—ever think of that?"

Most kids have, but he hadn't been in the Jungle long. His guardaddy, a sander who'd gotten tired of losing jobs, had drifted in a year earlier, lured by rumors that the dream-deepening beige crystals were cheap and plentiful. Ronnie'd been trying to scan our world since, but it was shockingly different from the secure, homogenous community in which he'd used to live. In a ho-com, everybody's family, because everyone works, plays, and talks alike. After a moment, though, he smiled. "Gee, thanks. What name should I use?"

"Uh-uh. You figure out what you want to be called, then you won't start thinking that you got done." I jerked my thumb at the line of olive-drab trucks. "Now, you want to direct the redistribution of the wealth here?"

His magnified eyes glowed, and his pointy chin bobbed up and down. I told him to climb onto the hood of the major's jeep, then called in my captains.

Eleven people ambled towards me; had I been less confident, or a stranger, I would have cuddled my back to a wall and made sure my safety was off. Most of them were taller than I was; all of them were older. Each moved with the laconic grace of a very wild, very vicious animal. Their

12

eyes never stopped moving. They'd survived as long as they had by seeing—and responding to—the tiniest flicker of threat.

Three of them—the skull-faced No-nose, Ralphie the medic whose long brown hair was tied back so he wouldn't tape it under the sulfa-gauze, and coffee-skinned Marianne, whose voice was almost as deep as her eyes—trusted me. Only one other captain did, and that was Shana, my communications specialist and lover, who was in the Com-Center across the street handling the ebb and flow of information.

Of the rest, some were reserved, like Tomtom and Billie, Amerind and Korean respectively, whose flat bronzed features were not inscrutable, but rather nonverbalized in patterns we couldn't read. And some were wary: Wheels McCafferty, Pete the Prick, and Maxwell, who were sure I'd fuck up, were waiting for their chance. Slow Squeeze, a Chicano, and Dirty Dan, a bewhiskered black, would take orders but pay no respect, and were touchy about race. Finally, Hairless was so universally hostile that I couldn't figure out whether he was my man or Catkiller's. Good with a gun, though. As were all of them.

"All right." Eyes lit on me, then skidded away, like sun-beams on a dusty windowpane. "Ronnie here's gonna handle the paperwork on the food; he'll tell you how much of what to take, and inventory your trucks before you pull out."

I had to break off for a minute. A shuttle from Pad 12, twenty k's offshore of Cleveland, was reaching for the sky above our heads. Its thunder washed across us; in a while there'd be a low, dusty wind. Didn't like the damn things. Bad enough they had to remind us, six times daily, that most of humanity could leave the planet behind like a worn-out campsite, and search for virgin worlds in space, but sooner or later one of those silver cocks was going to turn pervo and rape Fedra Three.

When its full-throated roar had dwindled to cloud chatter, I continued, "Don't give this kid any shit. He's doing the best he can. All right, get to it."

Some of the guarparents in the Jungle aren't too happy about our use of their children: they say childhood should be a time of running and playing, a time when each bounc-ing step shivers with the potential to become a seagull's soar because nothing is on your shoulders to weigh you down.

13

Maybe they're right. But can you have a childhood like that outside of a ho-com? No-nose spent much of his recovering from the trauma of a knife's slick slice; I spent a lot of mine helping him plot his revenge.

Shit, I'm only twenty-two, my childhood wasn't that long ago. What I remember most vividly is the running—not happy games of tag, nor showboat chasing of fly balls, nor backwards pumping coverage of wide receivers—not for me. I ran to stay free. My first twelve years were steady darts through sidewalk swarms, behind me heavy, pounding feet: shopkeepers, leapers, big brothers, rival gangs . . . at times it seemed like everybody in the world was chasing me down the broken streets . . .

At the end of all that running, what awaited me? School, of sorts, with rock-starred windows and radiators that hissed heatlessly. The clubhouse, an empty storefront that nobody wanted badly enough to risk evicting us. And home, where the pursuers chose to wait for me one day, where my guardaddy told them "Over my dead body" and they accepted his terms. . . .

Yeah, happy childhood days. Any Jungle kid who doesn't lead that kind of life deserves a handshake, a medal, and hubcaps for his wheelchair.

The little kids are useful—the organization isn't so complex that a Ph.D. has to do its paperwork. Nine-year-olds can keep the censuses up to date, poke and pry for things in need of repairs, and carry messages. Shit, somebody's got to do all that—and few Zulus have the time.

So you find a kid like Ronnie, and you say, "Kid, I need help. You wanna work for me?" He gazes up at you out of wide, warm eyes; his head bobs till it blurs; finally, he sputters, "Yessir, yessir, thankyouthankyou, yessir." Once you've given him the safe jobs, and the dull jobs, and the easy jobs, you find you've got room in your day for the others.

Some guarpars call it exploitation. Well, maybe it is. Yet we're giving them a real education in how things work, and that should count for something. I mean, nobody says schoolteachers are exploiters, even though they've gotten together to make it illegal for a kid to skip school. How many of them would be drawing paychecks if high school were optional?

We're showing these kids that they *are* important. We prove to them daily that their actions can improve the quality of their world. So maybe that world's mean,

14

cramped, and dirty. So what? We're teaching them that they can change it. Call it hope.

Nine-thirty. Ronnie had almost finished apportioning the trucks. Each captain would have three to take back to his grove: a better than average day.

Sweating men, stripped to the waist in the morning sun, staggered under hundred pound bags of flour, cases of canned goods, and equal quantities of whatever else Big Unk had declared to be "surplus" that week.

"Slow Squeeze," shouted Ronnie, his voice an agitated bird song over the herd beast grunts of the men, "your trucks are ready."

"*Si,* in a minute." The barrel-chested Slow Squeeze was busy holding two angry men at arm's length. All three were up to their ankles in dried peas.

"C'mon, Slow Squeeze, your trucks are in everybody's way. Please?" His thick glasses were dotted with sweat, and smeared from the hands that continually brushed his thick black forelock.

"All right, kid, all right." He shoulder-slung his rifle and headed for the trucks, drawing his men from wherever they'd been through sheer force of personality. Slow Squeeze'd make a nova Jungle Lord, if the opportunity ever arose. Selfishly, I hoped it wouldn't. To have him carve out a territory of his own would weaken me: not through the competition, but through the loss.

The last truck was ready to roll by 10:38. I flagged it to have a quick word with its captain. Up on the running board, I stuck my head into the cab. "Hairless."

"Yeah, Bander?" His reddish-brown eyes were small, set deep in puffs of sallow flesh. I've always disliked him for that.

"You double-check this time?"

"Yeah." His voice seemed cold.

"And you got everything Ronnie said you got?"

"Yeah." No mistaking it; icicles hung from his tonsils.

"Good, good." Our eyes locked until he realized that he was verging on insubordination; he broke off the contest. A bead of sweat popped out of his baldness and ran down the side of his face. "So this time there won't be any mush-mouth about the surplus?"

"No." He coughed stagily, and shot me a quick sidelong glance. "None at all, Bander. I'll have it to you tomorrow morning."

"Do that," I said, stepping down. Hands on hips, I

15

watched him head for his two square blocks of slums. "No-nose!"

He came out of nowhere to stand by my side. It's something he does frequently. You never see him approach. He's just there, two seconds after you've shouted his name. "Yup?"

"Take Ronnie into Hairless' grove, spotcheck both his latest census and today's rationing. If you find any serious discrepancies, take a full team in and investigate thoroughly."

He ran a hand through his bushy Afro, then inspected it as if he'd expected something to be stuck to it. "We got a problem with Hairless?"

"I hope to hell we don't, but . . ." I shook my head. You can't share your troubles with your subordinates; even if they're your friends, it only disheartens them. "Do what I told you. Report back to me, ah, tomorrow morning."

"Right." Calling Ronnie, he turned away.

The surpluses were important because they were, with the exception of corpses, our only export. Usually we can get along without cash money, since the basics are provided free by a government that feigns concern, but when you want something else—like plastiglass to cover a broken solar collector—you need those crinkly pieces of paper or the man won't let you carry it out.

Fortunately, the convoys brought a lot more than we consumed—Jenkins had been submitting inflated population data to HEW and banking the difference. So I split the surplus with my captains, letting each keep half of his leftovers. He was free to do what he wanted with them, although I'd advised everyone to keep an emergency reserve. The other half came to me. Half of that went into the Jungle's stockpiles; the rest was trucked, à la Jenkins, to the market web.

So maybe it wasn't legal—but we needed that crinkly, and Big Unk wouldn't front it unless eighteen lawyers had slaved for a year and a half to complete the damn forms.

A jeep snarled at my back like a watchdog ready to pounce. Instinctively leveling my rifle, I pivoted. Amusement spread across two military faces. "Want a ride?" offered the major.

"The Jungle isn't *that* big. Thanks anyway."

"Have it your way." Before telling O'Rourke to move off, he asked, "Do I get my trucks back tomorrow?"

"Yeah, ah, around dinner."

16

His crows' feet tightened in thought. "Unless they call a surprise mobilization tonight, that's nova."

"Well, if they do, give me a call."

"Sure." Not one to take ritual seriously, he laughed at my mock salute and purred away. Nice jeep: solar-powered for sunny weather, with an auxiliary methane motor for darkness. Only the army and the trucking firms could own vehicles like that. Everybody else got by on photo-voltaic cells with a standby battery. People who drove at night ran up monstrous recharging bills.

I hadn't told the major the complete story when I'd spurned his offer. Sure, I was going to take a roundabout way to my HQ, which was right across the street, but I'd prefer to walk even if it were longer. The brief jaunt does for my ego what an inaugural parade does for the president's.

Everybody knows me. At introspective times, I realize that their recognition is just acknowledgement of my power; nonetheless, it does feel good to be greeted by everybody from children comping randoms to old men dozing in the sun. Some do it because they fear I'll be nasty if they don't, but . . . hell, it feels so *good* I don't care. " 'Morning, Bander." "Hiya, Ban." "Hello, sir." Etc.

I kid myself that they appreciate me. I know I'm kidding myself, that they don't like anybody who wields power over them, but . . . then I ask myself if it matters. I have to say no. What matters is that they see me among them; that, if the spirit moves them, they can tell me what's wrong.

Not many have the cojones to do it, but it happens. And I make sure I listen. Feedback from the crowded streets is rare, but without it . . .

My late predecessor paid no attention to it. Aloof, greedy, and callous to the pain he caused, he ran the numbers, sold the drugs, and promenaded the pretty women. He was easily the most potent figure in sight, and his problem was that he knew it.

His arrogance mounted like a starship leaving Earth. He stopped caring when his boys did the residents; he claimed for himself a few rights that had vanished with the Feudal Age. Alienated people abounded, among them No-nose, Marianne, Ralphie, and Shana. It was easy to organize a cabal. And, since a lot of people were flamed off that he'd let his Zulus rampage during the Food Riots, it was even easier to rip the power from his hands.

He didn't care and he wouldn't listen. It was inevitable that he couldn't foresee us dancing on his grave.

I decided early not to repeat his mistakes. Not for me the total reliance on henchmen's reports. I'd walk the noisy streets, stare at the multicolored faces, and check for myself the sagging buildings in which lived nine thousand six hundred forty-seven of my people.

Want some statistics? Sixty-eight percent were over the age of sixty. Fifty-two percent had subnormal IQ's. Forty percent had physical handicaps ranging from quadriplegia to chronic asthma. Thirty-eight percent were emotionally unstable. Thirty-one percent were addicted to sand, heroin, go-gas, or alcohol. Twenty-four percent couldn't speak English. Twelve percent couldn't read or write in any language. Two hundred sixty-five percent. There is some overlap in there. . . .

Common denominators? Poverty. Resentment. Insecurity. Fear. Anger. And complacency.

Jungle dwellers are generally bored and dissatisfied, though all too few of them ever learn how to channel their dissatisfaction into legal self-betterment. Mostly they prefer to be left alone. They've traded in a lot of dreams for the right to live out of Big Unk's pocket, and not many of them want to go helping another person piece together his dream. Asked to give of themselves, they groan and faint and disappear.

I managed that place with eighty, sometimes a hundred, Zulus. Some concentration camps have been run with a lower guard-to-prisoner ratio . . . half my problem was that the guards wouldn't leave the prisoners alone . . . maybe twenty of my Zulus could be counted on to go out of their way to avoid doing a dweller. The rest, well . . . had a lot of coughing down there.

It's dangerous even to humble someone whose gun keeps you in power, whose gun could deprive you of power, but it's necessary. Tension between subgroups is essential. A leader depends on, and helps, his supporters, but he has to assist the people at the bottom, too. The quickest way to lose them is to let a bureaucracy develop.

There is no such thing as a good bureaucracy—only deepening shades of bad. They're the cancer of the body politic. I just wished I were a better doctor.

Strolling up Chestnut Street, I stopped for a second at Old Al's garden plot, where once had been an office building, a big one, that somebody hit with . . . we're still not sure what it was. A baby nuke? Ripped the damn building

18

off its foundations and tilted it back into the courtyard. Wiry Old Al was delighted.

After staking out an area roughly thirty meters by ten, he spent a month with a wheelbarrow clearing it of coarse chunks of concrete, then another month with shovel and rake and homemade compost. He planted a million, zillion flowers and willed them into life. He had blossoms from March through late October, and would probably still have his arthritic knuckles in the gravelly soil if he hadn't tried to do it in the November rains. . . .

I didn't go to his funeral. I couldn't afford to have my Zulus see me cry. A Jungle Lord is not supposed to do that, not even when the man in the box is his truest, wisest friend.

Old Al took me in when I was thirteen, after the street gang chasing me had settled for coughing my guardaddy. I'd dropped out of school by then—which he didn't mind, said schools were devices for homogenizing thought—and he decided somebody had to oversee my education. He nominated himself and, after disenfranchising me, was elected by a unanimous majority of one.

I lived in his cluttered apartment for five years, bedding down in the windowless room that housed his books. Thousands of them. Old, new; big, small; hard, soft; handwritten, printed, microfiched (he didn't care for that, said he never could get cosy with the readout screen). I'd plowed through most of them by the time I was eighteen. Old Al said at that point that I'd learned to ask the right kind of questions, and he was ready to award me my diploma: a pen and an empty notebook.

So I stood by his garden a minute or two, picked what I hoped was a weed, pinched back the leggy stalk of what I hoped was a flower. Old Al had taught me a lot, but by the time he'd started green-thumbing it, I was running the Jungle, and horticulture was something I'd never learned.

Damn. He'd have liked to have his showplace kept up.

I heard a commotion, and looked up Chestnut Street. A small crowd had gathered a block away, at its intersection with Aster. I couldn't see what was flaming them, so I hurried over. Time-waster or not, if it upset people, it was something I should know about.

When I got there, Dirty Dan was kicking the curb in disgust.

"Whatsa matter, Dan?"

19

"Dead man." His double chin pointed to the body; as always, his skin bristled with a three-day stubble. "Never seen him before."

I elbowed my way through the gawkers. Nobody had covered it; blankets, coats, even newspapers are scarce down there. You don't mess up the little you have on meaningless courtesies.

The dead man had been in his midfifties; his light-brown face was plump and his hands were unscarred. The ripped clothing had once been of good quality. His lips were drawn back over clean, even teeth; his brown eyes stared at the sky, as if to watch for vultures. He'd been beaten to death. He hadn't liked it.

"How'd it happen?"

"Damned if I know." Dirty Dan was worried, and with cause. The deceased had come from the outside, and his death could draw the frogs. They laughed at what we did to ourselves, but God help us if we damaged one of their taxpayers. At times like that they applied the doctrine of hot pursuit.

"What do you mean, you don't know?" I pointed up Chestnut, to the sandbagged checkpoint on Lily. "You're supposed to have two Zulus there all the time. Where were they?"

"They say they *were* there. They say he musta come up Aster, and he musta got done right quick."

"That's bullshit and you know it. Look at how messed up he is. He kicked at getting coughed, and if your boys hadn't been sleeping they'd have heard."

"Maybe he just got dumped here. Maybe somebody over in Catkiller's did him, and—"

"Don't give me that shit. Any car coming in is customed from top to bottom, right? So how'd they lug him in?"

"Bander Snatch, I tell you—"

"Shut up." Tapping my right foot to vent some of my anger, I gazed off at the cloudless, smeared-blue sky. Some garbage birds off the lake were circling overhead. Damn fools figured a crowd meant a picnic. "This costs you your gayshake profits for the next two months."

Trying not to let me see his involuntary relief, he argued, "You take those, I can't pay off—you're opening me wide up!"

"What the hell do you think this does to me?" The gas-head couldn't see that body-clogged gutters made me more vulnerable than a few unpaid Zulus did him. "Don't let it happen again," I said, recording the incident in my notebook. "Next time I might look for a new captain."

"Sure, Bander Snatch." The corners of his bloodshot eyes were moist; he liked his extra crinkly. "What now?"

"Any ID's?"

"None."

"Sonuvabitch. Cart him to the east side docks tonight, go out a way, and drop him. Make sure he stays under." It was almost noon, and I was tired. My stomach was reminding me that I hadn't eaten since dawn. I started to leave, then thought better of it. "He goes in with everything he's wearing now, scan?"

"Sure."

"And find out who did it. If it's somebody from this Jungle, I want him coughed, too."

As if I hadn't already had all the problems I could handle in one morning, Catkiller and a group of his men came strutting down Aster. I don't like Catkiller. He's taller than I am, better built, much handsomer, and he's got slate-gray eyes that turn into ice cubes on command. That may sound unimpressive, but believe me, it's much easier to be a hard-assed authority figure when you can view a person like he's a piece of shit that a dog dropped onto your rug.

His constant scheming to do me hadn't improved our relations, either.

" 'Morning there, Bandy," he called, staring at my slightly bowed legs to make his insult clear. It's something he does whenever we meet, and it's one more reason why I despise him.

"Hey, Kitty." I smiled angelically into his empty eyes. "Did you come down here for a reason? Or did they finally chase you out?"

His bodyguards stiffened, and their beefy faces begged permission to enlighten me. He denied them with a minuscule shake of his head. "I'm here to register a complaint, Bandy." His voice was as smooth as a dagger blade. "You magicked a convoy this morning and didn't cut me in on it."

"You've got your own convoys, Kitty."

"They're not big enough."

"Neither are mine."

"I want a cut."

"Neg that."

Without realizing it, we'd closed in on each other. Our faces were inches apart. Too rapidly for me to stop, he put

21

the backs of his hands on my chest and pushed them up and away. I flew backwards and down. He laughed. So did I. My assault rifle was trained on his gut.

"Shouldn't have done that, Kitty."

He had enough presence of mind to stand very still. "If you look up Aster, Bandy, you'll see you're covered from my rooftops."

And truth, I was. My quick glance found rifle barrels glinting in the sunlight; distance obscured them, but it did look as though every one was aimed at me.

"Well, well, well," I mused. "A stalemate. I lose you, they do me coldest, right?"

"Right."

"So I gotta figure, is it worth it to me?"

That drove the color out of his cheeks. To somebody like Catkiller, nothing is worth your own life. "Bandy—"

"You know, my man," I said dreamily, as though he hadn't opened his mouth, "the way I see it, I can hope that their reflexes are slow. None of your gangers is smart enough to run your Jungle. If I survive, I take it over. If I don't, No-nose does. Sounds pretty damn good to me." I gave him my ugliest smile, and let the rifle sight cut small circles in the air. "Whatcha think, Kitty?"

I didn't hear his reply. A large, heavy figure dropped on top of me and blotted out the sun. The gun was wrenched from my hands. "What the fuck—" I screamed as I came up.

Sergeant O'Rourke shrugged apologetically. "Sorry, sir. Major's orders."

I looked to the curb. The major sat behind the wheel of his jeep, unkindness in his blue eyes. "I gave you credit for more brains, Bander Snatch." His voice was equally unkind. "I don't mind if you and Catkiller lose each other, but there are unarmed civilians on this street. Pull that trigger and they die, too. Now get up."

I did.

"Catkiller," he continued, "you've got exactly ten seconds to get your ass back into your own territory."

"And then?" A hint of a sneer surfaced on his lips.

By way of answer, Dourscheid gestured to a handful of GI's, deployed with rifles at the ready. Then he said, "One—" Catkiller turned and ran. His musclemen followed close behind.

"Thanks, Major." I went up to the jeep. "I'm afraid I wasn't thinking too clearly."

22

He looked at me as though I were speaking Etruscan. He did not like the endless feud between Catkiller and me—possibly because Catkiller got along better with the bureaucracy than I did, and if the major were ever forced to intervene, he'd be ordered to tilt toward Catkiller. "Give him his rifle, O'Rourke, and let's get the hell out of this shithole."

As they rolled up Aster, the bad feeling entered my bones. I jerked my head and sniffed the air. It's one of those unconscious things you do when something's gone wrong but you don't know what, where, or how. My nose darted from side to side as I tried to pick out the evil. No good. It wasn't that close.

"Dan," I said, already moving down Chestnut, "clean it up quick, and send two rifles to HQ yesterday."

"Sure, Bander Snatch." His frown was puzzled. He doesn't see me running that often. Nobody does.

That day they did. I was desperate. I'd localized the taint; it was in the first grove, where the HQ building sat. I sprinted down the sidewalk, dodging a kid on a beat-up black bicycle, making a grandmotherly type hug the wall as I dashed past. Her expression was reproachful.

Across Rose and through the alley. There was no debris in the courtyard to trip me; Marianne ran a tight ship. Something had happened to Shana. I knew it. I couldn't tell what, yet, but something was sour.

Shana's my therenback. Our jectry's hard to explain, but it's got nothing to do with her sun-gold hair or her fine, fine hull. And truth, her face is not a Monalisa: her nose is broken, and her cheeks are scarred from a knife she couldn't duck. Her left arm's fused at the elbow, too. When we get some crinkly together, I'll buy a specialist or two. She says I can bring in all the orthopedic surgeons I want, but no plasticizers: the stiff arm's inconvenient, but the scars aren't. She's sorta proud of them.

So like I say, it's not her looks that plot our jectry. It's something else: an ultraspecial closeness, a rare mutual sensitivity. I scan her moods without studying her face or hearing her voice—I just sit back and . . . I know them. Sounds flimsy, but I'm always right. As she is when she does it to me.

I swooped up the building's back steps. The cracked plaster flew by me; the bannister swayed back and forth under my hands. "Shana!" I shouted as the staircase trembled, "Shana!" I was hoping she'd stick her head out and

23

snarl, "What the *hell* are you doing making so much noise?" I hoped so hard it hurt.

She didn't. She wasn't there. And that scared me. Shana is *always* there; she lives at HQ. She doesn't ever go out because she's the communications chief, and her sense of responsibility is awesome.

The ComCenter was devastated. Armchairs lay at odd angles in pools of scattered stuffing. The computer and the holovision were heaps of crushed circuitry. Boards had been pried up from the floor; plaster ripped from the wall. Even the toilet had been shattered. Not a single thing had been left in one piece.

I went to the hall for the pay viphone. Numbly, I punched my lawyer's number. Through a fog, I said, "Jake: the leapers got Shana. De-ice her."

His whiny voice asked, "How do you know?"

The ruined ComCenter reached out to oppress me. "Her office is torn to shit, and she's gone."

"So?" His shrug filled the screen.

"So only frogs do that when they're looking for something. Anybody else, they use torture." With shaking hands, I replaced the receiver, and pressed my forehead against the cool, crumbly wall.

It had been a very bad morning, but I had the feeling there was worse to come.

II

Pounding feet and harsh pants seeped through the bewilderment that plugged my ears. They were half-familiar, but half-terrifying as well, like wind whistles incorporated into a nightmare. I whipped my M-33 off my shoulder and leveled it at the landing.

Marianne's meter plus sixty swung around the newel post. There was grimness on her dark face, and it deepened when she spotted my assault rifle. Thirty-three years old, she'd survived a long time in a position whose incumbents died young.

The moment was curiously frozen. I knew that she would dive, raise her own rifle, and initial my chest. I knew that I should say something to relax her. I knew all that, yet I stood disoriented, paralyzed.

She, thank God, glanced at my face. Her breath whooshed out; the tension gushed from her body. "Good way to catch a cough, Ban," she grunted, peering into the ComCenter. "Jee-zus! What hell happened here?"

My throat wasn't working; my hands made a helpless gesture.

"Uh." Her hard brown eyes raked the chaos. "They do Shana?"

Again the gesture.

Softening momentarily, she took a half-step towards me, but her Zulus began to crowd onto the landing. We both knew she couldn't publicly console her commander. "Sid-down, Ban," she growled.

Reality was thawing the shock; I negged her advice. "S'okay, Marianne."

"So what happened?"

"Frogs? There's no blood, but a lot of mess. Besides—" Shana's rifle lay under her desk; a faint acridity clung to it. Ejecting the magazine, I counted the shells. One was missing. "Besides, anybody but leapers, she'd have been ready."

"Yeah." Crisply, clearly, she gave two of her men instructions to find witnesses to what had happened.

They'd have little success. Two of the other three corners at Carnation and Larch belonged to Catkiller, none of whose people would talk, and the third was the HEW warehouse. Moreover, the buildings adjacent to HQ were vacant due to fire damage.

"What else?" she growled, mostly to herself. From the crowd by the door she picked out a teen-aged boy. "Billy Burntknees," she rasped, and he approached with a hesitant air. He was—had been—Shana's aide. "Straighten this place yesterday; find out if anything's missing."

Why had Shana been alone? All the other captains had been across the street at the time, but there should have been Zulus at the front and back doors. She wouldn't have sent them away. She knew better than to leave HQ unguarded.

Kicking the lead plate on the front of her desk, I thought. Bad thoughts. Pictures of blue uniforms flooding the room, overwhelming her, swirling around the contours of her body as they searched her, and then washing her away. To a blue car with a vertiginous light show on its roof; tires screech on concrete as the car shakes free of the Jungle. Somewhere, they book her, print her, shower her, give her blue cotton overalls, and clang shut the iron door of her cinder block cell. Shit.

The tendons in Marianne's neck stood out; her ear tilted to the web-hung ceiling. Her square, tough hands quieted the others. As the room hushed, a hollow knocking from the armory overhead grew in volume.

She gave a hand sign to two of her men, who dashed out on cats' feet. In a minute they were back, with Gunfreak hanging from their shoulders. His head dripped blood.

The instant flutter of rifle-readying was stilled by one Zulu's report that the armory was as normal. The only thing out of place had been Gunfreak, whom they'd found hog-tied and gagged with cleaning rags.

26

"What happened?" she asked, as somebody righted an armchair for him.

Before answering, he gaped at the reddish-brown stains on his fingers, then probed his matted hair again. "Dunno," he said. "Helluva noise—grabbed m'gun and started down—whole fucking world lit up. Couldn't move when I woke. Kicked on the floor till ya got me. 'Ts all I know."

"Shit." She had more questions, but the two she'd sent into the neighborhood returned. "Yeah?"

Gordie, a nineteen-year-old black who was at least 180 centimeters, announced, "The border guards at Carnation and Chestnut passed a carload of leapfrogs at eleven o'clock. Twenty minutes later they let 'em out again."

"Six of 'em?" I asked.

"Uh-huh," he said. "Checked Rose and Larch, too. Those gasheads let in another carload. Same time of entry, same time of exit."

"Anything else?"

"Three people saw both cars come into the courtyard out back, through the alleys on Chestnut. Lotsa leapers went up the back steps here. Nobody noticed anything unusual when they left, though."

"Yeah." Some people follow sports. Others watch rocket launchings. Jungle dwellers study frogs. You never know, even after two years of benign neglect, whether they're going to keep on ignoring you. So you get that paranoidy feeling when you see them through your window, and you breathe quick and shallow all the time they're around. Funny nobody saw Shana in their midst, though. "The back door guards?"

"In the Food Room, asleep. Couldn't wake 'em. Gassed, I guess."

"All right. Jake's working on it; as soon as he finds out where they're holding her, he'll de-ice her. . . . All right," I repeated more decisively. "If they took her, they had a reason." I called Billy Burntknees over. "Tell the other captains what's happened, and that we hold a council of war in fifteen minutes." He scuttled to the hallway and started phoning. "The rest of you, uh, get this place cleaned up."

Marianne lounged against the doorframe; her M-33 was ready and her eyes roamed the staircase. I walked around the room, occasionally stopping to tell someone where something belonged, more often stepping past them as if

27

they weren't there at all. And to me, they weren't. Nobody was. I was somewhere else, thinking of Shana.

By now they'd have her stowed away. She'd be sitting on a hard iron cot, listening to the others jeer a passing guard, smelling the jail-house stinks of sweat and vomit, piss and shit, all overlaid with a disinfectant that only added another stench to the air.

Damn her anyway. Even before the Food Riots, when we were both part of the old gang, I'd told her, "Look, what's in it for you except a way to get badly lost?" but she'd laughed, and asked if the same didn't hold true for me.

Shouldn't mix romance with power. Right from the start, she had no objectivity about me—or I about her. I was loathe to discipline her; she was reluctant to criticize me. I'd rationalized, of course: told myself that she couldn't get hurt, not at a desk in the ComCenter, that she'd always done a nova job as ComChief, and that the others would speak up if they thought I were slipping.

She'd had her own ultimatum: "I'm your ComChief and you're my lover," she'd said, "or we're nothing to each other. Scan?"

What would you have done? Greedy bastard that I am, I'd shrugged, and agreed.

Respectful Billy Burntknees stood before me, with his arms folded behind his back. I almost bumped into him. "Yeah?"

"I've called the other captains, Bander. They're on their way." He smiled, warily, and gestured to the room around us. It was surprisingly neat. "I haven't found anything missing. Shana didn't keep nothing illegal here anyway. Just records and stuff."

"Thanks." Why the hell had the place been torn apart? Had they been looking for something they'd thought was there? Or had it been a spasm of official malice, for the sheer enjoyment of knowing that we'd have to clean it up?

I was feeling helpless again, as though I were going through incomprehensible motions which someone had told me were mandatory. I watched my captains trickle in; their worry and puzzlement deepened my gloom.

A curiously unreal atmosphere settles on you when a close one is missing. You pace, glancing at your watch as if its face could grow a mouth and answer your riddle. You pace some more, realizing that there's work to be done but finding yourself unable to concentrate on it. You pace, and

28

your mind wanders through a self-hewn labyrinth, circling, repeating, "Where, what, why, where . . ."

They were all waiting for me, but I didn't know what to say. For half an instant I had the sensation that I, a lion tamer, had walked into the cage *sans* gun, chair, and whip.

The Jungle was America's GULAG, and these were the camp's elite. They were the hardest, the meanest, and the smartest of those who could not—or would not—play the game by society's rules. Their eccentric energies were too disruptive; ho-coms could make no niche for them. So they'd drifted to the Jungle like rattlesnakes finding the only sun-washed rock in the area.

Make no mistake: only three of those people could be considered my friends. The rest were my subordinates, and that only because I'd convinced them, one at a time and all together, that I was the toughest of all. Show too much weakness, though, and I'd be flat on my back, trying to keep their fangs from my throat.

"The frogs took Shana this morning." My voice was flat and not a little hollow. "I have no idea why. Do any of you?"

From the cynical circle of faces came the chorus of expected negatives. Another uneasiness passed over me. Had one of them dealt with the leapfrogs to save himself? What if— I choked it off.

"All right." I cleared my throat and reached for the Jungle Lord voice. "They micro-shredded this place, but Billy Burntknees says Shana didn't keep anything here. What about you all? Do you know if there was anything here to interest them?"

Heads shook like flowers in a breeze.

"Then could they have been trying to do one of you, and just been looking in the wrong place?"

Questioning glances shot back and forth. Pete the Prick, scratching his brown hair, asked, "What do you mean, Bander?"

Patiently, I explained, "Has one of you attracted too much attention with your side-ops? Was one of you a little too blatantly criminal? Why the hell are they bothering us?"

Comprehension spread through them slowly. Marianne got it first. "I haven't bought guns or ammo for six, eight months, now—and the last time we were sterile all the way. They're not onto that, I guarantee it."

"Dirty Dan?"

He stroked the whiskers on his chin. "They're not flamed off by my lousy two gayshakes, believe me. Haven't had a mad customer for over a year. Not me."

"Me neither," volunteered Billie. "My tumblers are clean, cheap, courteous, *and* cut the frogs in on every stunt. The Twenty-third actually *likes* me—they're not going to be doing us."

Slow Squeeze, after putting in his standard plea for higher juice, said the same about his loans; Tomtom said the sand swipers had promised to ignore him if he limited his clientele to long-time addicts; Pete the Prick said the randoms take had been way down for months, so . . . and so it went, around the circle, each insisting that the law couldn't have been annoyed by his side-op.

"Well, look," I said, once they'd finished, "they're obviously after something. I want you each to check your treehouses, see if anybody's been scoping around. Hunt up your good guys—all of them—find out what the fuck this means. If they're about to do us, we gotta know what for."

The helplessness was back in force. For the first time in years, I had to look at the microscopic size of the Jungle, and realize just how tiny we were to the outside world. An amoeba must feel pretty cocky when there's no other amoeba around to mess with it; poke it with long needles, though, and it'll drop its pretensions to glory. The goddam world was so big, and there were so many angles from which so many agencies could insert their knives, that I honestly didn't know which way to turn.

"Bander," said Ralphie quietly, "you thought maybe those leapfrogs were Catkiller's in costume? You know, snuck in to flame us off, maybe get us to gig a few of the real ones?"

"Yeah," said Hairless, puffing himself into belligerency. His eyes gleamed with suppressed nastiness. "This has gotta be a trap."

"Sure," I said, "but what the hell kind?"

"It's a Leah trap," asserted Billie, pronouncing it like the girl's name. "They're trying to put it up us 'cause they don't want the people to have any power—this is a tactic to disrupt us, that's all."

The phone rang, interrupting whatever she was going to say next. I waved her into silence as Billy Burntknees went for it.

"It's Jake, Bander," he said, bringing the receiver into the room.

30

"Thanks." I looked at the rest. "Hold it down, now." I took the receiver, and gave the stretched cord a tentative tug. "Jake?"

"Neg, Ban." His voice was tremulous, as though he feared I'd reach through the line and strangle him for not finding her.

"Whaddaya mean, neg?"

"They don't have her."

"They *say*," I snorted.

"No, really." He was earnest. "The quickest way for them to lose their case would be to keep Shana from me. I call, and say, 'Do you have her?' They know I've got the call taped; they know if they say 'No' when the answer ought to be 'Yes,' that's it, the courts'll usher her right to the front door. Believe me, Ban—they haven't got her."

"What if they're trying to make a case against us, huh? Not against her, just against us?"

"Still no good. If they're holding her for any reason at all they've got to tell me." He let himself swell just a little. "Frankly, Ban, even if they're *not* holding her, just talking to her, they'd let me know. Really. My good guys in Leah are *true*. They wouldn't do me."

Yeah, sure, I thought, but aloud said, "Jake. We got witnesses who'll say there were frogs all over when she disappeared. Now, if what you say is true, what the hell were those fucking cojones-crunchers doing?"

"Easy, Ban, easy." Worry had reconquered his tongue; my news threatened his self-esteem. "Look, I don't know anything about that. I talked to some people who said they don't know her, haven't iced her, aren't holding her—"

"I suggest, Jake," I said, in a voice as cold as Catkiller's eyes, "that you call a few more people and find out why those bastards were down here."

"Why the worry?" He was relying too heavily on the familiarity he presumed he had with me. "Look—your favorite skinshaker disappears, so what? There's others. And the face on this one, it—"

"Jake." I was surprised that frost hadn't formed on the black plastic mouthpiece. "One more word like that and you will wake up dead tomorrow."

Though a ghastly sound chattered through the receiver, he didn't hang up. Jake *likes* being scared shitless. It's about the only thrill he gets . . . his other clients are all too boo-class to be anything but respectful. His mind's fucked up, but hell, he's *good*. The best. And his pervostreak doesn't endanger us too often. I'll bet he's a bastard with his wife and kids, though. "S-s-sorry, Ban."

"Jake. You will find out why the frogs came. You will find out why they took Shana. You will find out where she's iced. If you do not, you will get on a TransSolar rocket and ride it past Pluto. Do you scan me?"

"Yeah," he whispered, gratingly, as though he had no air left in his lungs. "I— I understand, Ban."

"Good." Without waiting for more, I tossed the receiver to Billy Burntknees, who fielded it deftly. "No luck," I told the room at large. "The frogs have that poor law-licker so trained he doesn't know his head's buried in shit."

"I'll bet he thanks them for letting him taste it," growled Billie, as she checked the clip on her rifle.

"Yeah, probably." It was harder to talk than I'd expected. I'd been waiting for Jake's call like a man overboard waits for the lifesaver. I'd been counting on him to answer at least one of my questions, and his failure had shaken me.

I leaned against Shana's desk, keeping both feet on the floor so I wouldn't drum my heels on the lead plating and expose my nervousness. "All right." I was speaking from the bottom of a well. "All of you, hit up your good guys, find out what's happened. Now." Throw the vultures their meat. "First one with the right answer keeps all his profits next month."

They scattered, leaving me alone in the empty ComCenter. I should have asked one to stay; my hand needed to be held. But who? Any who understood my desperation would have taken maybe ten seconds to decide it was his turn to be Jungle Lord. That's the way it is. You perch on the top, and your balance isn't too hot even when everything's nova. Let trouble bubble up, and you're so damn wobbly that they can knock you over just by kissing your ass too hard.

Shit, it was quiet. Shana should have been there, chatting on the viphone while keeping one ear tuned to the police radio. She should have had messengers scurrying in and out; she should have been tapping piles of notes into the computer and—

Without warning, I slipped into a dream world. There was no sound, no smell, no son of a bitch to kick me in the butt and tell me I was alive. Though my eyes were open, they might as well have been torn out: I couldn't see anything but blackness. Something surged up inside me like a jet of water looking for the fountainhead. Terror. What the hell? Why was I reacting like that?

Rubbing my hands on Shana's desktop seemed to help. For a minute the fiberglass felt canvassy, but as the hallucination faded it spun into slickness. The worst was over. Temporarily, at least.

My boots made hesitant scrapes on the warped boards as I went to the phone. I took it off the wall, jabbed out a number with a shaking finger, and gritted my teeth. My voice was relatively steady by the time the call got through, but I cut the picture. Didn't feel like seeing. Or being seen.

"Newsroom, please," I told the receptionist.

"Just a moment," came her nasal whine.

"Newsroom."

"Mike Calder."

"Who's calling, please?"

"Bander Snatch."

"Who?"

I hate lines like that. "Just tell him the name. He'll talk to me." My knuckles turned white, with anger and with embarrassment.

Calder's gravelly voice came on a moment later. "Hi, Ban. What's up?"

"Got a problem, Mike. You help me, maybe I can do you a favor."

"What kind of favor?" he asked cautiously.

"Well, there's this reel of film . . ." Calder's wife, in her college days, had been in need of some quick crinkly. Maxwell, captain of my eighth grove, had found her unusually photogenic. She'd starred in eighteen or twenty of his porn pics.

Calder didn't want them in circulation. Apparently he didn't mind his wife's past, but his colleagues were connoisseurs of grainy blue movies. He'd spent the first year of his marriage tracking them down; by the time he found who controlled them, I'd become Maxwell's boss. We'd worked out a deal. For a steady stream of routine favors, I'd let them gather dust. For a major favor, like the one I was about to ask, I'd give him every print of one particular movie. And I mean all. I have ethics.

Sharply, he drew in his breath. "Anything." I've often wondered if he burns them—or keeps one print for his personal amusement. . . .

I explained the problem, and asked him to scope out what he could about Leah's interest in my Jungle, my Zulus, or myself. He signed off, swearing that he'd do his best. I could practically see him mopping his sweaty forehead.

I made more calls. A guy in the mayor's office had to be reminded that we hadn't thrown away the gun smeared with his fingerprints. A woman at the Ashtabula Jail wanted to forget that she'd hired us to do the therenback who'd gone without her. A police lieutenant in the Twenty-third got very upset when I said we would cut off his subsidy if he didn't come up with something. And there were others, none of them very polite, none of them very willing, but all of them frightened to death of one thing or another.

What does a voodoo doctor feel when he pushes pins into dolls?

It was almost nightfall before replies began to whisper in. Straight line neg, said one. Couldn't find a thing, said another. Nobody's ever heard of a shaker named Shana, said a third.

I hadn't bothered to turn on the lights. The ComCenter has cheap fluorescents running the fifteen-meter length of the sagging ceiling, but they have no housings. Nothing worse than being there alone, at night, with all of them lit. When you chase away the shadows, you banish their cosmetic illusions as well. In the midst of a crowd, it doesn't matter—you pay attention to the people bumping into you. But alone, at night, holding the ancient viphone so you can lift it on its first ring . . . you can't ignore the cracked plaster, peeling paint, and chitinous scampers along the baseboards.

Footsteps sounded in the armory; Gunfreak was inspecting his wares. Not knowing what was about to happen—or even what had already happened—I'd warned him to be ready for anything from a leaper raid to a full-fledged war with Catkiller. After making sure that his bandage was firmly in place, Gunfreak had shown his yellow teeth in a humorless smile.

I went to the window, and peered into the night-drenched alley. Cigarette butts glowed like fireflies. They were ready, too: a few because they honestly wanted to help me, more because their main joy in life was blowing off the back of someone's skull, and the rest, the majority, because they didn't have anything better to do.

The phone rang. Whirling, I almost tripped over a waste-basket hidden in the shadows, but still managed to pick up the receiver before the third buzz. "Yeah?" I snarled into the impassive mouthpiece.

"Caccarolli here, Bander Snatch." My pet frog, the one we'd been paying to ignore us.

"Whatcha got?"

"Not much." He cleared his throat: nerves. The hungry little man was afraid of losing his stipend if what he had wasn't enough. "The police you saw down there came from Township One. I scoped around there—but cautiously, you know? I had no right to be asking questions, and if they get suspicious—" Having established the lengths he'd gone to for me, he went on, "Anyway, I couldn't get a damn thing. Nobody who went on the raid was around when I got there, and nobody'd give me their names so I could check them out myself. Sorry, Bander Snatch, that's the best I could do."

I let my head hang for a minute, till I heard him saying, "Bander Snatch? Are you there?"

"Yeah, I'm here. Thanks. You did your best. You're still on the payroll." I had the phone back in its cradle before he could tell me how nova that made him feel.

Township One. Way the hell up in the northeast corner of Fedra Three. What had they been doing in my Jungle? It didn't make sense.

I ran through the list I keep in my head, the one that tells me what contacts my good guys have. Couldn't find anybody who could help. Only one option. Visit the T-1 frogs myself.

I hollered for No-nose and Billy Burntknees, turned the Jungle over to the former and the ComCenter over to the latter. No-nose was disturbed by my order to put the whole Jungle on Red Alert, but Billy Burntknees was excited. Whatcha gonna do? The ones who can do the job don't want to; the ones who want to, can't.

Taking No-nose by the arm, I led him into the quiet of the hall, and explained that it was purely precautionary. I swore that I was 99 percent convinced that the night would be peaceful, but that I'd be derelict in my duties if I ignored the one percent. Brown eyes gleaming, No-nose ate it up. He patted the butt of his rifle, softly, as he did everything, and promised that he'd be wary.

Billy Burntknees had summoned a car, a magicked yellowcab with a diesel engine. It was waiting when I'd clattered down the stairs. Running such an engine without the proper permit was prohibited, but since the fuel was harder than hell to get legally, the leapfrogs almost never customed anybody.

From the knot of Zulus and captains in the courtyard, I picked the best driver and the three best guns. The Zulus rode in the back, and spent half the ride bitching about whose M-33 was in whose rib cage.

Slouched in the front seat, I let Wheels McCafferty pick his own route; he was not only a captain, but my chief smuggler. While he turned off Larch onto Boulevard B, I listened to a mournful newscaster describe the terror-bombing of the Arc de Triomphe. It was a tactic I might use if I couldn't de-ice Shana any other way. Or if . . .

Shana's dead, ran my thoughts, *Shana's dead*. That's what the episode in the ComCenter must have meant: she was dying, and I . . . something must have melted down. She must have tried to get away, and they pulled the trigger, and she fell face forward in a litter-choked gutter. That's why they hadn't told Jake—they were afraid I'd ape the French guerillas and do them all till they were lost in hell.

We sped through the night, and the broadcast blurred with the rush of tires on tired cement. Lights smeared by. Boulevard B took us past T-17, where yesterday's singers condescended to tomorrow's. The music from two hundred cafés lapped at the edge of the road. T-16, its windows blazing because painters partied at night. Right onto First Avenue, and the breeze off the lake blew algae-rot through the car.

Some twenty minutes later, Wheels asked, "You want it right out front?"

"On their doorstep. Just make sure you can move out quick if need be."

His headshake said I'd reminded him to do something he specialized in; I patted his bony shoulder and apologized.

Then we went in. Across the large, high-ceilinged lobby spread Mad Dog, Bob, and Gordie, rifles leveled, faces rushmored. Their postures announced that as long as everything was on-key, nothing would happen, but whoever got excited would be lost the coldest.

The frogs were not happy, but of the seven who watched our entrance, only the desk sergeant reached for his gun. Funny how it's always that kind. The street strutters were just propping up the walls as they eyed us. I had to say, "Relax, man, relax. We're not here for trouble, just questions."

He didn't say anything, but his automatic sank back into its vinyl holster.

"That's better. Let me introduce myself. I'm Bander Snatch, from T-25. I'm here because some of your boys were in my Jungle today. As it happens," I went on, playing it as neutrally as possible, "my communications chief was kidnapped at approximately the same time they were in the area. I would like to talk to them to scope out if they saw anything."

He wasn't buying a word of it. Maybe he'd been ordered not to. "Nobody from T-1 was down at your place today." His thin, pale face bulged with clamped muscles.

"Hey, no games, huh? I *know* they were down there. I just want to know who they were."

"Calling me a liar, boy?" He didn't deliver that line as though he meant it. One of the streeters might have been able to pull it off, but he sure as hell couldn't. He was just a comperkid with stripes.

"Sergeant," I said, politely because I didn't want to provoke him more than I had to, "I don't call people liars. What I will say is this: if you are not lying, you are ignorant of the facts. Possibly someone neglected to inform you of this afternoon's events, or else someone deliberately misled you. So, no sir, I am not calling you a liar. Just tell me who went on the raid."

That approach didn't please him, either. A purple flush rose above the blue collar. He stood. Leaning forward, he put all his weight on his underturned knuckles. His fatigued desk creaked. "Get outta here," he snarled.

"Once I get my answers, Sergeant, I'm gone."

"Listen, ganger, if you don't gedouda here, I'm gonna—"

"Call the frogs?" I asked wide-eyed. "Oh, heavens to Betsy, don't do *that!*"

One of the strutters, sprawled on a heavily initialed plastic bench, chuckled. I turned to ask if *he* knew anything.

"Not a thing, my man," he said grandiloquently.

"Somebody here's gotta know—who would it be?"

He scratched his temple to give the appearance of deep thought. "Well, now, I would presuppose that the captain might have an inkling of all this."

I studied him carefully, peering into his deep brown eyes, scanning his dark brown skin for telltale scars and Jungle tattoos. He was no ho-commer. He'd grown up poor, looked around, and headed straight for the boo-class. Traitor. Fedra Three needed people with cojones like his, especially down in my part.

He studied me right back, and I could tell where his

37

mind was at: he was looking down on me, smug because society wouldn't go out of its way to crush him, as it would me; scornful because I didn't have the brains or the guts or the backbone to claw my way up a similar path. I could have shot the bastard.

And he knew it. Slowly, he swung his feet onto the scuffed stone floor. I could see him calculating the angles, figuring how he'd leap and roll and do me with the cannon strapped to his waist. His eyes were full of glee at getting the chance to enlighten a representative of his childhood.

"Siddown, Johnson," barked a new voice. It came from the staircase to the right; easily, unflusteredly, I turned my head.

It was the captain, big, blond, and middle-aged, looking like God would if He caught Lucifer shitting on the Pearly Gates. "What do you want?"

"Five minutes and the truth." Our eyes locked like bar-wrestlers' arms.

"If your men put down their guns," he decided at last.

"If we've got your word on a safe-conduct out," I countered. Hard to tell how close to his word he'd stick, but usually, if you watch your behavior once they've promised, they'll let you out alive.

"All right," he snapped, brushing back his yellow-gray hair. "Get up here."

I sauntered across the broad room: it didn't seem a good idea to show too much deference. He stayed in the pool of light atop the stairs, glaring at my leisurely climb.

"Got an office?" I asked, "or do you want to chat out here?"

His head jerked towards a partly opened door; the silver-trimmed black lettering on its frosted glass said, "Theodo-sius K. Jones, Captain."

"Thanks." We had a moment's delay while we worked out who'd enter first, then he snorted and plunged ahead.

"What's it about?" He dropped his eighty kilos into a squeaky swivel chair, and folded his hands on the green metal desk. I took an armchair in front of him.

"The raid on my Jungle—in T-25—this afternoon. Some of your men went on it. I want to know two things: Why was my communications chief kidnapped, and where is she now?"

"Can't help you," he said, leaning back. The chair groaned. "Don't know a thing about it."

"Do you neg your men were there?"

38

"Yup." Without shifting his hazel eyes, he took a cigar from inside his suitcoat. He bit off the end, spat out the stub, and shoved what was left into the corner of his mouth. Content to chew, he let his monogrammed desk lighter go on serving as a paperweight.

"You want to play it that way?" I mused. "Fair enough. Then I'll play it this way: I'm fully convinced you know all about it. I'm three-quarters convinced that you arranged it as a gashead grab for headlines. I'm half convinced that Shana's in this building."

"That's bullshit." His teeth clenched; the tip of the cigar wobbled.

"Maybe so," I admitted, "but it's the best info I've got, and—unless I get some that's better—I'm going to act on it. You know how I'll do that?"

He didn't want to dignify my pause with a reply, but I wouldn't go on until he did. At last, he grunted "No."

"Then I'll tell you—I always front my plans to the authorities; official cooperation makes things much easier. I'm going to take my Zulus, and at last count 160 could handle an M-33 without shooting themselves, and I'm going to bring them up here, to T-1, and we're going to burn you out. Is that clear?"

Red, wrinkled face scrunched up, he thrust his lower jaw forward. "Are you outta your fucking mind?"

"Nope." Feet up on his desk, I gave his scowl my sunniest smile. "The way I figure it, you'll do us all in three or four days . . . 'course, in three or four days, we can gig a lot of frogs, and burn a lot of buildings . . . but, hell, you're a tough guy, you won't be caught crying over a couple dozen dead leapers. Will you?"

Jones had so many words fighting through his throat that they got in each other's way. None of them came out. His jaw worked and his tongue flapped, but all I heard was "Aayargh—"

"On the other hand," I said, ignoring his fist-waving fury, "you could tell me what you know. We'll fade into the Jungle and never bother you again."

The offer irritated him. Like most of his peers, he figured Jungle dwellers were scum, and Jungle Lords were the filthiest of all. The words floating in his head flashed at regular intervals through his eyes: "Degenerates," "sanders," "tumbler trainers," "pervos" . . . He fumed until I said, "Well? Is one of your men worth the truth?"

Frogs must be sentimental about each other.

"All right," he grated, his temper on an obviously short leash, "two federal agents requisitioned two cars and ten riot-equipped patrolmen this afternoon. They were gone about two hours. When they came back, they had a woman with them: blond, 170 centimeters, scarred face, maybe 60 kilos. That her?"

"That's her." My finger tightened on an imaginary trigger. "Where is she?"

"I don't know." He spread his weathered hands. "Honest to God, I don't. They'd left their own car here; when they came back, they hustled her into it and drove off. Bastards didn't even stop to thank me."

"All right, I believe you. What agency were they with?"

"That's the funny thing." He leaned forward, and for a moment I ceased to be his adversary. I was simply someone who could be expected to scan how unusual the situation was. "They were FBI, but . . . the Bureau had attached them to the Justice Department's civil rights division, which had lent them to HEW. They claimed to be working out of the NIH."

"NIH?"

"National Institutes of Health." He remembered to shoot me a suspicious glance, then decided hostility wasn't worth the effort. "Level, now. You got some kind of plague down there, or what?"

"Damn." Frowning, I tapped the arms of the chair. "Not that I know of. We're short on doctors, of course, but Ralphie runs sort of a clinic, and the hospital's in T-23 for anything more than a cold. Besides, I saw Shana this morning; she was in perfect health. Sonovabitch. Did they say why they were taking her?"

"They didn't even tell me they were." His tired face was as worried as mine. "Look, from what I know about the Jungles, I wouldn't send men into one unless there was an earthquake. But these agents said it was a yesterday case, and they needed an escort. They didn't say anything about a kidnapping, or even a warranted icing." His eyes flickered up, alight with genuine curiosity. "*Could* it have been a straightforward arrest?"

Fuck it, cooperate all the way. "It could. She was working with me, and damn near everything I do is illegal. But she was only in communications. I don't see why the hell they'd be interested in her."

"Information on your activities?" He was offering it as assistance.

"*My* activities? Hell, I've got one of the smallest Jungles. I haven't made real trouble for years. Besides, I keep the Twenty-third current on everything we do. Fifth Army, too."

"Then damned if I know." Shoving his chair away from the desk, he rose.

I stayed put. "How about scoping around for me?"

"Neg that." He shook his head. My expression prodded him into an apologetic explanation. "Look, first, I didn't follow the rules and regs on this one. There are thirty-seven forms to fill out when assisting a federal agency, and I ignored them because they were in a hurry. I could get broken for that. Second, they warned me it never happened —and that a good memory would earn their revenge. Now, I don't want your whatchamacallems, Zulus, tearing up my township—but better them than the Feds. Scan?"

There's a limit to how far you can push. "Scan." I stood. "And thanks—I won't forget your honesty."

"Staying out of T-1," he said, as he led me down the stone staircase to the lobby, "will be remembrance enough."

Once we'd reclaimed our rifles from the sullen desk sergeant, we headed to the car. Wheels relaxed when he saw us strolling, and pulled away on electric instead of diesel. "Where to, Bander?"

"Does the NIH—National Institutes of Health—have a building in Fedra?"

He thought a bit, slowed for a light, and said, "Not that I know of."

"What about HEW?"

"Aw, Christ, they've got a hundred."

"Well, hit 'em all, but leave the warehouses for last."

The light changed and we started the bleakest ride of my life. The fair weather had fled inland; a light rain off the lake had taken charge. The wipers chunked rhythmically; the tires hissed; every time we came to a new building, somebody had to get wet. It wasn't an exhilarating rain, like the kind that dares you to sprint through it and makes you feel nova for having survived. It was the depressing kind, which oozes its way into your bones and there makes a cold nest for itself.

Through it all, the radio announcer sold gum and computers and soft drinks and vacation trips to the moons of Jupiter. His voice was brisk, cheery; he'd obviously never

41

thought that some of his listeners might not have the crinkly for his goods.

As we pulled away from the thirteenth or fourteenth place, I said, "This isn't getting us anywhere."

"So?" asked Wheels. He was the only one who was dry, and he could have gone on all night. He loved to drive.

"Stay here a minute, be quiet, lemme think." Think, hah! I had no facts to think about, except that she was alive. That was almost certain. She'd reached T-1 in one piece, and manacled as she must have been, Big Unk's boys would have had no reason for losing her.

So how would I find her? She was out there somewhere, unless they'd thrown her on a plane to Washington, but "somewhere" took in a lot of buildings and a helluva lot more people.

The gloom of the afternoon had altered subtly; it still held a sense of solitude, wrapped tightly with silence, but there was light . . . soft and diffuse . . . for some reason I felt imprisoned in a padded cell: alive, unharmed, and unaware of what was happening outside.

"I want to try something, Wheels." It's difficult to sound assured when you're afraid you're acting like a gashead. "Cruise slow and steady. Follow my directions. They'll be things like left, right, back, forward—maybe streets, but not always. Got it?"

"Yeah." Hands on the wheel, he stared across the front seat, totally mystified. "Whatever you say, Bander."

"Go straight down Second for a while." The morning after the Food Riots, Shana had been missing. Since our relationship had then been a secret, I'd decided she hadn't been snatched to aggravate me. I'd walked through the pockmarked streets, warily, and I'd listened for her voice. I'd heard . . . something, so I'd turned a corner, climbed precisely three sets of stairs, opened the sixth door on the left, and found her unconscious under a pile of rubble. I planned to try it again.

"Take the next left." The car was quiet, and dark. We were on Boulevard A headed east. Ignoring the odors of wet, unwashed Zulus, I— "Right." —made myself a dowsing rod, and waited for the quivers. Route 322? Out of Fedra? "Left." Heading away from Ashtabula, now. Widely spaced clusters of illumination revealed the ho-coms; even their lights seemed aloof and introspective. Vague sensations tugged me this way and that— "Back up and take the last left." —like spirit hands guiding me through the night.

"Holy shit!" Wheels burst out, braking hard. "The whole fucking army!"

"What?" Rubbing my forehead where it had hit the padded dashboard, I opened my eyes. Our lights glared at a roadblock manned by crouching, battle-ready soldiers. A score of M-35's drew beads on our hearts.

Slowly, I opened the door; more slowly, I stepped outside. Rain fell on my bare head. My scalp prickled as droplets inched down my hairs and swamped my pores. I waited for someone in authority. The headlights were silvery cones full of squirming fish.

The big, burly form that loomed out of the darkness to my right clarified into a familiarity: Sergeant O'Rourke. We gaped for a moment, frowned as if on cue, and matched each other's mutter of "What the hell are you—"

We broke off. "Is the major here, too?" I asked.

"Yeah," he rumbled, "wanna talk to him?"

"Please."

"Okay. Leave your Zulus behind."

I waved reassuringly at the car, and set off down a winding driveway that curled away from the road. We passed through wrought-iron gates in a barbed-wire-topped stone wall. The trees were a row of leaky umbrellas.

Two minutes later, we mounted the front steps of a large brick building. The major stood just inside the front door, sheltering himself from the rain.

"Bander Snatch," he said, opening the door and extending a hand. "What brings you here?"

"Looking for Shana. Big Unk carried her off this afternoon. Had a hunch she was here." Another glass door led from the vestibule into a lobby lined with uncomfortable armchairs. The faded red carpet looked like it had served as a parade grounds. Across the far end of the high-ceilinged room flitted two female figures in white. "What is this place?"

"Lomala Research Institute. Sort of a hospital."

"What are you doing here?"

"Orders," he shrugged.

"You didn't need the trucks?"

"No, but get them back to the post tomorrow."

"Yeah, sure." I mopped my forehead, drew in a long breath. "Is Shana here?"

"I don't know." The wrinkles around his blue eyes tightened briefly.

"Well, how about scoping around for me?"

43

He thought it over. "I'll check. What's her last name?"

"None. Just Shana."

"Wait here with O'Rourke." He pushed through the glass door and crossed the threadbare carpet. At a desk at the far end, he spoke to a nurse, who flung out her right arm. He nodded, and went in that direction.

"Jesus, O'Rourke, what hell's going on here?"

"Damned if I know, Bander." He'd relaxed once his CO had left. "We were called in this afternoon, told to take up a position around the place and keep everybody out. Orders are to take interlopers alive, if possible, but to shoot if necessary." He grinned. "So don't try nothing, huh? Hate to have to do you."

"Yeah, sure," I muttered, not in the mood for banter. "Nothing you'd like better. But don't sweat it. We don't operate so well in forests and on lawns. Not our style. You wanna come down to the Jungle, though, we can play tag in the burned-out buildings."

"Neg that." He glanced through the glass, then stiffened. "Here he comes."

The major was with a white-jacketed man, probably a doctor, who had trouble matching Dourscheid's long stride. About my height and weight, he had olive skin and a night-black mustache. His slender hands moved like snakeheads as he argued with the major.

The door opened. "They've got her, Bander Snatch."

"What's the matter, Big Unk lose her a little?"

"Ask Dr. Gastine here."

The doctor scowled. "The woman known as Shana," he began, in one of those finicky, fussy voices I hate so much to hear, "has been admitted to this hospital."

"Who admitted her?"

"The Federal agents who arrested her."

I flamed off loud. "If she's been iced," I demanded, my step forward checked by O'Rourke's thick arm, "why the hell wasn't her attorney notified?"

"Because the law," he retorted, stroking the silky hairs of his mustache, "permits us to hold a suspect incommunicado for seventy-two hours—"

"BULLSHIT!"

"—when there are reasonable grounds for believing the suspect to be insane."

III

With a bland, bureaucratic disregard for the anxiety they'd caused, Dourscheid and Gastine refused to say anything more. My frantic questions were met with metronomic head shakes that only fanned my frustration. They stalled for at least ten minutes, until the doctor's belt beeped and he sighed with relief. "Dr. Pajalli has arrived," he said. "He will explain."

They escorted me through a bewildering series of glossy corridors. The building was far larger than its facade had suggested; I couldn't have retraced the route if I'd had to. At last they stepped aside and pointed to an iron-banded wooden door. I swaggered in, scuffing my bootheels on the thick ivory carpet. Despite the room's aura of power consolidated, I was ready to bluster, but a glance at Dr. Pajalli stopped me.

He stood behind a huge square of polished mahogany that floated 75 centimeters above the floor. The desk was bare, save for a human brain imbedded in a block of lucite, and it seemed to bisect him.

He was 150 centimeters tall, wearing long brown hair spiked with streaks of gray. His eyes held me like a lepidopterist's pin. Ebony, they were hard and cold, and scoped the interior of my soul.

His long, hairy fingers arched out from his palm like spider's legs. While he spoke, they toyed with the lucite block. He was terse.

"The woman called Shana is my hostage." His voice complemented his eyes perfectly. "I hold her to ensure

45

your cooperation. If you participate in certain tests, she will be released at their conclusion. If you refuse, she will be disposed of as I see fit."

"What kind of sand have you been shooting? You can't—"

"I can," he broke in. "A man was found dead in your area this morning. Witnesses will testify that she murdered him."

I appealed to Dourscheid. "Major, this gashead is—"

"—my CO, for the moment." He folded his arms across his chest and inspected the rug for uniform softness.

"Bander Snatch," cracked Pajalli's whip-voice, "it is in my power to have your lover declared insane. Should I do that, I could treat her, experiment on her, or institutionalize her for life."

"NO!" I slammed my fist onto his desktop, which shrugged it off. His furry fingers steadied the brain cube. "She wouldn't survive one of those places, and you know it!"

We all did. The institutions harboring the incurables were scattered in desolate areas where their residents could not interfere with "normal" citizens. There were several in the ice-bound wastes of Alaska, more in the Yucatan jungles, a few on coral islands in the Pacific . . . all places where the abandoned could run free, at no cost to society, and with no chance of return.

"Alternately," he continued, "I could declare her_sane. She would then be tried for murder, and would, almost inevitably, be found guilty."

"She never left the ComCenter, Pajalli, and we can prove it!"

"Who will believe a Jungle Lord?"

I winced, and bit my lip. No one would. We could parade a thousand Jungle dwellers through the courtroom, and not one of them would be a convincing witness. Especially if the jury came from Fedra Three.

"The possibility must be considered, however," he went on. "Should she be acquitted, she will find herself on the far side of the world, without friends, money, or documents. She might survive. She might even return, in a decade or so. On the other hand, you *could* cooperate."

That did it. "All right. You think you've done me. But I've got 160 Zulus who'd love to run a meltdown on this place. You got Shana in here somewhere, and believe me, even if you do have that damn army out front, they're not going to keep us from de-icing her. Now bring her here and let us go!"

"Bander Snatch," said Dourscheid, in a flat, just-following-orders tone, "only four of your Zulus know where you are. They can be lost. No-nose, he might scope this place out. He does, and he tries anything, and we turn your Jungle into a gravel pit. You scan?"

Desolation ebbed through me. I was a beached shark, and it was low tide. But I had one last play: there was a gun inside my tunic, and a sheath knife inside my left boot. I went for them. Shock widened three pair of eyes. "Get her down here."

A fireball exploded between my ears. I fell to my knees. My fingers opened. The gun and the knife thudded softly onto the rug. A peculiar noise welled up in my throat. I pitched forward, and everything went black.

When I came to, three expressionless faces gazed down at me. Dourscheid held my weapons. Pajalli fondled his damn brain. Gastine said, "You're ours, Bander."

"All right." I was furious, but helpless as well. And my head hurt. Later, I'd find a way to cough them all and get out. For the moment, though: "I don't seem to have any choice. What do you want me to do?"

Pajalli balanced the lucite block on one corner and spun it like a top. "Dr. Gastine will arrange for a comprehensive explanation." The brain in the plastic blurred as it whirled. Just like mine.

In the hallway beyond the heavy door, I asked my ex-tacit ally how I'd been done. He said he didn't know, but things like that happened around Lomala. Then we shook and he said good-bye, his lined face as inscrutable as ever. When he walked away, his shoulders seemed slumped . . . as though they bore a new burden.

Gastine brushed off the same question with a brief "You'll see," and led me to a tiny cubicle. "Wait inside," he said, just before he closed its door. It made two clicks: the second was a lock.

Beams of light, broken by thick wire mesh, fell on a comfortably padded armchair. Shrugging, I sat in it.

I was disgusted with myself. Trusting the major, I'd allowed myself to be suckered into the oldest trap known. If I'd stayed outside, threatened to lose a civilian or two, I might have been able to deal. As it was, I'd blithely charged in, and wound up on ice. With a migraine, to boot.

A synergistic compound of depression and fear settled

over me. I was impotent. I might be in danger. Others were going to determine my fate, as well as Shana's, and I didn't know them. They were cool clinicians, and we were rats for their maze.

The fixture overhead, which had originally looked like a fluorescent, began to shed warm, friendly light. Once I relaxed, its intensity dipped. The cubicle had become cosy; I yawned, and slouched. I rubbed my itchy eyes, and let them shut.

In my head awoke a dream that had no plot, no characters . . . a static image, a vision of a rainbow pyramid. Its colors—red at the top, violet at the bottom—shaded into each other indiscernibly. My mind's eye gaped at it, and I drew closer.

Gradually, the pyramid became a collage of evenly spaced single-colored particles. I focused on one that was topaz blue, and initially brilliant. It enlarged until it split in two. The new dots revolved around each other, then one spun up into the orange. Room was made for it, and its hue became that of its neighbors. The other stayed put, dimmed, and went out.

I scratched my temple and wondered what was going on. That was not the kind of dream that usually wanders through my head. I tend to see people, faces, and teeth.

The pyramid began to change; the colors no longer blended. Lines appeared, and widened. Strata formed. I picked out a particle for close observation: it, too, was born in brilliance, grew, and split—but the new continued to orbit the old, even though it was a different shade. The father faded, and still the child stayed, struggling, palpably, to imitate its sire.

The process accelerated; the rainbow disappeared. Replacing the cohesive entity were layers upon paper-thin layers of multicolored dots. Before long, the gaps between layers were thicker than the layers themselves. A wind came up . . . the pyramid collapsed. A few particles still hung in the air, high above the rest, trying to summon up a shape for the rubble to assume. The effort was too much. They, too, fell, and the dream dissolved.

A far-off voice was speaking: ". . . enter a contest which one wishes to win, one may enhance his chances for success by seeing to it that potentially more capable competitors are disqualified before the contest begins . . ."

I blinked. There wasn't room in the cubicle for a second person, except on my lap, but I couldn't see a speaker. As

48

the wall might have been one, I pressed my ear against it. I couldn't hear any better, so I sat up and relaxed.

". . . sponsoring organization may, on the other hand, wish to award its prize purely on the basis of achievement in that contest. In this case, one may assume that the winner represents the best that the talent pool is capable of producing."

A new picture formed in my head: two men wearing mountain gear stood below a sheer rock face. They measured each other with the eyes of rivals. Then a voice counted off, "One, two, three, GO!" They leaped forward. Almost immediately, one raced ahead of the other. The loser raised his arms in fury, displaying handless stumps.

The door to the cubicle jerked away. A huge black face thrust against mine; its eyes were like portholes and its voice like an organ. "Do you scan what's happening?"

"Not a bit of it."

"Sonuvabitch," he said, withdrawing and slamming the door.

"Then let's take it from a different angle," said whoever'd been talking about contests.

I shrugged and looked around. Still nobody. Sandy dream.

Boxes, each with two jutting pipes, stretched to the horizon. One pipe from each dove into a crystal stream; the other reached for the clouds. The submerged one on the nearest slurped. A moment later, a bubble formed on the upraised pipe, then broke away and floated off. It was beautiful. When it burst, as all bubbles must, it left behind clean air tinged with love.

The next was blue with green specks, rather than blue with red specks. Its bubble was less attractive, and its aftermath less pleasing.

The third was like the first, in both appearance and performance.

The fourth, purple under ivory, blew a sticky brown bubble that fell to the ground, where it bounced until it found a spike on which to impale itself. Its stench curdled my stomach.

Suddenly I was lifted into the air. Half the boxes resembled the first and third; the rest, of a hundred shapes and colors, produced an inferior bubble. I was puzzled. Turning to the box next to me, I asked, "Why do you have so many that can't make good bubbles?"

The box replied, "We have to have a thousand—we always have."

"Ah," I said, not scanning at all. Higher I rose. The crystal creek ran between two walls. On the far side of each were other boxes, at other creeks. On the right, they manufactured fertilizer; on the left, charcoal. Among each were some blues with red specks. "Now that color there," I said, pointing out one, "makes a nova bubble. Why not take it off the fertilizer line, put it on the bubble line?"

"It must find its own way there."

"But there's a wall in between."

"Yes, there is."

"Well, who built the wall?"

"The bubblemakers."

"Which bubblemakers?"

"The ones who care more about making bubbles than about the bubbles they make."

"Uh-huh," I said, and when the cubicle door swung and the black face hung, I snarled, "No, goddamit, I still don't know what the fuck's going on."

"Ah, shit," he said as he left.

His voice mingled with another's in the hall outside. It alternated between anger and derision; the other, though fainter, had a stubbornness, a cultured ability to dig in its heels and stand fast. The discussion, evidently, was between equals who looked down on each other.

Apparently the black man won, because he flung back the door and snapped, "Out!" Moving slowly, I rose, stretched, and yawned in his face. It was hard not to hit him and run, but Shana was still on secret ice. "What's up?" I asked him.

"Ah, it's these goddam artsy-fartsy intellectuals with their incomprehensible symbols—they flame me off, y'know?" He jerked his chin to the right, and we sauntered in that direction. "Me, I prefer straight talk. They claim, though, that their imagery implants ideas just as thoroughly, while avoiding the buzz-word syndrome."

"The what?"

"Buzz-word—a word that has so many connotations that its true meaning is lost." He started to gesture, but his hands were manacled to a thick leather belt encircling his waist.

"Oh."

"In here." His chin indicated a slowly opening door.

I frowned, remembering a click as the doorknob had

been turned. "How'd you do that?" I asked, pointedly staring at his hands.

His leathery face split into a wide grin. "Tell you later."

"Yeah."

"In."

It was a stuffy, wood-paneled room dominated by a round conference table. Around the ashtrays and the memo pads sat the apparent remnants of a defunct sideshow.

One birdlike specimen in a wheelchair wore a sculpted vinyl helmet which held a miniature keyboard against his tremulous lower lip. His tongue, pale and narrow, licked a key; the chair twisted so he could see me. Another, to all appearances a normal, middle-aged white male, spasmed every three minutes, and shrieked in a guttural foreign language. A woman in a well-tailored green dress, like an insurance salesman's, suddenly rose to slap the man who sat next to her, saying, "One more time and I cut them off, you bastard." Fingermarks glowed white on his round, pink face; he twitched out a few foolish grins, then raised his eyebrows. Something about him was familiar.

"What's going on?" I hissed to the black, whose handcuffs made him a full-fledged member of their company.

"Later," he whispered.

Once I was seated they stared at me, asking nothing, stating nothing, simply staring. My eyes skipped around the circle of faces like a bumblebee hunting for pollen. I was looking for friendliness, sympathy, what-have-you. I found none, but at least there was no overt hostility.

A draft of fresher air heralded Gastine's arrival. He was accompanied by a younger man, also in white, whose carefully manicured hands also clutched a clipboard. It was obviously a badge of rank. Those already sitting nodded to them, and mumbled greetings under their breaths. The doctors, smiling and patting shoulders, found themselves chairs on opposite sides of the table.

I realized that there was no one between me and the door, and that I could be tearing through the halls before anyone could stop me. I started to tense. The younger doctor raised his blue eyes and said simply, "Don't."

I didn't.

Gastine tugged a ballpoint from the several in his pocket, and scribbled on his clipboard. "Well, Bander," he said heartily, square white teeth flashing, "we're here to explain what Dr. Pajalli didn't." He caught the light of imminent interruption in my eye, and hastened, "Things will go much more quickly if you simply listen. Please hold your questions until we have finished."

I could do nothing but shrug assent.

"Point One: The Semiperfect Society. You may not realize this, Bander, but living conditions today, even in the FDRA's, are vastly superior to—"

"I read a lot of books," I said. "I know things have gotten better."

"Very good." Eyes on me, he paused, as if to readjust his style. "Nonetheless, let me recapitulate several of the more significant factors: (a) The L5 colonies have spread prosperity by supplying us with endless amounts of electricity and metals. (b) Population growth has ceased, which combined with (c) the Fourth Green Revolution, has eliminated famine. (d) Advances in medicine have made disease obsolete; only the degenerative ailments remain, and these respond favorably to implants and transplants. People are healthier. (e) Computer technology, and (f) modern transportation webs, have replaced the majority of urban concentrations with small, homogenous communities. (g) Space now serves as a vent for the fractious energies of the world's nonpoor."

"Tell that to the French bombers," I retorted.

"Now, there," he said, resting his elbows on the table and leaning forward, "is a good example of what I mean. The guerrilla warfare in Paris is being waged by an estimated two hundred cadres or less; the serious revolutionaries are gone, off founding utopian colonies."

I conceded his point. It was a good one.

"Point Two: The Skewed Fault Line. In 2135, scientists at the National Institutes of Health realized that no society on Earth has experienced significant external stress since the Indo-Pakistani War of 2063. The semiperfect society had dampened internal stress virtually everywhere. An unfortunate result of this unprecedented contentment is that no governmental structure has been seriously tested in well over fifty years."

That didn't seem to be worth bothering about, and I said so.

"But there you're wrong, Bander." He glanced back at his paper; he didn't look at it often enough to be reading from it, but too often for it to contain simple subheadings. "Bureaucracies are reformed *only* when it is obvious to *everyone* that they are provoking crises, rather than resolving them. Very few on this planet have been modernized in

52

the last century. They are dinosaurs which can respond appropriately only to stresses which the semiperfect society has rendered obsolete."

"You mean like riots in Fedra?"

"Exactly. That problem has been with us since Roman times. However, most citizens of this country—and others—live in a new social order, the ho-com world. Entire subcultures have sprung up like mushrooms, and each is utterly homogenous. Really, the only heterogenous subcultures left in America are found in the FDRA's. Everywhere else, one lives, works, and plays with people who do the same things he does. One does not need to interact with outsiders. Consequently, communication between subcultures has diminished, and mutual understanding has deteriorated."

"What you're saying," I said slowly, trying to transfer the words from my brain to my mouth without disrupting their pattern, "is that the ho-coms are tied together by power lines, market webs, roads . . . and not much else, right?"

He looked at me with some respect. "Exactly."

"So that like one good jolt could maybe disintegrate the whole system, because, say, a legal ho-com doesn't give a good goddam about an auto-assembly one, right?"

"Precisely, yes. You catch on very quickly."

I shrugged. The image had come from the dream in the cubicle.

"Point Three: The Theory of Approaching Trouble. At its simplest, it restates the old adage that, 'This, too, must pass.' Earth as a whole, or one of its societies, will encounter potentially destructive stresses sometime in the future. The possible sources of such trouble are innumerable. They will, however, exert force along the Skewed Fault Line, and then—"

"—the meltdown does us all, huh?"

He closed his mouth and rubbed his mustache, licked his lips, dried them with his fingers. "Yes. Very succinct. Point Four: One Possible Solution. If we prepare for all contingencies, we can avoid societal collapse. At the moment, bureaucrats in the Office of Civil Preparedness are doing their best to hypothesize problems and ways of dealing with them. We believe that this approach is futile. It can only further institutionalize societal responses to problems that will demand great flexibility. We feel we should develop a means of mass-producing leaders who can identify, and rectify, the flaws in the semiperfect society without having to resort to rulebooks written one hundred fifty years ago. Such mass-production would commence whenever it seemed necessary or even desirable."

"You mean like right now?"

"Well—" he made a small gesture with his hands "—doing it now might lessen some of the hidden tensions that have built up along the Fault Line."

"Sounds like a good idea to me." The warm, dead air provoked a yawn. "Sorry. Nothing personal."

"Of course. Point Five: Determining the Prerequisites to Mass Production. We studied the leaders in government and private industry, isolating and quantifying common individual characteristics. Among the study's more interesting results was that leadership is an elusive idea. However, even so, we discovered that a number of power-wielders were apparently unqualified, in terms of our preconceptions, to hold positions of authority. Closer examination revealed that while some of these were, indeed, incompetent, others with an equal lack of tangible 'credits' were performing superbly. That led to two insights: first, that our leadership development system is faulty, because it allows incompetents to creep in. Second, that certain unknowns compensate for apparent lack of qualification."

"This part seems pretty obvious," I said.

"In summary," admitted Gastine, "it does. But it did lead to Point Six: The Coincidence of Paranormal Talents and Leadership. You see, we scrutinized every leader who looked like a boob on paper but who performed well in real life. The computers couldn't analyze it, so we went at it another way: we talked to them, over and over and over, as well as to their friends, relatives, employees, etcetera, and kept asking, 'What makes you/that person a success?' We didn't get anywhere until we talked to Janice Ticplat." He nodded to the insurance-type woman, who patted her fluffy gray hair and took up the spiel.

"Well, you see, when they asked me that—I was working for Senator Thaolt then—I almost didn't tell the truth, I mean, it seemed so *silly*. I'd never mentioned it to anybody, of course, because if you go around talking like that people look at you as though you were, well! Anyway, I was very embarrassed about it, so when the young man asked me, I started to lie, but he swore up and down that the confidentiality of the report would be preserved no matter what, and that I could say whatever I felt was the truth." During her pause for breath, she focused her bright blue eyes on me. Something in their depths did not match her scatterbrained speech. "Well, I blushed and protested and finally let him wheedle me into saying, 'The senator's a success because of the green fuzz around his head.' Of course, I didn't understand why that got him so excited, but it did, and he thanked me and thanked me again, and the next thing I knew, I was working for Dr. Gastine."

"What Ms. Ticplat had done," explained Gastine, "was to see, paranormally, the dissipation of paranormal energies. We then sent her on other interviews, and in several cases she reported seeing a similar, uh, aura."

"Then they run into me," interrupted the emaciated man in the wheelchair. His voice was hoarse and gasping; one of the devices attached to his chair was breathing for him. "I tell 'em . . . green, blue, red . . . I see all kinds of fuzz. . . . In fact, I say . . . this was at a meeting . . . that guy over there's got some blue fuzz. . . ."

"The man Mr. Ench had so distinguished—" Gastine's olive hand gestured across the table "—was this doctor here. Close examination under hypnoserum revealed him to be mildly telepathic."

So *that's* why he'd said, "Don't." Even as I thought it, he nodded.

"Now," continued Gastine, oblivious to our byplay, "we can give you a demonstration, if you'd like."

"Of what?"

"Of paranormal talents. For example, Ray—" he nodded to the black man "—has telekinesis, the ability to move objects from a distance without physical intervention. This gentleman here—" he pointed at the guy who shrieked and spasmed "—has a form of telepathy; he cannot communicate with it, but . . . he caused the incident in Dr. Pajalli's office."

"The fireball?" My eyes widened. "*He* did it?"

The shrieker himself replied, "Ja. Haff you recoffered?"

I touched my temples. "Sort of. You really did me."

"It vas necessary."

"Hmm." I turned to Gastine. "You can skip the demonstration; it'd be . . . um, redundant."

The other M.D. winked at me.

"Very well." He glanced back at his clipboard. "That brings us to Point Eight: Recruiting Volunteers for an Experimental Training Program. We had one telepath and two 'spotters,' but that was not enough for a successful project. We needed more, whom we could examine at great length. Unfortunately, most of the leaders we'd interviewed refused to participate in our research."

"Dr. Pajalli, however," said the telepathic doctor, "had a solution. He maintained that there were vast numbers of leaders outside government and industry; he said that they would be more amenable to our plans because more, ah, pressure could be applied to them." He blinked, as if to invite comment.

"He scans realfine," I muttered glumly.

"Naturally, we looked for them in positions of symbolic or extralegal authority—that is, as leaders of social or fraternal organizations, and among the Jungle Lords of the four FDRA's. The only problem was finding them."

"I come in here," said the man Ms. Ticplat had slapped. The fingermarks had faded into a pinkness only slightly brighter than the rest of his skin. He still looked familiar; I furrowed my brow and tried to remember where I'd seen him.

"The convoy this morning," I said, conjuring up a memory of an overweight soldier in a constricting new uniform.

"Right!" Being remembered pleased him. "See, I ain't like Ench or Ticplat—I don't see no colors or fuzz or any of that crap. What I do is, I look at a person and I . . . well, it ain't *quite* what I do, and I can do something else entirely to cute little shakers like Ticplat here, but what I always say is, I blow a wind through their mind, and if I feel something in the way, the person's got a talent." Smugness settled on his flushed fullness. "Now, Ench and Ticplat can't see no fuzz 'less the person's actually *using* his talent, but I can feel it no matter what. And I did. You got one."

"Which?"

"Probably telepathy," answered Gastine, "since Mr. Ench has seen a blue, uh, aura around you."

"All right." I was getting fed up with the whole lecture bit. "That explains how and why you singled me out. Why'd you grab Shana?"

The pleasure with which Gastine answered labeled the idea as his own. "Three reasons: first, as an initial test—your ability to locate her indicates your powers and their intensity; second, she makes an excellent hostage; third, paranormals tend to associate with other paranormals, and we felt it would be worthwhile to test her, as well."

"Yeah." I rubbed the glossy surface of the table; my skin

56

oils left circular clouds on the polish. "All right, so you've recruited us. What are you going to do to us now?"

"Again," said Gastine, "it's very simple. We will test you thoroughly, partly to develop a simpler method of identifying paranormal talents. We will also perform some experiments intended to teach us how to enhance paranormal talents."

"Enhance, huh?" That would be nice . . . much easier to run a Jungle if I could read who was thinking of doing me.

"And, finally, with your permission and cooperation, of course, we'll try to inject you into our leadership system in the hopes that you will improve it."

"You want to make *me* one of Big Unk's boys?" The idea was ludicrous.

"We think you might improve things, Bander. There are a lot of duds in government. The more competition they get, the less likely they are to be promoted. Then, of course, your background is, uh, rather different from that of most bureaucrats. You might bring new ideas, and new flexibility, to the system."

"You've told me how everybody is going to benefit from all this," I said slowly, "so what do I get out of it?"

He was ready for the question. "During the testing period, your rewards will be minimal: we will ensure that no one usurps your position—the army will prop up your surrogate—and we will provide certain material aid to your, uh, Jungle."

"The way you said that," I mused aloud, "makes it seem that afterwards, I could be in line for some nova crinkly. Is that the way it is?"

"Yes."

"Well, amplify, man."

"No."

"What?"

"You may not be eligible, and I don't want to raise any false hopes." He looked around the table, as if to see if anybody had anything more to say. No mouths opened, so he nodded. "Very good, then. We're finished here. Ray will escort you back to Dr. Pajalli."

Manacles clicking, the big black man rose, and walked to the door. I followed, and in the hallway, asked him, "Why do you wear them?"

"So I do things with my mind, 'stead of with my hands."

"Such as?"

"Throw your wallet on the floor," he ordered me.

Shrugging, I tugged it out of my pocket and dropped it to the carpet.

"Now watch." He pinned it with his bloodshot eyes. Slowly, his thick eyebrows meshed, and sweat pebbles grew on his high forehead. "Not me, man, the wallet," he whispered.

Picture a warped rectangle of black plastic lying on red plush. It's still and silent, till suddenly, one corner jerks! Then the diagonal corner waves, and a second later the whole thing lifts off the floor and wobbles through the air, like an odd-shaped bat, or a very heavy piece of wind-litter.

Disturbed, but wanting to be on-key, I snatched it and shoved it into my pocket. Tele . . . tele . . . whatever, was really impressive. Be nice if I could learn it, too. "Nice trick," I said, wishing that my voice hadn't sounded quite so hoarse.

"I'm getting better at it." He shook his bushy head and the sweat flew in a dozen directions.

"Uh-huh." There was more I wanted to ask, but we'd come to Pajalli's office. The big brass doorknob spun itself eerily, and Ray motioned me in.

"So, Bander Snatch," began the tight bundle of purpose behind the suspended desk. Late at night though it was, his smooth East Indian face showed no stubble. "Are your questions resolved? Is the situation lucid?"

"Sort of," I admitted, approaching him as though I belonged there because I refused to show uneasiness to anyone.

"Wonderful," he said. "Pull a chair up to my desk, and write a letter."

"Hey," I snapped, "you may have done me, but I'm not your secretary."

He chuckled. The sound was clearly something he'd been taught, rather than ever having felt. "I apologize for the ambiguity. I wish you to write your second in command, informing him or her that you will be away for the next thirty days, and so forth."

"What's the 'and so forth'?"

"I do not plan to dictate the letter, Bander Snatch, nor do I intend to censor it. I had thought you might wish to instruct him, or explain to him the army's role in maintaining your authority, or the like."

"Yeah, that's an idea." I dragged the chair to the side of

the desk; its feet left furrows in the deep ivory rug. He'd laid out a silver-trimmed pen and, under the brain-block, a sheet of paper as stiff as cardboard. "What's this about material aid to my Jungle?"

"We will provide some," he said cautiously. "What did you have in mind?"

I daydreamed of all the things that the Jungle didn't have . . . shaking the visions out of my head, I next thought of all the things we *had* to have. "How about demolition and construction crews?"

"Too much."

"Then just a construction crew?"

"Still too much."

"Dammit, you—" I realized anger wouldn't help. "All right . . . how about you send down four people to teach us some shit?"

"What kind of, er, instruction did you have in mind?"

"Plumbing, electrics, carpentry, and masonry." I ticked them off on my fingers, then glanced up at him. "Emphasis on repairs, mostly. We're doing it all by ear, and—"

"No problem. They will report to your deputy first thing in the morning."

"All right." I scowled at the blank sheet of paper, then gingerly tugged it out from under the lucite. "What the hell kind of letter . . ."

He stood aloof, as though I hadn't said a word, and never would.

With a curse, I started writing.

Dear No-nose,

I found Shana. She's OK. Don't worry. The Feds iced her just so they could ice me, too. But don't worry about me. I'm OK.

I'm doing sort of a deal with them. They want to test me for some things. I said OK, if they'd send some people down to teach us some of that construction shit. So four teachers are going to show up looking for you tomorrow. Stop all the construction and get the workers in to listen to them. This is shit we got to know.

You're in charge of the Jungle while I'm gone, which'll be about a month, I think. If you got any trouble with people trying to take over, let Dourscheid know—he's going to keep me in power while I'm gone. All right?

I know you can do it, so do it well, unless you want your ass kicked when I get back.

Bander Snatch

I signed it with a resigned flourish—resigned because I knew that despite Dourscheid, when I went back to the Jungle I'd find myself entangled in a power struggle. Thirty days is enough to get a taste for it. Damn. We'd been such good friends. "Here you go," I said to Pajalli.

"Excellent." He skimmed it briefly. "I'll have this delivered to your men, and they can take it to this No-nose person."

"Yeah." In a sudden fury, I snapped the pen. Droplets of ink fell like black rain; the thirsty ivory rug drank them in. "Now what do I do?"

"You?" He raised one eyebrow. "It is quite early in the morning. I presume you are tired. Would you object to sharing someone else's quarters?"

"Since I don't know the someone, I can't hardly answer that, can I?" I said sourly.

"And if I informed you that her name was Shana?"

IV

Gastine looked from his clipboard to the incised numeral, then checked his clipboard a second time. "This is it," he said, reluctantly fitting his magcard into the plastisteel door. I'd had him listed as a potential good guy, but I wondered why he wanted to keep us apart.

Briefly, I thought of losing him with my bare hands, deicing Shana, and getting the hell out of Lomala, but one glance at the burly sentries guarding either end of the corridor negged that idea. I'd have to reconcile myself to thirty days of guinea pighood. *Shouldn't be hard*, I thought. *Easier'n ninety days in Al's library.*

The door was thick, apparently soundproofed. Beyond was a cubicle with a similar door on the opposite side. "What's this?" I demanded.

"An airlock of sorts," he said. "That one will not open unless the outer one is shut." He touched his mustache as if to conceal his mouth. I'd been noticing the way he kept licking his lips.

"Thanks," I said curtly, stepping inside.

About to tell me what was bothering him, he shook his head. "We will assign you better quarters in the morning."

"Yeah." I erased his unhappiness by pulling the door shut. It hissed into its air-tight seal and squashed my eardrums. I swallowed hard. Gastine's key locked me into the darkness. As I fumbled for the inner knob, I cursed the missing bulb. In a multimillion dollar research hospital, such small details shouldn't have been overlooked.

The second door swung into utter blackness. My ear-

61

drums relaxed as the pressure dropped, but my eyes went crazy searching for light where there was none. "Shana?" I called, quietly, in case she was sleeping.

No answer. Calling again reminded me of pitching pennies down a bottomless well: silence claimed my words at once, and returned not even the faintest of echoes.

Christ, I thought. *What a mess I've gotten myself into this time.*

Nothing for it but to trip over her. Unzipping my boots, I placed them against the door. On hands and knees, right shoulder to the wall, I started a circuit of the room's borders. My ears were alert for the susurrus of Shana's breathing; my nose sniffed for the elusive scent of her skin.

In the end, my groping left hand found her first.

"Shana?"

"Ban?" Her head couldn't have been more than a foot away, but her voice floated to me as though across a canyon.

"Speak up."

"I *am,*" she replied. "It's this place—it sucks up noise."

So, I thought glumly. *That's* why my frustrated fingers had balked at defining the fabric on the walls and floor. They'd thrown us into a . . . what'd they call it? I read it somewhere . . . a sensory deprivation chamber, I think. No light, odors filtered out of the air, sounds absorbed by special insulation . . . "How long you been here?" I shouted.

"Since this morning—right after they grabbed me."

The bastards. Why had they wanted her in here? For that matter, once I'd let them ice me, why hadn't they moved her? They could have given us beds in a ward. Pajalli had told me to rest up for the next morning's tests, but how he expected us to . . . unless *this* was a test. The hairs on my neck prickled. It'd be just like that sly cocksucker, to put me off guard so he could study me more easily.

The velvet blackness infuriated me. I hadn't hassled frogs, threatened bureaucrats, and almost melted down with the army to settle for Shana's face in Braille. I needed light; I wanted to *see* her. *Dammit,* I thought, *tomorrow I'm going to—*

Two lights flashed: one baby spot for each of our faces. Shana winced at the sudden brightness, and tried to duck out of the beam, but it clung to her like a suction cup.

Interestingly, there was no diffusion. It lit only her face, while the wall behind her was as dark as if light had never been. The architect must have gone to great lengths to keep the room's air free of dust particles.

I opened my mouth, stopped, and let it close on its own. The lights had been too fortuitous to be coincidental; somebody must have heard me. Yet since I hadn't spoken aloud . . . the conclusion was inescapable.

Pajalli's research concerned the identification and development of paranormal talents. Everyone I'd met earlier that evening had claimed at least one such power. Shana had been kidnapped, and used as bait to trap me, because the researchers felt that we, too, had extrasensory talent. What could be more fitting than for the project's telepaths to eavesdrop on us?

With the thought came a perception: on the fringes of my mind lurked a shadowy figure, hand cupped around its grossly distorted ear. I closed my eyes. Other figures appeared, all avidly listening to what I was thinking.

Some high-sense would have helped. Once the soft white drug, which looks a lot like powdered sugar, is sprinkled on the tongue and absorbed, it goes to work sharpening all your senses to beatific acuteness. It does the same to appetites, too, but in that dark, silent room, I could have withstood the hunger and the thirst, if only I could have focused on the phantom invaders.

My eyelids struggled up. I studied Shana's scarred face, more rushmored than I'd ever seen it. She knew, too. So, perhaps, had Gastine, which would explain his reluctance to lead me here.

A giggle from the outskirts of my mind goaded me into further thought. Shana had been here all day; the listeners must have been gnawing at her from the very beginning. Sensing it, she'd donned a casual pose that probably didn't blind them to the tension that boiled within her. *The bastards,* I thought, *the boo-class little bastards.*

The giggle became a guffaw. I chose to ignore it.

"Snow Tiger." That was my name for her. I'd pored over dozens of Al's books before first applying it, but I'd found nothing else that conveyed—to me, at least—the deadly grace and hard-eyed realism that she shared with that beast. "How goes it, Snow Tiger?"

An odd smile cracked the stone. "It's nova, Bander Snatch."

I frowned. By using my digger name, she'd rejected my invitation to intimacy. She calls me Condor when we're alone, and serious.

I reached out. My fingers brushed her shoulder and found it bare. Puzzled, they ran down her side. She was nude. More of Pajalli's psychology?

"Why don't you take off yours?" she suggested easily, while her blue-green eyes wig-wagged her alarm. "You don't really need them."

"Snow—" I cut myself off, and scoped for an explanation. It came to me in a minute.

She was a proud woman, and an honest one. Her refusal to relate on our deepest level could only have meant that the eavesdroppers were inhibiting her. She didn't want them to see what would ensue once she called me Condor.

I knew it couldn't be that the sex we'd have might be interrupted. She hadn't gotten flamed off over that in years. Nor would she fear that her throaty cries would be overheard. Privacy is the first thing that poverty takes from you.

So it had to be something closer to her reality, and I knew like I knew our jectry was the finest that I wouldn't discover it until we were alone.

My frayed nerves creaked under the additional stress. Letting my head hang, I hunted in the darkness for my hands. My fingers were almost visible, were achingly close to perceptibility. They reminded me of the shadows that haunted my mind.

Why don't you leave us alone? I thought, not hopefully so much as experimentally.

A chorus of derisive laughter answered my question.

It's not polite to listen to private conversations, I reasoned.

More laughter, harsh and mocking.

I'm asking you all, for the last time, please go away.

To listen to them, you would have figured me for a comedian. And maybe in their terms, I was. I certainly wasn't showing any sophistication in the use of the talents that Gastine had said I might have.

All right, I'll play it your way.

A curiosity-spiked silence trembled on the horizon.

Not knowing what powers I had made it difficult. I remembered what the big black man had done with the doorknobs, so I concentrated on the nearest figure and visualized its head twisting. Nothing happened. I imagined a

64

fireball blowing off its skull, and got the same result. A fantasized punch sailed right through it. Snickers began to shatter the silence.

Fuck it, I thought. Shana's hand touched my knee lightly, encouragingly. I glanced over to her. Her impassive face seemed concerned, but again her eyes belied her expression. She wanted them gone.

They'd laughed at me, had they? Those super-educated, super-intellectual gasheads had laughed at me for being wet behind ears I'd only just learned I had. Anger geysered through my body. My cheeks heated up; my eyes slitted into hard lines. I'd do them. I'd enlighten those baby-fuckers for laughing at a Jungle Lord. I'd given them fair warning, which was more than I'd have done in Fedra. Whatever got put up them would be their own damned faults.

You hear me out there? I snarled.

The jiggling figures froze.

Well, hear this, too: you've pushed your way in where you're not wanted, and I'm throwing you out. Now, get!

Amazingly, the nearest shadow disappeared. Confidence surged in my veins.

The rest of you, move it!

Another form stumbled back, but didn't fade away.

You asked for it. I lowered my eyelids and painted a picture on their backs: a long, green-scaled beast, with wings, and talons like meathooks. I gave it an asbestos tongue and a fiery throat; a saber-tooth's fangs and a gargoyle's face. I named it Bandersnatch, and its laugh was that of a hideously insane killer.

Burn them, I ordered it.

Two more hazy outlines disappeared. Bandersnatch, a hundred tons of impossible meanness, lumbered into the air and set sail for the one eavesdropper who stood his ground.

The razor-edged wings banked and the monster stooped. The figure threw up its arms, threw lightning at my beast. Bandersnatch bathed its chest in the cold fire and screamed its delight. Thunder burst around its ears; it tossed back its head and sang the melody. The figure started scrambling for safer ground. My monster would have none of it. It caught the mind-raper, took him high in the air, and ate him.

We were alone.

"Well?" I lifted one eyebrow a centimeter.

Shana let out her breath with a whoosh. The carefully

constructed poise began to collapse, piece by piece by artificial piece. It was hard for her; she's not the kind to emote
over a stubbed toe. But she was alone with me, maybe the
only person in the world she trusted for more than fifteen
seconds at a time, and the day had been a succession of
drawn-out horrors.

First, though, she asked, "Did they use me to grab you?"
I shrugged. "Walked in."

"Oh, you idiot!" Plainly, she thought I'd endangered the
Jungle.

"No-nose is in charge, it'll be okay."

"Sure, but—" She gritted her teeth. "They won't let you
go, and even No-nose can't run the Jungle like you can."

"Thirty days, they said."

"And you believed them?" Her voice was furious. I
could tell she was working up to a real explosion.

"Hey—they leveled with me on almost everything else."

"Well, they lied to *me*—this guy said he was a law-
licker, came to see you—he got up close and grabbed my
rifle and then frogs just *poured* in!" Tears of earnest anger
glinted in the corners of her eyes. "They tied me, and
gagged me, and the next thing I knew they ripped off my
clothes and tossed me in this hole. Ever since, they've been
snooping around and it felt like worms were chewing on
my brain . . ."

Fury set her teeth chattering, and destroyed her coher-
ence. Her face was contorted; though darkness cloaked it, I
knew her lean body was cable-taut.

"The fuckers!" she screamed. The room swallowed the
words as they left her mouth, and that extra insult was
gasoline on a blazing fire.

The spotlight followed her as she jumped up and beat on
the wall. I couldn't make out what she was saying, but her
meaning was clear: she was damning Big Unk for snatching her, Pajalli for sucking me into it, me for letting it happen, and the telepaths for the scavengers they were.

She pounded and bellowed and kicked for five more
minutes, then slumped down. Lips drawn back in a grimace that stretched her face into a horrid mask, she shuddered. Then shivered. Then shook with a hatred so intense
that her features blurred as they whipped about.

It was over in a minute or two. Inevitably, depression
followed. "It's no use," she said dully.

"Hey."

"It's not."

66

We sat in silence for a moment, while I forced my exhausted mind to scout for new eavesdroppers. There were none.

"Can I let loose?" she asked.

"Will it make you stronger?"

"Afterwards, yeah, but . . . can you handle it?"

I took a minute to think it over. We have a thing, Shana and I. When the struggle gets too much, we quit, we drop all the way to the bottom and let ourselves understand just how meaningless we are. It's like wallowing in self-pity: once you climb out of it, you're stronger, because you realize the world will ignore you unless you fight for what you want. The only problem is, to do it quickly, you need a second person to guide you through it.

Saying nothing, I took her hand. She squeezed it till my knuckles cracked.

It wasn't her fault; her best efforts could not have prevented either her kidnapping or my icing. That knowledge seared her. It jeered at her delusions of importance, scorned her pretensions to power, laid out in awesome detail her unimportance to Big Unk.

Tears, slow and quiet, trickled down her cheeks along paths of scar tissue. I knew where she was heading, not through telepathy, but through the instinctive understanding that I'd developed during our years together. Though it frustrated me, there was nothing I could do. Not yet.

Smaller and smaller she grew in her eyes, like Alice who ate of the magic cakes. Though a tough, street-wise woman, she hadn't posed more than a moment's difficulty to the bureaucratic body snatchers. It was like when she'd been a teenager, unable to stop the two-gang meltdown that claimed her first beloved. Or when she'd been a young girl, when the tumbler trainer had chased her screaming through a schoolyard.

Those half-remembered shadows mingled with the bloodless vampires who'd sucked at her mind that day; to them, she was as easy to handle as a new-born. She knew it. She felt it. She believed it. And that sense of infantile impotence, in its turn, became the anguish of the microbe that measures itself against infinity, and realizes its own insignificance.

Sitting crosslegged, vacant eyes staring at the invisible ceiling, she rocked back and forth as she keened her misery.

It was time for me.

Spine against the padded wall, I maneuvered her onto my lap. She was taller; her chin grazed my cheeks as her teardrops watered my forehead. Though the room was warm, she was shivering. Her vision had frosted her bones.

"Hey," I said softly, "I'm here." An atom alone in emptiness needs a companion, needs the reassurance of something its own size. That's why molecules form. "I'm here," I repeated for the first of many times.

I stroked her shoulders, upper arms, and back. It wasn't sexual, sensual, or even truly physical. I was trying to kindle spirit-warmth, to penetrate the black night of her soul and to help her survive until dawn. I massaged her cold flesh murmuring, "I'm here."

"Thank you," she whispered at last.

The worst was over. Her awareness of my proximity would gradually dim her perceptions of the vastness that lay outside.

I put my mind on patrol, to watch for telepaths crossing its border.

Her sobs had lessened to sporadic throat-catches. My calloused hand, brother to the evening breezes, ranged the smooth skin of her back. It was no longer clammy.

"It's okay, Shana." Right arm around her shoulders, I sent my left hand to wipe the dampness from her cheeks. Her face was like sculptor's clay. My fingers traced the scars to her jawbone. Her breathing softened; her limp muscles remembered their tone. Something akin to gratitude flickered in the blue-green waters of her eyes.

She was almost ready. From the hollow of her collarbone, my hand dropped to her tear-spattered breast. Cupping it, arousing its nipple to hardness, I nibbled at her chin. She shifted her weight to give me room to grow.

I kissed her, gently but insistently. She couldn't be jerked back, not after her journey, but she couldn't be allowed to tarry in the depths, either.

Once I'd made sure that no one was approaching my mental perimeter, I formed an image in my mind. "Snow Tiger," I said aloud, "Snow Tiger, look."

The image was of her name-beast. Perched on a white-coated ledge of rock, it stretched in the sun and refused to worry about the hunters below. Its proud jaws opened and its lazy tongue curled in the crisp air. Then, raising its haunches, it summoned its mate to satisfy it.

Deep in her throat, she laughed. "Look yourself," she said.

Silhouetted in the misty distance were two flying forms: one the Bandersnatch that I'd sent to harry the prying telepaths; the other, that of a condor. The condor flew just above the Bandersnatch's tail. It seemed to be trying for a midair miscegenation.

"Uh-huh." I smiled. My hand swept circles around her navel, and the circles grew warmer with each caress. Under the soft skin of her belly, iron muscles hardened.

Then down to the swell of her hip. Her left arm stirred like an animal sensing the spring; it went behind my head and made a pillow for my neck.

"Condor," she said hoarsely, and somewhat embarrassedly, "I— I'm—"

I cut into her apology with a kiss. Her tongue teased mine.

"Don't worry," I said as we broke. "It's what I'm here for."

My hand crossed silken roundness to lose itself in her pubic hair. She caught her breath. Her thighs imprisoned my wrist. Beneath my fingers, she was hot and wet. Her grip on my shoulders tightened.

I rubbed faster. Her eyes closed; her chin knifed my cheek. Her breath, quickening, singed my ear. The intimidating universe dwindled into a luminous setting for her burning radiance.

She thrust herself backwards, pulling me down with her. We untangled our legs with breathless giggles. Her fingers clawed at my belt.

A moment longer, and another. She tugged at me, threatening to tear it off if I didn't use it immediately. Instead, I kissed her with all the warmth and caring and love that I could muster.

Even the stars disappeared. She watched the universe form. She *was* the universe, and pulsed with all its primeval glory.

The time had come. My knees fit between hers as easily as they always had. She gasped as I slipped inside her; her legs held me while her fingers savaged my back.

Deep I plunged, and deeper. My mind stretched to its limits: one part vigilant for intruders, the other totally absorbed in Snow Tiger's writhings. I wished, as I drove her closer to orgasm, that our minds could fuck as well as our bodies.

She hit her peak and her moan seemed to last forever. I

grunted sharply. Her arms and legs were mangles that wrung me dry.

When we'd finished, her husky voice thanked me. She understood what I'd done.

Exhausted and panting, I sat up. The dry air stole my sweat, stole my stink. I didn't care. I'd kept the mind-rapers away from Snow Tiger so she could have her moment of weakness in privacy, so she could reforge her soul in safety. I'd stood with her, guarded her, and guided her. I was done. There was nothing more I could do for her that night.

Meditatively, I stared into the darkness, into the very uncertain future that I couldn't escape. Then I shrugged. It's the small victories that count in the long run.

I ran my finger down the cool line between her breasts. She chuckled, stretched, sent out sentinels of the mind.

And then she did it for me.

V

The absurdly tiny figure behind the floating slab of mahogany made no attempt to rise when we were herded in. Only Pajalli's midnight eyes moved; they seemed to be waiting for us to commit a *faux pas* on his rug.

There were two ways to play the situation: I could humbly, obediently "Yessir" the man to death, and hope that subservience would garner charity; or I could be hard-assed, and hope that he would treat me like a man.

My hesitation over choosing a role cost but a tenth of a second. Then, hitching up the beltless gray pants they'd issued me that morning, I strolled to his desk. Shana's mind stayed close, ready to offer support if I needed it. "You wanted to see us?"

He blinked; I'd scored a point. "Yes," he said flatly.

"You're seeing us."

He descended from the chair, stood, and planted his long hands on either side of the embalmed brain. "You killed one of my telepaths last night."

"Me?" I was surprised that the eavesdropper had physically died—who'd have expected it?—but the astonishment I professed was more than I felt. It's a game every Jungle dweller plays with every authority figure. Admit nothing until everything is known. Make the man tell you what he knows, first. Then, if it will help you, fill in a few blanks for him. "*I* killed one of your telepaths last night?"

"One of you did." His spidery fingers waved, admitting that he could have been hasty in singling me out. "I want to know which."

71

Non sequiturs tend to daze them, so I said, "You don't look like a leapfrog."

"Leapfrog? No, I—" He shook his head; his graying hair brushed the dandruff off his narrow shoulders. "If you're asking whether I have requested the police to investigate, the answer is no."

"Why not?" Shana applauded my question on the level only we could hear.

His eyes narrowed, and his very pink tongue, serpent-like, tasted the air. "Enough, Bander Snatch." He climbed back into his chair. "Let me begin again," he said, clearly struggling to control his temper. "A telepath is dead, and I have reason to believe that one of you killed him. I want to know who, why, and how."

"Sorry," I said, keeping my face blank. "Can't help you."

"And you?" His eyes lit on Shana's broken nose, and stayed there as if fascinated. People in his world got such things fixed.

Shana's smiles are always stiff, because the scars on her cheeks force them into awkward patterns. People meeting her for the first time often assume she's haughty. In certain circumstances, that can be desirable. "Sorry," she said, almost whispering.

"I did not resort to threats," said Pajalli, "because it was my wish to settle this matter in private, but if you two are not more cooperative—" Letting it hang, he sniffed delicately, ominously.

"Gee, Doctor—" I did my best to appear troubled "—I'd help you if I could, but . . . Shana, can you help him?"

"Huh?" Her blue-green eyes went from face to face with the frank bewilderment of one who's lost track of a conversation. "I'm sorry, I was doing my hair and I didn't hear you. Could you repeat it?" Her thoughts chuckled softly.

While she pulled her blond hair flat against her head and tied it in a ponytail, I said, "Shana, do you know anything about a dead telepath?"

She sucked in her breath, primarily to gauge Pajalli's reaction to her well-curved hull. There was none, and not because her coveralls were shapeless. The man was a monk.

"Enough." Pajalli's level voice was coldly angry. "I do not enjoy melodrama, but you will either tell me what happened, or my staff will interrogate you. They will use a polygraph, truth serums of various intensities, and telepathic probing. It will not harm you, but it will waste everyone's time. Please. Honesty will reap no retribution. That is a solemn promise."

I studied his dark, smooth face. He *could* get the truth easily enough, if he were willing to invest his staff's time and effort. Besides, no law prohibited the thinking of nasty thoughts, even if a person happened to die while you were thinking them. "All right," I said, half-sitting on his desktop, which took my weight without giving a centimeter, "I did it."

"How and why?"

I described the previous evening, emphasizing my warnings, and the dead man's refusal to vacate. I also stressed the fact that he had entered my mind, and not the other way around.

Tiny ears poking through his long hair, Pajalli nodded, then astounded us by saying, "I apologize for the conclusions to which I leaped. You were well within your rights. He should have known better. I also regret my hostility, which stemmed from the scarcity of telepaths. I had considered nothing but the loss to the project that this man's death represented. I am sorry."

"It's okay," I said, as nonchalantly as I could.

His bleak eyes flicked up. "Do not do it again. Telepaths are too rare."

"Sure, sure."

"Unfortunately, it would be next to impossible to exercise adequate control over their . . . nocturnal amusements. No matter what I say, someone will repeat last night's misadventure. Therefore . . ." Thoughtfully, he toyed with his pet brain. "Have you any idea why that man died?"

"Neg."

"Let me explain. Each mind has a set of rules which governs the . . . creativity within that mind. While these rules are internally consistent, they are not the same from one mind to the next, although they may be very similar. Do you understand me thus far?"

"Uh . . . huh."

"Going from one mind to another, therefore, is much like travelling from one universe to another: one must expect that the 'natural laws' of the former universe no longer pertain, and that the possibilities inherent in the future are constrained solely by the laws of the new universe."

"If you say so."

"It would appear that the eavesdropper did not believe he was in danger. . . . Apparently he did not understand that once his mind was within yours, *your* rules determined the range of the possible."

"Yeah, so?" That earned me a mental kick in the shins; Shana didn't think flippancy was appropriate. When I glanced at her, she was frowning.

"Well, when that beast of which you spoke soared into the air, he did not believe it. But he was nonetheless subject to it. Therefore, he died. This is unfortunate, but perhaps inevitable, if you do not establish better methods of dealing with intruders."

"Such as?" I asked.

"For example." A hint of sheepishness colored his cheeks. "I am not a telepath myself, so you must understand that my advice is purely theoretical, and must be translated into the practical in whatever ways best suit you."

"Sure."

"Very well. You might consider enclosing your mind—with a wall, a moat, a building of some sort—so that anyone wishing entrance would need to request your permission."

Ducking inside myself, I saw my mind sprawled on a rolling plain, like a Kansas wheatfield. As soon as I visualized a wall encircling it, it was there. "Wait a minute," I said, coming up and out, "a wall, or a moat, they could fly over. A building they could break into."

"If that's the manner in which your mind functions, then your objection is valid." His hand gestured impatiently. "It was merely a suggestion. Do whatever satisfies you. I was simply suggesting a methodology."

"All right."

"Very well. I have disrupted your schedules more than I should have, but I am pleased that we have resolved this problem." He pushed a button; the door opened and Gastine entered expectantly. "Dr. Gastine," said Pajalli, in a conclusive sort of way, "will escort you to where you are meant to be." He nodded briefly and the interview was over.

The testing began immediately, plunging us into a three-day blur of needles, dials, and white-jacketed doctors who pored over printouts. Shana and I met in the halls only by accident; at night we shared a bed, but nothing else. We were too tired, and dazed, to compare notes. I didn't think of No-nose or the Jungle even once.

Our routines were stopwatched. A loud bell would shatter the early morning peace; thirty seconds later the auto-bed would roll us to the cold and unyielding tiles while blinding lights flashed spitefully. Four minutes to splash in the sinks, two minutes to hustle to the cafeteria, eighteen minutes to gobble breakfast . . . everything, from nose-scratching to taking a leak, was metered out in precise units.

They were running physical and psychological tests simultaneously. In between counting and measuring and weighing everything they could touch, presumably in an attempt to find a physiological basis for my talent, they battered my mind with pages of ink blots, and hours of word associations.

Accompanying me everywhere was an orderly. He was a big, hulking brute called Mosstooth, which, thankfully, was a digger name, rather than an epithet. From the morning bell to the evening collapse he'd guide my steps; always, he'd have buried in his palm a clipboard that he scrutinized at every opportunity. Tacked to it was my schedule, and Mosstooth's Mecca was a world in which every train ran on time.

"You've got three minutes, forty seconds, Bander Snatch," he'd say. "Want to sit here in the lobby and have a smoke?"

"Don't mind if I do," I'd say, but just as I'd get comfortable he'd consult his watch and say it was time for another urinalysis.

I didn't mind the physicians too much. Their learned poking and prodding was, after all, meant to determine my basic fitness, and health—my own—is something I've always been interested in.

Some tests, though, did seem less than helpful. One beaver-toothed M.D. wired me like a Christmas tree, plugged me into a computer, and put me on a treadmill. As an incentive, the treadmill was enclosed, and the wall towards which it flowed was "live." Every bump earned me an electric shock.

I'd come out of something like that exhausted, dragging, wanting nothing in the world except a cool drink and a soft chair, but Mosstooth'd take my upper arm and haul me along the antiseptic corridor to another maniac's testing center. "No time to waste, Bander Snatch, we're forty-two seconds late for your next series."

"Gimme a break, Mosstooth," I'd say. "Lemme catch my breath—won't do no good if the damn shrink can't understand me 'cause I'm puffing and panting."

"Haw, haw," he'd guffaw. His playful back slaps felt like rifle butts. "You're real funny, Bander Snatch. You're a pleasure to escort."

"Thanks," I'd grunt, fleeing to the wood-paneled lair of a mind-warper who'd fill me with drugs and cross-examine me about sibling rivalries.

During the minutes that the printout hadn't stolen from me, I worked on my mind shield. A domed stadium it was, with a roof that vaulted high and a sturdy beam for my Bandersnatch's perch. On the one opening I hung a sign; it read: "Closed for repairs." As far as I could tell, the shield was impregnable. And with my monster ordered to look for strangers . . .

"Come on, there's a guy wants to measure your inner ear pressure."

"Lemme finish the cigarette, Mossy."

"No time, Bander Snatch." The great hand would pluck it from my lips and flick it expertly at the instaburn. "Let's go."

By the morning of the fourth day, my nerves were ready to snap. I'd been pushed, pulled, opened, closed, and otherwise fiddled with so many times that I'd ordered myself not to take any more shit. Mosstooth, more sensitive than his lumpish face would have suggested, was treating me with kid gloves. Maybe in the long run it would have been better if he had maneuvered me out of the corridor, even if that meant slinging me over his shelflike shoulder.

I was slumped in a plastic cup-chair, head back and eyes puffed shut, when a shadow fell across my face. An unpleasantly familiar voice rasped, "Well, well, if it isn't my old pal Bandy."

I do not like to be called Bandy. My knees may curve away from each other, but it's for me to mention their mutual aversion.

Suppressing the urge to snap my foot into the speaker's crotch, I raised my eyelids. "Catkiller." The list of faces I would rather have seen approached infinity. "Why are you here?"

"Ask Big Unk."

"You were brought here?"

"Yeah." He gave the lobby's faded carpet a contemptuous sneer. "You think I'd be here on my own?"

I said nothing.

"They snatched my woman, figured that'd draw me, but hell! How was I supposed to know where she was?"

"Well," I said, unable to resist, "some of us know these things."

"True." He pursed his lips. "But the rest of us aren't so pussy-whipped."

"What?"

"I heard about your hunt for that shaker of yours," he continued. "At the time, I figured it was 'cause you couldn't run your Jungle without her whispering 'Do this, do that' in your ear."

I bristled. "And now?"

"And now I see you sitting here, with your ugly guar-daddy telling you what to do, I figure I was right."

Mosstooth laid his warning hand on my arm. Shaking it off, I got to my feet. "You care to tell me more of what you've been figuring, kitty?"

"Well, sure." He smiled down at me. "I figure you got to have somebody telling you what to do, or you would sure enough not know what hole to stick it in."

Anger flashing like heat lightning, I tightened my voice to a speartip and thrust: "Least *I* know enough to stick to *women*."

He's been touchy about that for four or five years, ever since the night he was so high-sensed that he tried to have sex with everything in sight. Any reference to it drives him into a desperate rage.

He exploded. Lips drawn back, he leaped at me.

I was waiting. My fisted hand sank into his gut. With a "GOOSH!" he lurched forward. Clasped hands found his neck and pushed it down, into my upjerked knee. I heard his nose break.

"Aw, that'll spoil your pretty face, kitty," I said, shoving his shoulders.

He toppled onto his ass, but was quick to recover, even though blood streamed from his nostrils. "I'll kill you," he hissed, drawing his legs under him and leaping up.

Mosstooth tried to intervene, but was brushed aside as though he were an hallucination. Cupping his balls, he sagged against the wall.

"Here, kitty, kitty, kitty," I jeered.

Breathing through his mouth with great gasping inhalations, he stepped forward, feinted, kicked at my head. My crossed wrists caught his ankle, but couldn't hold it.

The battlejoy was welling up inside me. I dropped my guard a touch to sucker him in. His hands stabbed at my face. I blocked them, but his knee jolted my ribs. I flew backwards, clipping my head on the wall.

Catkiller danced in, hands and feet blurring through a dazzling array of feints and jabs. His speed worried me until I caught its pattern and adjusted. Then it was less bewildering; he actually seemed to move more slowly.

I let three punches bounce off my shoulders, dodged another bony knee, then came off the wall with a shout. I penetrated his guard like a pin through a balloon, and my stiffened hands chopped at his neck and face.

I avoided the pressure points. Knocking him unconscious would have spoiled my fun. I wanted him awake and aware while I ruined his good looks forever.

Teeth shattered under my hands. Blood gushed from them and from his nose. Just for the hell of it, I cracked his cheekbone. I was debating whether or not to rip off his ears when a dozen meddling hands pulled me away.

"I'm not finished," I hollered, but they wouldn't listen. Catkiller did, though. The fear in his slate-gray eyes pleased my soul.

"Lemme go!" I demanded.

"Shut the fuck up, you gashead." It was O'Rourke whose hands pinned me to the wall; his round face was a storm-clouded moon. "Whatsa matter with you? You gotta try'n lose this guy every time you see him?"

"Hey, he started it," I said lamely.

"Yeah, and you wanted to finish it, huh?" He looked from me to Catkiller. "You were doing a nova job on him, too. Whadja do, get lucky on your first punch?"

"What do you mean?"

"Well," he drawled, like a man who's seen it all, "I've watched Catkiller a couple times. Another minute he woulda recovered, and then, my little Bander, youda been chopped to shit. Hell, you're all fucked up as it is, and he wasn't nowhere near his best. You got some kinda suicide urge?"

"You think so, huh?" My flushed cheeks threw off a sunlike heat. "Lemme go, I'll *show* you I can cough the bastard."

"And get Pajalli and the major on my neck? Neg that."

Over his shoulder he jerked his chin at his men. They started dragging Catkiller to a waiting room.

The other Jungle Lord had recovered some poise. With a shiver-type motion, he shook the soldiers off. Straightening, he pivoted, and stared into my face. The flesh around his eyes was cut, and already beginning its black swell, but the eyes themselves were dug from Pluto's snow. "You're a dead man, Bander Snatch," he said. Then he spun on his heel and marched into the room.

O'Rourke watched him go: one hard man eyeing another. "He means it."

I forced my split lips into a grin. "Don't worry. Not about me, at least. Catkiller's always promising what he can't deliver."

He snorted. Mosstooth hobbled up, slapped his khaki back, and thanked him for breaking it up. "I'll take care of Bander Snatch," he finished.

"You do that," said O'Rourke, "if you can."

"Come on, Bander Snatch, Pajalli wants to see you."

"Yeah." I followed him, not seriously worried. Hell, all the doctor could have done was throw me out of his project.

I had more important things to ponder. O'Rourke had triggered something . . . he'd figured I'd stunned Catkiller with a lucky punch, but it hadn't happened that way. Catkiller had been at the top of his form, and. . . . But wait, if he'd seen Catkiller before, and had felt that Catkiller was moving slowly . . . no, I distinctly remembered that I'd deciphered Catkiller's pattern . . .

Ivory rug slid past my feet, and I raised my head in surprise. We'd come to Pajalli's office already. His cheeks were blotched with purple. He was standing in front of his desk, his hands behind his back. "You are trying my patience, Bander Snatch," he announced, in a voice throbbing with threat.

I had troubles enough without flaming him off, so I held up my hands placatingly. "Hey, look, I'm sorry about the fight, but given the circumstances there wasn't much else I could do. Catkiller's the kind of sander who you got to hit over the head a few times if you don't want him figuring how to put it up you when your back's turned."

His black eyebrows rose incredulously.

"No, listen," I said, "there's been bad blood between me and Catkiller for years. If I hadn't lost him in your lobby, he'd be thinking of ways he could do me. I mean, he figures, I'm alone here, no Zulus to back me up, he can knock me around, enlighten me some, and then when we get out he can magic my Jungle, you know?"

His mouth goldfish-gaped, then slowly closed. The man simply did not understand Jungle politics.

"All right," I said in frustration, "I'm sorry I did it, and I won't do it again. There. Good enough?"

His fine-boned head bobbed; his hand emerged to gesture at the door. Mosstooth and I backed out, almost bowing.

"Whoo," said my escort when we were on the safe side of the thick door, "I thought he was gonna have a stroke right before our eyes."

"Yeah." I smiled briefly, regretted it, and pointed to the clipboard. "What's next?"

Never happier than when he could refer to the schedule, Mosstooth flipped through page after page of small type. "Uh . . . you're all finished with the initial tests. In fact, as soon as I show you where Room 872-B is, you're all finished with me, too."

"Damn. How come?"

"Because from now on your schedule's real simple: report to 872-B at nine every morning, break for lunch, then return there till five at night. No more corridor-hopping. So you don't need somebody who knows his way around."

"Oh." I blinked, suddenly realizing that for all his officiousness, Mosstooth had been a friend in a place where I hadn't many. I'd miss him. "Well . . . okay."

"This way." He turned down the long, low-ceilinged hall. "We take the elevator to the eighth floor, unless you like stairs."

Remembering all I'd climbed in the Jungle, I decided that even if the hospital's eight flights wouldn't strain my legs, riding would be more luxurious.

And it was.

"Here we are." He spun to his left, marched some ten meters, then stopped. "In here."

The small room was softly lit by sources concealed behind translucent wall and ceiling panels. Like the entire hospital, it was carpeted, and the walls were coated with a brown vinyl. The furniture was odd: a deep armchair that looked inviting until its wires became apparent; an examination table inset with a computer; a wall-hung viewscreen; a blackboard; and a bookcase filled with books, magazines, and things resembling toys.

A little man with skin like parchment was mounted on a stool before the blackboard. Hopping down as we entered, he smiled at us. His hands fussed with each other nervously. "Good morning." His birdlike eyes flitted across my bruised face. "I am Ralph Eaton, your instructor."

Mosstooth said, "This here is Bander Snatch, Mr. Eaton." He patted my shoulder in what he intended to be an encouraging fashion. "Go to it."

"Yeah." Turning, I looked him up and down. "You're ever up in the Jungle, Mosstooth, give me a call, hey?" I thrust my hand at him, and let him squeeze on it.

"Will do, Bander Snatch. Take care of yourself." Painfully crunching my hand one last time, he disappeared out the door.

"Now, Mr.—"

"No 'Mr.'," I said. "It's Ban, Bander, or the full Bander Snatch."

"Ah, Ban, then." He flashed a nervous smile; the teeth in his mouth had obviously started in someone else's. "What we'll be doing here is attempting to decide just which powers you have, and then defining the limits of those that you do have. If you'll take a seat—" His wrinkled monkey's paw swept through a grandiose arc and pointed to the armchair.

"I don't like the wiring," I said.

He flustered easily. "I'm very sorry, of course, but—"

"I have no choice, right?"

"Yes, exactly." When he favored me with another sweet smile, I looked askance at him. He made me want to slip away.

"So what are they for?"

"For instructional purposes—" he licked his lips "—for grading purposes, and for, well, for your rewards and your punishments."

"Punishments?" I let my voice climb.

"Well, yes, of course, a student who knows he cannot be punished will hardly make all the effort he is capable of." He sounded astonished that his dogma had been questioned.

"And I don't have a choice."

"I'm very sorry, but you have none whatsover." He simpered.

Christ. "All right." I sat on the chair's edge and let him hook me up. A cap covered my head, gloves second-skinned my hands, and socks hung baggy around my ankles. Each item was thick with wires to the computer in the table. To get the socks on me, he had to take off the ones I'd been wearing. I did not like the way he stroked my feet.

"What's all this for?" I twisted my ankle out of his leathery fingers.

He assumed an extra dignity, as though my withdrawal had been an accusation. "We shall investigate your powers," he huffed. "Your earphones will describe how another person uses the power which I will request you to use. You will attempt to perform the task I set. Is that clear?"

I shrugged, awkwardly.

"We will start with telekinesis." From the shelf he lifted a large glass jar, the lid of which was soldered on. Inside lay a single white feather. "Telekinesis," he explained pompously, "is 'far-moving'—that is, the power to move objects from a distance, without any physical contact." He set the jar on the stool, then pushed both closer to me. "Listen to your earphones; speaking is a person who has this power and who uses it well."

He pressed a button; a relay flipped and a low-voiced Midwesterner said, "I can use TK in either of two ways: as if I had another body that I could remote-control, or as if I were within the object I'm TK-ing. The only limitations that I've discovered are that I have to be in sight of what I'm working on, and that I can't do with TK what I can't do with my real body—I mean, I can make an ashtray seem to fly across the room, all right, but I'm only 'picking it up' with my invisible body and carrying it. If I get inside that ashtray, about all I can do is to rock it, to tilt 'my' weight first this way, then that."

The tape ended; Eaton's voice asked: "Is that any help?"

"Hey—" I made a face "—how should I know?"

"Very well," he sighed. "Let us begin."

"Sure. What do you want me to do?"

One shriveled finger tapped the jar. "Lift that feather."

"How?"

"With your mind, the way the voice told you to." He thumbed a second button. Across the gray viewscreen spread glowing green numerals: "$100."

"What's that?"

"Your incentive."

"Say what?"

"If you move the feather, you will earn one hundred dollars. If you don't, you will be fined one hundred dollars."

Thin biceps standing out, he hoisted himself onto the examining table. "Go ahead."

Hell, I didn't know what to do. Staring at the feather, I imagined my mind reaching out to it, feeling it, blowing on it so all its lesser feathers split. Then, with a pinch of imaginary fingers, I lifted.

Unfortunately, it didn't move.

He was pleased to see me fail. "If you don't do better by five o'clock," he said, suppressing a smile, "that'll cost you a hundred dollars."

"I don't have a hundred dollars," I pointed out.

"Well, we *know* you're a telepath," he said primly, "and these tests will be arranged so that you will be able to pay your fines through your earnings from telepathy."

I moaned softly. It was going to be a long twenty-seven days.

Late that night, I sat crosslegged on the stiffly starched sheets of my bed. Next to me, the even rhythm of Shana's breathing invited me to join her in dreamland. It was tempting, but I had something to scope out.

The fight with Catkiller had harassed me all day. An inexplicable itch, it kept pushing itself into the foreground and shouting, "Study me, study me!"

I'd finally given in. Being a Jungle Lord teaches you to trust your instincts, even when they seem to annoy you without cause. Deep-gut hunches that go unheeded often leave you lying in a gutter with a knife-holed back. Your subconscious, you see, notes and correlates all the things that your main mind hasn't time to worry about.

Playing the fight back in my memory, I tried to slow its speed so that I could scan what was happening.

I broke Catkiller's nose and floored him.

He charged me, hitting too fast, too hard.

I was in trouble; I concentrated on his attack.

I found a pattern in it.

I filled the pattern's blanks and then I was in control.

I— What?

I reran that scene again. And again, and again, Finally, I grasped what I'd done. At the time, it had seemed simple— and natural—to fight with one eye on the future. From one action, I'd extrapolated the next. Knowing where Catkiller's fists would be, I could be elsewhere, as though he were a statue.

But that wasn't all. Everybody who fights does that kind

83

of guessing, yet half of all fighters lose. No, O'Rourke was right. Catkiller should have demolished me.

Unless . . . a hunch began to rise within me, like yeast in bread. It came at such an odd angle that I hesitated to consider it. Then I sighed, recrossed my stiffening legs in the opposite direction, and let it into my forebrain.

I hadn't simply arranged to be somewhere Catkiller's claws weren't. I couldn't have moved so quickly. Actually, what I'd done was . . . I'd found the pattern's blanks and filled them.

Let me put it another way. If your nose hurts, you tell your hand, "Hand, caress my nose," and it does. Its motion, though apparently smooth and easy, is composed of millions of tiny jerks resulting from the expansions and contractions of your muscle cells. Your reflexes handle those cells on a level so deep you're not aware of it. Your subconscious brain emits a series of orders in the proper sequence, and with the proper interval after each, to make it all happen at the speed and intensity that you desire.

What I had somehow done to Catkiller in the corridor was to widen the temporal gap between each two orders. The sequences took longer to complete. His deadly fists did move slower.

I had filled the pattern's blanks and then I'd been in control.

The next morning, I almost described it to Eaton, but something held me back. More Jungle Lordism, I'm afraid. You always keep something up your sleeve, even if only your arm, because you *know* the other guy's doing the same.

So I didn't mention it to Eaton. Or to Pajalli, when I saw him later in the day. Or to anybody else who worked in that insane research institute.

What I did was, I suffered.

As I entered 872-B, the wall screen glowed with the single word: "Sex."

"Sex?" I took my seat, and tolerated Eaton's touch.

"Yes. If you fail, you will get none tonight."

"You'd put Shana and me in different rooms?"

"Oh, not at all." His hands played with each other. "The computer will run a hypnotape that will leave you impotent for the following eighteen hours."

While I was trying to digest the implications of that, he began to introduce me to pyrokinetics. He'd stacked gasoline-soaked sticks in a white ceramic baking dish, and he wanted me to ignite them through force of will.

"You're crazy," I protested. "What the hell kind of sand dream is long-distance arson?"

"Watch." He laid one shriveled finger on his right temple, and closed his watery blue eyes. A moment later, smoke threaded its way through the sticks. Poof! The pyre blazed orangely. Black smoke smeared the ceiling.

"Uh—"

"It's simple." Grinning at me, he blasted the flames with a portable fire extinguisher. "I drenched them in gasoline for you, but I, personally, can start a fire almost anywhere." His grin broadened unpleasantly. "Your paints, for instance."

His finger groped for his forehead, but before his eyelids shut all the way I said, "I believe you, I believe you."

He pouted briefly. "Ah, well, perhaps another time . . . but do, I beg you, remember this if you feel the urge to be recalcitrant."

"Yeah, sure, whatever you say."

When I tried the trick, I was a complete flop. No matter how hard I concentrated—and I had the motivation—I couldn't get it lit. Eight headache-spawning hours proved that I didn't have the power.

By the end of the day, I was as limp as the wires. "I just can't do it," I said, removing the gloves, and kicking off the heavy socks.

Eaton heaved a synthetic sigh, and activated the computer. "Very well, but you'll have to take your punishment. I hope Miss Shana does not mind."

The tape was a *bzzt*-ing beep in my ears. I started to get mad. It was all psychological. They were trying to make me make myself impotent, and I didn't want to play their game. Not with Eaton's wet smile hanging eight inches before my face. What was it with that creep? Was he happy I'd be hungry because he didn't have any little gayshakes to play with?

When he'd finally set me free, I stormed through the twisting halls to our room. *Dammit*, I thought as I jerked back the institutional sheets, *I'm going to prove that that leather-skinned queer is*— But despite Shana's best efforts, I couldn't get it up. It wouldn't even quiver.

The next day, the word was "Power." The goal was levitation. The result was failure.

At five o'clock Eaton shrugged; the computer clicked sadistically. Before I could protest, I was deep in a machine-inspired fantasy.

My ankles were linked together by an iron chain that joined them to the collar around my neck. On my hands and knees, I was scrubbing a vast stone floor. I had no brush, no sponge, no cloth. I was using my bare hands, and blood streaked the rough soap.

Catkiller was my overseer. He'd lean casually against the far wall, whip in idle hand. At regular intervals he'd saunter over, criticize my work, kick me with his pointed boots, and crack the whip across my bare back. Then he'd return to his post to lounge until his next inspection.

Helpless, indignant, in pain, I could do nothing but push the soap. Spread it. Rinse it. Push—

"That's all for today." Eaton tugged the cap from my head.

I blinked. I rubbed my eyes. My back was hunched, and begged to be balmed. "Yeah."

The following days tore my head apart. The nights weren't long enough for it to heal. Twenty-four days. Twenty-four sessions with the palace torturer. Twenty-three nights of maddened dreams.

Wires hum and computer clicks. Inflated Eatons, peering down from Olympian stools, juggle my mind in hands the size of beds.

Pebbled words burn the viewscreen: MONEY (we'll let you win every other time because we can take it right back). SEX (I really don't see *why* it should upset you, he simpered). POWER (work, Bandy, work! Feel my whip. Work!).

Insane commands: Look into the future. Visit Pajalli's office without moving. Become a Siberian tiger. Make me flap my hands like a bird. Burn this (*I* can, he jeered). Hold this and recount its past. Heal that man's wounds. Turn this greasy lump of lead into gold. Grow new flesh over your cut. Lift that feather.

On and on and on. Everything blurring, folding, collapsing time upon itself to draw yesterday and tomorrow into the crease of an eternal today. Electrodes rub skin raw. Fungus grows between toes that live in insulated socks. Ass is seat-sore; back is stiff; legs twitch and jerk at night because they miss the long walks through Jungle streets (never expected that).

Twenty-three nights alloy with twenty-four days because nowhere are there windows. Fluorescents pour heartless, heatless light over everything. Everybody looks like a corpse. Except Eaton, who looks like a mummy.

MONEY (read my mind). SEX (read the future). POWER (read the past).

The warped machine dangles me in the bitter wind. Cold bones stroke my wrists and calves. I wake up tired but fear the sleep of dreams. And Shana is little solace because she has her own tormentor, her own mechanical sadist, her own complex series of chill-sweat nightmares.

At five P.M. on the last of my thirty days, the intercom chimed softly. "Dr. Pajalli wishes to see you in his office," Eaton said after answering it. Unhappily, he disentangled me. I'd been trying pyrokinetics again, and he'd been hoping to see me writhe through another punishment trip. Age always despises youth.

Pajalli controlled himself better, though. Hirsute fingers cradling the lucite horror, he nodded to a chair. "Sit down, Bander Snatch."

"All right." I complied, and while I waited for him to explain, I reveled in the chair's unthreatening comfort.

"You have provided us with much invaluable information," he began, "and I cannot overemphasize our gratitude. To make it tangible, however, I would like to offer you a proposition."

"What's that?" My mind was crowded with fatigue, but it still had room for suspicion. Pajalli had already kept me iced for thirty days, and I had a feeling he would try to extend them.

"Quite simple, actually. At nine A.M. tomorrow, you will have to choose between returning to your, ah, Jungle, and continuing in our training program for telepaths."

"No choice at all, Doc." Did he think I was sanded? I hadn't forgotten his promise. And the longer I waited, the harder it'd be for No-nose to step down. "It's back home for this boy."

"Ah, but you haven't heard me out." He folded his hands and smiled, but the expression had been manufactured for the occasion. "It would be virtually impossible for us to develop your telepathic ability beyond its present level. We have not the knowledge. If you leave us, your power will be forever weak."

That was discouraging. Shana and I could communicate

87

without too much trouble, but frankly, when we were together, it was easier to talk like normal humans. And I'd been hoping to find some practical applications for what I could do. "I'm not sure I understand what you're saying."

"What I am saying is that I would regret, intensely, the stagnation of your talents."

"So?" My shrug was heavy, and resigned. "If I can't improve them, and you can't either—"

"There is a third method."

"What's that?" My pulse quickened ever-so-slightly.

"Some years ago," he began, and I knew I was in for a lecture, so I set my feet comfortably on the ivory rug and mustered my patience, "a survey team found an Earthlike world with a native intelligence."

"Happens all the time," I interjected.

"Yes—but this particular race is telepathic."

I sat up straight, and stared into a double image: Pajalli's delicate features were reflected in the mirror polish of the floating mahogany. "How come I've never heard *that* before?"

"Very simple, Bander Snatch. Prior to publication, survey data are classified documents. It was decided—" his ebony eyes glittered angrily, as if he had not participated in that decision "—that relations between our worlds would be, ah, difficult. It was felt that excessive xenophobia would ensue if our people believed that their thoughts were being monitored."

He sighed; it was a comment on mankind's flaws. "To continue. The aliens—who call their world Arkslsnagl, by the way—were as curious about us as we were about them. Once they understood the alleged necessity for limitations on Terran-Arkslsnaglian contact, they suggested that we use their planet as a training ground for telepaths."

"What's the place like?" My interest was genuine; so was my willingness to entertain the idea of visiting it.

He spread his hands. "I have never visited it. The expedition's reports, however, say that it is strikingly Earthlike. No life suits are required. Much of the native life can even be considered edible."

Better and better. "What kind of cities do they have?"

"They have none. They claim to be nontechnological."

"Huh?"

"They prefer an uncluttered life, which they maintain gives them time and opportunity for philosophical meditations."

I couldn't imagine a less likely environment for my kind of person—no cities, lots of philosophy—I'm an urban activist, not a rural contemplative. And yet there was allurement to the notion. "You want to send me up there?"

"I do not want anything," he corrected icily. "I am offering this to you as a means of developing your talent. No more."

I chewed my lip. It *would* be fascinating, and maybe even useful, to spend time in a telepathic society. . . . "If I go, who pays for it?"

"We do. We pay your passage out and, if you return, back."

"*If* I return?" I echoed.

"They warned us that their, ah, curriculum would be rigorous," he admitted. "The price of failure appears to be . . . death."

I rose, while wistful regret tried to hold me down. "Neg that, then."

As though I hadn't stirred, he said, "Should you return, we will pay you one million dollars."

"Say what?"

Honest amusement crept into his eyes—puppeteers enjoy working the strings. "One million dollars."

That was a whole lot of crinkly. "Shana?"

"She cannot go. Her talents are too insubstantial."

"She's a telepath, too," I protested.

His eyebrows lifted. "Just barely."

"But—"

"Enough for now. Tell me your decision tomorrow at nine." He balanced the block on its edge. "We will honor it no matter what it is." The lucite spun like a gyroscope on a leash.

So I trudged upstairs to our impersonal quarters and I told Shana about the offer. She'd had a hard day; she wanted time to think. In silence we descended to the cafeteria, where we picked at tasteless trays while the staff hummed and chattered and ignored our brooding oasis. Then we rode the quiet elevator back to the shadow-swathed room. Neither of us made for the lights.

"I don't know, Ban," she said at last, sinking deliberately into a narrow, sterile armchair. "That's a huge pile of crinkly—you could do so much with it."

"Yeah, but . . . off-planet? Maybe getting myself lost real cold?"

Her eyes had no color in the gloom—just a suspicious, blink-birthing shine. "What are your odds of surviving in the Jungle?"

"You got a point there." If I went, there'd be no meltdown with No-nose. And if I came back . . . there were places to live besides the Jungle. Sitting on the bed's edge, I reached across an incredible distance for her hand. It was icy cold, and limp. "What's the matter?"

"It's going to be . . . hard, without you."

"Hey. I haven't—"

"You have, don't pretend you haven't. You just want me to tell you it's okay."

"I wouldn't say that."

"I would." She pulled her hand away, and sat in the painful dusk of impending apartness.

"Snow Tiger—"

"Oh, Condor . . ." Tears—of exhaustion, of rejection— fell without hindrance.

"Hey."

"Sorry." Sniff. She shook her head in an autumn flurry of blond.

The carpet was thin and fibrous beneath my knees. I laid my hands on her lap, palm up, so she could cover them with her own. "Look—"

"You look." She knocked on the door of my mind shield. I opened it; she stalked in. "See this? And that? And that?" Pointing scornfully to sections of the stadium, she made things creak and wobble.

"So?"

"You could do better, much better, if only you knew how . . . and you *want* to learn, I *know* you do."

Touching my shield, she'd found my soul. I couldn't bear being stunted; I couldn't waive the chance to nourish my talent. Not even for her. Bleakly, I knew my selfishness. Numbly, I lowered my head to her waiting hands. Hands that gave more than they took. Hands I didn't deserve.

"I'm sorry," I whispered to the fingers of compassion.

"I know," she said, with such understanding that I, leaving, yearned to stay. "I know."

And we slipped to the floor, where we mingled with the shadows and each other. Her tears became mine. My hunger became hers. And the great dance of life moved slowly, sadly, through the bat-wing ghosts of the future.

VI

Five of us waited in the small, cool reception room next to Pajalli's office. Since we were all the same kind of people—hard, wary, scarred—there was no idle chatter, no low-voiced confiding in the stranger who shared the lamp. Our glances were unconcerned, yet measuring. Our backs were to the wall at all times.

Pajalli's well-groomed secretary was as cool as we were. Young and thin, he pushed his computer as blithely as though we were a boys' choir dropping in for a quick chat with the headmaster. Whenever Pajalli buzzed him, he'd listen a minute, then most courteously say, "Mr. Flame-friend, he'll see you now." His beardless face showed no nervousness, not even when Carla the Crusher practiced her karate moves.

The phone took him from his correspondence. "Mr. Snatch—"

"No 'mister,' " I said, rising from the armchair's upholstered warmth.

"Yes, sir." Thup-thup-thup-beep! He'd lost all interest in me the moment he'd transmitted the message.

Pajalli called for my decision before I'd half crossed his carpet. I let him wait till I'd closed the gap.

"A million in crinkly if I survive, huh?"

"Yes." His eyes darted to the frozen brain, then back to my face. He could have been looking for points of similarity.

"All right, I'll go."

"Are you certain?"

"Yeah." I made scuff marks in the carpet's pile. "Hell, why not? Can't make a million in the Jungle without the frogs getting all flamed off. I'll try it."

"You are aware that once aboard the ship, you'll not be able to turn back, are you not?"

"Yeah."

"Very well." He pushed a tablet across the desk, and atop it laid a pen. It was a perfect mate to the one I'd destroyed my first night there. "A waiver, releasing us of all responsibility for your physical well-being. Please sign where indicated. Press hard, there are copies below."

Running my eyes down the dense columns of fine print, I wished I'd asked Jake to be present. Legalese confuses me. I narrowed my eyes and read more carefully. There was no mention of money, and I said so.

"That is only the waiver. The contract itself is here." He slid another tablet over to me, and the print on that was even finer. "Forgive the nit-picking attention to detail, but Lomala's legal department . . ." He made a small, helpless gesture with his hands.

"Yeah, I know." I scrawled my name on each. "My own law-licker's the same way." I returned the tablets to him and, after a second, the pen as well. "Now what?"

"Are your, ah, affairs in order?"

By way of reply, I snorted.

"Have you made a will?"

"What's to bequeath? I'm wearing my clothes, you're holding my rifle. . . . I don't have anything else but influence, and that's probably gone already."

"I'd not realized." He uncovered, and pressed, a button set into his desk. Though it made no apparent sound, the corridor door swung inwards, and Gastine joined us. "Dr. Gastine will escort you to Pad 12. He will brief you, and answer any questions you may have, on the way."

Gastine's mustache twitched as he smiled a greeting at me. "Are you ready to leave? Or would you like to say good-bye?"

"I'm ready now." Ignoring his inquisitive eyebrows, I headed for the softly lit corridor. I knew he'd been referring to Shana. He'd expected me to spend a last hour with her, but I refused to admit to anyone that she'd asked me, early that morning, not to do it:

"Ban," she'd said, her hair a golden spray on the pillow's puffed white, "say good-bye now, when we're alone."

"I'll get you once I know when I'm leaving."

"Uh-uh."

Comprehension had come quickly, if reluctantly. The room had been quiet and secure. We could say what we wanted without feeling the pressure of an impatient car, or a down-counting rocket.

Maybe it's best to part in the morning. Walking away from someone you love leadens your gut. If you do it early enough, the minutia of your daily routine will distract you, so that when you have time to look in on your sorrow, you find it somewhat dissipated. When you do it at the end of the day, though, the heaviness lingers through the small hours of the morning, and deepens your soul's lowest ebb.

Leaving your lover's like chopping off part of yourself. If other things busy you until the scab's formed, then it doesn't hurt so much. If you sit there and concentrate on the oozing blood . . .

So I'd slid my fingers into her soft, fine hair, and I'd kissed her, and I'd told her that I'd be back soon. With a funny little smile, she'd said that would be nova.

Then I'd breakfasted alone.

The memory was shattered by Gastine's strong fingers. They encircled my arm, and propelled me into an antiseptic examining room. "One last thing," he said. His olive cheeks, flushing slightly, hinted at embarrassment. "We'd like some of your sperm."

I made a grimace of distaste. "What for?"

"In case—" he broke off to clear his throat, and to lick the trim fringes of his mustache. "To be honest, it's in case you don't come back. We don't want to lose your chromosomes: it's still possible that telepathy is genetically determined."

He closed the door, and another doctor appeared from a room within. Gastine explained what had to be done; the other guy nodded, scrubbed his hands under a u-v faucet, and set about doing it.

Mildly, I resented being treated like a prize bull, but I could see Gastine's point. TP was rare, and Lomala couldn't risk depleting the gene pool by committing all good telepaths to Arkslsnaglian uncertainty. Of course—through my mind, and immediately out of it, flashed the thought that with my sperm deposited in their bank, they wouldn't need me any more—of course, it would have been simpler, and more enjoyable, if I'd had children in the normal way, but Shana . . .

It wasn't something I could have asked her. My abdication would unsettle the Jungle, and for her to have gone pregnant into the maelstrom . . . uh-uh. Power-wielding Jungle women can't afford children: it would set them up for a choice that no one should ever be forced to make. In a no-holds-barred subculture, kids are natural—and obvious—hostages.

"Done," said the doctor as he disappeared back inside. "You can pull up your pants now."

After doing it, I followed Gastine out the door, down the long corridor, and into the spring air. Far from feeling immortalized, I was depressed by a vague but pervasive sense of guilt.

It didn't spring from worry that the Jungle would collapse without me—I had confidence in No-nose and Shana, for one thing, and I felt our organization was strong and flexible. I knew that my departure would trigger a power struggle, but my return might have done that anyway. My mood didn't seem to have anything to do with the Jungle because, frankly, I just didn't care any more.

I was going to the stars, where I might die. Could you fret about your hometown in that situation? Especially if you weren't ultrafond of it?

Yet the guilt wouldn't flake off. We were five kilometers towards Cleveland's Pad 12 before I understood why: leaving depressed me because it acknowledged failure. I'd always detested the Jungle, but I'd never seen any way out of it—in a world of specialists, I had no marketable skills. So I'd stayed, channeling my hatred for the squalid environment into a determination to rule it, and to improve it. I'd won some power, tried to apply it . . . and failed to make my Jungle better than the one I'd grown up in.

I *wanted* to leave. I was glad to drop an unmanageable responsibility. I was deliberately seeking a way to make myself more valuable to a world I'd never known. In response, my subconscious, aware that I was seizing the first chance to flee that I'd ever had, had been enumerating my inadequacies, and slyly suggesting that I'd fail in my next endeavor, too.

Fuck it, I thought savagely, and glared through the windshield. The ten-o'clock sun climbed behind us, its dispassionate eye blinking at the metal toys that raced the length of Interstate 90. "Ready to brief me?"

"Sure," said Gastine. "There's not much to say, though. You'll be set down in a wild area of the planet. Somewhere else on Arkslsnagl, a beacon will be emitting a telepathic signal. When you hear it, proceed to the beacon, and follow its instructions for summoning a rescue craft. Simple?"

"How's that going to develop my telepathy?"

"Getting to the beacon will require you to interact with the native intelligence. If you don't establish some sort of telepathic rapport, they'll kill you."

Stated that baldly, it evoked despair. "How many you sent there?"

"A dozen."

"How many have come back?"

"None . . . but," he hurried to add, "only one of them, to our knowledge, is actually overdue."

"Oh, that's just nova." I slumped in my seat. "How do I establish this rapport?"

"I don't know." He took his eyes off the road long enough to give me a look of wry sympathy. "That's up to you, Bander. You're the telepath, not me. But I'll tell you something—you're the best we've ever had."

"Thanks."

"You're welcome."

Glum silence filled the air; I turned my face to the window and stared at what flowed by. The highway embankments rose ten meters on either side, effectively blocking my view of what lay above, but I had a feeling we were already between metropolitan areas. Hard to say why. There was less traffic, for one thing. More sky bulged between the overhead bridges, for another. Mostly, though, it was that the shortcropped grass on the embankments looked greener and healthier, as though it were rooted where it belonged. Down in the Jungle, grass is a shy stranger—feet kill it, smog chokes it, shadows starve it.

"All right," I said at last. "Why couldn't you do the same at Lomala?"

"We would if we could," replied Gastine, "but it's too hard. We don't know enough; telepathy is so subjective that we can't establish viable equations and parameters. We could say, 'Achieve this much or we kill you,' sure. But the thing is, we couldn't judge you objectively. The Arksls-naglians can."

"Uh-huh." The road to Pad 12 loomed up on the right; Gastine nudged the machine into the appropriate lane and slid easily onto the approach ramp. The sun swung round to pour through my window. "I still don't scan."

"It's like this." He slowed to pitch a coin at the toll machine. "We'll pay you a million dollars if you can become a functional telepath. Since we're incapable of judging, we'll let the Arkslsnaglians do it for us. You earn the money by surviving. Now do you get it?"

"I guess so."

The parking lot was a madhouse of mirrors: a thousand strips of chrome and glass, each filled with tiny sunbursts. Gastine crept between two yellow lines, pressed a lever to align his own solar cells, and got out. "Coming?" he asked.

"Might as well," I said. "Want it locked?"

"Nah."

Pad 12's terminal was crowded with hundreds of suitcase-swinging travelers. The ones coming out were tired, rumpled, and bored; the ones going in seemed suspended in anticipation. All of them looked harassed, especially when the loudspeaker system announced a flight in not-quite-audible tones.

"This way." He pointed to a corridor that bore above its mouth the large sign: "Space Shuttle VI."

"What station do I connect at?" There were seven of them at last count, all identical.

"Rafschpuer." He flashed my ticket at the guards, who let us move through them into the metal detectors. Lights flashed approvingly and the stainless steel gates parted.

"What do I do when I get there?"

"Nothing."

"No, what I mean is, how do I make the connection?"

"You're not traveling first class," he laughed. It was a sympathetic sound, but it held a note of apology. "Believe me, the baggage handlers will get you on the right flight."

"Baggage handlers?"

"You're going in cold sleep, Bander."

I frowned. Total strangers would freeze me down and box me in. I'd been envisioning portholes, asteroids, sophisticated conversation in the lounge . . . what I'd get would be a glorified shipping crate. "Hey!"

"Sorry. We *could* send you first class, if you wanted . . . but your contract says you'd have to front us the difference in fares. In here." He gestured to a door; I decided to ignore its sign.

He'd made sense. Space travel was expensive, which was one reason why Jungle dwellers resented those who indulged in it. People who vacationed on Ganymede . . . how could they be contrasted with the others, the ones who didn't have the crinkly for a crosstown bus trip?

I didn't like the baggage handlers, or their workroom.

Gastine didn't seem pleased with the situation, either, but he stood chatting with me, trying to put me at ease, until somebody saw he didn't have a ticket and told him to get the hell out. We shook hands by the door. He stuttered slightly as he said, "B-Bander, I . . . " He swallowed hard. "When you came to Lomala, I didn't like you, Bander. I was really delighted with the way we pulled your strings. But now . . ." He fidgeted, and his cheeks flushed. "You've got a lot of courage. I hope you make it. If you do, well—" He grabbed my hand again, and pumped it hard. "Good luck." Then he was gone.

I stood by the door for a long few seconds, and found myself wishing I'd gotten to know him better. . . . Hell, I couldn't even remember his first name.

"Are you this, uh, Bander Snatch?" The voice behind my ear was reinforced by a light jab to my shoulder blades.

"Yeah," I said, pivoting, "I am."

"Awright, strip, step into that cubicle there, and hold your breath when the light turns red."

"What for?"

"You wanna go to—" he checked my ticket "—Arksls- nagl, or doncha?"

"I do."

"Then do what I say, or you don't go nowhere." His grease-stained hands tugged the brim of his hat, as if to draw my attention to its faded gold insignia.

"All right." I took off my clothes, and held them uncertainly. He scowled and grabbed them. "Thanks." I entered the cubicle. He slammed its cold door on my ass. The light at the tip of my nose—it was a tiny cubicle—was green. A relay chuckled solemnly. The light blushed red; I caught my breath. An instant later, everything was a mad whirl of soapy water and penetrating subsonics. It drained away quickly, and the light reverted to green.

The wall in front of me was hinged; it opened into a transparent "corridor" that led to a long, narrow box. "What the hell was that?" I shouted through the plastic, pointing back to the cubicle.

"Gets the bacteria offa ya skin," he explained. "Now in there." He nodded to the box, which bore a disconcerting resemblance to a coffin.

"My clothes?"

"Ya'll wake up wearing 'em," he promised. "Now in, quick, 'relse ya miss ya flight."

"All right." I eased myself over its rim. "Now what?"

"Lie down, 'n don't worry." He toed a floor switch. The lid of the box dropped from its berth near the ceiling. My eyes widened and my muscles tensed. It seemed to be falling too quickly.

"Hey—"

"I tole ya, don't worry." The lid touched down so lightly that there was no sense of impact. Its inner surface glowed. By my ear buzzed a small speaker: "Awright, now ya gonna get put to sleep—don't worry 'bout nothing, and don't hold your breath."

A heavy pink gas began to fill the box. Spreading from the far end, it curled up over my toes like an incoming tide. Its touch was pleasant. I watched it—holding my breath, I admit—until it crossed the bridge of my nose and swirled in my eyesockets. At last I inhaled its sweet murk, and started swiftly on the road to sleep.

I'll never know whether I heard it or dreamed it, but right before I lost contact with Earth, a faint and forlorn voice said, "I'll be waiting."

Climbing a hill of smooth black soil, no boulders, no flora, no fauna. One lonely shadow thrown forward by strong white light. The inner ear appeals for balance. Climbing without feet. Empty conversations drift and swirl in the valley below, mounting the incline on convection currents triggered by light that isn't hot, but isn't cold, either. Climbing. A steep slope, forty-five or fifty degrees maybe, yet the feet don't take part, depending on unseen helpers who push the body up a greased sluice. The air thins. The temperature drops. The distant voices soften.

The summit flattens into a plateau stretching to all horizons. Two steps forward—feet still not moving; nice trick there—and the light disappears. Pacific silence reigns.

A desert dark and cold. Eyes adjust to the dimness, find phosphorescent puffs along the skyline, no rainbows anywhere. The ground is unperturbed by shapes of life or other. Impossible to take cover, though the night is a cover itself, but footsteps would be harsh crunches in the still air. Except these feet remain soundless, while the solitary traveler has come kilometers from the plateau rim.

Alert for predators, rods and cones on golden time, tympanic membrane quivering even though no carnivorous paws approach . . . paws? Tentacles? Mucusoid ooze? Odd place. Stalkers would make noise, yes? Yes. Please? At least let them be visible, assuming they must be at all. Better yet—

White line slashes sky. Feet still hang uselessly, but the line becomes an arc becomes a sphere and the ground slants down.

Another hillside, same as the last, ol' black dirt barren except for body gliding down it towards the world's largest honey factory, leaning forward, wanting to yield to gravity's call, but held back by invisible barriers, skating down into beezy busy buzzing. Alone.

BOOK
TWO

I

I spasmed awake: a match had ignited in my windpipe. Either that or I'd just finished a ten-mile dash. My lungs were sucking in all the air they could, and rejecting it without letting it enrich my bloodstream. I didn't like it; it had laced my last dream with a stiff shot of terror.

Twisting wildly, to knock the squatting bug-eyed monster off my chest, I sat up. My hair and my shoulder tips brushed smooth tautness. I still couldn't breathe.

Forcing open my eyes snapped sleep's last grip on me. One look around the tent's prosaic interior cut off my adrenaline supply, which brought on the physical dullness that hits whenever I thrash my way out of a nightmare.

It's a mental letdown, too: one second I'm enlightening the distilled essence of evil, and the next I find it's just that my legs are tangled in a sheet. Reality's insignificance flames me off—I don't like my subconscious to indulge in epic fantasies. Life's rough enough as it is.

Sighing, I pushed my naked foot through the tent flaps. Clean, cool air rode in on a sunbeam. I lay motionless until my lungs slowed down, then I crawled out. It's a bitch to leave a pup tent feet first; I wondered why whoever'd cocooned me in it hadn't realized that.

Once outside, I saw why I'd been choking. The intake grill on the battery-driven air filter/heater was clogged with dead leaves, stirred by the night winds and plastered against the grill by the unit's suction. Strike two against the person who'd dumped me there. A chimpanzee would have found a better place for the gizmo than at the edge of a bed of leaves.

The third strike was called while I was getting dressed. The whole tent collapsed. It hissed. It bubbled. It melted. By the time I'd strapped the sheath knife around my waist, the thing was completely gone, including the air filter/heater. Only a damp, slimy film was left on the ground. Even, as I watched, the gunk soaked into the forest floor, and that was that. Talk about biodegradable.

Carefully, I lowered myself onto an outcropping of black rock covered with bird shit. The jagged roughness under my ass was my only link with reality.

Admittedly, Pajalli hadn't said they'd outfit me for a safari, but I had figured that I'd start with more than a suit of clothes and a knife. I mean, he wanted me back, didn't he?

A delightful insect, with a hair-thin body and lace wings like a drunkard's eyeballs, settled gracefully onto my left wrist. Daintily it rubbed two of its eight legs together. Then it bit me.

I cursed, slapped it into a bloody smear, and cursed again. My wrist *hurt*. The skin turned sickly white. A minute red dot at the stinger's point of entry expanded into a two-centimeter circle. A bump formed in its middle. Then *that* spread. Within a minute, the whole back of my wrist was puffy, swollen, and painful as hell.

To say that I was unhappy would have been an understatement.

I wasn't sure just what difficulties I'd been expecting to find between me and my one million dollars, but it wasn't what confronted me. I'm a city boy. The closest I'd ever come to nature had been watching a dog piss on a patch of scraggly brown grass. Now, I had known—from movies, books, and holo-vee—that forests didn't have sidewalks or slums or Jungle Lords, but . . . I'd never really thought about what they did have.

From where I was sitting, I could pan across a whole damn landscape filled with nothing but trees. Tall ones, short ones, skinny ones, fat ones. That wasn't bothersome. In fact, it was so much like holo-vee that it actually reassured me. I'd seen hundreds of adventure pics set in even weirder forests, and the good guys had always come out on top. But . . . the things that began to catch my eye were the things that directors had never shown in closeups.

Five meters away, greenish-gray dead leaves rustled. Nothing wrong with that—except the air was still. And whenever a papery curl fell away from the noise, sunlight's shafts bounded off a twenty-centimeter length of metallic blue. We had cockroaches in the Jungle, but never like that.

To my left was a tree. It looked normal, except for twelve parallel scratches in its shaggy bark. When I inspected them—which was difficult, what with looking over my shoulder so much—the first joint of my little finger sank all the way into each scratch. Now, that's something they don't show in the movies, unless the story concerns the beast that does that to helpless trees. And if that's what's happening, then the hero cannot be threatened by the sharp, shiny claw that's rearranging a pile of crispy leaves.

That was my problem. I couldn't cast myself as anything but the hero. And why not? That's what I'd been all my life. At least to myself.

Crouching on that stone, scanning the suddenly ominous forest, I knew I'd made a helluva mistake. So maybe Bander Snatch was a hard-assed Jungle Lord who knew his way around the gutters and the alleys. So what? Ol' BS didn't know shit about forests.

Ol' BS had listened to Pajalli; calculated how far a million'd go; and figured that since he'd never had any serious problems staying alive before, he never would. Gashead. Shame he hadn't been as skeptical as Shana.

Gastine had leveled with me. He'd told me nobody had gotten off this planet alive yet—but it hadn't struck me as *real*. Nobody'd had the cojones to kick my predecessor out of his Lordship, either.

I'd envisioned myself strolling through the forest like it was my Jungle: cool, poised, in command. The natives'd treat me like my Zulus had. Eventually, I'd find the beacon and warm up the radio. Then I'd sit on a log, scratch my ass and pick my nose, and wait for the ship with the crinkly. Nice fantasy, Ban. You blew it.

The forest had become very menacing. The pools of shadow that had momentarily been a welcome change from sun-scorched streets were now dank and dangerous. The overgrown wrens had sprouted hooked beaks and daggerish talons while my back had been turned. Even the ground had changed, from a foot-easing sponginess to thinly disguised quicksand. I shuddered.

Time for a quick inventory. I had a six-inch permasharp knife, a pair of boots, a pair of pants, and a loose pullover shirt. I raised my eyebrows at the clothing: Pajalli had laid

105

out a lot of crinkly when he'd bought them. They were duraweave. Soft, smooth, and virtually indestructible, they couldn't stop a laser beam, but nothing else'd cut through them. I'd considered getting some for my Zulus, until I'd discovered it would have been cheaper to build ho-coms for the entire Jungle. Even the army can't afford to buy it.

Last item on the inventory was me: 168 centimeters, 63 kilograms, in dynamite shape for just about everything. Especially running.

That would be my strategy. I was deathly afraid that I wouldn't get out of the mess I'd gotten myself into, and I planned to stay that way until the Lomala ship lifted off. Only craven cowardice, I decided, would prevent me from taking foolish risks—like letting cute pink bugs play with my wrists.

Fear is wonderful stuff, if you don't need an impressive facade. It keeps you out of dark alleys, and away from people with glazed eyes and twice your strength. When you don't have an image to maintain, remaining intact is nice. I figured I could stay that way, if I could control the fear-injection valve so that I'd tremble just enough to choose the safest way of behaving.

I shivered. I wanted to double-time my ass off that planet.

No hungry eyes glowed in the looming trees, so I began to concentrate on perceiving the beacon. I had to blank out my mind. Thoughts could interfere with the signal: sometimes distorting it, sometimes jamming it completely. I had to pretend I was an ancient street lighter, from the days when they used gas. Scurrying inside my head, I had to snuff out every single flame of thought. It took a while.

Finally came blackness. Lush, velvet ebony swallowed me. Darker here than there, as though it had been folded into itself, it seemed to reach to infinity on all sides. I hung in its middle, a lonely spark adrift in a great sea, and I listened. I listened harder. I listened harder still, till impatient frustration kindled a fire that chased the night away.

I was back among the forest noises, and angry. I'd done everything I'd learned about TP, and I hadn't heard Lomala's fucking beacon. Maybe *that* was why the other telepaths hadn't made it back—they hadn't been able to find the escape hatch. Assuming, of course, that it really existed. And assuming the Lomala cocksuckers had remembered to turn it on.

"Damn it!" I shouted, bouncing to my feet. My anger

106

raced through the trees, startling birds and small animals until it had thinned into a whisper. I kicked at a rotting branch, and jumped back from the cloud of tiny flies it disgorged.

I felt like throwing a temper tantrum, but a sleek brown shape chose that moment to flow around a gnarled tree. About 60 centimeters at the shoulder, it looked like a stretched-out mountain lion. As it glided towards me, its amber eyes were fixed on my face.

Absurdly, I was remembering Pajalli's comments on the edibility of the native life, and wondering if Arkslsnagl and Earth shared common ancestors. Just in time, I recalled that I was supposed to be a coward.

Stepping away smoothly, I drew my knife and held its curved blade low and rising, the way No-nose had taught me. I was not pleased. A knife was not my weapon. I believe strongly in the virtues of a loaded assault rifle.

The cat came on, its paws so deft that there wasn't even a faint crackle. Its silent approach made me want to spin and sprint. The more I thought about it, the more sensible it seemed. My legs were longer. Given my fear, they'd move just as quickly as would its. Faultless mathematical reasoning proved that I could put a helluva lot of distance between us. The urge strengthened. I was just about to whirl when my back slammed into scratchy bark.

The cat paused, and cocked its head, almost as if it were working up a new plan. I hadn't changed mine, but peripheral vision told me that the tree was broader than I was. I'd have had to scramble around its trunk before I could put on any speed, but my stalker would attack if I showed it my back.

I froze. The eyes of the animal that wanted me for lunch were large, and round, and patient. Its jaws parted slightly, to show a pink tongue and hard yellow fangs. It needed a bath in a bad way.

Totally oblivious to our drama, an antlike creature made its many-legged way down my arm, exploring what it thought was a different kind of branch. My hand came up to swat it, but my eyes couldn't leave the cat's. The ant kept going, up my wrist, along my fingers, onto the hilt of the knife.

An idea struck me. I waited until it had pulled itself to the tip of the blade, then I flicked the knife and sent the ant tumbling into the cat's face.

It must have hit an eye. The cat tossed its short-maned

107

head, blinked half a dozen times, and snarled angrily. The urge to flee fled; I decided I had to take the offensive. After one quick muscle ripple, like a pianist running down the keys to check the instrument's tune, my mouth warped into a smile. The tip of the knife moved in little circles. My left hand assumed a better guarding position. My feet slid out easily, pulling my back away from the tree trunk.

The cat was displeased. Its tail fluffed, arched, and swayed like an irate cobra. It raised its right forepaw; six translucent claws scarred the air. It backed off a pace.

Suddenly I faltered. All my soul begged me to run, and I started to accede. I hadn't gotten a quarter of the way around the tree when the predator, with a happy growl, leaped.

My left arm swept up instinctively. Claws dug into my biceps, but couldn't penetrate the duraweave. The cat stood on its hind legs as my arm raised its forepaws. Then my right hand darted forward, plunging the razor-sharp knife through hide and bone, and tore upwards. A twenty-five centimeter gash spurted blood. Its claws raked my side. It died.

Shock washed over me, and I dropped to the ground. Forgetting all about ants, birds, and everything else, I let down my chin and quivered for a good ten minutes. It wasn't a totally negative feeling: the sickness of what-might-be is far stronger than what-might-have-been. Mostly, I trembled with disbelief, both at what I'd done and at where I was.

The paranoia started then, when I huddled among the roots of an alien elm and realized—no, *believed*—for the first time, that the Lomala Research Institute had sent me to a place where I could actually, physically, die.

It's hard not to claim that my suspicions flowered at that moment. They didn't, really; that was merely their germination. But, as when an acorn planter visualizes the adult oak, so I saw in that brief instant the outlines of the plot against me.

Lomala had decoyed me to another planet by promising me one million dollars if I could return. They'd given me a knife, a set of clothes, and the promise that there was a way out. They'd told me that all I had to do was find their beacon, and luxury was mine.

Bullshit.

I'd listened for that damn beacon, and it wasn't pumping TP waves into the air. Or . . . three possibilities: one,

108

there was simply no beacon. Two, there was one, but it wasn't turned on. Three, it was there and operating, but not on my wavelength. As far as I was concerned, all three possibilities yielded the same conclusion: Pajalli didn't want me to escape. He wanted me lost.

My logic had been flawless up to then, but I couldn't understand why Pajalli wanted to do me. Though Arkslsnagl was an exquisite death trap, why spring it on *me*? He hadn't had to go to all that trouble just to get me out of the way.

So I put that aside, like a dog saving a bone for midnight gnawing, and I opened my eyes. Bugs covered the carcass of the cat. I watched for a while, listening to the dance of tone-shifts in their buzzing, until my stomach remembered that it was empty. With a grunt, I struggled to my feet. I seemed to recall that if you rubbed two sticks together for long enough, they'd burst into flames. Or something like that . . .

Charred cat lay heavily on my stomach. Though too early to tell if the stuff were edible, it had tasted all right. Of course, its flavor might have been enhanced by two hours of stick rubbing, but I didn't really care. I made a mental note to eat more slowly in the future, and stood up.

I had to find a stream. My hands and face were filthy; the thick layer of dirt, grease, blood, and crushed insects was beginning to irritate my skin. Besides, I was thirsty.

After listening for a few minutes, in the hopes that any water in the vicinity would announce itself, I shrugged and headed down a winding forest path. Probably a game trail, it was bare and hard-packed, as though generations of hooves had taught it the futility of producing life. From my point of view, that was wonderful. I didn't know what, if any, venomous creatures lived there, but if they were like the ones on holo-vee, they'd stick to bushes and clumps of grass—places that I, a conscientious coward, would not investigate.

A sphere of silence encompassed me. If I stopped, or was so stealthy that my feet didn't scrape, I could hear distant bird calls, and now and then the voice of a larger animal. But nearby, the only sound was that of the wind forcing its way through the foliage. Even the insects were quiet.

I didn't like it. It made me feel . . . well, when I was in sixth grade, because nobody else had a good suit of clothes, I was picked as the emcee for a school program. They gave me some cards to read, and pushed me onto the stage. The house lights had been doused, but the audience was still chatting. As it became aware of my short, stout figure nervously approaching the microphone, it hushed. Staring into the dark, buffeted by the pressure of their eyes, I had the eeriest sensation: that they were waiting for an error so they could throw things. I'd seen it happen in cartoons and old movies, and I was afraid. Not of the pain, but of the object I wouldn't see coming, thrown by a face that would never be more than a shadow. That's how I felt in that forest, as silence preceded me down the trail.

After two kilometers, a placid brook ran up to the path. Its water was clear, and sparklingly inviting. With many sidelong glances I knelt to drink. Almost as an afterthought, I shed my clothes and plunged into its cool embrace. When I gingerly sat on its pebbly bottom, wavelets lapped my collarbone. The sole problem came afterwards: I couldn't figure out how to dry myself. Eventually, I brushed off what I could with my fingers, and let the clothes sop up what was left.

The trail paralleled the stream and the two directed my feet. Far from having an instinct to explore, I just had nothing else to occupy my time. So I ambled through the leafy shade, alert for cousins of my breakfast, and wondered vaguely what the hell I was going to do.

Within a kilometer, my thirst was resurrected. Though practically bloated, I had an indistinct notion that desire persists after need has been filled. I stooped, swirled water over my tongue, and spit it out. The thirst didn't die.

I had a hunch that a chemical in the stream might have been causing it, but if that were so, I'd be helpless. It had tasted okay, yet it was so different from the brownish-green, malodorous liquid that trickled from the taps back home that I couldn't swear that the two were, at bottom, one and the same. For all I knew, water was supposed to be gruesome, and the stream ran chuckling with wine.

My tongue was swelling. My lips were dry. My throat felt like a dust field after a drought. I tried to swallow, but couldn't: I was too parched. Cursing hoarsely, I stepped towards the brook. Overhead, the branches shook.

With an effort, I wrenched my eyes away from the bliss-giving water. A mottled green loop, scaly and as thick as my leg, hung just above the obvious drinking spot. A truly gigantic snake, it was more than likely interested in dining on me.

110

I didn't stop running for a good ten minutes. When I did, my thirst was back to a tolerable level, and wasn't demanding that I hasten to the stream. Funny how fear'll do that.

It wasn't much longer before dusk darkened the forest. A lifelong urbanite, I was so bemused that it was nearly night before I realized that yes, this is sundown, and no, there's nobody to turn on the street lights. I started looking for a place to bunk.

Nightfall worked on me like a sleeping pill. I paused for a massive yawn, then rounded a bend in the trail. A series of ant hills, damn near two meters high apiece, stretched into the gloom. If it hadn't been for them, I would have slept right there. Yawns ripped through me so quickly that none were satisfying. Just as I'd ease into the relaxing tail-end of one, the urgent inhalation of the next would begin. Staggering past the ant hills, I could barely keep my eyes open: my lids were lead shutters, and my eyeballs burned mercilessly.

It was no use. I had to bed down before I passed out in the trail. The sinking light showed a small clearing just beyond a hedgelike bush. Fighting to stay awake, I swept soggy, moldy leaves into a pile, and watched the ants scurry in annoyance. I flicked one off my finger after it had nibbled at me. Luckily, I was so tired that I hadn't felt its pincers.

A huge smile creased my face as I collapsed. The wind was cool, and gentle. It opened a gap in the dark-leafed ceiling and ushered in a shy astral glimmer.

Being alone, where nobody could hear and mock, I chanted softly, "Star light, star bright/first star I see to-night/wish I may, wish I might/have the wish I wish to-night." I wanted so many things . . . something inched down the bridge of my nose. I picked it off, and squished it in midwriggle.

Giggling with the silliness of exhaustion, I wished for an aardvark. Between wakefulness and sleep, in that state where thoughts are as vivid as dreams but as pliable as sculptor's clay, I fashioned an anteater. Tall at the shoulder he was, with a bushy tail and an impossibly long tongue. Smirking at my fantasy pet, I gave him steel claws and an appetite bigger than himself. "Welcome to Aardvark Heaven," I told him, as I drifted into the sleep where dreams would rule me, and not vice-versa. "The ant hills are over there. Have fun." I could just picture him, shuffling, sniffing, sticky tongue a deadly dart. After a few minutes, he'd tire of munching on stragglers, and would head straight for the biggest hill, the roof of which he'd tear off, the passages of which he'd slurp clean, the inhabitants of which he'd—

"Hey!" I was erect and very, very awake. Sleep had decamped like an unfaithful lover, abandoning me to an ant-ridden pile of leaves. But . . . face close to the ground, I could barely make out individual shapes. None of which belonged to ants.

I'm not sure what triggered the idea, yet I knew, as surely as if I'd spoken to an angel of the Lord, that my fatigue had been induced by a TP attack. Launched on me by the ants. For the purpose of devouring me while I snored.

The thought was so horrible that for the next half hour I concentrated on nothing but building a fire. It came more easily than it had earlier; soon I had a crackling blaze. As well as a headful of disturbing notions.

Four times that day, I had had trouble with the wildlife. In each instance, I had wanted to do something foolish. I'd let the pink bug alight on me. I'd thought I could outrun the lithe cat. I'd insisted on slaking an already-quenched thirst. And I'd damn near slept in the ants' hunting ground.

They were all using TP on me. The Arkslsnaglian predators were fogging my brain with false desires, so that I'd leave myself vulnerable. So that they could eat me in peace.

At that moment, I understood why the Lomala Research Institute was out to do me: I was telepathic. Their talk about changing the system was patent mush-mouth—the system had given them their power and prestige, and any rule change would jeopardize their holdings. TP would blow their stable, conservative world apart; they had to stamp it out. Thus the Institute had organized a program to identify and isolate anybody with the power. They'd lured us out of the bushes with promises so they'd know at whom to shoot.

And now I could see why they'd stranded me so far from home. They'd told me—my God, how many times had they told me without my ever listening to the meaning behind their words?—they'd told me that I was blessed with a sizable potential. And instead of cutting and running, I'd beamed with pride.

They were afraid of me, and of what I might do to them if they overtly attempted to kill me. They had known that if they tried to liquidate me, I would have been outraged.

Pragmatic scientists all, they would have calculated, down to the last decimal, the radiation that would surge from me during my death throes. They would have estimated its effect on those whom I would have blamed. Hadn't I already coughed one of them? So, after hemming and hawing, they would have said, "The risk factor is too great. We mustn't execute him here. It would be better if he died somewhere far away, preferably by accident." So they'd marooned me on a planet infested with telepathic wildlife, a planet where even if I managed to survive, I wouldn't be able to do them any harm.

"Fuck that!" I bellowed to the fire-lit trees. I was on my feet, pacing, occasionally shaking my fist at the sky, as if someone up there were watching me. Defiance roared in my soul; I sensed man's kinship with the great apes. I was *not* going to die just because Lomala's social scientists didn't want their apple carts upset. I was going to get off the planet, get back to Earth, and—

Leathery wings fluffed the air above my head. Warmth flowed down my arms and legs. When the bat swooped, I smiled, and held out my hand. It was such a cute, friendly thing that I couldn't resist. It reminded me of a teddy bear I'd had as a child, even though my pillowmate hadn't had such sharp teeth— I jerked my hand away. The bat hissed its frustration, banked, and glided back. Again the warmth and friendliness. Its open mouth was filled with shadows.

I dove beneath it. My splayed right hand skidded into the glowing coals and I screamed. And screamed again. And in the haze of the moment's anger I blamed everything on the circling bat. My hatred boiled up; I visualized seizing it, tearing its membranous wings from its rodent body, crushing its hollow bones beneath my foot— the bat was gone. The night was cold.

"Who are you trying to kid?" I squatted by the fire. My hand throbbed so badly that I was able to scrape the ash and dirt off it without amplifying the pain. It would have felt good to douse it in the stream, but I wasn't up to the short walk through the darkness. I had enough ideas about what could be lurking in the undergrowth to keep me where I was.

The rebelliousness seeped out of me like air through a balloon's pin-prick. Shoulders sagging, I gazed into the restless flames. Lomala had been astute: I would die in exile, just as they had planned, because I could do nothing else. Escape was a pipedream.

113

The question was not whether I would die, but when. Surviving the predators would take constant alertness, which would leave precious little time for things like feeding myself.

The old me, the Jungle Lord, sketched a possible alternative: A Tarzanlike existence in which I, through spite and sheer toughness of will, managed to become King of the Forest.

But I snorted. The will that I'd need would be sapped, suckered, and seduced by anything I tried to subjugate. Even if it were possible, who wanted it? Living in a tree house, battling big cats, chasing away ants . . . who needed it? Jesus, what'd happen if I got sick? Or broke something. Or . . . God forbid, what did Cheetah do to Tarzan when the ape-man grew gray and arthritic?

Uh-uh. Even if I fought off wild animals, and loneliness, and decades of toil, I'd come to nothing but a bird-pecked pile of unburied bones.

But dammit, I thought, *dying in an alien jungle!* I must have seen a thousand holo-vee shows with that theme—and so what if I was in a forest instead of a jungle? The only difference was that if I hung onto life in a forest, I'd get the chance to freeze my ass off come winter.

All right, I thought, stirring up the embers because branches crunched in the nearer shadows, *so I don't want to be banal. But Tarzan or the lost explorer, either way, I will be* . . . Sparks climbed the spiral staircase of the updraft. Watching them disappear, I realized what I had to do.

Suicide. It was the only rational option. Given that I was going to die, I could at least choose the time, place, and manner. It seemed the least I could do to maintain my dignity. And, to be perfectly honest, all other ways of dying struck me as far more desperate.

It was settled. I even knew how I'd do it: I'd find a cliff, sheer and massive, a natural monument that dominated its district. I'd blot out my mind, as the Institute had taught me, and topple down its face. True, I'd never have a grave—but what man could have a finer stone?

Content for the first time that day, I added an armful of sticks to the fire and went to sleep. And dreamed that Shana was next to me.

Fire protected on Arkslsnagl as it did on Earth. When the dawn set the birds to squawking, I was there to greet it.

I got to my feet and stretched. My bruised left arm hurt

the most, but my burned hand and stung wrist were close seconds. Everything else was stiff—beds in the Jungle weren't what the princess would have liked, but they were a helluva lot more comfortable than bare ground. Wind-piled leaves look soft, but I'll take a waterbed any day. Besides, the leaves itched.

After making sure the coals were out, I limped to the stream to wash. Old habits die hard. My cleanliness didn't make a bit of difference—nobody was going to see me, and the smell might even repel carnivores—but being clean was so ingrained in me that I grimaced involuntarily at the thought of not washing. Even the chance that the trees swarmed with snakes couldn't keep me away.

The water was colder than the morning; I splashed it on my face and shuddered at its icy kiss. Then I scooped some up in my cupped hand and drank. My teeth tingled and numbed, but it tasted good. I never knew what I'd been missing before Arkslsnagl.

A breeze sprang up and rustlcd the leaves. It was a nice sound, a soothing sound—another one of the things urbanites lack. I leaned against a tree trunk and let the morning whisper in my ears. As a fringe benefit, it dried my face, and brought me the odors of the forest.

They smelled good, even the ones whiffed with decay. It was *honest* decay. Whatever it had been in life—a bush, a snake, a bird—it had lived the best it could, according to its own lights. Whereas down in the Jungle, it smells of corners cut, money saved, courtesies ignored.

I had to figure out what to do. Late at night, it had been easy enough to talk of jumping off cliffs, but in the first pale light of day I realized that I didn't even know where the nearest was.

Trees surrounded me like an army of occupation. The obvious course would have been to climb one and look around, but the on-key Jungle Lord wasn't eager to trust his sixty-three kilos to things that swayed so much in a light wind. Besides, things might live up there. Etiquette—and that keenly honed sense of fear—urged me not to disturb them.

The stream rushed and swirled and made soft liquid laughter. I stared at the slim silver fish darting back and forth in its clearness, and after a while the obvious seeped into my soggy brain. Streams run downhill.

And cliffs lie in higher ground. The rocky brook at my feet flowed from that higher ground. All I had to do was trace it to its source, and somewhere in that neighborhood would be my death cliff.

I set out at once, walking warily. My pride in myself demanded that it be I who ended my life, not a hungry beast that resembled something out of a nightmare. Knife in hand, I stuck to game trails and the open ground. When I had to pass through underbrush, I poked it with a long stick first.

It slowed me down considerably, but I didn't care. I wasn't out to set a speed record. I was just trying to make sure I'd be alive for my own suicide.

For the first week, before city muscles had accustomed themselves to forest hiking, the treks were short. Every five or ten kilometers, I'd find a grassy clearing, scan it for ant hills, and camp for the night. I developed into a nova lean-to builder; they didn't ward off the rain, but they did provide a flimsy security. Growing up in the Jungle teaches you to prefer a wall at your back.

The second day, shortly after a flying thing had tried to make away with my hair, I found a better way of starting fires. The thing—it had a beak as long as my hand, and talons that could girdle my waist—was lying on the ground, wiggling from my first blow. Cautious about approaching it, I threw the knife. I shouldn't have. It is not my weapon, and I am not accurate with it. The spinning blade, after missing the little fucker by a meter and a half, caromed off a rock. My first thought was SHIT! My second: HEY! The blade had raised a spark, and as if imitating its sudden spurt into life, my brain had raised an idea.

After dispatching the thing with a small boulder, I experimented. If I brought the rock and the knife into rapid contact at the right angle and the right speed, a spark leaped out. I gathered a handful of dried leaves. Directing the spark into their midst was a bitch, but half an hour of practice taught me how to do it regularly. Soon I figured out how to breathe the tiny spark into full-fledged flame. The rock became a welcome weight in my pocket.

Loneliness attacked in force on the third day, after the novelty of the situation had worn off, and after my fear had eased a bit. That morning I caught myself saying "Hello" to the multifaceted reflection in the stream.

While waterbugs skated circles around my stream-face, I realized that for the first time in my life, I was absolutely alone.

Growing up in the Jungle only *seems* like solitude. People surround you, of course, but they're too busy with themselves to take the time to be with you. After a while, you learn that only by appealing to their self-interest—say, by scoping out some good high-sense, or by planning an interesting job—can you cluster them around you. They may not care two shits about what happens to you, but hey! It's better than talking to a wall.

In the alien forest, though, I had even less companionship. Nobody to talk to, nobody to listen to, nobody even to watch. Just trees, and bushes, and wild animals that might or might not want to eat me.

You don't realize how much of your daily routine is based on other people. It doesn't even have to be an interaction, just . . . feeling down, saying, "What the hell's the use?" you see somebody else plodding through the shit. It doesn't inspire you, exactly—but you do say to yourself, "If that cocksucker can keep on, so can I." Rivalry—or jealousy—keeps you going.

In the forest, there's nobody else. And the temptation to lie down and die can become overwhelming.

Only my stubborn desire to die at the time and place of my choice remained. I wanted that craggy cliff for a gravestone. I wanted to show . . . myself? . . . that I was tough enough to survive on Arkslsnagl if I wanted to.

The suicide had to be my *choice*. The toughness of life couldn't force me into it; I refused to allow that. I'd jump, sure, but only because life was *futile*. The pride of the Bander Snatch would permit nothing else.

I stirred the stream with my hand. My mirror image shattered; the frightened skaters drew quick lines from the center. The heaviness in my chest rose with me. Gritting my teeth, I stood in a shaft of sunlight and forced it out of my heart. Most of it went. The yearning for Shana wouldn't budge.

Upstream, then, back trail blazed by another circle of ashes, another swaying lean-to. Soon the forest would claim them, and all traces of my passing would have been erased. A depressing thought, in one sense: a man likes to leave his mark. But in another sense, its honesty appealed to me: the forest took what it needed without reverence for half-forgotten notions.

My belly was grumbling again. I probed the undergrowth for small beasts that wouldn't fuss too much when I killed them. My diet, for the three days I'd been on Arkslsnagl, had consisted mainly of frogs and lizards—not because I liked them, but because the mammals moved too quickly. The only time I could catch one was when it attacked me.

The game trail led to a clearing. I looked for bare, rocky spots—places where lizards would sun themselves. My mounting hunger made me impatient. I kicked through the long grass, stick in hand, hoping to rout something that a quick swipe would stun. Then I stopped.

I *was* hungry, but . . . an extra dimension to the nature of my appetite seemed reminiscent of my earlier mishaps with the predators. It was like *this* much of the emotion was genuine, and the rest was artificial.

I whipped out my knife. The long grass was still, except where a vagrant breeze played with its seedy tops, and the underbrush rimming the clearing was motionless. Scattered bird and bug noises sounded all around, from the sun-gold treetops to the black/green shadows beneath.

The craving increased as I stepped forward, and dropped off when I took two steps back. Uh-huh. Something was luring me on.

I had a choice: advance and see what it was, or retreat and hope it wouldn't pursue. Sunlight warm on my hair, forest smells in my nose, I let my stomach decide.

Excelsior!

Beyond the clearing was a tree. From its gnarled branches hung smooth-skinned fruit, packed in scarlet clusters the size of my fist. Cautiously, I picked one, and slit it open. Its aroma was different, yet hauntingly familiar, like the face of a childhood friend whose life followed a divergent path.

The knife blade cut a small square and raised it to my tongue. It was juicy, and cool, and . . . while not good, exactly, not disagreeable, either. In time, I could get to like it.

I carried half a dozen more clusters into the clearing, and picnicked in the grass.

Nice world, I thought, spitting seeds past my toes. *The fruit tells you when it's ripe.*

TP seemed commonplace on Arkslsnagl, and I wondered how its evolution had differed from our own. Probably just chance. Ten billion years earlier, one freak cell in the ocean had developed an extra talent that gave it an edge over those without it. So it had eaten the others, and its offspring, inheriting the trait, had gone on to overwhelm the world.

Why, then, did the animals still have eyes, and ears, and noses? The best I could do was (a) why does humanity have an appendix? and (b) the more senses, the better.

I'm no scientist.

A presence stalked into the clearing and stiffened me. My head, periscoping above the fronds of grass, whipped this way and that. Something nearby was hungry. And big. And mean.

Knife drawn, I looked for heavy disturbances in the grass. There weren't any. Sonovabitch. The monster was waiting for *me* to move.

Sympathizing deeply with a cat-chased mouse, I picked out the nearest tree. A few deep breaths, for steadiness and for extra oxygen. The monster took the opportunity to creep closer, and I could smell its blood lust. Its thoughts were simple, repetitive, graphic: claws tearing through furry hide; teeth sinking into bloody flesh.

I burst to my feet and ran like hell. I wanted that tree trunk at my back in the worst way. The hunter's thoughts sharpened, strengthened, and almost paralyzed me with their intensity. I stumbled on. My frantic eyes searched for my attacker.

Suddenly the carnivorous thoughts vanished—imploded like a cracked shell under pressure—and a small form sprang out of the grass a foot before me. Fear sizzled the air. It zigged, it zagged, it disappeared. I gaped after it foolishly.

A rabbit. I had almost shit my pants over an Arkslsnaglian rabbit.

As inanity faded, excitement grew. The rabbit had camouflaged itself with a predator's thoughts so thoroughly that I had been convinced it was hunting for me.

If a rabbit can do it, I thought, *why can't I?*

Sure, why not? For the three days I'd been on the planet, I'd been having constant troubles with the local carnivores. Half my waking hours seemed spent in flight. My sleep was a patchwork of hasty wood-stocking, frantic firefeeding, and eyes glowing beyond the fire's light. If I could avoid all that hassle . . . then I kicked myself, because the aardvark episode should have made the whole possibility clear the first night.

Think bloody. I entered the forest's cool dimness. *Think bloody*.

I used, of course, the Bandersnatch: wings tucked close

to its side, bony head and hideous beak thrust forward, cold eyes avid for the slightest sign of edible life.

It worked. It was hard to maintain a vivid image for more than a moment, but that was sufficient to fluster everything in the immediate vicinity.

Nothing, but nothing, was willing to chance a meltdown with the Bandersnatch.

Unfortunately, it cut off my food supply. The birds and the bats and the shrews and the weasels that had been leaping out to feast on me had disappeared. Few of the fruit trees were beckoning. My belly complained, loud and often. My mind told it, *Shut up, better empty than in something else's.*

After a few days, though, even that argument lost its impact. I had to try something different.

I built a four-sided shelter, got inside, and roofed it over. I formed an image of a small animal, lying helpless with a broken leg. The broadcast was simple: pain, fear, stuck. Pain, fear, stuck.

The brother of the cat that had attacked on the first day strode into the clearing ten minutes later. After pausing at the edge to sniff the air, it stalked towards me with its tail arrogant.

My shelter puzzled it. It grew frustrated, and tried to paw the sticks away, but the tough vines that lashed it together wouldn't break.

A weasel popped up, blinked at the cat, and pulled its head down. Too late. The cat had seen it, and was already leaping. From the agitated grass came a high squeak and a snap.

Closing my eyes, I awoke the Bandersnatch. Its cruel beak snapped at the cat's neck. With a startled squall, the cat bounded to the forest fringe. I claimed its dinner for my own.

A few more days sensitized me, and I learned to "hear" other minds long before they drew near enough to be threatening. Relieved, I shelved the Bandersnatch, and saved it for the approach of something big. Almost immediately, my menus improved in quantity, quality, and variety.

Another sensitivity surfaced: the ability to feel what lay behind the masks the various animals broadcast. If I heard a rumbling hunger, and sensed the blind urge to kill, I could tell whether it was an honest-to-God predator, or an herbivore trying to pull a fast one.

That was very helpful. My legs appreciated it.

120

One goal for which I strove was to become mentally invisible. I held my mind shield in place most of the day, hoping that it would enable me to pass among the animals without frightening them.

Thus did I come to understand why the beasts weren't noseless, blind, and deaf. When the wind was wrong, or my feet were clumsy, they took off. A human might be willing to disbelieve his senses—as when he sees pink elephants—but animals aren't that dumb.

The ground was gradually steepening, as if the mountains were preparing me for their majesty. That was fine by me. Loneliness still hovered like a ghost. TP competence had made life more predictable. I had less and less reason to savor the passing moments. Time for me to die.

One morning around the start of my third week, I was puffing up a brambled slope behind which I'd seen a snowy peak. As always, I was listening for other minds. I heard one: big, and nasty, and disgruntled. It did not feel like a rabbit lurked behind it.

Resignedly, I summoned the Bandersnatch. I wouldn't eat for a few hours, but with that nearby, hunger wasn't such a high price.

Scales glistening, the evil-tempered being eyed the landscape with reptilian contempt. Just for the hell of it, it ripped a small tree out of the ground and tumbled it through the air.

Unfortunately, big nasty wasn't buying. Instead of turning tail, it came to investigate, heralding its presence with a flourish of earthquakes and hurricanes.

Too much for me. Humus squished underfoot as I started running/falling down the slope. I hadn't gotten ten feet before a loud roar trembled the air. A huge tree blocked my path; I spun and snuggled up against it.

Big? Nasty? Believe me, never have those words been so accurately applied as on that morning. It had eyes like most animals have heads; its teeth were like a portcullis. Its reddish-brown fur was thicker than Pajalli's carpet. When it stood on its incredible hind legs, its pointed ears brushed branches seven meters high.

And it was coming right at me.

The knife in my hand felt like a paper clip. The Bandersnatch swooped back viciously, but for all the effect it had, it could have been trying to reason with Big Nasty.

Closer it came.

My knuckles were white; my asshole was stuttering.

Over and over I mumbled, "I don't believe it'ssobigthere's-nothingsobigit'sobigsobigsobig."

It hunched forward, and swung a two-meter paw. Claws like overgrown bayonets lanced out. I forced my back against the bark and pretended I was moss. The claws just barely grazed me. The duraweave wouldn't tear, but it didn't have to. Those claws *hurt*.

Six hot wires seared my chest. I screamed. The beast raised its paw for a return swipe and I screamed again. The claws criss-crossed the first marks; the agony doubled; I caught a whiff of mental laughter.

The fucker was amusing itself.

Out of nowhere bubbled a fear-swamping anger. Getting coughed was despicable—though I may have resigned myself to death, I had intended it to be death on *my* terms—but being toyed with was worse.

It may sound silly, perhaps even pompous, but as the monster positioned its paw for a third slash, I was thinking, *Dammit I'm a man and I have the right to die with dignity!*

Fire burned me again and I lost control. It didn't matter that the beast was four times my size. It didn't matter that I was going to die. All that mattered was that I would no longer watch myself be sliced to death.

I screamed, not in pain but in anger. My knife pin-pricked its belly. Hatred enflamed my soul and I hurled it at the beast's savage mind. The Bandersnatch stooped to help.

It batted away the Bandersnatch, met my hate with its own. Emotions ground together like emery wheels. Sparks flew and minds shrieked.

It flicked the knife out of my hand, breaking my wrist. The extra pain amplified my thoughts.

I thought death, and destruction, and great bodies shuddering the ground with their fall.

(I found—)

I thought fire, and flame, and smoke, and heat, and singed fur.

(—the pattern's blanks—)

I thought teeth and claws and blows like sliding mountains.

(—and I filled them.)

I thought trees snapping and winds whirling and the gods standing up to keep score.

(I found the pattern's—)

I thought it all and put it behind the beast's fiery eyes—

122

(—blanks and I filled them!)
—and then I let it explode.

When I regained consciousness, Big Nasty was dead.

But not alone: snuffling morosely in its reddish-brown fur was a scale model of it, a . . . my mind groped amid the pain for the word . . . a— a cub. I lay motionless and watched.

The size of a teen-age human, its fur was the same shade as its . . . mother's? It was trying to rouse her; whimpering softly, it pushed its nose into her side again and again, occasionally backing off to scratch the soil, lower its head, and butt her corpse.

Listening to its worried complaints, I sensed its bewilderment, its fear, its . . . its loneliness. Its emotions were so remarkably human that for a few dazed minutes I wondered if I weren't clothing its reactions with my own. But when I purified my mind, shut down all my thoughts so I could hear its the better, I knew it was no mistake.

I knew also—and the irony was tinged with bitterness— that I had personally precipitated the entire fight. I'd been too quick to unleash the Bandersnatch; I'd angered the mother because she'd thought my monster would prey on her child. Cub. Why was it coming through so humanly?

And why did I feel remorse? I shouldn't have; I'd just barely escaped with my life. Battered, bruised, bleeding . . . why did I feel that by killing the mother I'd assumed responsibility for the child? CUB! dammit.

Its big head perked up, and twisted about. Soft brown eyes focused on my prostrate form. With a hesitant sniff, it lumbered over to me, and gently nudged me with a clawless paw. Its mind reached out, asking "&%#$*&%?" The only other time I've sensed that same tentative tremulousness was when someone asked, "Do you love me?"

What could I say but "Yes."

With a satisfied grunt, it sat on its haunches, and began industriously to lick my face. I made no move to stop it; I was too busy trying to figure out what to do.

If I let it be, it would starve to death. That wasn't right. Death is inevitable for all creatures, but suffering isn't. If it hadn't been for my goddam cocksure summoning of the Bandersnatch, its mother would have been alive to care for it, and to teach it how to fend for itself.

I owed it. I could either replace its mother . . . or take it up the cliff with me.

Stiffly, I pushed myself to my feet, and scratched the cub

123

behind its perked ears. "Come on," I said, and started walking.

It stopped when it came abreast of its mother, and put an unintelligible request into my head: "$#%?" Lying against her flank, it made a forlorn sound.

"She's not coming," I groaned. "Come on."

"$#&?"

Shaping the "NO" firmly and simply, I slid it towards it. And it understood. Sadly, reluctantly, it followed me up the winding path.

The next morning I spotted the cliff: five hundred sheer feet of granite solemnity. That afternoon I found a trail up its side. The bear cub panted along behind me, pausing only occasionally for a backward glance. It hadn't quite accepted the fact that its mother would never bring up the rear again.

The trail was steep and rocky; it was a bitch to get up it, especially with one wrist roughly splinted. At times I even had to push the cub. Not that it was afraid of heights—it just saw no reason why it should scale them.

At last we made it. My hands were scraped and bleeding; my legs quivered helplessly. I plopped down on the edge, and looked into dizzy nothingness. A stiff wind blew me back.

With both the cub's paws in my hands, I began to blank out my mind, to spare myself the sight of uprushing rock and the millisecond flash of agony. It was going to be tricky—I'd have to erase all but the muscle control necessary to throw us both over the brink.

Slowly, the blackness crept in. The cub whimpered as I wrapped it in velvet. A minute. An hour. Darker and darker. Just two minute sparks and—

"Come find me, Bander Snatch," sang the beacon.

My eyes burst open. I couldn't believe it. I was afraid to believe it. It had to be a trick. Lomala wanted me dead . . . didn't they?

"Come find me, Bander Snatch," it sang again.

Luckily, the plain below looked inviting.

II

The descent called for backtracking the torturous route of the morning. Even going down it wasn't easy. The strength I'd needed to haul myself from one rock to another was now needed to keep from falling. The cub—I'd started to call him Baby Bear—didn't improve my mood, either. Balancing superbly, he clung to his perches with casual ease, but still saw no reason why he should move from one to another. He wasn't hungry. The sun was warm but not hot. No enemies endangered us. Why not stay put?

By the time we got to the trail that led to the plain, I was in bad shape. My fingers were stiff, swollen, and bloody; my arms trembled weakly. My right wrist throbbed against its splint. I had to sink down on a fallen log and rest before I could go on.

The cub studied the way I arranged my body, then sat in clumsy imitation. I put my elbow on my knee and my chin on my fist. With a happy snuffling noise, he did the same, even though he didn't have much of a chin. I untangled myself. So did he. I crossed my legs at the knee. He tried, but couldn't—his legs were too thick. I laughed. He radiated dejection.

"Hey, Baby Bear," I said, putting a hand on his massive shoulder. The thought behind my laugh had hurt him: smug superiority coupled with malicious pleasure at his failure. "Hey, man." Rubbing his fur gently, I tried to transmit the genuine concern I felt for him. No good. "But we're *friends*."

That cheered him somewhat. Ears perked, he raised his

125

snout. His golden eyes stared into mine, almost as though he could translate the pattern of flecks in my irises.

"Let's go," I said, rising.

He had other plans. He swung his shiny muzzle up. My gut rumbled, with the fuzziness that said it came from somewhere else, which meant Baby Bear had put it there.

"Hungry, huh?"

It rumbled louder.

"Well . . ." My knees began to unhinge and the world turned misty as he demanded his supper more loudly. "All right, all right. Ah . . ." I glanced around. The forest was full of game, but we had made no attempt to disguise ourselves and had probably chased everything away.

The life-scented breeze blew right at my face. I climbed over the log and squatted, calling Baby Bear to my side. "Ssh," I said to him, as I rid my thoughts of their human taint. Another minute and they were those of a wounded rabbit, torn by bird claws and stunned by a sudden fall.

Within seconds, a small black animal with more teeth than a shark skittered out of the underbrush. It stopped on a patch of bare ground; its pink nose sniffed the air. Apparently reassured, it moved another foot closer.

Just as the silence began to prey on its nerves—a wounded rabbit makes an agonized squeaking which I couldn't mimic—I guided the Bandersnatch in from behind, swooping low to the ground. Toothy at once bounded forward, over the log. It spitted itself on my knife before it knew it was there.

"Here you go, Baby Bear."

Grunting, he knocked it loose and watched it fall to the bed of rotted wood. He flipped it over, clawed it, lifted it by its heels, and swallowed it whole.

The beacon surged to the lower limit of audibility, and I rose. "Come on, let's go."

Hunger somewhat appeased, Baby Bear shambled after me.

It's funny how quickly situations can change. Until I'd beaten Baby Bear's mother, I'd been deathly afraid of every noise in the forest. Now, with my confidence reestablished, and with two hundred some kilos of immature killer waddling behind me, I felt like I was back home again.

The cub was no threat to me—or to anything else, for that matter—but his odor and his brain-print protected us better than a circle of barbed wire.

The forest began to thin out the next morning. Tree

126

stumps, old and new, sprouted all around. Fewer dead leaves crackled underfoot; the ground was covered, sometimes to considerable depths, with pale chips of wood that had flown from a lumberjack's ax. Baby Bear's motions became hesitant, as though I were taking him somewhere he didn't want to go.

I pushed on steadily. If he followed, I'd welcome his company and keep my promise. But if he chose to stay . . . frankly, I didn't stand a chance of dragging him.

The parallel between my relationship with the cub and Lomala's with me became our third companion. I, too, had had my old world destroyed by an outside power. I, too, had followed that power with initial eagerness. I, too, had gotten so far and then balked.

I hate to flip-flop opinions. When I like something, I want to keep on liking it. When I hate it, I don't want to stop. And yet power-wielders have to be as flexible, as malleable, as molten plastic. Nothing stays in place. Things shift, change, mutate . . . what's nova one day is abhorrent the next. It's frustrating—life is much easier when you can let a single set of emotional reflexes guide you forever—but it's the only way to stay on top of things.

Lomala's image was altering again. The pendulum hadn't swung all the way yet: I was still suspicious of their motives, and of their good will, as well. But since their beacon existed, maybe everything else they'd claimed would be true, too.

Baby Bear whined with displeasure when we emerged from the last fringe of forest.

"Hey, man," I told him, "it's okay, you'll get used to it." He couldn't understand the words, but the emotions they conveyed penetrated his heavy-boned skull. If I wasn't worried, he wouldn't be, either. That simple.

A strong, dusty breeze filled the corners of my eyes with moisture. Blinking, I scanned the belt of scrub, a no-man's land between the forest and the fields. Not twenty meters from me were the remnants of a small fire. The fields belonged to the native intelligence, then.

Yet no fences broke the smooth roll of tilled land. Four distinctive crops waved in the wind: a berry, a grain, a gourd, and the fourth either a leaf or a tuber. Each had its own vast expanse of field.

When I went to sample the berries, a buzzing grew in my ears. No, not my ears, I realized, in my mind. Low-pitched and formless, it beat the rear-bottom of my brain like a crashing surf, and loudened as the forest fell away. Baby Bear, responding to it also, pawed his ears in bewilderment.

"Damfino, BB," I said. "Let's sit."

Our bench was the bank of a small run of water, apparently an irrigation ditch. Baby Bear sniffed its placid surface suspiciously, clawed it with gentle, fascinated strokes, and then strode in. It was shallow, but he was able to roll onto his back and submerge all of him but his nose.

The buzzing unnerved me; head in hands, I studied it. Couldn't get a clear picture. It was like being ringed by a huge swarm of bees whose black hives blended with the nothingness. I sighed. Time to repair the stadium. Easy enough: just visualize it, create a thousand workers armed with sprayers and cans of fiberfoam, then, godlike, order them to insulate the place. Sit in the ruthless sun, feel the sweat spring from my temple hair, watch the little men spread six inches of quick-drying foam on the walls of the stadium in my mind.

Ah, success. After three or four minutes, at the most, the background noise had been muffled to the thinnest of whispers.

That had to go, too.

Hah! Put another dome atop the one that's already there; leave six inches of dead air in between, and . . .

Silence. Beautiful, luscious silence. Deep enough to sink in, soft enough to soothe, warm enough to run naked through.

All that was left was helping Baby Bear.

The hairs on my neck prickled suddenly, warningly. I raised my head. An Arkslsnaglian stood before me.

If Terrans descended from apes, Arkslsnaglians have ursine grandparents. Though not quite two meters tall, his body had the same massive stockiness that Baby Bear's had. And yes, his face curved into a snout, though he had a definite chin, and his gleaming brown eyes lurked deep under bars of bone. A half-pelt ran from his eyebrows over the top of his head, down his neck, across his shoulders, and down his arms. Thinning out at his wrists, it left his six-fingered hands hairless. He wore boots, a jockstrap, and nothing else.

"Ah . . . hi." Instinctively, I nodded.

He nodded back, neither surprised nor startled. He seemed to be saying to himself, "Another one, huh?"

Baby Bear reared out of the water, and the farmer spun

128

at his liquid snort. Then, quickly, he snatched an imple-
ment, a razor-sharp pickax. Holding it across his barrel
chest, he inched warily to the ditch's edge. His intention
was obvious. And ominous.

"No!" I said, not remembering that we didn't speak the
same language.

He kept on.

"No, dammit!" Brushing past him, I splashed through
the water to Baby Bear's side. Body between the two anta-
gonists—for by now BB was snarling—I shaped in my
mind a picture of BB and me walking hand in hand. It was
like a kindergarten finger painting, and I blushed when I
opened my stadium to offer it to the farmer, but it was the
best I could do on the spur of the moment.

He stopped. The skin over his eye ridges wrinkled. Off
the dome of my stadium-screen ricocheted a rapid-fire series of thoughts, all going too fast for me to do anything
but notice.

Helplessly, I spread my hands. The gesture meant nothing to him. *I can't understand you*, I thought. Equally inef-
fective. I cast around for an image that might reach him,
and settled on a blur. With deliberate gradualness, I slowed
it down until it appeared as a stream of separate pieces.
Braking it even more, I caught one of the pieces in my
"hand."

Nodding, he lobbed a thought at me very slowly.

Elated, I grabbed it—and found it a Chinese puzzle of
alien complexity. Nothing about it made sense. I turned it
over and over, trying to find some way to unlock it. Neg.

The farmer's sharp teeth showed as he scowled. I could
understand: he'd gone and baby-talked me, and I hadn't
understood word one. Then his features lightened, and his
lipless mouth twisted another way. I hoped he was smiling.

His gesture was as incomprehensible to me as mine had
been to him. He clenched his long, sharp teeth, and
painted across my mental sky a picture of surpassing subtlety: he and I walking through the golden fields to an old
house.

Borrowing his brush, I sketched in a crude figure of
Baby Bear.

He erased it.

I replaced it.

He rearranged the figures to show Baby Bear and me
leading the way, while he held his weapon at the ready.

I nodded.

From the treeless ridge, the house was a duplicate of the one in the farmer's image. Its wood was rough and weatherbeaten; on the outside, at least, it had never known paint. Nestled among a grove of shade trees, its three stories looked oddly squat: the doors and the windows, while not much taller than ours, were at least twice as wide.

The farmer led us to a bench beneath the trees. A few faces formed behind the dusty windows. The front door creaked open.

The being that emerged was old and venerable. The little of its pelt that remained was pale silver. Its skin was a fine mesh of wrinkles, spotted here and there with dark blotches. It came haltingly across the yard, and the farmer hastened to offer it an arm.

Clad in a dull red tunic that fell to its knees, and beneath that tight pants of midnight black, it radiated motherliness. I decided it was female.

Her thoughts were startlingly vigorous. They rattled off the dome of my stadium like baseballs falling from the sky. For the third time, I spread my hands and emoted incomprehension.

As if on command, the farmer released the old lady's arm and disappeared into the house. A moment later, he returned, a wide wooden chair in his calloused hands. She sat immediately, arrogantly sure he'd positioned it correctly.

Her faded brown eyes were old: bloodshot, watery, crusted. They probed mine for a century, until at last she made a noise like rushes bending with the wind. Her hand fluttered a fraction of a centimeter.

My stadium collapsed; the rubble disappeared. My mind was softly naked on a forbidding plain. An arrow of light sought the center of my being; I tried vainly to dodge. It found me, penetrated, and suffused outwards, filling every nook and cranny. I was petrified. My back was a waterfall of sweat, and my heart thumped like a mad drummer's solo. From my center rose two words: NO HARM. I believed them because there wasn't anything to do but believe.

I surrendered to the light, which ran wild in my castle of thought. Its illumination was ubiquitous, but one globe was discernibly brighter. It shot from one section to another, like a steel sphere in a pinball machine, stopping on dimes,

130

twisting impossibly, bouncing, spinning, circling, diving. I half-expected to hear *ding*ding*ding*.

Then it withdrew. I was alone.

"Do you know?" asked a voice. "I harmed you none."

"Yeah." The conscious reacts to changed circumstances more slowly than does the subconscious. "Hey—"

"No, I speak your language none. We have birthed a brief half-breed. For a time, a very short time, it will resonate twice for once, and once for each. It will be inaccurate—the multiple greens will be one—but it will speak."

Listening, I understood. She'd left a piece of herself in me—no, that's not right—she'd fused herself to me. Imprinted on me, so to speak, a replica of the energy patterns that were she. It wasn't true to scale: everything was skewed and distorted because it couldn't parallel my mind otherwise.

"How does it work?" I watched that thought flash through the switchpoints and I *saw*— she'd spoken of resonating, but only because I knew no closer terms. "Never mind, I see."

"How unfortunate."

"Why?"

"It offers you life," she replied. Her regret chilled me.

"And you're sad about that?"

"Your people sport greatly." Behind those words flickered others: hunt, fight, bloodgush.

"Is that what happened to the rest?"

"Not all. Not yet."

"Well, why—"

Before I could complete the thought, her "voice" cut through my mind like a fine-tuned laser beam. "We are honor," she said. "An oath is a mountain, not to fall for a whim of pleasure." Again the last word lingered in a dozen places, all unpleasant.

"Oh." I fiddled on the bench, aimlessly crossing and recrossing my ankles. "Well, uh . . ." A confusion of questions demanded to be asked. I tried to order them—ask questions in the right order and you can sometimes learn enough peripherally to skip later questions—but in vain. Abandoning all pretense of logic, I grabbed the most pressing: "How do I stay alive?"

"Dually, Hairless One: learn to shade the green, and fill my wish."

"And if I can't do one or both?"

"One last fingerhold: hounds and hunters do tire." Her face blended patience and anticipation. She wanted me to run before the chase, but she could wait.

"All right." Folding my arms, I slouched. "So how do I learn?"

"The hour is early, Hairless One, still early." Her thin hand waved at me; it was nearly translucent in the slanting sunlight. "First we talk."

"All right." I patted Baby Bear gently; he'd been showing signs of restlessness. My touch calmed him. My whisper calmed him further.

"How did your path join the beast's?" asked the old lady.

"Well . . . I promised to take care of him." That sounded strange, even to me, so I explained that in my remorse over killing his mother, I'd vowed that I wouldn't let him perish for want of a parent.

"I know." Her large eyes blinked several times, slowly, a though marking stages in her mental digestion. "Did you attack the she-beast to prove manhood?"

"Uh . . . I didn't attack her, she attacked *me*."

"Then her death is the delta of her foolishness." The tone—the color?—of her thoughts denied any obligation on my part.

"Yes, but . . . it was also my foolishness. I sensed her anger, and could have left the area, but I persisted . . . if I hadn't been so damn cocky, it wouldn't have happened."

"From where view you the beast-cub?"

"You mean Baby Bear?"

"Yes."

"I like him. He's not real bright—can't hold a conversation or anything—but he's not hard to handle, he's not dangerous, and he's, uh . . . he's a companion, you know? His odor keeps hungrier animals away, and he's warm to sleep next to at night. What can I say?"

"At what cross-path will you kill him?"

"Kill him?" I echoed bleakly.

"Yes." She sketched a picture of a man and bear locked in bloody, mortal combat.

"Never." My tone was less flat than my response: Arkslsnaglian culture might demand a ritual man-beast struggle, and I'd prejudice my chances if I insisted on keeping Baby Bear alive.

"And if I wish its death?" Her face was an oft-folded sheet of blank paper.

"I don't know."

"Kill him you would?"

"Hey, I told you, I promised——"

"What oaths do you swear?"

"If there's a good reason . . ."

"And if I speak of such a reason, but speak not the reason itself?" Tensing, she leaned forward slightly, as if my answer would be crucial.

"Look," I blurted in exasperation, "I'm a stranger here. I don't know your laws, your customs, anything. It would have to depend on what Baby Bear was doing. If he were eating up little kids, I'd probably agree. If he were just sitting under a tree, not bothering anybody, I might argue. It all depends, you know? If I figure you're giving me an order just to watch me jump, well . . ." I shook my head slowly, unable to finish the sentence.

"I know." Her face seemed forbidding, as though a sudden frost had touched it, but her thoughts were warm. "Go now. I wish talk your . . . friend."

"Huh?" I glanced from her to Baby Bear. "You mean *him*?"

"He friend your, isn't?"

I looked into his chocolate child eyes. "He's the closest thing I've got to it on this planet."

"Then leave us."

"All right." I rose, and stretched. Her bench had been as uncomfortable as any bench anywhere. "Where should I go?"

"With Ubsan." She made me realize that I should walk to my left, and I did. The farmer awaited me at the corner of the house. He nodded, then led me towards a small outbuilding some forty meters away. The background noise that I noticed earlier again buzzed in my ears. It was louder now, as though the mythical bees hovered above my ears. Instinctively, I raised my hands to them, but when that failed I recalled my stadium.

The maddening buzz faded as I locked the insulated door. By then, Ubsan and I had almost reached the outbuilding. With a funny look, he motioned me inside.

It was dark—pitch black once Ubsan swung the wide door shut—but the floor was heavily carpeted and the air smelled fresh and clean. Perhaps a touch too reminiscent of the sensory deprivation chamber at Lomala, the room nonetheless had an amiable ambience.

Ubsan growled under his breath. My domed marvel disappeared. The buzz was back. For the second time in an hour, my mind was alone and naked. Angered, I slapped the stadium up again. Ubsan snorted it into oblivion.

"Gimme a break!" I shouted at the darkness.

He made a sound of gentle inquiry.

I re-erected the stadium.

He tore it down.

I— I— I— I—

—don't know how long I was so tethered, but when he finally untied the mental leash, I was incapable of building anything in my mind.

On the roof of my skull formed a picture: Ubsan's dark stockiness, lit by a sourceless light. The background was nonexistent—I had the impression that it was black, but I couldn't take my eyes off Ubsan.

Something *ping*ed against my being.

Another view of Ubsan, this time from the side, like a Leah mug shot.

Ping.

The slide show speeded up; I saw my captor from a thousand different angles. With each flash came a *ping*. It was like having hail bounce off your head.

The picture changed. The new one, showing Ubsan and me together, was accompanied by a *pong*. Again flickered a series of still shots, each from a slightly new angle, each of slightly shorter duration, each with its own painful *pong*.

Baby Bear joined us and the *pong* became a *pow*. Faster and faster burst the light; louder and louder grew the *pows*. It was starting to hurt. Groping through the darkness, I grabbed Ubsan's arm. "Hey, stop it!" I demanded.

He paid no attention—he understood me not at all—the vicious barrage fell all around me.

"Dammit!" I pushed him, lost contact with his leathery skin, heard him tumble over backwards.

A new picture: me, sitting quietly, my mind devoted to the thoughts that streamed into it. The *pows* were *blams* and the pain increased.

I couldn't take it any longer. Ubsan's breath rasped two or three meters to my right. My legs tensed beneath me. After a huge inhalation, I leaped and landed on him. My left fist counterpointed the last *blam*.

He rolled; I followed. My hands found his thick neck and tried to encase it. My broken wrist resigned. I seized an ear instead. He gasped in pain and anger. I tried to rip it off, but his strong hand immobilized me. The pressure mounted, forcing my fingers to uncurl. They moved away from his head—towards me—behind my back. Ubsan was panting. He ground my face into the thick carpet, pinned my wrists painfully with a pair of fingers. His acrid sweat spattered the nape of my neck. I heard a snapping, as of elastic, and then felt a cord grip my forearms. In seconds I was securely bound.

Breathing heavily, Ubsan paced around the room, dissipating his energy into the booted feet that shuddered the floor. Then he approached, and squatted. Breath hot on my neck, he patted my shoulder, telling me he wouldn't hold a grudge.

I certainly would.

Because despite the fight, despite my obvious agony, the language lesson continued. Even after my conscious mind blanked out, my subconscious was harried by his thoughts.

When I came to, the front yard bench was hard beneath my back. The old lady was just withdrawing from my mind. Her after-image lingered, warm and friendly, like a morning breeze on a summer's day.

"Your friend speaks well of you," she said.

"Huh? Oh, oh, Baby Bear. Uh . . . that's good."

"For you, yes." A sigh slipped through her lips. "For us—" unrequited hunt-lust burned savagely hot.

"So what now?"

"Now?" Her hand gestured to the gathering darkness. "Sleep. Tomorrow . . . tomorrow will be dealt with tomorrow." Unsteadily, with much reliance on the arms of her chair, she pushed herself to her feet. "You and your friend will eat, and then sleep."

"Fine," I said. "Where?"

"Follow Ubsan." She turned, and hobbled slowly towards the door.

Ubsan had been at my side for some time, but the old lady's presence was so impressive that I hadn't noticed him. Now he pointed towards the back of the house. I followed. The outbuilding had been lighted; within, a heavy meal graced plates scattered across a cloth spread on the floor.

"Come on, BB," I said.

He bounded inside, stopped, then fell to all fours. Muzzle pressed into the dark brown carpeting, he whimpered in disbelief.

"What's the—" I'd crouched, and my new vantage point combined with the light to show me that the "carpeting" was fur. Bear fur. "Oh."

I couldn't stay in there. I felt itchy, and obscurely ashamed. I carried a couple plates out to the porch. Ubsan scanned quickly and took a few more. I got the cloth and, with much tugging, BB, too.

We ate in the open air, while the cold stars sprinkled the twilight sky. The dinner was good; the night was warm. I finished with a belch and BB licked the plates morosely.

The dinner made me sleepy. I couldn't go back inside; I spread a blanket on the porch and BB sprawled beside me. Ubsan made a gesture I didn't understand, but I figured it was a shrug and smiled at him.

He nodded, patted BB on the shoulder, and stood. A picture formed in my mind: BB and I stretched out, smiling, snoring. I think it was Ubsan's way of saying, "Good night."

I wish he'd left earlier, though. If he hadn't tarried by my head, I might not have noticed that one of his boots was adorned with a small tattoo. It was a heart, with the word "Rosie" inside it.

I didn't sleep well.

III

The next few weeks passed . . . "slowly" would be half accurate.

The minutes carried me like a lethargic freight train. Ubsan and the other villagers were teaching me their language, in the painful, repetitive fashion that he'd used the first night. My part was passive, was to imitate a sculptor's rock. While I sat on the porch of the outbuilding, legs crossed till the ankles hurt and the toes grew numb, they'd coalesce images into meaningful balls that they'd backhand off the roof of my mind.

The process nourished a blinding headache, a perpetual mistiness in the eyes, a ringing in the ears . . . by the end of Day Two, the question was no longer would it be effective, but rather, would it be fatal?

So the minutes passed slowly, as did the hours, as did the days. When night fell, and I was a limp lump of sweaty flesh ready to collapse onto the nearest blanket, I could barely remember which sunrise had wakened me. Along with everything else, it had receded into the dim past.

But even though it seemed like I'd been on Arkslsnagl all my life, if I shifted my perspective fractionally, I'd feel that I'd just landed. It was almost as simple as setting the angle of my head: cocked to the right, the days marched out of memory like fence posts sinking into the distance. My Jungle life—my real life—lay way the hell off, past the point where the posts disappeared. But cocked to the left . . . ah, then, every dreary day spent crosslegged in the steaming sun folded in upon all the rest and vanished, like raisins sprinkled onto oatmeal.

In part, the reaction was due to their refusal to let up on me: they didn't *need* to let me rest, because they could teach me as efficiently when I was sleeping. Maybe more so, for when my mind sagged into unconsciousness, it couldn't resist their incursions. I fought to retain my alertness—and hence my integrity—for a week, then lapsed into a semistupor that persisted like monsoon clouds. And the dreams that frequented it, you wouldn't believe.

The villagers worked me over in shifts, because that mode of teaching—that constant giving—drained them quickly. Each tutor lasted less than three hours, then would be replaced by another, and another, and another. . . .

At one time or another, almost everyone in the settlement labored in the vineyards of my mind. Only the Old Lady didn't; she was above such mundane things as work. Though she ran the place, singlehandedly and almost despotically, the others wanted it that way. They must have. She was so obviously frail that one good slap would have killed her. Two days of neglect would probably have done the same. The community could have deposed her—and disposed of her—simply by withdrawing its services. There was no way she could have forced them to do anything they didn't enjoy. But it never happened. They catered to her as though she honored them by her parasitism.

No one else was exempt, though, and I met them all. There were Ubsan and his four or five children, who ranged from knee-high to tree-high; there were Obben and Irthda, both lineal descendants of, and possible successors to, the Old Lady. Also Egano the cook; Sepol, who farmed with Ubsan; and a dozen or so others. Though I didn't think so at the time, they were good teachers. Patient and helpful, few of them would go easy on me.

To be honest, I did suspect that they got a perverted kick out of being harsh. Irthda, in particular, shaped images of unparalleled ferocity: regardless of the subject, they were of damn near epic proportions, and their colors . . . the colors in her images flashed brighter than fire. Burning their ways into my head, their vivid after-images glowed for hours. Learning from her was like staring into the sun.

Obben, on the other hand, was always gentle, although I occasionally got the feeling it was because she had no faith in my ability to learn, and hence didn't put herself out. Her

138

palette dripped pastels; the balls of thought which others hurled, she lobbed. The pain was less, far less—and when she couldn't help but hurt me badly, she'd pat my head as if to brush it away. On the night shift, too, she was more considerate: usually, if I were asleep, my tutor wouldn't leave the house. He'd lie in his bed and rifle the thoughts across the yard. I couldn't blame them—it was just as effective, and easier on feet tired from a day in the fields. But Obben was different. She would come. More than once, tangled in the mesh of a particularly gruesome dream, I'd fight my way into panting wakefulness to find my head pillowed on Obben's soft, capacious lap. She cared, even if she did give the impression of a rich lady talking to her Pekinese.

The kids were the best, though. The adults' sheer size was intimidating, and it's hard to learn when you're nagged by the fear that a mountain will fall on you if you don't. Also, the children's personalities had fewer sharp edges. And their thoughts were easier.

Children are too fresh to be overly complex. Their vocabularies may be broad and deep, and the words they drop may leave you gasping, but their thoughts are simple and . . . well, childish.

Even their grammar is simpler, probably because of the number and type of relationships that they can perceive. They lack experience, so they see things in direct, A-B terms. He hit me. You're big. I'm hungry. And so forth.

Since the Arkslsnaglian language is telepathic, consisting of crystallized thought patterns, the simpler the relationship enclosed/encoded into the ball, the easier it is (for me) to grasp. And since the children's thoughts were naturally simpler . . .

We played games, the alien kids and I. Mind games, mostly, because in the physical ones I would have had an advantage—not size or strength, but coordination and, again, experience.

One in particular I grew fond of. They had a name for it, a spherical twist of discrete thoughts that *sploing*-ed as it hit your mind. Translated literally, it reads: "First one to erase the thing that shouldn't have been drawn gets to do the next picture." *Sploing.*

Its rules were simple. One person in the circle of players would create a thoughtball, which he'd shoot out only once. Since normal conversation usually involved multiple emissions of each thought, to ensure its being understood in all its pristine complexity, it was challenging even to notice the thoughtball when you had only one glimpse of it.

It exemplified, of course, a relationship—and in this game, they were artificially complicated. The object was to pick out the one extraneous item, the one which had no logical or conventional relationship with any of the others. You won by being the first to return the ball to the group with that extraneousness eliminated.

It was not an easy game. I don't think I ever won.

Ubsan and the others generally gave me two or three hours a day with the kids—they knew it was important for me to be able to comprehend *somebody*. But after "play time," as Ubsan called it, they dragged me back to the grim business of remembering the meanings attached to the thoughtballs that turned my mind into Swiss cheese.

The days blended into each other. Morning passed through a haze of suffering and concentration to become night. Night had no particular significance, for me at least, because it signalled no surcease. The others laid down their tools, enjoyed their heated discussions, rested with their loved ones. I sat on the porch, with BB my roving shadow, while my teacher of the moment crashed against my mind. A rock on a beach can at least look forward to ebb tide. I didn't have even that.

And yet . . . the damn routine was working. Concepts grew easier to recall, harder to forget. The comprehension of familiar phrases became instinctive; subtlety began to insinuate itself into my tutors' discourses. I basked in the sunshine of their approval, for that and only that robbed their thoughts of barbed frustration.

Learning to speak, on the other hand, was a bitch. I developed the ability almost by accident (come to think about it, that's probably the same way a child gets to babbling. Hear things often enough, and you can't keep yourself from repeating them).

The rain was pouring down. It drummed on the porch roof and splattered the muddy ground. The weather had been lousy for four or five days, chilly and cold, and my spirits were eroded. The patches of moss growing in Baby Bear's fur didn't help any, either.

Irthda was luminescing the interior of my head. I was blinded, singed by her passion. The rain-chatter hampered my concentration, like radio static garbles transmissions. Thirty or forty times she'd imaged the same thoughtball; all

140

of its components were familiar, yet I couldn't catch their interrelationships. It was definite misery: Irthda, easily the least tolerant of slow learners, was really flamed off, and I do not speak metaphorically. With each repetition her colors brightened, and deepened, until at last the ceiling of my mind shrieked at me.

"Oh, God," I muttered, while I shook my head and wished for the rain to stop. A sunny day was what I needed. Clear sky, with maybe a lace trim of clouds around the horizon, and the sun beating down, and the ground dry underfoot, and—

Irthda's bone-sunk eyes registered surprise. -What did you say?-

"Huh?" on one level, but -I want the rain to stop and the sun to come out- on another.

-You spoke to me.-

"I did?" but inside, down deep, I stood with my hands on my hips saying, -By damn, I did.- The feeling was intensely good.

Interestingly enough, Arkslsnaglians do not use mind shields. From what Pajalli had told me, as well as from my own experience with Terran telepaths, a thought screen had seemed to be the first thing one had to devise. But the Arkslsnaglians would have nothing to do with one. Whenever I tried to put up my own, they tore it down.

Though at first I couldn't figure it—I was new at the game, but I didn't want people messing around inside *my* head—after a while it became clearer. The simplest analogy is this: very few Terran urbanites walk around in earmuffs, even though they'd protect our eardrums, because they would also filter out noises that we might want—or need—to hear. By the same token, a mind shield isolates one Arkslsnaglian from another.

An alternate way of translating it is this: just as we have a cultural taboo against invading the privacy of other people's lives, the Arkslsnaglians have a taboo against invading the privacy of other people's minds. Our taboo is weaker: microminiaturization makes realizing your victimization difficult, to start with, and then figuring out who bugged your telephone is a paranoiac's paradise. On Arkslsnagl, there's no difficulty sensing a peeper, and not much more in identifying him. Each brain is uniquely patterned. When you extrude a spy tendril, it's marked with your characteristics. If they're acquaintances, the spied-upon can immediately recognize the snooper. If they're not, his memory will retain the pattern so that others can make the identification. Like fingerprints, almost . . . except that the average Earthman couldn't recognize his own prints, much less someone else's.

In addition, the Arkslsnaglian code of ethics has a real kicker: it is considered inhuman for one being to spy upon another. It doesn't sound like much, but . . . remember, their culture is *alien*. ALIEN!

The reasoning goes like this: one does not peek into the brain of his peer. If one does, the peekee is not the peeker's peer, which raises the question, then, of which is the superior and which the inferior. If the peekee is inferior, then the peeker is morally justified. If it's the other way around, he's not.

For example: it's quite all right to listen to a draft animal pulling a cart, because it is an inferior. If, however, you ease your way into someone else's mind while he/she is meditating, then the culture assumes that you are saying either (1) the other person is an animal, and therefore fair game, or (2) you yourself are an animal.

To muddy the confusion a bit . . . if the victim complains, he/she has established her/his status as a human, for animals don't complain after the fact. A complaint, therefore, definitively establishes the peeker as an animal. Because one human does not do that to another.

Simple? But if the peekee does *not* complain afterwards, then he/she is kept in the stable until he/she does get off his/her ass and bitch some.

Since any animal that tries to probe a human mind is usually slaughtered as soon as possible, very few Arkslsnaglians will even consider violating the sanctity of another mind.

And since, as the saying goes, necessity is invention's mama . . . the burly, debate-prone Arkslsnaglians walk around with naked minds.

Through this entire period, I continued to deepen my rapport with Baby Bear. It was communication on a completely different level—whereas with the Arkslsnaglians I exchanged symbolic thought patterns, with Baby Bear I swapped sensations.

It's not hard to do. The vocabulary is limited, of course, but to communicate a given sensation (and therefore to arouse its subsequent emotion) calls only for awakening it in yourself, amplifying it, and passing it on. Pass it on . . .

shorthand for "establish sympathetic physiological resonances in the brain and body of the being with which communication exists." It's not quite that technical; on the other hand, it's not as simple as "pass it on" implies, either.

We reached a certain cramped fluency. The basic negative emotions—hunger, pain, fatigue, anger, fear—were the easiest, but we were *together* so often that positives entered our repertory. Through trial and misunderstanding, we found that many of them had to be twisted around: for example, I couldn't say "I like you" to BB, because its upshot, once it had permeated his system, would be a sudden wave of affection whipped up by his echoing my "I like you." If you've ever been caressed by a 200-kilo bear cub, you'll know that it's less enjoyable than one might presume.

When I wanted to communicate such an idea, I had to reverse it: "You like me," or make it passive: "I am liked by you." Once it had entered Baby Bear's system, he'd take it for his own. He'd feel loved, and all would be well.

So time slogged through the rainy season. My wrist healed, my beard grew, and I got better at understanding the Arkslsnaglians. I even reached the point where I could talk without inviting too much laughter. I never did get used to that. I don't like being laughed at—does anyone?—but especially not when the merriment's occasioned by something I can't control, like problems with a foreign language.

It could have been three months, or it could have been six. I was lost, they kept no calendars, and the temperature didn't vary much. Either Arkslsnagl had a very long year, or no axial tilt, or we were on the equator. Precisely which remains a mystery to me. Once I asked them if it would snow, but Ubsan's response was so puzzled that I gave up.

One bright morning, when it was Obben's turn to mangle my mind, she came to the outbuilding to take me on a guided tour of the farms. I wasn't excited by the idea—excitement comes reluctantly to the semicomatose—but I'd passed the point where I thought arguing with those monomaniacs would do any good. I said okay, and whistled to Baby Bear.

Instantly, Obben objected. Her impatient thoughtballs were coherent, and rationally interconnected, but the undershapes suggested that BB disgusted her. Arkslsnaglians seemed instinctively hostile to the bears, reminiscent of our feelings about snakes. I couldn't be sure—language and

143

culture continually intervened to ward off certainty—but they acted like people holding a grudge against others who'd played on them a particularly vile practical joke.

I'd asked Ubsan about it once, in the middle of a language lesson. He'd scowled across the porch at BB. His eventual answer, rid of the patterns tacked on for emotional effect, was: -They're the ones who showed us how to be and they did it just so they could have the forest to themselves.-

-How to be *what*, Ubsan?-

-How to be, how to be.-

Yeah. I put it down to unreasoning prejudice, and when people asked me not to bring BB, I shrugged and agreed. It was easier than arguing, especially since I had no status except that of tolerated pest/guest.

BB was sprawled half on, half off the porch; I went to him and eased my fingers into his luxuriant fur. (*Yawn*) *Sleepy. Sun warm. Dirt soft. Don't want to go. Want to stay. Wind sings.*

Rubbing his huge skull, I repeated the message until he fell asleep. Then, stifling a yawn of my own, I set off to the rolling fields with Obben.

It was a nice day, one of those lazy mornings when you're too itchy to stay in one place but not in the mood to go anywhere fast. We strolled. *She* strolled; I had to half-skip to keep up, since she wouldn't slow down. Arkslsnaglian legs are too damn long—even just moseying along, they cover ground at a ridiculous clip.

She led me through the sunshine to a treeless ridge that overlooked most of their farmland; from there, she pointed out their crops and the fields in which they grew. It was a quiz, in a way: after she'd named a crop, I had first to visualize it, and then to identify its manifold uses to her people. The city boy performed as expected. I got things backwards and upside down, which seemed to displease her. I could feel her coldness grow.

Soon the sun was high. The birds that had been circling glided in for a siesta. Obben, gazing across the fenceless fields, wouldn't respond to my persistent queries. Finally she turned, to show that Jekyll had become Hyde. Her gentleness and patience were gone. Her size and strength, which had up until then been simply a part of her, were subtly emphasized to contrast with my own. Her breathing was uneven, as if an inner excitement had seized her.

The command mode in Arkslsnaglian employs alternating thoughtballs: the first describing the action to be performed, the second delineating the alternatives.

-Take off your pants.- Obben didn't bother to sketch in an alternative. Every other ball was a black hole of menace.

-What for?- I asked, using the relationship network to show that I was merely curious, and not defiant.

-For sex.-

My horniness was an established, if secret, fact. Months had passed since I'd last been with a woman—the inability to remember exactly how many didn't lessen my appetite any—and I hadn't even masturbated since leaving the forest. Though not the most modest of people, I somehow hadn't been able to play with myself in the middle of a language lesson, and the damn lessons had never ceased.

Even so. I was not avid for sex with Obben. I'm not fond of perversion, for one thing, and that's how screwing an alien struck me at the time. For another, she had at least thirty centimeters and a hundred kilos on me—it would have been like fucking a mattress that breathed, and I've never been into that, either. And finally, although I'd never been exposed to formal sensitivity training, I had been a Jungle Lord, and I'd learned heuristically that different groups had different ways of doing things. The Arkslsnaglians had never discussed their attitudes towards sex, which suggested a taboo. I did not want to do anything that'd anger them. The tattoo on Ubsan's boot was warning enough.

So, staring at the coppery flush above her broad cheekbones, I said, -Thanks, but no thanks.-

-Strip.- The ice-black "or-else" echoed doomfully.

-Look, Obben— -

Her hard, flat hand clipped me topside the head. Stunned, I fell to the ground. She knelt. Her shadow covered me. One hand, flattening my shoulder blades, pinned me. The other fumbled for my belt.

I fought back as best I could, even though I couldn't believe that it was really happening. With kicks, punches, and handfuls of scrabbled-up dirt hurled in her face, I resisted. My blows bounced off her muscle slabs like raindrops on a pane of glass. My old standby, the Bandersnatch, swooped at her gleaming mind, but she threw up a screen at which he could only squawk. Then I tried the blank-filling trick that had finally done Mama Bear, but Obben's nervous system telegraphed its messages behind impermeable tubing at which I beat in frustration.

Hot sweat rained down on me; I jerked at its acid touch. Soon it wet my ass and upper thighs.

The waistband of my pants trapped my ankles. If they hadn't been duraweave, they would have been in shreds. Obben rolled me onto my back as easily as a circus strong-man overturns a pillow. The fingers of her left hand immobilized both my wrists; her right hand pressed my knees against the ground.

The sun was cruelly hot and bright. Obben's head eclipsed it, drenched her face and mine in shadow while acquiring a corona of its own. Her top-set ears made a blasphemous image: Satan's horns with a saintly halo.

Growling, she flashed a command full of unfamiliar terms. She repeated it pictorially, if pornographically: my cowed prick was limp, and she wanted it hard. I tried to cooperate—I knew she was listening; I had no choice—but nothing happened. It's hard to think erotically when a she-bear's panting tongue drips saliva onto your face.

She sat on my knees, took my prick in her hand and pumped it. Her fingers were rough, unkind. I responded anyway.

Then she raped me.

When she was finished, she rose and walked away, not pausing, not looking back. Bruised and violated, I lay in the mocking sunlight and watched her broad shoulders sink under the edge of the ridge. When she was gone, I staggered to my feet and pulled up my pants. Had there been a stream nearby, I would have washed myself, first, very, very thoroughly. As it was, I let half an hour die before I started home.

Though it wasn't the first time I'd been raped—I'd been taken by a few aggressive gayshakes in my boyhood, until my gut-shooting the last had earned me a hands-off rep—it was the first by a female, and the first to which I had no ready response. In the Jungle it was easy: you either purged your mind of the memory, or you got even. But on Arkslsnagl . . . I didn't know the rules, and felt too humiliated to ask. Talking to the Old Lady might get Obben punished, in which case I should do it. On the other hand, Arkslsnaglians might feel Obben had a right to my services, and might discipline me for opening my mouth.

Life among aliens can be interesting. You never know whether it's a street beneath your feet, or a high wire.

Stiffly, I followed the winding dirt trail home. I was in a

146

state of confused anger, but the walk didn't cool it. When I arrived at the house, I still didn't know what to do.

Baby Bear was lying in the leaves under the outbuilding porch; he sat up when I came into view. Shambling over to me, he snuffled at my hand for goodies. I rubbed him between the ears instead. Then I went inside and strapped on my knife.

The settlement seemed deserted. Nobody was in the large yard. The back windows of the house were shuttered. The first sign of life came when Sepol and Ubsan returned from the farms. Neither of them looked at me, not even when I waved. After storing their tools in the shed beside the outbuilding, less than twelve meters from where I sat, they disappeared into the house.

It's hard to determine motivations, especially when your emotions are running high. Had they been aloof because Obben had wanted me, rather than one of them? But that presumed that they knew what had happened, and *I* hadn't told them. Could it be, then, that they behaved that way every evening, and I'd just never noticed before?

I waited on the porch for one of the teachers to come. The back door stayed closed. Even after the light had faded and the sun had set, my mind's peace stayed unbroken. My stomach began to rumble, but nobody brought dinner. In a while, BB joined me to complain about the same thing.

"I know, I know," I whispered, stroking his fur to calm him. "We'll just have to be patient."

Still no one came. One by one the lamps in the house fell to sleep, until ghostly black squares stared across the yard. The sky was sprinkled with haughty stars that made no move to help us.

I dozed in spurts, expecting one of my tutors to come on line for the lessons. Nobody did. They left me alone. And, for the first time since I'd emerged from the forest, my dreams were not spattered with thoughtballs and mental images.

At first there was a vacuum—a void—a stream of ebony emptiness, cool and refreshing, that swept away the debris of acculturation as it flowed. Drinking from it, I felt myself begin to heal.

Then Shana marched down a shadowy street, hair blowing in the wind, and the open-mouthed hulks of once-fine buildings whistled softly. "Shana!" Her back stiffened. "*Shana!*" She walked on. "SHANA!!!" I called again.

She turned in annoyance. "Can't you shut him up?" she demanded.

I looked where she was looking, and my eyes found Ubsan. Apologetically, he said, "I'll try." When I started to call her for the fourth time, he jerked the leash in his hand. Fire bit my neck. Shana thanked him with a radiant smile, and rounded a corner. I tried to follow but the leash wouldn't snap, the leash only throttled. Finally Ubsan got angry. His tattooed boot broke my ribs. "You're mine now," he bellowed. "Mine! Sit. Sit!"

Sweat covered my body at the dawn.

Across the yard, the back door rattled on its crude, heavy hinges. Ubsan emerged. Rubbing my eyes, I sat up and waved. He ignored me.

My stomach was a hollow pit teased by flames. I could barely think for its lamentations. It was BB, demanding food in the only way he knew. I crossed the porch and tried to soothe him. He was hard to mollify, but the clamor in my belly subsided after a while.

"Come on," I said, clattering down the warped steps. "We're going to find out what's going on."

Ubsan was opening the shed door, his back to us. He must have heard us approach, but when I tapped him on the shoulder he pretended not to notice.

Tired, hungry, and exasperated, I would not put up with that kind of shit. Grabbing his pelt, I yanked viciously. His face snapped up to eye the dawn sky. He made no sound. I pulled harder. He fell towards me, breaking my grip, and bounced up immediately. His hands rose like snake heads, like threat personified.

BB didn't like my being menaced. His lips drew back from his fangs; his stocky body quivered with his snarl. On his hind legs he waddled forward.

Ubsan was unarmed. His eyes showed fear. He began to back away.

I saw my chance. I had to plant a complex idea in BB's head, and quickly. I commenced with a memory of Ubsan bringing us food, and repeated it until I was sure that BB remembered it, too. Then: *Push him, hold down, scare him, he bring food.*

The cub responded magnificently. An instant later, Ubsan lay flat on his back while two hundred hungry kilos smashed his shoulders. Drawing my knife, I forced myself into the tiny space between their heaving bodies.

Ubsan took a swipe at my mind, causing pain and confu-

148

sion. His thoughts thudded into me like rifle bullets. My roof was a kaleidoscopic nightmare of conflicting imagery. I could barely see for flashes of blinding light. Stringing two coherent thoughts together was virtually impossible.

My knees folded and my face scraped the gravel before the shed. The pain fertilized Ubsan's barrage. Chaos was born. I couldn't remember what it was I— I— I— I—

I was watching Pajalli play with his lucited brain while he berated me for having killed his telepath. He was telling me, "Each mind has a set of rules . . . going from one mind to another . . . one must expect that . . . the possibilities inherent in the future are constrained solely by the laws of the new universe."

The physicists say that if you race to the edge of the universe, you'll find that you're hurrying home—you cannot get there from here, because it's curled in on itself.

If a universe can be that way, why not a mind?

With that my mind dissolved, spun, re-formed. The center was the edge and the edge was the center and Ubsan's thoughts couldn't begin to penetrate. They zoomed directly back at him, and startled hurt exploded across his face.

I creased his throat with the knife, and tried to talk. My thoughts couldn't get out. I had to pause, restructure, then ask: -Why?-

-Why what?-

-Why is everyone ignoring me?-

-Why should we not?-

-You didn't before.-

-Before we thought you might be human.-

-And now?- A thin line of blood had risen under the blade.

-Obben had her way with you despite your objections.-

-So?-

-Yours was not a peer-to-peer exchange.-

-Oh.- I was catching on. Evidently rape was in the same category as eavesdropping: one human didn't do it to another. -I see. Should I complain to the Old Lady about it?-

-She won't see you.-

-Why not?-

-She sees only those ignorant of their attackers' identities.-

-Ah.- That's how it worked. -So what do I do?-

-Live as an animal.-

-I'd rather not, thank you.-

-Then prove your humanity.-

149

-How?-

-A true human wouldn't need to ask.-

-I see.- Rising, I grabbed BB by the loose skin behind his neck. He didn't want to get up—he hadn't been given his breakfast yet—but after a flurry of sense-swaps he finally shuffled away from the prone Ubsan. I gestured with my knife. He stood, shakily. He took a step towards the shed but I cleared my throat and pointed to the house. He hesitated. I twisted the knife so its blade caught the sunlight and ricocheted it into Ubsan's eyes. A centimeter further and the blood was visible. Sunlight. Blood. He got the message.

And so to deal with Obben. As Ubsan's shoulders scraped the frame of the back door, I realized that she had to be inside. No good. BB and I could intimidate a single Arkslsnaglian, but a whole settlement would simply laugh. I couldn't barge in on them no matter how much I wanted to.

But my mind could. Squatting, I cut it loose and sent it forth. It zinged inside, and touched Ubsan's. -Where's Obben?- I demanded.

He looked across the crowded kitchen. Along with six or seven others, she was sitting down to the dark-polished breakfast table.

-Thanks.- I sprang from him to Obben. She felt me enter; her food-laden fingers stopped halfway to her mouth.

-Get out,- she said flatly, expecting the blind obedience she'd get from a draft animal.

-Fuck you.- I found her nervous system, but the impermeable tubing still swathed it. After a pause, I searched for the quirk in her private universe that allowed such tubing. I couldn't see any way of altering it.

Her attempts to kick me out were meeting with little success. Due to their moral code, the Arkslsnaglians have had little experience with invasions of mental privacy. And it's through experience that you learn to react reflexively in a crisis.

I traced the tubing to its junction with her mind; I smelled the stench of fear that masked the background mutter of an empty stomach. Brushing the fear aside as though it were a curtain, I reached for the hunger. Nothing insulated it.

Grass is good, I thought, I amplified, I grafted onto her appetite center. *Very good. Better than anything else.*

150

She struggled furiously, but I held firm and kept on pumping. *Good. Green. Healthy. Good.*

A prestorm silence trembled while she regrouped. Then, to the accompaniment of thunder and lightning and roaring winds, she hurled her entire mind at me. I let it blow me clear out of her head. I flailed dramatically for balance. I dove back in. She stopped me cold at the border—

—just as I'd hoped. With a twist and a wriggle and a heartbeat's worth of time, I enclosed her mind in her own impermeable tubing.

Obben lunged at me, unaware of what I'd done. Her fringes broke against the tubing. Astonishment flickered through her being. Then anger. Minutes later she glowed with horror and hatred and agonized frustration. I waited. I watched. I made sure that the damn tubing would hold and then—I'm not sure why—I opaqued it. It seemed somehow fitting.

Urgency gone, I sauntered to her appetite center and reminded it of the magnificent taste of good grass. Her massive body rocked back and forth, then suddenly erupted. Her chair crashed backwards. Without a glance for the others, she marched to the back door, through it, and out onto the lawn. There she dropped to her hands and knees and began to chew at the grass. I waved to her, but she didn't see me.

While I was still recovering, Ubsan came outside, two huge bowls of food balanced precariously on each palm. Obben, grazing placidly, blocked his path. He kicked her.

-So you are a human,- he said.

-Yup.- Taking the bowls, I gave BB his share. -Thanks.-

-It is what you merit.- He sat on the porch rail. -You were impressive, and original. One could admire you. Perhaps even come to like you.-

-I appreciate the vote of confidence,- I said, through a mouthful of greens.

-?-

-Never mind. I like you, too.-

When we were finished, he scooped the empty bowls off the floor. -The Old Lady would like to see you.-

-She's taking me back into the fold?-

-Yes.-

-Where is she?-

-Out front.-

-Let's go.-

He led me back to the bench where I'd sat for my first interview with her. She was already in her chair, which floated in a pool of early morning sunlight. -Hello, Hairless One.-

-Hello, Old Lady.-

-You've spoiled our hunt.-

-Sorry.-

Her fingers fluttered dismissively. -Obben will do as well.-

I raised my eyebrows.

-Grass will not suit her. She will soon weaken, and die. She is of no use to us now, so it is right that she provide us entertainment before she goes.-

-That's one way of looking at it.-

-Yes.- She nodded. It was apparent that her brain, sharp as it was, had momentarily lost the thread. -You will recall,- she began eventually, -that when you came I said there were two things you had to do.-

-Learn to communicate, and perform a task.-

-Yes. You have learned to communicate well—-

-Thank you. What's the task?-

-It would have been the death of your companion.-

-Would have been?-

-It would have been to prove your humanity. But now . . .- An image of Obben hung between us. -Now, I think you have proved it sufficiently. We will take you to your beacon.-

IV

Ubsan and I were on the road an hour before sunrise. His cart, an ancient, creak-wheeled affair with a wooden bench that left splinters in the unwary, was pulled by the three-horned beast that also did plow duty. It was skittish, and obstinately unhappy about Baby Bear's proximity, but Ubsan was a mean hand with a whip. After a few jolting minutes, the beast steadied down, or at least resigned itself.

The weather was good. The stars, fading as their shift ended, were still sharp enough to promise a clear morning. It was cool, but not chill. I felt fine in my duraweave, and Ubsan never wore more than his jockstrap. The breezes that would flutter my hair during the day hadn't awakened yet. We were the only motion in a static green land.

-Why did we have to leave so early?- I asked. Not that I wanted to linger—an eagerness to get back among friends was growing in me—but the day was very young.

Ubsan concentrated on the reins and whip for a moment longer, then cautiously leaned against the bench's rough back. -Obben provides sport this morning; it was thought you should be gone.-

-Why?-

-Were you there, you would hunt, as one, with the people.-

-Mm.- Yes, that might provoke hard feelings. Though the Arkslsnaglians were honest—they hadn't changed any rules to keep me from proving my equality, which some people back home would have done—they did have their pride. What I'd done to Obben upset a lot of their smug assumptions, and from their point of view, my helping to chase her through the fields and the forest would have been too much. -Why were you assigned to take me?-

Arkslsnaglians do not believe in flattery, or even in diplomacy. -No one else would go.-

My cheeks reddened. I made a few meaningless foot shuffles while I regained my composure, then asked— because I was curious, because I thought I could be objective—what the others didn't like about me.

-It.- He jerked a thumb over his shoulder at BB, who sat erect and sharp-eared in the bed of the cart.

-Why?- The cub had been around the settlement long enough for them to get used to him.

Ubsan, not replying, looked at me across a chasm of ignorance. I didn't know enough about his people. He didn't know enough about mine. There was no place for him to start his explanation.

-Sorry.-

He waved a hand.

-Lousy road.- Not even gravel covered its unkempt, weedy surface. The wheels churned through twenty-centimeter ruts that straddled its middle. It appeared it would be impossible to get out of the ruts if another cart came from the opposite direction. I asked him about that.

-It is never a problem.-

-Never?- We bumped around a shrub-screened curve, and I began to see why. The ruts, like incised railroad tracks at a switchyard, split. Ubsan flicked the reins and the beast bore to the right, to a small clearing beside the road. Pulling up there, in the shade of a massive tree, it settled down to switching the flies off its ass. -Why are we stopping?- I asked.

He pointed up the road with his whip. From a distance floated the wispy thoughts of an approaching carter. -He told me he was coming.-

To the ultramodern, high-tech side of me, the ponderous, delay-prone system made little sense—synergy's impossible when the parts can't become a whole—but the part of me that had been born on Arkslsnagl applauded. By all means keep the communities separated, by time as well as by space! Self-respect is more important than comfort, although Terran ho-coms did provide a fair amount of each. But the Fedra's—the densely crowded Jungles—they shrank the individuals into anonymity. Who can respect a person no one knows?

154

My thoughts were broken by a spurt of excitement almost orgasmic in its intensity. Ubsan's knuckles whitened on the handle of his whip. BB's ears perked up. The draft animal stirred, and grunted uneasily. -What's that?-

-The hunt.- He made a sighing sound, an echo of the treetorn wind. It was the noise of taciturnity.

-Oh.- I stared at the cloudless sky and listened to the chatter of the winged things around us. One with green-specked wings darted through the flies annoying our locomotive.

A cart rumbled into sight; its driver gave a sign of recognition to Ubsan. Then he brought his whip down across his animal's back, startling it out of its lethargy. They were past the layover in less than a minute.

-The road is now ours,- Ubsan said, as his own whip came into play.

-How long is this going to take?-

-Long?- His puzzled expression rejected my attempt to transliterate an English idiom.

-Sorry. Ah . . . how many days must we travel?-

He wiggled his fingers. -Five? Six?-

-I see.- I fell back against the seat, and watched the landscape rock past. It wasn't very interesting. Though picturesque enough—cool, green, and alive—its relevance to me diminished the closer I drew to my goal. The farms were even worse: vast stretches of monotonous fields, interrupted here and there by hunched-over farmers on inspection tours.

Not what I wanted to see. I was impatient to get home, to find the old friends, to be with Shana again. Opportunities to think about them all had been rare; this trip was really the first time since emerging from the forest that I could call my thoughts my own. And they turned, almost automatically, to the people and the places I'd left behind. God, I wanted to see them again.

The Obben hunt flashed sporadically, superimposing a tangential urgency on my own. Mostly it was Obben herself. The others weren't using their telepathy because it would have given them too great an advantage. She'd stay calm for hours, then suddenly erupt in paroxysms of panic.

I didn't like it. There was no way I could guard against it. I'd be drowsing in the warm sun and the easy sway, and abruptly my every muscle would tense. My heart would fire a quick burst as adrenaline spurred it. BB'd snarl. The ox'd stutter-step. Then Ubsan and I would grimace briefly

155

before lapsing back into the rhythm of the journey.

Occasionally the children came through, too, probably because they couldn't keep a tight enough lid on themselves, what with the excitement and the suspense. Since some were very young, I wondered why they participated, but Ubsan's explanation was hardly illuminating.

-It is part of being a person,- he said, and opened his mouth to sigh.

The third day had dawned before he tried to amplify that statement. We were picking berries by the side of the road while we waited for another cart to pass. He began talking, almost to himself, though his thoughts were clearly beamed at me.

-Any animal can kill,- he started off, -and all do.- His incisors split a berry in half. Its juice left a bluish film on them.

-This kills?- I patted Three Horn's sweaty flank.

He pointed to the grass that stuck out of the beast's mouth. -Is not depriving any being of life killing?-

-True,- I admitted.

-Animals kill to live: to defend their own lives, or to maintain them. We do not. We kill because . . .- Incomplete thoughtballs were rare, and indicative of a relationship so complex that the speaker wasn't entirely confident he could express it in its fullness. -We kill to remind us that we can kill. Because of what we are, we must remember death.-

The other cart trundled past. Ubsan tossed the rest of the berries into his mouth and clambered back up to the bench. Dark stains marked the corners of his lips.

We rode in a silence that stretched like a rubber band, growing ever tenser until a distant thought-scream broke it. -Obben.- The wail rose in pitch and desperation, spiralling up, *up*, UP through the sky into nothingness. I strained to hear more, but there was no more.

-Animals know life alone,- he resumed. -They know what they must do to protect and maintain their own lives, but something in their minds keeps them from understanding it. To them, there is only one life—their own—and everything else is background. To us there is more, yet to remember that, we must kill, and in the killing remember, for it is this that makes us human.-

I had neither answer nor comment, so I let a wordless hour jostle by. -Ubsan,- I said at last, stiffly, -there is a mark on your boot. It is familiar to me.-

-Is it?- He twisted his foot to get a better look at it. -I have wondered about that, Hairless One. Is that a natural mark, or an artificial one?-

-Artificial.- I cleared my throat. -We call it a tattoo; it's a . . . a form of decoration, or adornment.-

-Ah!- He chuckled to himself. -The one who wore it needed such adornment; his face was ugly enough to frighten even your friend here.-

-Ubsan . . . how did you . . . -

-Following most closely, I made the kill.- A sound from deep in his throat denoted pleasurable reminiscence. -Your men are strong and cunning, Hairless One. I trailed him to a clearing not far from the settlement. Had I come ten breaths later his trap would have been prepared. As it was, it nearly caught me, but I am blessed with a certain quickness of eye. The rock hurtled past harmlessly. Then, ah . . . but does this pain you?-

I shrugged. Though he didn't precisely understand the gesture, the variety of thoughts orbiting it aptly expressed my confusion.

Did it pain me? Well, no . . . and yes. The man who'd loved Rosie was a stranger whom I wouldn't have known if he'd resurrected himself and stood before us. I had no personal interest in him. Had I been back in my Jungle, and had he tried to do me, I would have ordered him coughed without a second's thought.

But out there . . . I don't know, the Arkslsnaglians were okay, yet . . . something about being among aliens makes even the most obnoxious prick from back home good to see.

There was another part to it that the old-time swashbucklers understood perfectly. Every killing is followed by a period of assessment: does something happen to the killer? If so, does the disadvantage of the vengeance outweigh the advantage of the killing? If not, then there's nothing, absolutely nothing, to keep them from sticking their knives into the next funny-looking foreigner who waddles along.

So did it pain me? I really couldn't have cared *what* happened to the fucker, if only it had happened on Earth. On Arkslsnagl I cared. His unavenged death made mine that much less of an impossibility, and thus it pained me deeply.

I pointed to the boots. -Why?-

-He was brave. He deserved to be honored.-

-You honor him by turning him into a pair of boots?-

-I honor him,- said Ubsan gravely, -by walking in his skin.-

Trees marched past in glum silence, and birds wheeled through the crisp air. There was no point in arguing with Ubsan. He thought he was honoring the poor bastard, and so, sure enough, he was. Honor's too intangible to be limited to specific phrases and gestures.

In the meantime, the signal beacon had grown louder. Though at the settlement it had been so faint that I'd had to entrance myself to hear it, four days of travel had brought me into the range where it was deafening. Completely in the mind, not all the ear-muffling in the world could keep it from driving me bat-shit. -Don't you hear it?- I protested.

-What?-

-That voice—"Come find me, Bander Snatch"—don't you hear it?-

-No.- He cocked his head to one side, and reached out with his mind, but still made the gesture of dissent. -There is nothing.-

Red ice chilled me. Black fire burned me. The Siren's voice summoned my very cells, and would destroy them if I didn't obey. -Well, forgive me, but I disagree.- I was in a bind. I had to shield myself, even though Ubsan might be offended. I explained the situation between bursts of come-hithers.

He looked at me as Mr. Average would a freak. His fingers wiggled doubtfully. -If it pleases you, Hairless One, dissociate yourself. Does it have to do with your fellow who preserves my feet?-

-No.- What could I say? The beacon's magnetism was real. My naked mind was rent by its violent flux. To that extent, then, I had told Ubsan the literal truth. But there was more. Deep inside, I was pleased—and relieved—to sever communications. Something in Ubsan's sidelong glance said that I was still on trial, and that his people were hoping I'd disqualify myself at the last minute. . . . Truth to tell, I was wary of giving him a clear shot at my back.

For two more days I rode the bucking cart. Doing nothing and saying nothing, I prayed with all my heart that inaction wouldn't set me up as the settlement's next quarry. In between times, I thought about how good it would be to play the returning hero. Waiting was getting harder.

At last we halted in the large clearing that surrounded the beacon. Around the base of the white stone obelisk rested herdsmen; their tawny, three-horned charges were grazing in its middle.

Ubsan nodded to the ten-meter needle, then made the nose-twitch of annoyance. Forgetting about my deafness, he'd tried to speak. Still twitching, he wrapped the reins around the seatboard. Then he dismounted, and motioned for me to follow.

My shielding vibrated under the stress of the signal beacon. No noise penetrated, but bits of soundproofing were already flaking off. As I crossed the clearing, an internal blizzard began to rage.

The others rose at our approach; I scanned them briefly. They were undistinguished: one young boy who smelled of manure; two filthy specimens who giggled, played with their exposed genitals, and couldn't focus their eyes; and one middle-aged male whose demeanor was far more dignified than his multipatched cloak. Ubsan strolled into their midst while I read the stainless steel plaques bolted to the obelisk.

TO SHUT OFF HOMING BEACON, OPEN HATCH
BELOW, LOCATE APPROPRIATELY LABELED
SWITCH, AND THROW SWITCH FROM RIGHT
TO LEFT. THE NOISE WILL CEASE AT ONCE.

Next to it was another, which read:

TO SUMMON RESCUE CRAFT, FORCE THE CHIEF
TO THROW THE APPROPRIATE SWITCH.

I sensed trouble, but didn't dwell on it—I was too busy searching for the appropriately labeled switch. Of the two dozen such switches, half wore engraved metal tabs. Carla McGinnis. Frostfree. Bitter Beer. Frank Lucenzio. Bander Snatch.

When the old-fashioned jackknife had flopped from right to left, the malevolent vibrations immediately vanished. With a sigh of relief I razed my shield. The hatch offered my forehead a smooth metal compress. While the Arkslsnaglians crowded up behind me, Ubsan asked, -Is it done?-

-Only the first part.- The sudden drop in pressure had bewildered my eyes, which hurt and swam in moist circles. I shook my head forcefully. It didn't help, but did give the illusion of doing something. Then I had a sudden thought, and opened the hatch again. My finger ran down the line of black ceramic switches. Only one had been thrown. My own.

-Nobody's made it this far?-

The man in the ragged cloak answered: -You are the first.-

The first. What did that mean? Ten or eleven other Terrans had started the test; one, at least, was already a skinless skeleton . . . or a pair of boots. Where were the others, though? Their absence—the uncertainty of their fates—marred my triumph.

-Are you ready for your last test, Hairless One?- asked Ubsan.

For one long moment I wanted to vomit. For the next, I wanted to kill him—them—everybody connected with that madness. Why wouldn't they let me go home to my friends? -Last test?-

-Yes, you have one more field to plow.- He made the ritual motions of introduction. The cloaked one and I bowed gracefully as our minds brushed fringes. -You must convince this chief to call down your compatriots.-

The chief, over two meters tall, had shoulders the way Baby Bear had fur: to extremes. I slapped my forehead while the sinking sun imitated my heart. -Ubsan, do I have to?-

-Nor must you return home.-

"Aw, Christ." I was tired in mind and body. -Can we put it off till tomorrow morning?-

-Certainly.- Astonishment tinged his answer. Time is flexible on Arkslsnagl. -The chief is in no hurry. He— - He paused to receive a message that to me was a heavily-accented blur -He says that if you would like to exercise your mind before you grapple with him, he will provide food and shelter until you feel ready.-

-Grapple?- What was it, rigged? He had arms like I had legs.

-With your minds, Hairless One, with your minds.- A liquid chuckle spilled out of his mouth. -We have respect for you, but to ask you to fight this man is something we will not do.-

-So what do I do?-

-Approach his mind—preserving your sanity—and make him understand that it would be best for all if you were assisted to leave.-

His words, though mild enough, were imbedded in an urgency pattern that alarmed me into asking: -And if I can't?-

His fingers wiggled. -It has been long since his settlement has hunted well.-

My eyes were birds before the cobras of his boots. Frost crystallized the pit of my stomach. It wasn't fair, dammit! The runty little Earthman, a neophyte telepath, was being told that if he couldn't mentally manhandle a chief—a fucking chief, for Chrissakes!—they were going to pin a foxtail on him and let loose the hounds.

I shook my head; made a stay-away motion with my hand. -I . . .- couldn't finish the thought. Baby Bear snuffling at my heels, I wandered away from the obelisk. I had to think.

The chief had offered me preparation time. I could take him up on it, learn the mechanics of his mind, polish some strategy, and then . . . but he'd be doing *exactly* the same thing, and it was a cinch that he'd learn more quickly, and more thoroughly, than I could. Neg that.

Yet if I challenged him right away . . . aw, Christ, it wasn't fair. The goddam switch had to be nearby. Maybe I could ferret it out if I . . . no. They wouldn't let me.

The sun kissed the horizon. The obelisk's shadow tip seduced the forest.

What the hell. Everything from start to finish is a risk that varies only in degree. I turned to face them. Their eyes gleamed out of the gathering darkness. I knew I didn't have to explain.

-Tomorrow, then,- said the chief.

-Fine.- I lost my fingers in the hair of BB's skull. -Rest well.-

-You do not require my hospitality?-

-Ubsan does,- I said without hesitation. -I must keep vigil.-

After a final bow, he led Ubsan to his settlement. I stayed in the clearing with my friend. Maybe it was foolish to be proud. A bed would have been kinder than the short-cropped grass; a warm meal might have renewed my strength. And yet . . . I had a strange reluctance to pass one night as the equal of a man who would try to prove the contrary. Time enough to be his guest once I'd earned his unqualified respect.

But I didn't sleep well.

Too soon came the morning to the midst of the clearing. Its restlessness woke me at once. Stiffly, I struggled into a sitting position. BB lay next to me, jaws parted and tongue

161

hanging half out. His fur glistened with dew. Nudging him in the ribs, I messaged that it was time to rise. After a few minatory grumbles, he got his legs underneath him and staggered to the woods for a quick bite to eat. My body stayed put, but my mind went with him. It was nice to ride somebody who didn't want to kill me.

-Are you ready?-

I spun around. Ubsan, the chief, and the two with slack faces were striding towards me. Behind them came the beast-boy with his nervous grazers; nothing, apparently, could keep the animals from their daily routine. -As ready as I'll ever be.-

-Good.- Ubsan was the referee, but a palpably ambivalent one. He wanted the chief to win because they were both Arkslsnaglians; he wanted me at least to hold my own, because I, after all, was his protégé, his personal alien, his . . . friend? So he'd explain the rules and make sure we abided by them. No matter how it turned out, he'd wish it hadn't. -You know the chief.-

-Yes, I do, but these two gentlemen?-

-Their minds will shield the chief's.- Though he wanted to say more, protocol kept him unhappily silent. I braced myself for a disagreeable surprise. -You must pick a path through their minds, first, before you may approach the chief's. Once you have come in contact with him, you will try to convince him to signal your fellows. I will warn you in advance that to appeal to his good nature will be useless. You must force him to yearn for your hasty departure.-

That was clear enough. -Is there anything I'm forbidden to do?-

-Yes. Neither of you may enlist the aid of another. There will be no physical contact. You, Hairless One, may not harm any third party.-

-Huh?-

-You may not attack the chief's family or friends.-

We bowed like judoists. His long shadow stretched across the emerald grass; distorted as it was, its shoulders were still intimidating. Then, with thoughtballs that spun like burned-out suns, Ubsan said, -Begin.-

My move. Whatthehell, it was all going to be in the mind, might as well be comfortable. I sat, and crossed my legs. The chief, after another bow, followed suit. His sidekicks stood, mutely scratching their cojones.

Tentatively, I extended a tendril until the first barrier loomed sleek and menacing. Involuntarily, I gasped. A

162

curved field of thought, its soft whiteness was apparently solid. I went around it—over it—under it—it was a perfect sphere. The chief's mind lay somewhere in its interior.

I had to break through. Drawing near its blurred surface, I realized that its milky skin was an illusion cast by its uncontrolled thoughts. Not one was anchored as it should have been. All were in motion, sweeping random, implacable circles around the shell.

Penetration would be akin to charging a machine-gun nest. I tried to track a single thought, but it moved so quickly that picking out its path was all I could do. I shuddered. If one of those sonsofbitches hit me while I was in its plane . . . my mind recoiled and the sphere dwindled.

I had to insert a tendril—a tentacle—a portion of my mind umbilically attached to the rest of me—inside that clouded mass. It would have been simpler, as well as much safer, if I could have shaped a scale model of my mind and remote-controlled it like a drone. But I couldn't. I had no influence over anything detached from me.

Yet the normal probe would leave the link between me and me—the umbilicus—very, very vulnerable. One of the other's wild thoughts would inevitably collide with it. I'd never experienced such an impact, but I was positive it would involve a whole lot of pain.

After again scrutinizing the mind before me, I came all the way back to the tangible world. -Ubsan,- I demanded, -what's wrong with that man?-

-Which?-

-The one whose mind is on the outside.-

-Oh.- He looked to one of the fuzzy-eyed ones, the one who was squatting in the grass and absently relieving himself. -He's insane.-

-Insane?-

-Yes. They do that, you see.- His hands made an englobing gesture. -Normally, we keep them stacked.-

The image set me to laughing. Gallows humor. The kind that takes your attention off your cold sweat, your null-g'd stomach. Stacked. Like dishes on a shelf. Like boxes one inside another. Like a fucking Chinese puzzle.

Back to the attack, and to basics. Every mind has its own set of rules. Everything in it must conform to them. *Nova*, I thought, as I extruded a new tendril. I'd learn the rules of that loonie's mind and . . .

It took a while to discover that he had one rule, and one rule only: ANYTHING IS POSSIBLE. After that it was simple.

Tapping his energy, I bored a tunnel through his surface and sheathed it with the same impermeability I'd found in Obben's head. It worked. Within ten minutes I was inside his shell. Behind me, thoughts flared in rainbow bursts as they crashed against the sheathing and died.

Where the first mind was alive in chaos, reflecting all that approached, the second was a pitted cinder. Its thoughts didn't spin, didn't soar, didn't cut electron orbits around its nucleus. Still and motionless, they were dank clouds on a listless day.

Its basic rule was pure madness: NOTHING IS POSSIBLE. I searched for a flaw, a weakness, a way to turn that heavy insanity upon itself like I had the first. My mind balked at its bleak despair, and found nothing.

NOTHING IS POSSIBLE.

My fingers slithered onto the hilt of my knife. *That* would solve the problem. One good wrist action, snap! A watery cough from the pierced madman. That would be that. With the core blown away, gravity fails. The doldrums would vanish like mist under a hot sun. Then I could stalk the chief's mind freely.

But I didn't dare. Ubsan had explained the rules, and even a slight tug on the knife would cost me a broken arm.

NOTHING IS POSSIBLE. My God, how in hell could that be countered?

Wait. There *was* a flaw. If nothing were possible, how could there be existence? Further, how could it have form, and density, and texture?

Below me, thoughts lay like shoals of beached fish. *You are,* I shouted, *you are!* Ranting and raving, with a preacher's passion and a dying man's need, I hammered the message home. My thoughtballs lacerated its passivity.

Hours later, it began to stir. Inching as close as I could, I listened. Slowly, the mind groaned out an amendment: EXISTENCE IS THE ONLY POSSIBILITY.

Success. Withdrawing to myself, I made the tendril a needle. Like a javelin thrower I hurled it at the madmind. Its velocity was incredible. Its point was sharper than a serpent's tooth. Its body was greased steel. It HIT! and I was through.

One more mind left, a sane one. A stubborn one. -Chief,- I said, -I want you to throw that switch.-

-I refuse.-

-Why?-

-My people yearn for the hunt.- Beneath his dignified

facade squirmed barely leashed lusts: for a headlong rush through the forest and the gut-punch of an adrenaline super-charge; for sweat-slippery combat ended by the hot gush of a fang-torn artery; for the hoarse ululations of the victor.

My stomach churned. It had been *my* body he'd broken in his revery. *My* blood on the leaf mold. I retreated to physical awareness. Slowing the wild beatings of my heart, inhaling the pastoral ambience of the early evening, I prepared a reply that I hoped would shake him.

Back in. -I might enjoy the hunt.- I hit him with a quick series of flashes, like sixteen-frame clips from a film: me, gliding lithely through the undergrowth, pausing here and there to lay traps. Them, breaking legs and puncturing feet as they blunder into what I've set. Me, in a tree on a branch with a rock. Him, stiffening, looking up, actually seeing the granite guillotine slice through his forehead. Me—

-You are arrogant, romantic, and totally unrealistic.-

-I just want to go home.-

-Your desire shall never be fulfilled.- Maggots ate through my eyes.

To hell with the banter. Bring on the Bandersnatch. There—*blink*—ten thousand meters up in the Arksls-naglian sky, he studies the ground. Pulsating light catches his eye. He circles, finds the center of the chief's mind, plummets towards it claws outstretched. He—

-*Totally* unrealistic.- With the gentlest of pressures, the chief nudged my monster to one side. He roared on. His new target was his creator.

-Hey!- I shoved him back on course.

Mind-flickers of amusement. And the meathook talons focused on me again.

-Fuck you.- Make the Bandersnatch *blink* out of there, *blink* into being on the horizon, low and fast, a bomber coming in under the radar screen, great green-scaled wings beating the air, tips nearly brushing the ground while the shiny claws flex, reach, flex—

blink and it was aiming at MY BACK GODDAMIT GET DOWN GET DOWN GET—

blink and he was gone and you can bet your fucking life I wasn't going to resurrect him, not when my foe could control him as easily as I could.

But it left me weaponless. The chief's mind was too well guarded for a head-on attack: I was straining at its boundary, unable even to begin a path of penetration.

Find the rules, see if—obligingly, they shone before me. Complex and flexible. Anything I could do, he could undo.

Withdraw, then. Float in mind-space, in the dull hazy gray that drifted through no-mind's land, try to comprehend . . .

I couldn't enter his mind. I couldn't hurt him from outside it. I couldn't do a damn thing. Maybe I should accept the hunt, run before it and try to . . . how many Arkslsnaglians could I lose, though? All of them? And if I did that, who'd throw the switch?

Wait a minute. Maybe there was a way. If I could just find out what he was afraid of, I could summon shapes, paint pictures, animate images to haunt him until he—

-I fear neither man nor beast,- he laughed, and truth rang firm.

I was impotent. I had plenty of strength, but no power. True power is the ability to arouse another's fear and to manipulate it—and through it, him—for one's own ends. But I had none, because the chief had no fear.

Nice try, Bander Snatch. You almost made it. You survived the forest; you survived the farm. You learned a language, a culture, an alien mode of thought. And it wasn't enough. Your friends' wait will never end.

Weightless in nowhere, I began to resign myself. When the inevitable confronts you, it's time to ready yourself to face it. I strangled a few regrets, then slid into the physical to say good-bye to Baby Bear.

The morning sun was in my eyes; I frowned and squinted. He was gone from the clearing. Moments later, I sensed him in the woods, hunting breakfast. His mind burned with hunger. His eyes saw prey. Leaves whispered beneath his paws as he approached it. His arm flashed, crashed, killed. A shimmer of pleasure ran through him as he began to eat.

About to share good-byes, I halted. His aurora was familiar, much like . . . *switch* and I examined the chief's mind, also shimmering . . . *switch* to Baby Bear and by damn! the glowing pleasure-fields were the same.

I had my answer. And my power.

-You would hunt me, would you?-

-Happily.-

-When you hunt, what are you?-

-What I am always.-

-When you hunt, you hunt together, yet alone?-

-Of course.-

166

NOW!   *switch/blink*   shimshimmershimshimmer
switch/blink -Compare.-

-I— -

-LOOK AT IT!!!-

-I disavow it.-

He could disavow it for the rest of his life, but I was
going to cram it down his throat. -Why would you hunt
me?-

-To kill you.-

-Why would you kill me?-

-To remember.-

-What would you remember?-

-Death.-

-Why would you remember death?-

Again he tried to evade my point, but I enveloped him,
and held him steady. -Only man knows death,- he admitted
at last. -We must remember we are men.-

-But when you hunt . . . . - Leaving the thought, I
picked up Baby Bear's mind, brought it next to the chief's,
and showed him.

-I— -

-You're not a man, are you?-

-Of course I'm a man.-

-Even when you hunt?-

-I . . .- He began to face the truth. His elastic shell
grew brittle, and porous.

Now I could move. Insert /here/ their portraits, and
wire in /there/ their hungers, and install /over-down/ the
mirroring monomanias of the hungers. Graft them in, tickle
some life into them, force them nose to nose so that they
could see their brothership, and then—

—the corporeal me eased his knife out of its sheath.
Ubsan made a startled, clumsy attempt to interpose himself, but the person with the knife was too quick. Before the
heavy body could snap the slender arm he had slit (*oh-
GodthathurtsmornIexpected*) his left palm and reburied
the blade in its leather tomb. The red-smeared hand
reached out to unfold like a rose beneath the nose of the
chief who—

—inhaled sharply, deeply. His lips drew back from teeth
that lengthened into fangs even as the one me watched.
And inside, his soul thickened, coarsened bestially, in response to the sweet aromatic warmth of blood.

An important psychological "mechanism" lay exposed.
Formerly covered by debris from a million years of muta-

tions and modifications, it glimmered uncertainly. It was like a switch. On: human. Off: prehuman. Unrecognizable except to those with insightful hunches. Not designed for direct manipulation, it clung to existence as a survival device. The environment could ease it either way, and did, when the occasion arose.

I seized it, on one level; I withdrew my hand, on the other. Exultation brightened my thoughts—I'd be going home soon. -I got you by the short hairs, Chief.-

-I sense your trespass. What is your power?-

-To rob you of humanity, now and forever.- Once activated by intent, the switch could be locked into place. In fact, it would never be unlocked. The animal would not submit to mind-tinkering, would rather die than comprehend—and respect—the multiplicity of life. -Will you call my rescuers?-

His thoughts were shot with purple, the color of defeat. -Yes,- he said. -Break off the battle and remove yourself.-

-Ubsan?-

-I have observed.-

I slid out and returned to purely physical awareness for the first time since the contest had started. After one startled glance at the night sky, I fainted. Later, when the undisturbable slumber had broken of its own accord, I found out that we'd been grappling for nearly four days.

An hour after I awoke, while I was sitting crosslegged in the grass with Ubsan, Baby Bear, and the chief, a snarling static began to fog our conversation. Ubsan sighed, and rose. The chief followed suit.

-We leave you now, Hairless One,- said my tutor . . . and my friend.

I said nothing, but my hurt surprise was evident.

-***fellows drive us off.- He pointed skyward, and as if in reply, a black speck appeared. -Their minds ***** undisciplined; they pain ***** presence.- He was shouting over the din.

-May your journ*******o greater underst******** bravery. My peo********t the hu************sed.- With a grave bow and a swirl of his tattered cloak, the chief strode to the far side of the clearing.

-******** One,- said Ubsan, scowling because he'd waited too late and now couldn't say what he'd wanted, -******* Lady and ********** you ******* again, we

168

**********.- Savagely, he kicked the grassy turf. Dew sprayed silver.

-Ubsan,- I began, but nothing could get through the mental mess. I stopped, did something about the obstruction in my throat, and then—customary or not, I didn't care—I embraced him, patted his shoulder, and gently pushed him towards the forest. Leaving him was almost harder than leaving Shana had been—at least when I'd said good-bye to her, I'd known we'd be reunited.

By the time the chopper landed, I had my mind shield wrapped around Baby Bear and myself. Two minutes later, after a short argument, the obelisk stood alone in its meadow, pulsing its signals into the wilds of a planet that might—or might not—shelter ten other Terrans.

And an hour after that, we were boxed and frozen, free to dream our dreams of ice and dark, while the sunship rode us through the interstellar night.

No ice.

No dark.

The hillside remains, steep and smooth, but its soil is rainbow dust, sprinkled with petals of fragrant satin. Gliding up it, no need for feet which are happy to be useless, shadows fall forward, pushed there by the warmth of a sun that's simultaneously orange, yellow, red, and white and blue, too.

Two shadows, almost of a height. One is three times the width of the other. Companionably, they bump shoulders.

A diminishing buzz rises from the valley bees. Listen close: they tell where the flowers are full, where the winds ride soft, where the life is good and its dances long.

The slope slips into a plateau once crossed at night, in fear. Nighttime still enthralls the highlands, but the sky! The stars! None of them close—a great glass bowl inverted over the altiplano keeps the brilliance at bay—yet how bright they are! The horizon is ringed in fire. An artist's palette has splattered the bowl. No ebony sombers that heaven. In God's pointillistic vision, every dot impinges on its neighbors, filling, thrilling, willing the darkness begone.

Flowers brush dangling feet; warm breezes whisper, murmur, chuckle to appreciative ears. Distant figures, cloaked in vagueness, soar on courses of their own, with fur and feather and scale glinting in the diffused glow.

The two sail on, spores blown by a wind ripe with susurrant scent, e(pro)vocative; the two yearn to linger and inspect, to laugh and be awed, but the wind blows until morning breaks with blinding bravado.

The hillside drops into a volcano's crater. Cool lava swirls in whirls of red, white, black, brown, yellow; noise is dinned out by a billion blacksmiths; life, strong and rich, exhales its aroma. Sight and sound summon. The two descend. Together.

BOOK THREE

I

There was a full-length mirror in the Thaw Room, positioned right before the exit. It was almost impossible to leave without confronting yourself. I didn't even try. Critically, I eyed the clothes I'd awakened wearing: a puff-cuffed blue tunic, a pair of skin-tight white pants, and glistening brown boots with high heels. A far cry from the duraweaves, and not quite what I'd worn in the Jungle, but it'd do . . . at least till Lomala paid me, when I could go buy something more fashionable. Maybe Shana would go with me. She always had a good eye for clothes.

Brushing back my shoulder-length hair—my beard had somehow disappeared in transit—I sauntered out. Noise slapped me hard. I recoiled from it, and from the harsh view lit by unsympathetic fluorescents: lines and angles, coldly artificial; people moving through private patterns, garishly attired; heavy planes of wall and ceiling and floor a synthemarble tomb. Then I wiped the startlement off my face and looked for the tight knot of friends come to greet me.

There was only Gastine.

When he stepped forward to shake hands, I paid less attention to him than to the rest of the crowded terminal. My eyes, refusing to settle on his olive face, kept bouncing off to dart around the long, high-ceilinged room. They found only strangers, camera-slung and heavy-armed, scuttling to the parking lots and boarding lounges.

"Where is everybody?" I asked with false breeziness.

His eyebrows pulled together, and the tip of his tongue

crept out to realign his mustache hairs. They were gray, as were the shrunken preserves of hair on his head. "Everybody?" he asked, filling the embarrassing silence.

"Yeah, everybody—you know, uh, Shana? No-nose? My—" Surprise flitted from his right eye to his left. "What, is my homecoming classified information or something?"

"Not exactly, Mr.—ah, Bander." He jerked his head and started walking towards the main exit. He set his feet down as though they hurt. "Come on."

I didn't want to follow. How the hell would my friends ever find me? We hadn't arranged any meeting places.

The inertia ran deeper, though. As long as I stood still, I could protect myself from pain. I could shield myself by excusing their absence—they musta gotten stuck in traffic, huh?—but any move towards the door would be an admission that nobody was coming. That my reception was over. That of the warmth I'd been anticipating, Gastine's limp handshake was all I'd ever get.

I shifted my weight from one foot to the other. The crowds swarmed by as though I were a misplaced pillar. Shoulders brushed me. Bags clipped my legs. Voices muttered instructions, flight numbers, and endearments.

Twenty meters downstream, Gastine halted, and glanced back. Even at that distance, the sympathy in his eyes shone through the cracks in the crowd. He wiped his forehead, bit his lip, and shrugged. Before he could return, I moved towards him.

And honest to God, it hurt.

Coming even with him, I mumbled, "Why?"

He had the tact not to ask, "Why what?" Hand on my shoulder, he just shook his head slightly. "It's been a long time, Bander."

"It's been what, nine months at the most? They forgot I existed in nine lousy months?" Exaggeration, but to magnify hurt is human.

His dark brown eyes snapped wide and wondering. "Nine months—Bander, you've been gone six years!" He pressed his face close to mine. "Didn't you know?"

"No . . ." I was shaking my head from side to side, like a brawler trying to clear his vision after a bad punch. Rip Van Winkle would have recognized the numbness. Things spiral through your ears and track muddy footprints across your brain, but you register them as noise. All around is random motion, Brownian motion, and during close-ups,

174

when a blur becomes a person, you don't see anything you can relate to.

Gastine was developing an odd expression; I figured I had to say something, anything, quick. "Holy Jesus Christ, six fucking years . . . why didn't anybody tell me?"

He smiled. It was that sheepish, pained lip-twist that says, "I wish I could help you, buddy, but I can't." He reached for my elbow. "Let's find the car," he said

So I trailed after him, docile as a stunned steer. My head swiveled from side to side with a clockwork regularity that drew stares from strangers. I didn't care. I was looking for the missing five years. They were around the airport somewhere. Probably in the lost baggage room, although since Gastine was leading me onto the heat-shimmered asphalt there was a possibility that they'd simply been parked out there. Sonuvabitch! Five whole years, gone, pfft!

We got to his car without finding them. While he fumbled with the keys, I leaned on its sun-baked roof and made circles on the glassed-in photovoltaics. No meaning to the moving finger's scrawl: just circles. Doodles. Time-wasters. I yanked my hand away. Already short five years, I couldn't afford to lose any more.

The lock clicked open. I cracked the door and hopped onto a plastic seat softened by the heat of the day. "Oh, shit!" I said suddenly. "Baby Bear!"

Taken off guard, Gastine jabbed the key at the ignition. And missed. "Who's Baby Bear?"

"He's my—" I choked down the word "friend" because I'd been acting gassed enough as it was "—my pet. I brought him back from Arkslsnagl."

He switched the motor on, and twisted around to back out of the slot. "Don't worry—he'll be in Quarantine until the health inspectors clear him. We'll arrange to have him delivered to you."

"Can't I go see him?"

His look said he had never owned a pet, or wanted to. "Why?"

"To let him know everything's okay." Dammit. For a minute, worry over BB had taken priority, driving the other worries away, but my own words had brought them all back. "Oh, shit."

"Now what?"

"Ah—" I waved a hand. "Time lag. Soul rot. I don't know. Ignore me."

"That's not such an easy thing to do," he said, putting the car in gear.

"Why not?"

"Well, with Pajalli dead, you're—"

"Say that again?"

"What?"

"About Pajalli."

"He's dead." His dark hands readjusted their grip on the plastic wheel. "It happened last what, January? Heart attack, late at night, we found him the next morning. I'm running Lomala now, but . . ." He blocked off the lazy sun with the visor. His fingers quivered. Nerves. Too much responsibility.

"But what?" I prompted.

"Pajalli was responsible for the program that sent you off. With him gone, the government, as well as our corporate sponsors, is getting fidgety. There are congressmen who'd like to eliminate our funding. They've already cut the TP program; they say that with five people overdue, the loss rate is too high. But now that you've come back, maybe you could . . . that is . . ."

"Exhibit A and all that?"

"Yes." He nodded again, and exhaled loudly. "But I want you to understand: you must evaluate the program *honestly*. Tell it the way it was; we won't push you to support it. Then, maybe . . ." A grimness straightened his lips. "We can talk about it later, if you'd prefer."

"I would." And he'd probably prefer to hear about Ubsan's boots later, too. I leaned my head against the window. Maybe the five years were out there, bobbing on the white-capped lake. "So what happened?"

"The time, you mean?"

"Yeah."

"You were in cold sleep for a *reason*, Bander. Our ships travel faster than light, but not instantaneously. The trip to Arkslsnagl takes two and a half years or so."

"Why didn't anybody tell me?"

He shrugged helplessly. "We thought you knew."

Damn. I probably *should* have known . . . or at least known to ask how long I'd be gone . . . Christ. "You better fill me in on what I've missed, then."

"Since you left?"

"Yeah."

His forehead wrinkled as he searched for subjects he

176

thought I'd care about. "Well, the Jungle was granted limited autonomy right after the Gang War."

"The what?"

"Well, after your friend Catkiller—"

"He's no friend." It was obvious that Gastine, forgetting our differences, had remembered our similarities.

"Yes." He cleared his throat. "At any rate, he precipitated the Gang War by taking a job—"

"You're kidding."

"Not at all." He concentrated on the thickening traffic for a moment, then returned to the topic. "It was with the Federal Government. Fighting broke out over the question of succession, and intensified rapidly. It engulfed three more Townships—23, 14, and 15. I believe one of your henchmen finally took over everything—a woman named Marianne?"

"Yeah!" I leaned back and chuckled, then broke off as the memories came alive. "Wait a minute. What happened to No-nose?"

"No-nose? I don't recall the name . . ."

"Oh." Cold emptiness evacuated my chest. If Marianne was running things, No-nose had been done. I'd turned the Jungle over to him, and he wouldn't have given it up to anybody, not even Marianne, if he'd had a choice. The only question was: had Marianne done him herself, or had she simply profited by it? "Swing through the Jungle on the way, all right?"

"Are you sure you want to?"

"Why shouldn't I want to?"

"Well—" he made an apologetic gesture, as if to assure me that no offense was intended "—your visit might be misinterpreted."

"How?"

"Marianne might think you were intending to, ah, resume control?"

"But—" Humbugging Gastine's suggestion would have been unfair. I hadn't consciously planned to stroll in and take over, but . . .

It's a pain in the ass to be honest. Instead of having a nice, solid self-image, you have to maintain a reflecting pool to fill the real shapes of your changing soul.

All right, the idea had poked its nose out of the dark corner of my mind. Guessing at the way things had to be, I'd wanted to show the folks that Ban was back in town, and to tell them that everything was going to be straightened out.

There in that speeding car, I understood that I'd been wrong. I'd always wanted things to be too static. Not that I'd ever resisted change, but that I'd never thought of it as something others could initiate. *I* had always been the active one; others had danced to my tunes. Or had they? No. Another illusion. An ego-lie.

I'd been involved in a lot of things, and I'd kidded myself into thinking that I'd been responsible for them. I hadn't. Maybe I'd been a leader, yes. But what is a leader? Somebody who blazes a trail through the wilderness? Or just the one who's perched on the crest of the time wave?

If I walked in there with my old attitudes, Marianne would cough me.

And she'd be right to do so.

I'd never understood. To me, the world had been a field of statuary through which I moved, shifting the statues' positions as the fancy took me. People had been objects for me to manipulate. I'd thought that when I wasn't manipulating them, they'd stay put so I could find them again when I remembered them.

"Oh, shit."

"What's the matter?"

"Growing pains." Two k's of silence sped by. "I think I'd better visit the Jungle," I said afterwards. "But thanks for tipping me off. I'll make sure Marianne doesn't get the wrong impression."

Route 322 ran sunken through the parklands of old Ashtabula; its off-ramp clung to its embankment. The Jungle began on top, at a sandbagged checkpoint on Boulevard A manned by two armed guards. We stopped and showed them empty hands. They motioned us out and brusquely ordered us to assume the position. I opened my mouth to protest, but Gastine gave me a look. I quickly spreadeagled against the car.

Rough hands jostled every inch of my body; I thanked the Lord that I was clean. After Gastine was also frisked, they did a rapid, efficient custom of the car.

"All right," snapped the guard, a teen-age girl who held her rifle like she'd grown up with it, "get moving."

Beyond the checkpoint lay desolation.

Fourth Avenue was clear, but badly potholed. On either side the buildings were scarred, burned, destroyed. Reddish-gray piles of broken bricks loomed everywhere. The few pedestrians looked drawn and tired. There seemed to be a shortage of children and dogs.

"What the hell happened?"

"The Gang War," grunted Gastine.

At the corner of Fourth and Carnation was a facadeless building. It looked like a three-story dollhouse whose angry owner had torn its front away. Inside, on the third floor, water-stained paintings still hung crookedly from the cracked wall. "What the hell were they using?"

"Everything short of nukes." He gave me a crooked grin. "With you and Catkiller gone, a lot of would-be emperors showed up. Your Marianne was the only one who didn't run out of ammunition."

It fit. She'd been my gunlord. "Where's her headquarters?"

"At Fifth and B."

Her place had been hit as hard as the rest, but they'd started to repair it. Scaffolding made a grove of metal bamboo on the sidewalk; we had to duck under tangles of rope spattered with paint and mortar. In the dim and dusty foyer, two guards stiffened, and leveled their M-33's. I recognized one: Ronnie, the kid who'd been No-nose' aide. "Ronnie!" I said, breaking into a smile. "Long time no see!"

He still wore glasses, but his nose didn't drip any more. His green eyes, as unmoved as chips of marble, inspected my front. "Hello, Ban. Why are you here?"

"That's a helluva welcome home." Queasiness stirred in my gut. I found myself gauging the distance between us, and figuring how to disarm him.

"Is it?" His eyebrows went up; his voice was faintly mocking. "Maybe it's 'cause of your good-bye present, hey, Ban?"

"What do you mean by that?" I asked warily.

"You hadn't gone off, we wouldn't't've had no Gang War." His face was so expressionless that it chilled me. His voice was as cold and as thin as a winter rain. The safety of his rifle was off; his finger moved restlessly within the trigger guard.

"I wouldn't do that," I said.

"Why not?" No part of him moved, but his tension mounted inexorably. "It don't matter, do it? You ain't nobody these days . . . Bandy."

Gastine blocked the doorway with his awkwardness, so I

179

couldn't throw myself backwards. The graffitied walls pressed too close. For half a second it was hard to breathe. Ronnie saw it—a spark of glee lit the depths of his eyes— but the sourness in my mouth came from sickness, not fear.

I'd run away. The community I'd been building had been ravaged. This kid—and how many hundreds more?— had matured into a man-eater. They get that way when the warfare smolders. They pull it all inside. To lessen the pain of seeing a buddy's body, they sever their connections with humanity. Their only trust is in a full clip. They kill for less and less: first, to revenge; later, to pre-empt; still later, to rid themselves of annoyance. Some of them get to where they'll riddle a man just to watch him die.

I felt sorry as hell for Marianne. Jungle Lord? The toughest, nastiest wolf in the pack was more like it. Her leadership was proven by her existence: nobody had co-jones enough to go for her. Yet.

"I'm going to lose you, Bandy." The frost had left his cheeks; a warm glow now suffused them. His nostrils flared to smell the blood that would be spilled. "Got prayers you want to say?"

He wasn't going to back off. He couldn't. He'd told his partner what he was going to do, and he was too young to realize it would cost him nothing to change his mind. Kids are like that. Their hardassed talk backs them into corners from which they have to come out fighting. If they don't die, they lose something: a sensitivity, a humility, a sense of proportion. And you can't tell them what they're doing because they're perverse as hell. You've got to take them quick, and hope you don't have to do them the coldest.

It would hurt to open my shield, but it was the least lethal way. I cracked the door, and—

—*his pants, I wanna see him pissis pants run off lose No-nose 'cause of him and Daddy too right through the fucking gut hours to die coughing and groaning bastard coming back like he's still top him 'cause I'm no kid and—*

And meanwhile, from every point of the compass chattered:

—*magicitthen! newpairwetfeetandtearingholesinmysocks brickrightthrough scarehelloutofthem nogoodtumblerthinks-shecanputmedown skinnylittledudebutIlike hisstyle whatthe-hellhasthatidiotgotmeintohecouldgetmekillednottomention-himself—*

I had to keep from wincing as the myriad thoughts
180

slammed into my head. To react to them could be to trigger, unintentionally, Ronnie's pent-up hatred.

His outflowing thoughts were slimy-cold, and redolent of long-dead bodies. To struggle for control of his mind would be dangerous; a reflex twitch could tear Gastine and me in half. So I hunted until I found the place where his finger-nerves gossamered into his brain. Then I visualized the inside of hell.

Yelping, he dropped the rifle. I caught it before it hit, swung it up, aimed it at him and his goggle-eyed partner. After a brief hesitation, his partner carefully rested her own M-33 against the wall, and raised her hands. Ronnie was too busy examining his unblistered palms to follow suit.

"I told you not to do that," I said softly.

"Jeesuz, whadja do, ya fucker?"

"I taught you a little something about the uses of power."

"Whazzat?"

"I got a gun, and you don't, and you really flamed me off, but I'm not going to do you. It's called mercy. And it's mercy that sets humans apart from animals."

He was completely bewildered, but I didn't care. Footsteps were carrying a familiar voice downstairs. It was Marianne. With a jerk of my head, I sent Ronnie and friend into the street.

"Marianne."

"Who— Ban?" The astonishment that disturbed her coffee cheeks quickly gave way to guarded calculation. Her fingers curled around the bannister.

"Yeah." It's a measure of instinct's strength that, though we'd parted friends, I wanted to keep the rifle trained on her heart. The cramped foyer seemed too much like enemy territory. "Dropped in to say hello."

"Why—" Her brown eyes watched the muzzle zero in on the wall. "That's very nice of you. Thoughtful." Her voice had a hardness I'd never heard before: a raspy restraint that hinted at a barely controllable temper. "So it was nova to see you. Good-bye."

"Anxious to get rid of me?"

"I could ask the same of you."

"I'm not."

"Good." She came down the last three steps. Her square, scarred hands scooped up the other M-33. "But in case you don't mean what you just said, let me tell you something.

181

You're not wanted up here. There's no place for you. Try to make a place, you'll find we're tougher than you ever were. So get out and don't come back. Catch a real cough if you do."

"Tougher?" I wanted to skim through her mind, to read her soul, but the background clamor would be too painful. "Crazier, maybe, but not tougher." I handed her Ronnie's rifle butt-first. "You don't measure toughness by the blood you've shed, Marianne. You measure it by the blood you could have shed, but didn't." I turned, and shooed Gastine out the door. All the way to the car, my back felt as big as a barn door.

Only her bitter eyes touched it.

We were fifteen minutes into civilization before Gastine found his voice. "You're a madman."

"We're still alive, aren't we?" It felt very good to slouch limply, and to let the breeze ruffle my hair.

"But you antagonized her."

I studied him through one half-slitted eye. "For a reason, my friend: I had to show her I wasn't afraid. If she'd thought I was, she'd of done me on my way to the car. My confidence made her think trap."

"Was it?"

"You were there."

"I meant your telepathy. Were you reading her mind or something?"

"Uh-uh." I let the eye close. "Too much background noise in the Jungle; if I'd tried, it would have scraped me raw."

"But with that kid—"

"That was different. He *was* going to kill us."

"You had to read his mind to know that, didn't you?"

"Uh-uh. Just his eyes, and his lips, and his fingers. When they said go, I changed his mind for him. That's all. Took me half a second, tops. Hurt like hell."

"Oh." He turned down a narrow, tree-lined street that dead-ended at the only building in the vicinity.

"This isn't the way to Lomala."

"We're putting you in a hotel; all our rooms are filled."

My turn to say "Oh."

He pulled over to the curb, grabbed his briefcase, and surrendered the car to a uniformed attendant. I followed him, through an attractively designed metal detector, into a small, plush lobby. The ReserPuter found my name in its

182

memory banks, and offered to trade me a room key for a credit card. When I fed it Gastine's, it demanded his authorization. He spoke his name into its microphone; it checked his voiceprints filed in the AmExMaster. Twenty seconds later it coughed, and thrust two plastic cards at us. The second was the key.

"Bander Snatch!" boomed a deep, strong voice.

I knew who it was before I turned. "Major!"

While our hands sought to crush each other, I saw the changes in him. His sandy hair was almost gone; his face was a little fuller. The wrinkles around his blue eyes were as deep as ever, but the shadows and the pouches had vanished. He must have learned how to sleep nights while I was gone. The biggest change was that he was in civvies. Staring at them, I asked, "You AWOL or something?"

"I'm *out*. Did my thirty and retired."

Gastine had conjured up an elevator and we all boarded. "So what are you doing now?" I asked.

"I'm here to recruit you." The ride was already over. We stepped into a carpeted hallway and found my room. Actually, since it had a lemon-walled sitting room with a sofa and four armchairs, it was a suite. Gastine dropped his briefcase on the coffee table; Dourscheid slid into a chair.

"Recruit me?"

He grinned, and began to unwrap a cigar. "I'm still with Big Unk, Bander Snatch, and I'm here to offer you a job."

"Job?" I gazed at him blankly, then turned to Gastine. "Do I need a job? I thought I was going to get a million dollars."

"Oh!" His hand flew to his mouth, as though to keep something in. "I forgot all about that." He scrabbled for his briefcase. Locks clicked and papers crackled. "Here we go," he said with a sigh.

The rubber-band wrapped package weighed half a kilo. Most of it was legal garbage—forms and releases and contracts—but in the very middle lay a passbook bearing my name. The first entry was for a cool million. Seven digits sure do look good. "Nice," I approved. "Thank you."

"We keep our word, Bander, we keep our word." His dark eyes worried the papers I'd discarded. "Those will have to be signed and processed before you can receive your bancard, though."

"Yeah, later. Now what's this about a job?"

Dourscheid, feet on the table, blew out a thick cloud of smoke. Gastine coughed and reached for the ventilator switch. "Do you know what an ombudsman is?" I had a fair idea, so he went on: "That's the position, and you're a natural. A telepath like you can tell whether or not a red-tape foul-up is accidental or spiteful or what. We'll give you an office in one of the Justice Department ho-coms, a secretary, and—"

"Uh-uh."

"Uh-uh, *what*?"

"I can't work in a ho-com. Too much noise."

"So we insulate your office." He shrugged. "Not that a couple hundred neighbors'll make more racket than your Jungle dwellers did."

"That's not what I mean," I said. "I'm talking *mental* noise—like static, only louder, and painful. You people don't know how to control your minds." Really, they didn't. Arkslsnaglians held their thoughts in tight, unobtrusive patterns similar to magnetic fields; Terrans sprayed them in every direction, like radioactive piles gone wild. On Arkslsnagl you could admire the form and vitality of a person's mind. On Earth, you had to hide from it.

"I don't understand," said Dourscheid. Gastine echoed his bewilderment.

"I didn't think you would." I sighed, and lowered myself into one of the armchairs. Its contours adjusted themselves to my body. "Set that aside for a minute, tell me more about the job itself."

"Basically," he began, addressing his remarks to the moist end of his cigar, "it would be what you make of it. You'd have a lot of power, the kind we've tagged 'reactionary power.' You can't use it to innovate, only to influence the use—or abuse—of other power. For example, somebody comes and says that the FBI is doing him. You would have the authority to order the FBI to cease and desist. Or whatever. There are limits, of course: only federal employees are in your jurisdiction, and you can't order anybody to take any action except that invested in his office by statute. In other words, you can only order him to do *his* job, not somebody else's. And of course illegalities are, um, illegal. Third, you can order any federal official to *stop* doing something. Fourth, all your decisions can be appealed to the courts, and overturned if the court so deems. Any questions?"

Rubbing my eyes—Earth air made them sting—I thought about what he'd said. "You mean I could order the President to stop waging war or something?"

"Exactly."

"That's crazy."

"Of course it is." He actually laughed. "Two other restrictions, though, reinstate some sanity: first, you cannot act except upon receipt of a complaint. That's important, so remember it. Second, before you act, you must discuss the complaint with the federal officials or agencies in question. Is that clear?"

I shook my head slowly and uncertainly. "It seems clear," I admitted, "but . . . I mean, it seems almost *too* clear. How the hell did this get passed? I can't see Congress giving anybody—"

"They didn't want to," he interrupted, "but the machinery, it's like it's breaking down. The lines of authority are completely tangled, nobody knows what anybody else is doing, and some of the laws on the books are two centuries out of date, but still enforced. People are getting flamed off, especially in the ho-coms, where they just don't want to be bothered by outsiders."

"Haven't they always been flamed off?"

He shrugged. "Sure, but up to now the government's held the trumps. These days . . . did Gastine here tell you about the Gang War?"

"A little."

Carefully, he tapped fine gray ash off his cigar. Without looking up, he said, "They sent us in when the shooting started. Ten thousand combat infantry. Pulled us out twelve hours later, because we'd have had to kill everybody up there to stop the fighting. Too high a price. That's one example. Want some more?"

"Uh-huh."

"Computers. Big Unk's got more of them than anybody in the known universe. Every scrap of information that anybody's ever given the government is in them."

"That's not trumps?"

"That info has to get *into* the computers, Bander Snatch. Lots of terminals are scattered around the country. If somebody who knows what he's doing gets to one of them, he can really fuck things up. For example—and this is super-classified—the IRS lost all its data on the year before last. Every bit of it. They don't know who did it, or how."

"Can't they get it back?"

"Sure, but they're barely keeping even with the data flow as it is. A resubmittal of all those forms would backlog it into the next century, as well as admit the IRS' vulnerability. But that was just an example. My point was that government's gotten so complex that it's easier and easier for the citizenry to screw it up. Your job will be to mollify the citizens so that they won't *want* to screw it up. Clear?"

I said it was, and we talked some more. He agreed that I could find an isolated house in the country, and work out of it, as long as it was near a transport web. "Shit, Big Unk's begging for people like you. Even the nest-featherers know what's happening. We'll get it approved, don't worry." Then, to my surprise, he jammed the cigar into the corner of his mouth and stood. "Have to take off," he said. "We'll get together, bullshit some, huh?"

Something in the way he said it told me it would never happen. Telepathy scared him in a way Zulus never had.

After he'd left, Gastine and I played with the paperwork on the million. There were waivers of this and releases of that, guarantees and sureties, signers and cosigners . . . by the last, my fingers were cramped and my eyes red.

As he was tucking them into his briefcase, I finally mustered the courage to ask about Shana. He didn't answer. I asked again. This time he looked up, straight into my eyes, and his tongue came out to rearrange the tips of his mustache. "She's with Catkiller," he said steadily. "She's his mistress."

"Oh, Jesus." I let my head loll back and stared at the ceiling. He couldn't have given me a worse reply if he'd spent the last six years thinking one up. "You're sure?"

"I'm sure."

A part of me sought to save face. "When you had him at Lomala, did you find he had any mental powers?"

"None, so far as we could tell."

"You're sure?"

"I'm sure." He snapped his briefcase shut. "I'm sorry."

Grunting, I motioned with my hand. He seemed to understand. Without another word, he touched me lightly on the shoulder and let himself out.

I went to the three-meter-high window and looked down sixty stories to the dots of motion below. The nearest building was four k's away. The sun was setting behind it. Headlights laid glowing threads on the ribbon of pavement. I studied the scene. With the right kind of leap, I could leave a great raspberry-goo stain in the exact center of the street. It was tempting . . .

. . . but, I confessed ruefully, too melodramatic. This wasn't my cliff. Nor was it my time. Suicide's a noble exit only when it causes less trouble than continued life would. In an alien forest light-years from home, it's a dignified alternative. In the parklike heart of old Ashtabula, it's a pain in the ass for the sanitation workers.

Besides, if Gastine were telling the truth, who would care?

Briefly, as I stared at the clusters of light springing up in the outlying ho-coms, I thought of going hunting. I could reclaim Shana—surely she'd come, once she knew I was alive—and if Catkiller didn't like it, we could fight.

And I would win. I knew that for sure.

But did I want to?

I missed Shana. I loved her, and I'd thought she loved me. Regaining her would restore to my life the extra dimension that completes a person.

And if she wouldn't come?

My pride would be hurt. Catkiller wouldn't pass up the opportunity to rub my nose in it. There'd be a fight. And I would win.

But why would I want to win?

Like letters etched on ice came the uncomforting answer: the only reason I'd want to cough Catkiller would be as revenge for his having mocked me, for his having made me feel inferior.

That was it. Shana had gone from me to Catkiller, and was still with him. That said a lot. Maybe he was better than I was, at least in relation to her.

Could I honestly kill a man because I was jealous?

Yes, I could.

But I wouldn't. I was too old for that nonsense, too . . . experienced. What Arkslsnagl had taught me about death had changed me, and my outlook. I couldn't kill a man just because he threatened my pride, not without overturning my mental equilibrium.

Chopping off everybody else's legs may make you the tallest kid on your block, but frankly, it would be a helluva lot better all around if you just got used to being short.

So I wouldn't go looking for the Catkiller.

I'd wait for him to make the first move.

That way I could call it self-defense.

II

"Upstairs, second door to the right."

The deliverymen supporting the waterbed frame were too tired to respond. On stumbling feet they stared up the wide staircase. Behind them appeared two more, with a refrigerator.

"The kitchen's over that way." I waved in the general direction of the northeast corner of the house. "Through this room and the next. There's . . . hell, I'll show you. Follow me."

Wheeling the appliance, they made little if any attempt to keep from scraping it on the doorways. Teeth gritted, I kept my acerbic comments to myself. The last thing I needed was a crew of insulted movers. They'd either strike, or take special pains to damage everything else. And the furniture had cost too much to get ruined in transport.

I was appalled by the quantity the house could swallow. It was like the horn of plenty in reverse: trucks had been disgorging themselves through the front door for two days, yet most of the rooms were barren.

There was no law that I had to furnish it perfectly within a week of purchasing it, but . . . on the one hand, I wanted to get the shitwork out of the way, and on the other, I honestly didn't have faith in my future. It's like when you find a big bill on the street: you snatch it up and spend it quick, before somebody takes it away. I kept waiting for somebody to come along and claim the crinkly I hadn't spent. Or for the money itself to disappear—as though the passbook entry had been made in invisible ink.

"Right in there—whoa, plug it in first—that's it, now just ease it back . . . great, great." As they swaggered out of the room, they grunted something that I pretended I didn't hear.

God, it felt funny to have so much living space. The house wasn't big, but ten rooms were nine more than I'd ever had to myself in my whole life. It'd take a while to get used to it . . . the whole works—house, repairs, taxes, furniture, etc., etc.—had cost a quarter of my bankroll. Not too much for five green acres two k's from the nearest ho-com. There were trees to the north rolling all the way to the lake, cornfields to the east and west, and a horse farm to the south.

I'd already met some of my "neighbors" when I asked their ho-com if I could use their marketweb tube. That was all I needed from them, since my house was solar-powered and the viphone/computer lines had been strung to it a long time ago. The Maintenance Committee, speaking for the 158 residents (82 advertising executives and 76 children) agreed.

I'd thought I would enjoy getting to know them. My contacts with their kind of people had always been interfaced through a frog, or a marketweb buyer, or an equally hard and suspicious type. To meet the upper middle class without that barrier would be quite an experience.

I was wrong. They expressed nothing deeper than polite interest in me, and apparently felt no urge whatsoever to discuss themselves. Once they'd ascertained that I was not connected with advertising, either as a buyer or a seller, that was it. I was irrelevant to them and to their world.

That's the major weakness of a ho-com. Each has its own reality, centered around the community's profession, and other realities are simply extraneous. Cultural diversity is good, and there's an homogenous community for just about every subculture, but . . . I get the feeling that the system lacks a centripetal force, and I wonder if that isn't dangerous.

"The big desk goes back in there; the little one stays out here. Yeah, that's right. The couch against that wall there. Great, great."

I'd met my secretary the day after accepting Dourscheid's offer—it was her taste that had chosen the furniture. She hadn't remembered, but it was actually our second meeting. The first had taken place in a stuffy conference room at Lomala the night I'd been suckered into this business. Her name was Janice Ticplat. A gray-haired lady in her late fifties, she had the energy of a teen-ager and the blue eyes of a starlet.

It looked like we would get along well together. Her quick mind, as well as her ability to answer any question I asked, made me demand why she was content to be a secretary. She replied that raising two children alone had taught her the consequences of being responsible. She said she couldn't handle the numb horror that comes when one of your mistakes ricochets through someone else's life.

I'd already decided that I was going to lean on her a lot. I needed an informant, in the anthropological sense, whom I could trust to keep me abreast of local mores, taboos, and mana sources. Janice seemed to fill the bill perfectly.

The phone rang; the screen showed Gastine, still twitching at his sparse mustache. It puzzled me that with all his tugging, he hadn't permanently depilated his lip. "Bander, your ah, pet, is going to be released from quarantine the day after tomorrow. Shall we keep him for you, or—"

"Can they deliver him here?"

"Of course."

"Then have them do that."

"Very good." He glanced down, probably at some papers on his desk. A nervous light came into his dark eyes. "When do you think it would be possible for you to, ah, testify?"

"Testify? Oh—that evaluation thing?"

"Yes. Before a congressional committee."

"What the hell for?" Even if I was a government employee, I didn't want to go to Washington. "You never mentioned Congress."

"We didn't know about it." His hangdog expression vouched for the truth of his words. He looked poised on the edge of a breakdown. "They want to talk with you before they fund any more of our programs."

"What for?"

Raised to the camera, his eyes were very bloodshot. "There seems to be some suspicion in congressional circles about the ah, fiscal integrity, of our volunteers."

"I don't understand."

"Then I'll be blunt. They think you took the ombudsman job so you could make a fortune in bribes."

"With a million in my pocket I need more?"

"They're not too happy about that, either. But later—I'll let you know once they set a date."

190

"Oh, yeah." I hit the phone's kill button; the screen blanked silvery. That was all I needed: a probe into my motives. With the right kind of leaks, any congressman could make me look like the blackest thing to come down the pike since the late Attila.

Muttering to myself, I returned to the front door, only to find that all the workmen had left. They'd finished their delivery by the simple expedient of piling everything in the living room. It cost me sweat, bruises, and the rest of the day to put everything where it belonged.

I rose early the next morning. The Arkslsnaglian schedule still affected me; I couldn't have slept longer if I'd wanted to. Not that I did—I was looking forward to my first day of Ombudsmanship.

In the kitchen, I skimmed the newsboard while I downed a pot of coffee. The news was gloomy—it generally is, when it isn't scandalous—but it was the first time since my return that my reading was not continually interrupted. It was interesting to see how some of the things Gastine had talked about during that conference six years ago seemed to be coming true.

Baja California had decided to become independent. France claimed that the last of its urban guerrillas had given herself up. A bill before the Senate would add eight thousand pages to the tax code. The drought that had been ravaging Egypt when I left was now menacing Brazil; meteorologists were predicting heavy rains in the autumn. The L5 cartel was raising the price of electricity.

The front doorbell rang, fuzzing the sports page with static. Have to get an electrician in. Reluctantly, I thumbed the newsboard off and tightened my bathrobe. I made a note to dress earlier in the future.

It was Janice, arms full of artificial flowers. She had enough to fill every vase in the house, and then some. After suggesting that she print up a key for herself on the computer, I told her I'd be upstairs, dressing.

Her distracted frown was for the reception room; she mumbled something about knowing she should have stayed to make sure things got put away properly. I left her to it, and retreated to my bedroom.

"Any clients?" I asked on my return, ten minutes later.

"Just one." As the room was both empty and disarranged, she had to add, "He phoned ahead. He'll be here in fifteen minutes."

"Uh-huh. Need a hand?"

"Uh-uh."

"Nova. Send the client in when he arrives." I paused to sniff the flowers—the label claimed the Tru-Tu-Lif scent would last a year, which I doubted—then passed into my office.

My Office. Sounded good. I'd had a number of headquarters, and even a War Room once, but an *office*. That had such fantastic connotations of elegance, of discretion, of velvet-gloved power . . . people who had offices didn't try to lose each other; they were reasonable, rational. . . . I settled into my authentic leather swivel chair with a happy sigh.

The curtains draping the full-length windows whispered apart at the press of a button. Little light came through, because they faced west, but the view of the barbered lawn rolling down to the willows around my yard afforded me a tremendous amount of pleasure.

Buzz, went the speaker imbedded in my desk, and I smiled as I flicked the appropriate switch. "Yes?"

"That gentleman is here to see you. A Mr. Samoth."

"Send him in."

An instant later he erupted into the office. A short, fat man with a very red face—so red it seemed blood should be spurting from his ears—he threw down a pile of papers and hammered them in place with his fist. "Just look at this!" he bellowed. "And I'd like to know why I had to come out here! We could have done this over the viphone."

"Please, uh, have a seat." To keep from replying to his last statement, I began tugging the papers out from under his swollen knuckles. I had no intention of telling him that, as a telepath, I had to be near the person I was "reading." "What seems to be the problem?"

"The problem?" he sputtered. "Just look, you'll see."

I looked. Most of the documents in the two-inch stack were marked IRS. Half were letters; half were forms. Picking a letter at random, I skimmed over it. It seemed they wanted money . . . so what else was new?

"I'm afraid . . ." I checked a few more. "Look, I don't understand all this crap. Why don't you tell me what's wrong, and we'll go from there."

"They're killing me! Look!" He jumped up, pawed through the papers for a particular letter, and thrust it under my nose.

192

"Yeah, okay, so they want, uh . . . $248,693.77." I shrugged. "Do you owe it to them?"

"*They* say I do."

"What do you say?"

"No, this is bullshit, I don't owe them that much, I can't— here, my checkbook!" He threw it down like a gauntlet. "My savings account." It thudded onto the pile. "Tell me, do I have the money? Can the IRS squeeze blood from a stone? I haven't got it; I can't pay it."

"Wait a minute, okay?" The CRT screen, obedient to my questing fingers, displayed the list of access codes Dourscheid had given me. I ran down the column until I found the one that unlocked the IRS files. "Okay, let's see now." Carefully, I tapped the numbers into my desktop terminal, then added Samoth's ID number after them. The screen blinked, and his file began to pass in review. "Hmm."

"Well?"

"Wait a minute." I hit the intercom. When Janice answered, I told her to key her screen to mine. "Can you make sense of that? Mr. Samoth says he doesn't owe anywhere near that much, but . . ."

"No." She tapped the viphone suggestively. "Joe Southworth over at IRS should be able to help. Shall I get him on the line?"

"Please."

Uneasiness attacked my pride while we waited for the call to go through. What was I doing, talking to a man I didn't know about a problem I couldn't scan? I was in over my head, and the bottom would probably drop even more before it leveled off. I should have taken the crinkly and run.

"Southworth." A thin blond came into focus.

"This is Bander Snatch," I said. "I'm a new ombudsman—"

"Yeah, I've been told about you. Need help?"

"Got a man here, uh, T. Lawrence Samoth, complaining about his income tax. Says he's been—"

"Ol' Tough Luck Samoth, huh? Wait a minute, lemme flash his file." His eyes darted away. A rapid clicking filled the speaker as he talked to his computer. "He give you a sob story?"

"He's right here." I had to grin at Samoth's expression. "So is his checkbook and his savings account."

"He bring his wife's?"

"His wife's?"

"Yeah, he— No, look for yourself." He rattled off a thirty-two digit number, which I dutifully punched in. "That's their combined statement of holdings, there— you got it?"

"I do." My eyes widened as I studied the figures. "Holy shit!" I had my machine bottom-line it. "Thirty-seven million?" My voice was edged.

Southworth relaxed. His smile came wide and friendly. "He tell you his tax bill would wipe him out?"

"Yeah, he did . . ." I glanced angrily at my client, whose forehead showed drops of sweat. "He had me believing him, too."

"Don't feel bad. He's done it to everybody. Need anything else?"

I ignored the heap of papers that still loomed on my desk. "Nah."

"Okay. Just remind ol' Tough Luck about the penalties for fraudulently providing a federal officer with false information." He winked at me, then signed off.

"Mr. Samoth?" I turned to him, trying hard to be polite.

"I heard, I heard." He was already scraping the documents off my desk, and sorting them into rough neatness. "I'm leaving, no need to show me out, I know the way." He waddled to the door and was gone.

When she came to close it, Janice gave me a rueful grin. "You'll get used to it."

"Jeez, I hope so." I leaned back in my chair, and set to work examining my irritation.

A beguiling song-and-dance had almost gotten me to support a tax-cheat against the IRS. And I was flamed off. I, who had survived into adulthood only by ripping off Big Unk, was pissed that somebody else had attempted it.

It was easy to say, well, I'd been poor and he was rich, hence I'd deserved a break and he didn't. But . . . where do you draw the line?

I couldn't shake the feeling that I'd betrayed him. Yes, he'd lied. Yes, he'd tried to use me. But what most mattered was that he'd been resisting the government, as I'd done all my life, and I hadn't helped him.

Before Arkslsnagl, I'd have shown him—for a small percent—how to turn his money into gold and bury it in his backyard, if that would have kept it away from the IRS. Even when Dourscheid had offered me the job, I'd been thinking in terms of subversion: I'd be the inside man

194

who'd aid people in doing things that Big Unk didn't want them to do. I'd keep the behemoth off their backs so they could live their lives.

And here I'd gone and practically thrown the guy out of the office!

Damn . . .

Buzz.

"Uh-huh?"

"Two things, Ban: first, Customs called, they'll be delivering your pet in three hours. Second, two people have come to see you—some trouble with the Immigration and Naturalization Service."

"Send them in, please—and keep an eye out for the delivery."

"Yes, sir."

The door opened to admit an attractive young woman dressed in sky-blue capes. Her hair was blond; her face was Slavic. Behind her, cloth cap twisted between nervous hands, limped an elderly man. "Mr. Snatch?"

"Call me Ban," I said, rising while I motioned them towards chairs. "How can I help you?"

"My name is Ann Torikowski. This is my father, Stefan Torikowski. He speaks not much English." She said something to him in their language, and he forced a smile to his thin, trembling lips.

"Please, sit." Once they had, I asked, "Now, what's wrong?"

"Well, my father escaped last year, during the troubles, and he came over here on a tourist visa that he got in Prague. He's applied for a permanent visa. But they won't give it to him. They say he has to leave. If he doesn't, they'll deport him back to Warsaw, but if that happens . . ." Tears swelled in the corners of her cornflower eyes. "The government thinks he helped smash the surveillance machines. It will *kill* him, Mr. Ban! And he's my father and we were separated for so many years and *please*, can't you help him?"

After her cold fingers had released my wrist, I obtained Mr. Torikowski's visa number and did my thing on the computer. This guy I was going to help. Big Unk wanted to send him back to Poland? That was enough to convince me that he should stay. Pure perversity. Plus a half-guilty sense that those of us who didn't have much power had to hang together to keep from being pigeonholed by the bland bureaucratic machine.

His file lit up the screen. I studied it closely. No logical reason for deportation was given. "You are a citizen, aren't you, Ms. Torikowski?"

"Oh, yes, Mr. Ban."

The law says that quotas and skill requirements will be waived in the case of a member of the immediate family of a citizen, unless the potential immigrant had a criminal record. Torikowski was clean. The INS officer who'd handled his case, however, had commented: "There are insufficient grounds for proving the relationship between Ann Torikowski and 'Stefan Torikowski.' Recommend denial."

"When was the last time you saw your father, Ms. Torikowski?"

Her shoulders slumped. "That's what the other man asked."

"I'm sorry to be repetitious, but I'd appreciate hearing what you have to say."

"When I was four," she whispered.

"Is your mother alive?"

"No."

"Do you have any relatives in this country who could swear in court that this man is really your father?"

She dug through her purse for a handkerchief, meanwhile saying, in a very small voice, "No."

Aw, shit. Her testimony wouldn't be any good, if she hadn't seen him in twenty-five years or so, and his papers wouldn't prove anything because papers can be manufactured. . . . "But you think he is, huh?"

"Yes, I do." Her eyes crept up my face. "If he isn't, how can I ever hope again?"

"I understand." I leaned back and stared at them both. Perched on the edge of her chair, she was dabbing at her swollen eyes and draining her reserves of strength. He was looking straight at the blank wall behind my back, very much the peasant who waits for the commissar's decision while knowing he can do nothing to influence it.

I was going to have to check it out, in the way that only I could. "Ms. Torikowski, please wait in the other room while I talk to your father."

"But he speaks no—" Her jaw dropped two centimeters as she heard what I'd said. "My father? You do believe he is my father?"

"I'll call him that till I know he's not," I replied.

She fretted herself to her feet. Hand on the old man's shoulder, she bent over to hiss Polishly into his ear. His cautious nod included a sidelong glance for me. "Will it be long?"

"No, I don't think so."

"I shall be there."

I waited till the door had clicked shut, then I half-swiveled in my chair. Catching the other man's eyes, I peered at their yellow corners while I collected my courage. Even though the ho-com was two k's down the road, enough thoughts would escape from its residents to pain me. And of course Janice and the girl were just a few meters away. But I had to take the risk, because I had no other way of proving Torikowski's identity, short of visiting Poland.

His eyes fell away. His liver-spotted hands stretched the band of his cap. His broad, wrinkled face had a certain bovine blankness.

One last deep breath. I cracked the clam shell of my shield and extruded a feeler. Scattered thoughts dinged it like hail. Striving to disregard them, I enveloped his mind. My eyebrows leaped in surprise: he wasn't emitting. Something covered his mind—shieldlike, but not a shield—wrapping paper?

I peeled back a layer. His mind lay tangled and forlornly yearning; its every part was twisted and contorted. Alarmed now, I inched up to it. Syllables rumbled through the space between us, thunder in an empty sky. "Stefan Torikowski" was repeated, clearly and crisply, but the rest was in Polish.

I could have closed then, and authorized his stay, but the mournful throbbing in his pretzel-shape urged me closer. And closer still. Despite my discomfort, I began to see how he'd been forced back upon himself, like wood twisted after a long steaming.

That bothered me. I had never scrutinized a Terran mind—a brief glimpse from a safe distance was all I could tolerate when only curiosity drove me—but Torikowski's seemed artificially wrong. Its chafing pain puzzled me even more. Why the hell was it wadded up like that, if he hadn't wanted it?

A mastery of Polish would have been a big help. As it was, I had to saturate him in a complex image, the gist of which was: "Old man in chains, I have a saw."

The reply was faint, a time-faded painting: manacled hands laid on an anvil.

Taking that as permission, I searched for a loose end.

There was only one, so tightly overlapped that my heaving accomplished nothing.

Buzz.

I jumped half a meter; my tentacle rubber-banded back inside. Torikowski remained immobile, but across his weary face flickered the hurt of abandonment. While my right hand told him to wait, my left found the intercom button. "Yes?"

"Deliverymen with your pet. They're early." In her voice was a hint of reproof. She obviously felt pets should not intrude on ombudsmanship.

"Oh . . . be right there." Quickly, I left the office, trying to avoid the sight of Torikowski's drooping shoulders. "Ms. Torikowski," I said as I entered the reception room, "please tell your father I'll be back in a minute."

"Yes, Mr. Ban." She hastened off to pass on the message.

"Where are they?"

"Back at the truck. Ban, what kind of pet is this, anyway? They were both carrying shotguns."

"Oh, Jesus." My feet swished through the shag carpet as I sprinted for the front door.

Their truck could have been used to pick up deposits from banks. One of them stood ten meters away with his gun leveled. The other, by the back door, seemed to be trying to figure out how to open the truck while keeping his gun ready.

"I'll let him out," I said, reaching for the handle.

"You sign first," he said.

"I don't sign till I see him."

"Where's your cage?"

"What cage?"

"The one you're gonna keep it in."

"Why should I keep him in a cage?"

He shook his head like an attendant humoring an inmate. "It's your life, buddy. Sign here."

Amused that even I could get snarled in red tape, I gave in. With the pencil he offered I signed the multicopy form. "Good enough?"

"Yeah. You wanna open her?"

"Please. Is it—"

"Press that button there and the door'll go straight up." He backed off five meters and aimed his shotgun over my shoulder.

Shrugging, I pressed. The motor whined protestingly;

198

steel scratched steel. Slowly, the door rose. A snarl drifted out of the fetid darkness. "Baby Bear," I said, "it's me." I reached for his mind, but before I could grip it the door had opened and he was bursting into the sunshine.

He was angry. His fangs were bared and his claws flashed menacingly. Nervous metal clicked as safeties went off. "Don't shoot," I called, without looking back. -You're my friend,- I thought, -you love me.-

He wasn't buying it. After a cursory scan of the vicinity, he clambered down from the tailgate and reared up on his legs. He'd reached adolescence during cold sleep; he now towered over me like a small tree.

-Friendlovefoodwarmth,- I broadcast again and again, all the while as motionless as a granite outcropping.

His tiny eyes glittered in their furry sockets. He lumbered towards me, massive paws raised high, then stopped as a familiar scent wafted out of the strangeness. After waving his arms in brief perplexity, he lowered himself to all fours. -You?- he asked.

-Me.-

Snuffling happily, he butted my shoulder with his head. I scratched between his ears and he growled his pleasure.

"All right, guys, you can take off now."

"Get him away from the truck."

The hostility in their mind-set triggered his early warning system. The hairs on his neck began to stiffen. I smoothed them, soothing him with honeyed thoughts. Grudgingly, he allowed me to lead him away.

Shoes scraped cement as the two dashed for the cab of the truck. I didn't look back—I might have gotten mad. Doors slammed. The motor r-r-ripped into life; gravel crunched and crackled. BB relaxed shortly after they reached the street.

He was going to need a mind shield. On Arkslsnagl, where people kept their thoughts to themselves, it didn't matter. On Earth it mattered. He'd be a nervous wreck in a week, if he weren't shot first.

So I went in. His simple mind couldn't maintain a shield as intricate as my own. The best it could support was a mental pelt which would ward off animosity about as effectively as his fur kept the rain away. Though it wouldn't solve the problem—I'd have to train him very carefully—it would help to minimize it. But what the hell, people teach German shepherds not to eat small children.

Janice, although impatient for me to get back to work,

allowed herself to be introduced to BB, and promptly went up a notch in my estimation. Accepting my statement that he was harmless unless frightened, she radiated soft, loving thoughts. BB, positively beaming, sat on the floor next to her desk, and tilted his head so she could reach the spot he loved to have scratched.

I guided her hand to the appropriate place, reminded her that he was semitelepathically vulnerable to nasty thoughts, and went back into my office.

"Sorry for taking so long," I told the two anxious people within. "I had to get my pet out of the truck because the deliverymen were scared."

"Have you reached a decision yet?" Ann asked timorously.

"Well . . . if I could have a few more minutes alone with your father . . ."

Again the worry lines faded at my using those words. "Certainly, certainly," she said, bustling out as though her spirits needed more room.

An idea for untangling the old man had come to me—as ideas will—while I'd been busy with BB. First I searched for his sleep center. Then I stroked it, and watched him untense.

A very physical way of describing a nonphysical occurrence is to say that minds deflate as consciousness ebbs. It's like a sponge that shrinks when its water has evaporated, only quicker. In twenty seconds, the snarl that was Torikowski had grown limp and flaccid. The loose end was no longer pinned by the overlap, and was easy to unknot. Once I'd laid the separate strands in neat, straight lines, I woke him.

The most striking difference was in his eyes. Before, they'd been glazed and dull. Now they were shrewdly alert. After a brief nod of recognition, he studied the rest of the room, and probably missed very little.

The "wrapping paper" still confused me. It seemed to serve no useful purpose except that of concealment. So, poised to halt if I caused any pain, I removed it. He didn't stir, except for one bright flash of teeth when I'd finished.

Thoughts stabbing me deeper, now that he was back to normal, I demanded to know who he was. "Stefan Torikowski," he responded immediately. I hit the intercom: "Send her in."

"Yes, sir," but the door was already opening.

The old face lost ten years at the sight of her. An aristo-

200

crat, now, he rose to kiss her hand. A long stream of Polish chuckled and gurgled. Her eyes flickered from him to me, as if I were the subject of the discussion. When he'd bowed his conclusion, she cleared her throat and turned to me, startled.

"My father tells me . . . very strange . . . he would like to thank you, and ask you to arrange an appointment with the CIA. He says he has much to recount, much that of most interest would be."

A burst of gutturals interrupted her.

"He says you do not understand what you have done."

"I don't, frankly."

She relayed that and he mulled it over. When he spoke, she shook her head in growing incomprehension. "He tells of a better way to converse. I do not understand, he riddles me. He says you speak directly through my middle."

Why did I have to wait for others to teach me how to use my powers? I nodded. A moment later, Torikowski's thoughts and mine flowed through the interpretive membrane of his bilingual daughter's mind.

I broke the connection within two minutes. The pain in my tentacle was bad enough, but the agony welling out of his memories was more than I could stand.

The six months prior to his departure from Warsaw had been spent in the basement of an innocuous building staffed entirely by innocuous people. They'd prepared him as a butcher does a chicken: after stripping away his original personality, they'd hypno-taught him in a dozen different subjects, and masked their super-sleeper with a peasant's dispirited exterior. Then, making him forget how they'd tortured him into his new shape, they'd convinced him that *they* were the true rebels. It had almost worked.

Why must people find ways to pervert technology?

"Janice," I said into the intercom, "Mr. Torikowski needs to see somebody from the FBI immediately. Have them pick him up here. He's got a lot to say, so tell them to send a Polish-speaker. Got that?"

"Yes, sir." Disapproval reentered her voice. "Sir, there's a police officer here who wants to see you about Baby Bear."

"Send him in as soon as these people come out." I cut the connection and stood. "Ms. Torikowski, I'm glad I was able to help. Why don't you and your father wait with my secretary? She can probably find you some coffee or tea."

She passed that on. Her father grabbed my hand and

squeezed it. His eyes impaled me, but he spoke to her. Confused, she shot a question back. He seemed to repeat himself.

"Mr. Ban," she began hesitantly, "my father says to tell you that you are a good man. He thanks you for with him sharing your soul."

"Pardon?"

"I do not understand it, but he said to say exactly that."

"Well . . . tell him it was my pleasure. . . . And tell him," I added, because his meaning had suddenly dawned on me, "tell him that I respect him."

We said good-bye. A funny little smile on my face, I went back to my chair and sat. So I'd left a piece of myself behind, like the Old Lady's "brief half-breed." I hadn't expected it, and I might have to be careful about it in the future . . . but Torikowski was a good man, too. He wouldn't abuse his insights.

"Mr. Uh—Snatch?"

Before my desk stood an LEA man, uniform cap tucked under his left elbow. Something about him . . . he was forty-ish, dark black, maybe 175 centimeters tall . . . I'd seen him before, a long time ago . . . sure! I snapped my fingers, taking him aback. "Johnson, isn't it?"

"Yes, sir." Accustomed to the quirks of the upper middle class, he stood motionless and courteously attentive.

"I thought so. We met, maybe uh, six years ago? I invaded your precinct with some of my Zulus." I grinned. "You almost enlightened me."

Recognition broke through the politeness. "You?"

"Yeah, me." Standing, I reached for his hand. "I got out of the Jungle, too."

"Sorta figured you might." Now he was confused, but wary. My status meant he wasn't supposed to hate me on sight any more, but he was too good a frog to be able to forget my past.

"I'm legit, man. And I earned my crinkly honestly."

He decided to reserve his judgment. "If you say so, sir."

"Can the 'sir' crap—it's Ban. Have a seat."

"Thanks." He set his cap on his knees. "About this pet of yours."

"Baby Bear?"

"If that's a baby, I'd rather not see a big 'un." He took a small notebook from his shirt pocket, and flipped through it. "One of your neighbors complained."

"Neighbors? I—"

202

"From the ad-com?"

"That's two k's away!"

"Well, your pet sort of towers over the corn fields, and through binoculars . . ."

"Some little old lady, right?"

"You got it." He was beginning to relax. "She thinks it's wild, and dangerous, and a public menace." He laughed shortly, as if to say she should only know about me.

"The yard's fenced in," I pointed out.

"Ban—" the leaper-ganger rapport had come alive, made only slightly awkward by the new me "—he could tear through that fence like it was tissue paper." Then he set the frog aside, and he himself asked, "I seen a lot of weird animals, but never nothing like *that* before. What is it?"

"He's a—" I frowned. I didn't know *what* BB was. "I brought him back from outer space."

Genuine interest filled his flat-nosed face. "Really? Shit, I've never—" remembering the circumstances, he returned to routine. "Did Customs clear it?"

"I smuggled him in under my coat."

Chuckling, he went on. "How dangerous is he?"

"Look, how about I introduce you to him? See what he's like, and report on that basis. While you're going through channels, I'll . . . yeah, I've got it, I'll throw a party and let the ho-com folks get to know him. How's that sound?"

"Say what?"

"You're acting on a citizen complaint, right?"

"That's what I said."

"But if you don't get any more, you don't have to do anything, right?"

"That's true." As he saw the light, he yielded to an approving smile. "I would like to meet him."

"Sure, come on." I led him out the back way, through the kitchen, and we found Baby Bear curled around the trunk of a small maple. He was snoring softly. -Hey, man, wake up.-

-Coolsoftsleep.-

-Meet a friend.-

-Grumble.- But he rolled over on his back and blinked at us.

"He's very sensitive to moods. If you're afraid, he's afraid. If you're not, he's not."

"Just like dogs." Crouching, he slowly extended his hand, palm up, fingers motionless.

Baby Bear eyed it with a spark of interest. -Food?-

-NO! Friend.-

-Hungry.-

-Hello now, food later.-

-Grumble.- He thrust his snout forward and sniffed delicately. His long tongue emerged to taste Johnson's wrist. He sniffed some more. Then, projecting complete boredom, he rolled away and fell back to sleep.

"He don't seem too dangerous, Ban."

"Told you so." Janice was at the back door, waving. "Looks like I'm needed inside, so unless you—"

"Just one last question."

"Shoot."

"Figure on using him for anything illegal?"

"What?"

"Gotta ask—mainly 'cause of who you were—care to answer?" Pen hovering over a blank notebook page, he winked at me.

"Tell you, Johnson: inside of two months, this neighborhood's gonna be terrorized by the biggest, furriest, goddamnedest Zulu you ever saw."

His laughter blended with mine, and for a moment all the differences disappeared. "N-O," he spelled aloud. "That's enough for my report—but there is one more thing."

"What's that?"

"Would it bother you to have a frog dropping in to visit your pet?"

"Any time you like." I took a step away, stopped, turned back. "Uh, Johnson?"

"Yeah?"

"All right to visit me, too."

I think he meant it when he said he would.

By the time I got inside, Janice had returned to her desk, and was taking information from a worried-looking man with thin brown hair. I got a good look at his profile before he knew I was there; I think I would have recognized that beaky nose in a blizzard.

"Ralphie!"

"Bander Snatch, sir." When he turned, he looked a lot older than his thirty-five years.

"Christ, feels like Old Home Week." We slapped palms.

"Heard you were running the show out here," he said. "Knew I'd get a fair shake from you."

"Thanks. I'll be right with you, let me just— Janice?"

She looked up from her computer terminal. "Yes?"

"Rush job. I want to invite everybody in that advertising ho-com to a party tonight. Try to reach them, huh? Also, their Maintenance Committee's got a truck; if you could order a case of every kind of liquor through their web/tube, they could bring it with them. Thanks." I motioned my once-upon-a-time medic to follow me, then stopped. "Order some party food, too, all right?"

She accented her resigned shrug with a grimace. "What time is this going down?" Her pen was poised above a pad of paper.

"Uh . . . eight?" I checked her face to see if that was a bad time, but her displeasure didn't intensify. "Thanks again."

"Oh, sure." Her fingers were flying over the keyboard of the terminal before I could step in my office.

"Sit down, Ralphie, what can I do for you?"

"Got troubles with a passport, Bander Snatch. Tried to get one, State Department said no way, not till the one I got now expires. Thing is, I haven't got one."

I frowned. "But they said you did?"

"Sure enough. I don't—never did—but the word is that the SecState's still down on the Jungle 'cause of its autonomy. They say he thinks that's messing up the Mexican negotiations, so any way he can, he's doing everybody who ever lived there."

"And you figure one way is by screwing up the passport applications?"

"Only thing I can figure."

"Hmm." I let my eyes unfocus while I thought it out. It seemed too petty even for the State Department, but some of those bureaucrats . . . I had to find out first, though, whether Ralphie was telling the truth. With extreme caution, I opened a peephole in my shield. "You giving it to me straight?"

"Sure enough." His hurt look was inconclusive, was, in fact, almost to be expected, but his mind pulsed clear and strong. He either had a rotten memory, or a true story.

"What do you want a passport for anyway?"

"Gotta go to a conference in London," he said diffidently, though it was obvious he wanted to be questioned about it.

"Conference?"

"On ho-com health care services run by paramedics with diagnostic computers—it's for my job."

"You got a job?" I couldn't keep the surprise out of my voice.

"Yeah, sure. Got the hell out of the Jungle during the Gang War. Man, I was too old for that shit. Reflexes slowing down, you know? Worked as a hospital orderly. Didn't pay enough to support us—I got a wife and three kids—so I studied nights, got a few promotions. I'm running a chain of clinics in the waterfront ho-coms."

"That's nova, Ralphie, congratulations."

"Yeah, well—" he shrugged "—still need a passport."

"Lemme see about that. What's your real name?"

"Tcazkuk, Ralph Tcazkuk."

"Maybe the computer can help." I fed it the right numbers, and it burped up a photocopy of the application of the "Ralph Tcazkuk" who'd been issued a passport. The picture on it vaguely resembled my old friend. I'd have to check the fingerprints, though. "Ever been printed, Ralphie?"

"Sure. When I applied for the passport."

"Does State still have your application?"

"No, they returned it." He fumbled in his coat pocket for it.

"Nova. Let's compare." After five or ten minutes spent hassling with the computer's convoluted programming, I managed to coax it into doing the comparison. It took a lot less time for the semisentient device to reply, "Negative. Sets made by different individuals."

"Told you it wasn't me."

"I scan." What had happened was clear, at least to me. Somebody—probably from the Jungle—had needed a passport—probably for a touch of smuggling—but had wanted one issued in someone else's name. The solution? Use somebody else's vital statistics; make it another Zulu's because they're mostly too poor to travel. It was a real freak of fate that Ralphie's life hadn't turned as sour as most.

"So what do we do now?"

"From here on in it's easy." I checked my list, then dialed the number of my liaison at State. It rang twenty or thirty times before I gave up. "Sonuvabitch! The bastard went home, and it's only—" quick glance at my watch "—four-twenty. Damn!" The intercom plastic was cool to my finger. "Janice? First thing tomorrow, put me through to Sirois at State."

"Yes, sir." Her impatience resented my interrupting her in the middle of arranging the party.

"Sorry. And thanks." I let up on the button, and turned to Ralphie. "Look, here's the thing: everybody at State's gone home already, we can't do anything more today. Are you in a rush?"

Pulling an unhappy face, he ran his hand through his sparse brown hair. "Uh . . . I need it in two weeks."

"Shit, we should have it approved tomorrow. Why don't you come by in the morning? Finish it off, we can have lunch together."

"Nova." He stood, I stood, we shook hands.

"Take care."

"You, too," he replied as he headed out the door.

We might have been more eloquent if we'd known we were saying our final good-bye.

III

"He's so *big*!" oohed the little girl. Staring up at Baby Bear's muzzle, she was about ready to topple over backwards. "He's even bigger than Alex!"

"Would you like to say hello to him?" I pitched my voice low, to cut through the chatter and the music.

"Can I? Can I really?" She jiggled with excitement, till a sobering thought struck her. "He won't eat me up, will he?"

"Not a chance. I'll just—" Hands under her armpits, I boosted her face to a level with BB's. -Another friend I love.- "Say hello, now."

She was too awestruck to speak. Her eyes widened into saucers as she gazed down the shiny length of his muzzle.

-Noisy,- grunted BB.

Instantly alert, I took a mental sampling of the back yard. It was like sprinting across a machine gun's field of fire. Even ignoring the pain, it was nerve-wracking: Baby Bear could easily turn paranoid enough to launch a pre-emptive attack on some kid who was pissing his pants in fear of him.

-Nice noise,- I retorted. -Friend-noise.-

His wet nose brushed the little girl's. Her guarmother, hovering a meter away, stifled a horrified gasp. BB's eyes flickered, measured her, returned to the child's. Solemnly, he blinked. She giggled. Her pudgy, tentative hand reached out. Her fingers mingled with the fur of his throat. "He's *soft*," she whispered in wonderment.

BB positively purred.

208

"I'm glad you like him." I swung her down and patted her head. "He likes you, you know."

"He does?" Bliss spread across her face. All it needed was jam stains.

"He does. And he'd like you to come back sometime, to play with him."

"Can I, Mommy?" She ran to her and tugged her hand. "Please can I?"

The guarmother eyed me with something akin to hatred. BB growled warningly as her emotions slopped over his feet, but at my signal he quieted. The lady's feelings were understandable: it was her daughter, for whom she alone was responsible, and she'd be damned if she'd let some off-world monster hurt her.

Alex, the mother's companion, was nearly as wary, but realized he didn't know enough to make a decision. He puffed on a joint as he stared at BB, willing to keep his mind open until events convinced him to close it. Swirling the ice cubes in his drink, he drew me to one side.

"Tell me, Bander," he began, in a crisp executive-type voice, "how dangerous is this animal?"

I spread my hands helplessly. "It depends on the situation, because he's extremely sensitive to moods. I've trained him to ignore fear, but I'm having some trouble teaching him to deal with hostility. He's not quite ready to believe that hostility doesn't *have* to presage an attack."

"You're giving him credit for an astonishing amount of discrimination."

"No more than he deserves."

"Hmm . . . well, you know him better than anybody, I suppose . . . but tell me, kids can be rough on pets—what with ear- and tail-pulling and all—how's he going to react to that?"

By way of reply, I pointed across the lawn. Behind BB stood a child of maybe three years, a fat little boy whose huge eyes sparkled in the twilight. With the air of a dedicated researcher, he was kicking BB's right ankle at five-second intervals. BB, looking down over his right shoulder, seemed to be wondering what to do.

I checked his mind. It held no irritation, just quiet amusement.

"Well?" I asked Alex.

"Impressive. But what's to stop him from—"

"—getting mad? Not a damn thing except his good nature."

He shook his head slowly, dropping his joint and crushing it under his toe. His every instinct ordered him to snatch the child out of danger; only his implicit trust in my judgment kept him still.

It was very interesting. Most of the eleven adults present—all members of the ho-com's Area Relations Commitee—were skeptical of BB's peaceful intentions, yet they allowed their children to be introduced to him anyway. I was beginning to realize that the apparent paradox in their behavior stemmed from their attitude towards me.

Their first assumption was that I was eccentric. In their terms, I had to be. I lived alone, which nobody did. My pet was the oddest living being they'd ever seen. And I wasn't in advertising.

To that they added a second assumption: that I could manage my own eccentricity, without harming innocent bystanders. Again, that *had* to be the case. I had money. I had a responsible—if irrelevant—position with the government. And nobody was trying to lock me up.

Therefore, went their reasoning, they would tolerate my eccentricity . . . at least until it began unmistakably to threaten them.

This was what made the ho-com world work. The parochial, insulated members of the boo-class would not interfere with the private lives of those who lived in other communities. When it came to business, of course, there were no wool-covered eyes, but . . .

You grow up in the Jungle, you live with the notion that the guy you're talking to just might be crazy enough to use a blade on you in full view of a dozen people who know him intimately. It's not smart—though they won't finger him for the frogs, somebody's bound to tell your friends—but the ability to comprehend consequences is *not* an inherent part of their makeup. And they'll get you if you don't watch out.

In an homogenous community, however, it's different. People can't drift into it: they have to fight for admission. They're under the constant scrutiny of their colleagues/neighbors. There's no room for the unbalanced. People do flip out, of course, but when that happens, they're gone in a flash.

Really. A ho-commer is far more likely to run you over while driving drunk than to harm you or yours through a perverted sense of humor.

Out there, it's not the adults who are dangerous. It's the kids.

BB, tired of being pummeled by a small foot, stepped away with a patient air. The kid clapped his tiny hands. BB looked over to me. I could practically hear him sigh.

"So what do you think?" I asked Alex.

"Tamer than our liquor account," he laughed.

Approaching BB was a girl, maybe ten years old, dressed in store-new play clothes. Her brown hair fell in pigtails. She pointed at him imperiously.

"Excuse me." Sensing trouble, I patted Alex' arm.

A wild-eyed lady burst out of the crowd around the bar. "LEAVE HER ALONE!" she shrieked.

BB's lips drew back. His fangs glistened in the fading light. With a low, angry snarl, he stepped forward and raised his paws.

The woman looked as feral as he did. Her dress whipped about her suntanned legs as she charged.

I couldn't take the time to think. Grass blurring under my feet, I raced towards her. Sickness numbed my gut. I wouldn't be able to intervene in time.

BB's talons had started their downward swing. I hurled myself into a dive. My outstretched arm swiped viciously at long, lush legs. She went down in a flurry of nylon. Before she could move, I'd thrown myself on top of her.

"LEMME GO!"

"What the hell are you doing?" I demanded, rolling her over on her stomach and pinning her arms behind her back.

She started to sob. "He'll kill her, I know it, he'll kill her."

"He won't kill anybody, lady." BB and the girl were behind me now. I raised my head, and intercepted a spectator's horrified gaze. "Oh, Christ," I muttered. I didn't want to turn. I knew what those claws could do. And the thought of a slender young body lying bloody in the dew-damp grass was more than I could take.

But it was my responsibility, so I forced my head to swivel. Abruptly, my muscles went slack. My mouth gaped.

BB, having lifted the girl through the air, was positioning her on his broad shoulders. His eyes were rolled far back so that he could set her down in the right place. His long, sharp claws gave her an exo-rib cage.

-What are you doing, man?-

-Friend sit.-

Her legs encircled his neck, and her hands rested atop his head. A maharani on her elephant, she waited for the peasants to pay homage.

I started clapping. After a moment of hesitation, the others joined in. The girl's mother still lay on the ground, grass-stained and teary, but the applause drew her head like rabbit scent does a dog's. Blindly, she looked right and left, then blinked furiously and focused on her daughter. The blood fled her cheeks, leaving them sallow and waxy. Her mouth groped goldfishlike, but anything she was saying, we drowned out.

"How'd you get him to lift you up?" I asked the girl.

"I told him to," she sniffed.

"And he understood you?"

"I'm here, aren't I?"

That put me in my place. "What's your name?"

"Kathie." She was too busy exploring a pair of fuzzy ears to look at me. After all, I was only a person.

"How did you talk to him, Kathie?"

"Well, I— again? You're greedy, you know that?" Hand burrowing into his fur, she began to scratch him. "The same way he talks to me."

I opened my shield for a second, and felt their minds caressing each other. Warmth and affection flowed in both directions.

She smiled down with the air of abstraction that characterizes crowned heads of state. She was doing her best to be courteous, but she did have weightier matters on her mind, and so we'd understand, but she couldn't devote more than a fraction of her attention to us.

Gastine would have to see this, I thought. He'd been grumpy about the cost of BB's passage, but if my pet turned out to be a telepath-spotter . . . I wondered what a functioning, immature telepath like Kathie would be worth to Lomala. Gastine probably had the exact figure scrawled on his clipboard.

Kathie's mother was getting to her feet; I gave her my hand. She clung desperately, as if unaware that the same hand had tumbled her on her dignity. "Is she all right?" she jabbered. "Is it going to hurt her?"

"Lady," I said, "the question is not whether Baby Bear is going to hurt Kathie, but whether *she* is going to hurt Baby Bear. Frankly, she's in the driver's seat."

212

"You're horrid!" she said, between sobs, gasps, and pants. "Get my baby down from there."

"Kathie," I called, stilling BB with a touch of my hand, "your mother's worried about you. She wants you to come down."

Her lips lost their happy smile. She was clearly annoyed by her mother's solicitousness; for half a second, I heard her wonder whether it was not time to pack her bags and leave home.

I shook my head. "Not yet, Kathie. Give it a few more years."

Her eyes narrowed as they probed my face. "How did you know to say *that*?"

"How did you tell BB to lift you up?" I parried.

Her hand started to shape an answer, then gave it up as hopeless. "I'll come down." Her voice was flatter, duller. She whispered to BB. Obediently, he lowered himself to the grass. His soft brown eyes followed her as she walked away.

-Kathie.- I shoved the word right between her ears. Her ten-year-old shoulders stiffened. She wasn't sure what I'd done, but knew nobody had ever done it before. -Come back sometime—*with* your mother's permission—and play with Baby Bear. He needs more friends.-

A smile zig-zagged across her face, like lightning through a summer sky, and then was gone. Her mother took her hand. She went without a word, pausing only to throw BB one last wave.

The party broke up a few minutes later. The Area Relations Committee was, if not ready to classify BB with the family dog, at least willing to tolerate him from a two-kilometer distance. The children, of course, wanted to stay and "ride the bea-ah, Mommy!" but their various guarparents were already muttering catch-phrases like "overtired," and "wouldn't finish his nap."

And that was that. No friendships had been formed, nor reciprocal invitations extended—the Area Relations Committee had come almost as a diplomatic mission—but no further complaints would reach the police.

Which was what I'd wanted all along.

Wasn't it?

I was grumpy the next morning, and the intercom jangled my nerves. I parted the drapes. Daylight scattered my wistfulness. "Yes, Jan?"

"A Mrs. Washington to see you, sir."

"Show her in, please."

The door swung away from an old black woman. Hunched at the shoulders, thin gray hair cropped into a short Afro, she trudged across the room as though it were but a waystation on the road to despair.

"Nice to meet you, Mrs. Washington. Please, sit down."

She lifted her face a millimeter at a time. Her mouth opened. Past yellowed, broken teeth creaked the words, "You too boo-class to help a po' ol' lady."

"What's the trouble, Mrs. Washington?"

"Big Unk say I dead. Cut off mah check." One hand clutched her purse while the other, a gnarled cluster of arthritic hooks, rummaged through it. She muttered under her breath until she'd found the letter. "Here. You see fo' yourself."

The heavy letterhead stationery, thumb-stained from much handling, was addressed to Ms. Esmerelda Washington. "Did they send this to you?"

"Mah daughter."

The message was terse: inasmuch as Mrs. Josephine Washington was deceased and her children were over the age of 21, their Social Security Assistance was being terminated as of the above date. "Did you talk to this—" I checked the signature "—Theobald L. Murchinson?"

"I talk to him, but he say I some kind of impostor. I told him I ain't dead yet, but he cut me off. Talk to some other people, they say come to you. I'm here."

"Now, you *are* Mrs. Josephine Washington?" As I asked the question, I parted my shield.

"Ain't so old I forget my own name." Her wounded pride shrieked its anger and its pain. "I'm Josephine Washington, same as it says there."

"Is this your Social Security Number here?"

"It is for sure." Again she fumbled in her purse for a piece of paper. Smaller and older, it was coated with fifty years of thumb smears.

I took it from her shaking hand, and compared its bleached numerals with the crisp computer type of the notice. The number was the same.

"Well, Mrs. Washington, this may take a while, but—"

"That's what they all say," she interrupted. " 'You just set in the corner and keep your mouth shut,' they say. 'We get round to you when we good and ready.' "

"No, Mrs. Washington, you don't understand—"

"I understand. Told mah daughter ain't no use coming here; told her they just gonna ignore an ol' lady who ain't dead yet—" Her clawhands swept across my desk, snatching at her papers, but succeeding only in knocking them onto the floor.

Picking them up, I struggled to control my temper. "Mrs. Washington—"

"You give me mah things back, I go away, leave you alone with your im*po*'tant things," she said bitterly. Her pointing finger was an antique pistol, knobbed with rust, useless for all but effect. "You give me them back, I say."

I couldn't take it any longer. She whined—she wouldn't let me finish a fucking sentence—my nerves had already been too taut— "GODDAMIT, LADY, SIDDOWN AND SHUT UP!"

Her eyes popped open and her jaw dropped. She stood statue-still for a moment, then tottered backwards. The chair barred her way. She dropped into it without looking. Her eyes misted. Tears began to trickle down her withered cheeks. "Ain't no call for you to shout," she sobbed. "I'm just an ol' lady never done you no wrong, you got no call to shout."

Her crying was more exasperating than her constant interruptions. Impatiently, I jabbed the intercom button. "Jan. Get in here and take this— this lady into the reception room. Keep her there till I've got this mess cleared up."

Two minutes later I was alone with my desk, my viphone, and a nagging guilt. I sat behind the first, picked up the second, and set the third aside. A guilty conscience won't go away; you can deal with it at your leisure.

"Social Security Administration," said the bored receptionist.

"Bander Snatch, Federal Ombudsman, put me through to, uh, Theobald L. Murchinson."

"Would you state you business, please?"

That flamed me off. "Only to Murchinson." My calls were supposed to be highest priority; *nobody*, but *nobody*, was allowed to screen them.

"Then I'm sorry, but—"

"Sister, your name tag and your ID Number are clearly visible. I suggest that you get him on the line immediately. Otherwise—" I left the fine details to her bureaucratic imagination.

With a nervous nibble on her pencil, she nodded. "Yes, sir."

The screen dissolved in a field of snow that regrouped into angular masculine features. "Murchinson."

"Bander Snatch. I'm the new ombudsman for this region."

"Right, right. Got a memo about you."

"Show it to your receptionist. Look, here's the story. Got a lady here who's been declared dead. The problem is, she's not. She needs her Social Security checks resumed."

Murchinson looked wary. "Name?"

"Josephine Washington, Mrs. Social Security Number 865-43-7373."

He played with his computer terminal for a minute. "She is dead. I have the report right here."

"Pretty damn lively for a corpse. Walking, talking . . ."

"It's an old dodge. Surprised you didn't catch it. They don't tell us that somebody's died, you see, and then—"

"I know the way it's done, Murchinson—I used to do it myself. But this time, at least, Mrs. Josephine Washington is very much alive."

"How do you know?"

"Trust me."

He looked ready to object, but something—maybe a flicker of humanity—changed his mind. "Tell you what. You send us an official order to reinstate that account. As soon as I receive it, I will personally sign the first check. Good enough?"

"Why do you need the order?"

"Because otherwise the auditors will nail my ass to the wall."

"You got it. It'll be in your data banks in thirty minutes."

"Thanks." He winked at me. "Tell the lady everything's going to be fine."

I threw the off button, and slumped in my chair. I didn't really want to talk to Mrs. Washington again . . . after a moment, I understood why.

I was embarrassed.

I'd treated her like a piece of shit, not a person. No apology could make up for my behavior. Oh, I could say the words—easy as pie, wham-bam, sorry, ma'am—I could even *feel* the words, but there was no way . . .

Yet I had to try.

Click. "Send Mrs. Washington in, please."

216

"Sir?" Janice hadn't misunderstood me; she was just giving me time to reconsider. I used it.

"Wait a minute—I'll come to her."

"Yes, sir." She sounded pleased.

Click. I closed my eyes for a second, rubbed them, then went out to the reception room. "Mrs. Washington?"

She wouldn't look up.

"First, I want to tell you I'm sorry I shouted at you. I had no right. You're a citizen, and a taxpayer, and as such you're entitled to courtesy." The words had come from nowhere, but they felt right. More, they seemed to hint at the full truth. She *was* entitled. Any citizen was.

Yes! We bureaucrats had been hired to perform functions and to provide services that the citizens chose not to do by themselves. Whatever their reasons for hiring us—our special skills, their lack of time, the nature of the task—the bottom line was that we were their employees. As such, we owed them honesty, efficiency, and deference. It was not the other way around.

Why had it taken so long to sink in? My job, above all, called for a person who instinctively believed that. Who relished the thought of knocking high-and-mighty bureaucrats off their thrones. Who wasn't trying to build a throne of his own.

"Second, Mrs. Washington, I've talked to the Social Security people. As soon as they receive my order, they'll mail you your check."

Her head jerked, and she gazed deep into my eyes. "You wouldn't do an ol' lady, would you?" she asked hoarsely.

"No, ma'am, I wouldn't."

She pondered the situation. "Why, then I guess I ought to thank you." She held out one ancient hand. I shook it gladly.

"They really going to get me mah checks again?"

"Yes, ma'am."

She stood, gathering her dignity around her like a coat. "That's real good, sonny, *real* good."

I escorted her out of the house, and watched her stride down the walk. Her step was springy, now, and she held her head high. Whether it was getting the check, or beating Big Unk, or just plain finding somebody who believed her, I didn't know.

And to be honest, I didn't need to know. The change in her was reward enough.

217

Closing the door, I asked, "Has Ralph Tcazkuk called?"

"No. I have his number, though—would you like to call him?"

"Yes, I would." I perched on the edge of her desk while she dialed. A young boy answered. His thin and pale face was splotched with red. His eyes were puffy. When Janice asked for Ralphie, he broke into tears and backed away from the camera. Another face came on.

"Can I help you?" An older man, gray-haired and grave.

"I'd like to speak to Mr. Tcazkuk. This is the ombudsman's office."

"Oh." He blinked several times. "Well, he's . . . he's dead. Last night. Ah . . . there was some shooting, and he got caught in the crossfire."

Janice fumbled through some condolences. When she'd signed off, we looked at each other and shrugged. Not indifferently: bemusedly.

"Shall I mark the case closed?"

"Uh . . ." I chewed on a fingertip. "You know, somebody out there still has a passport in Ralphie's name."

"Does it matter?"

"I don't know . . . notify Sirois, that'll keep whoever it is from using it, but . . ." At the back of my mind was a bleak foreboding. "Get the computer to tell you the address of the present passport holder."

"All right." She fed it the right question, and retrieved the answer.

"Is that the same as Ralphie's?" I asked.

"No. Completely different." A frown creased her high forehead.

"Six Seventy-five Maple . . ." The street was more than familiar: I'd used to live on it. But 675 . . . "Jan, get into the Fedra files, find out if there *is* a 675."

Two minutes later, the answer flashed out at us. *No.*

"What now?" she asked.

"I don't know." I studied the smoothness of the ceiling while I picked at the puzzle. I needed more pieces. "Call Marianne."

"Marianne who?"

"Marianne. No last name. She's the current Jungle Lord."

Four levels of command tried to shunt me aside, but threats and promises finally brought her stone face before the camera. "What?" was all she said.

"We need your help, Marianne."

"Fuck off."

"I'm *asking*, Marianne, asking."

Her eyebrows rose slightly. "You? Ask?"

"Yes." Briefly outlining the situation, I shot through the computers a photocopy of the phony Tcazkuk's picture. "I want to talk to him. If you could locate him for me, I'd be very grateful."

"You would be?"

"Yes."

"All right. We'll do what we can at this end. You return the favor."

"Sure. How?"

"Get the government to hurry up on its deliveries."

I signalled Janice, who taped the information. "What is it, food?"

"No. Uniforms, guns, and ammo for our police force. Also two helicopters. Then there's the construction equipment and the materials for rebuilding. Plus a whole pile of other shit that they promised us when we signed the peace treaty. None of it's come through yet, and we're getting flamed off. Can you goose them into action?"

Cautiously, I said, "I thought Catkiller was getting paid to be the liaison."

"When we can find him, he says he's bogged down in red tape." She snorted. "He's probably figured a way to magic Big Unk, and he's got no time for us. Will *you* do it?"

"Yeah, sure, I'll start on it right away. Do the same with the picture?"

"You got it." For a moment, her face relaxed into a smile. "Ban?"

"Yeah?"

"Thanks, huh?"

. . .

IV

Early morning in the Jungle. Black shadows on gray concrete. A line of rose against the eastern sky. Footsteps the
only sound: some slow and weary, the heavy trudge of exhausted nightpeople; others fast, decisive, impatient to ar-
rive before . . . before they can be recognized?

I was one of them.

It was strange to return. Stranger still to slip through the
desolation with no other escort than Baby Bear. I remembered being fourteen, when No-nose and I would glide
through the promise of dawn, trying to get to the opportunities first.

The pavement was broken. The air was rotten with garbage, cement dust, and long-dead lakeshores. The dark
streets were full of cover. BB followed me through them as
though we were in his environment, not mine.

Marianne had phoned late the previous night, explaining
that she'd had to wait till her ComCenter was empty before
she dared contact me. "The guy in the picture is Wheels
McCafferty—"

"Damn! I shoulda recognized him. What'd he do, put on
weight?"

"He's eating good these days. Nobody's too sure, but
they think he's working for Catkiller. Which is why I'm
telling you to back off."

"What?"

Dropping her voice, she'd told me that my erstwhile rival was about to cut himself a large slice of pie—the grape-
vine had no details—and McCafferty was presumed to

220

be a part of his operation. Nobody knew more: the word on the streets was that long noses would get chopped off. . . . "So stay out of it, Ban. Besides Catkiller and his men, the kids down here hate you. I won't be able to protect you if you come in."

"Gotta talk to Wheels, though."

"It's a good way to get yourself lost."

"Yeah, I know—but I don't have a choice."

Her eyes had flickered to either side, as though searching for hidden listeners. She'd leaned closer to the pickup to whisper, "Well, walk soft, huh? And take a gun, for God's sakes."

"Thanks for the warning. I'll be all right. Really."

I would be. The area had changed in the five lost years, and feelings against me ran high, but I had Baby Bear for an early warning system. While the shield around his mind kept the background chatter of ten thousand Jungle dwellers from driving him berserk, I'd fine-tuned it to pass plans of aggression against us. If somebody was going to open fire, BB would know about it the instant the sniper made up his mind.

-Come on.-

-Feet sore.-

The pleasant thoughts I aimed at his toes diminished some of his annoyance. Frankly, I could sympathize. My own feet resented the demands I was placing on them. I hadn't tortured them on cement in a long time.

-Watch it.-

We froze against a half-tumbled brick wall. A drunk rounded the corner and wobbled down the sidewalk, head rolling loosely. He saw us. He gaped at BB's unearthliness. He drew himself erect and staggered on by, muttering under his breath. The words lost in his alcoholic slur probably established a cause-and-effect relationship between the rotgut he'd drunk and the monster he'd seen.

I almost chuckled as I waved us closer to our goal.

After much wheedling, Marianne had given me McCafferty's address. She'd told me he was known to be in town, since he'd been seen driving a dark, bearded Hispanic to a meeting with Catkiller. I'd been pleased. I had a few questions to ask my ex-chauffeur.

Like: who'd arranged his phony passport?

Like: what had he been doing to need one?

Like: why had Ralphie been coughed?

We darted into the decayed foyer of the building where

he lived. Glass shards crunched under my boots; BB hissed as one bit into him. -I'll take it out in two minutes.-

-Grumble.-

The row of battered, oft-broken-into mailboxes yielded Wheels' room number: 213. Second floor. I mounted the steps like a wind-goosed cloud, making only one sound: the click of a safety. BB scampered up with equal stealth. Nice thing about semidomesticated carnivores, they never lose their cunning.

The staircase fed into a corridor, and I peered around its corner. It was empty. -Wait here,- I told BB.

-Foot.-

-One minute.- Every Fedra apartment house was identical to every other. 213 was straight ahead; its windows overlooked the courtyard. I scurried to it on silent feet, acutely aware that any of six doors could swing back to clear a field for shotgun fire.

But they didn't. -Come on.-

-Foot?-

-Maybe.- Reaching for the knob, I frowned. The door frame was splintered, and wood chips littered the cracked linoleum. I pushed on the door with my toe. Rustily, it creaked open.

One deep breath, and I went in, gun ready. My head snapped from side to side. My eyes devoured everything they touched.

First impression: Wheels was a pig.

Second impression: His apartment had been pretty classy, until somebody with a grudge had turned it into a pigsty.

Third impression: The leg jutting into the living room had probably belonged to McCafferty. I hoped he was still attached to it.

He was, but it wouldn't do him any good. His 167 centimeters were liberally splashed with blood, and I knew he was face up only because they'd overlooked one of his teeth. Tufts of red-ended black hair lay all over the kitchen floor. My stomach lurched as it realized that the white thing in his crushed hand was one of his eyeballs.

The fuckers hadn't even had the decency to finish him off.

"Wheels, can you hear me?"

He gurgled, low and so full of agony that I had to re-swallow burning acid. Then I had to do it again, because

222

my old driver was not going to talk to me. They'd cut out his tongue.

I'd have to enter his mind.

I plopped backwards into a kitchen chair, leaning my arms over its high plastic back. Its support was welcome. I shut my eyes to the blood, and my ears to the moans. After struggling with my own intense reluctance, I cracked my shield.

A string of hand grenades blew up in my face. My shield slammed shut.

Sweat drenched every part of my body, and quickly cooled into clamminess. I'd seen people in Wheels' condition before—any Jungle dweller has—but I'd either left them for dead or ordered a medic to work on them.

I had never tried to interrogate one.

Abruptly, my stomach abdicated. I found the sink half a second before I lost my breakfast. The dizziness was so strong that I had to clutch the faucets. Waves of cramps kept me crouched for what seemed a very long time.

When I'd rinsed my mouth, and splashed my face with cold water, I turned back to McCafferty, fully expecting to find that he'd died. He hadn't. Game little bastard. For a minute I considered pressing my rifle to his temple and pulling the trigger.

But I couldn't. Not yet. He had information I needed.

I sat down again and worked out a plan. I would have to be rapid—so rapid that the various steps would occur automatically—yet delicacy was essential. One false move inside his head would wipe away what I'd be looking for.

My knuckles whitened on the chair back. I took three deep breaths, closed my eyes, and screwed their lids down. Then—

—the shield split and my tentacle cobra-struck into—

—quad .50's spitting death in a dozen colors.

Dive! FREEZE swoop TIME! Wheels' nerves slowed their mad mouthings enough to let me pick my way through air pregnant with copper jackets, but not before one of them had chewed a path through my tentacle. The hole was leaking energy. I was threatening to unravel. Shit. My strength was dissipating so quickly that my cross-section of time was being pulled back into the continuum. I had barely reached McCafferty's muzzle when it snapped home. I heard myself yelp.

But I was in, and with a writhe and a twist I'd found his pain centers and disconnected them.

I managed to retract into myself before I fainted.

BB woke me with his injured paw. My eyes focused on a brownish blur, then found the piece of glass glinting in its sticky bed of blood. -Be brave.- I squeezed it out; BB raised it to his mouth.

Wheels was still alive. His moans had ceased because he could feel no more pain. As I picked myself off the floor, I forced my mind open again. The abnormal behavior of his thoughts was striking: instead of spraying out from the center, they whirled around it in tight orbits. At first I was glad.

-Wheels.- I approached his scale model of a solar system. -Who did this?-

Silence.

-Who hurt you?-

Extended silence. His thoughts *weren't* travelling in orbits, but in dense spirals whose outer rims blended with infinity. They moved faster with each passing second.

-McCafferty, WHO HURT YOU?-

Not words, but a face answered me. Out of the blackness loomed a bald skull that swelled to monstrous size and towered over me. Its small eyes were reddish-brown, and almost buried in folds of sallow skin. It laughed and laughed and laughed before it spun away.

I knew that face. He'd once been one of my grove captains. We'd called him Hairless.

-WHO ELSE?-

My shout added energy to the system; more welled up from below, from the physical side. The spirals snapped into straight lines. In ten seconds not a fragment of Wheels McCafferty was left.

He was dead.

But I knew his killer.

"Dammit!" I broke my grip on the chair and stomped into the living room.

BB gave me a questioning whine.

"Oh, yeah, sorry." I went back to the kitchen—taking care to avoid the huddled corpse on the dirty linoleum—and checked the refrigerator. On the bottom shelf were two pounds of steak in a cellophaned wrapper. I stripped off the plastic and carried the meat to BB. "Eat well, you ghoul."

Snuffling, he settled down to his snack.

While he ate, I sat on a cushionless couch amid mounds of shredded foam rubber. Had Hairless searched the place,

224

I wondered, or just vented his malice? The dismal mess reminded me of the day that had led me on this trail, when I'd returned to HQ and found Shana missing. I'd asked the same questions then.

After a few minutes of rest, and a few more of thought, I hunted for the viphone. It was buried under a pile of pornographic books that had been swept off the shelf; when I cleared the rubble away, it was stubbornly going *beep* *beep* *beep*. With a sigh of relief that Hairless hadn't torn out its wires—but then again, why should he have? He obviously hadn't expected Wheels to use it—I punched in the number of my office.

"Good morning," trilled Janice, "Ombudsman's of— hi, Ban."

"McCafferty is dead. I'm going to try to find his killer."

"Have you called the police?"

My grin was involuntary. She clearly didn't comprehend the Jungle. "They don't operate down here. Vengeance is private. Have you come up with anything?"

"Well, I just got in a few minutes ago, but—" she glanced to one side to consult her notes "—the DoD says they made the first deliveries on schedule. Marianne, however, said that was . . . incorrect."

I could just imagine what Marianne had called it. "So what are you doing?"

"We're tracking down the invoices, to confirm where and when the deliveries were made. The DoD says they went to a warehouse in the Jungle; Marianne disagreed with that, too."

"Uh-huh." I scratched my forehead as I thought. "Look, you keep at it, see what you can come up with. In the meantime I'm going to find Hairless. I've got a feeling—no, dammit, I'm convinced—that this ties directly in with that passport shit. Two sudden deaths are just too convenient. If I have any luck, I'll call in. All right?"

"Ban—" As she bit her lip, her eyes fell away. "Be careful, all right?"

"Sure thing." I hoisted the rifle into the camera's field. "I won't take any ridiculous chances."

When I called Marianne, she said to the best of her knowledge, Hairless was three years' dead. She couldn't help find him. I'd have to do it myself.

My technique was simple, if unorthodox. I'd torn a cover off one of Wheels' books, and trimmed it to the dimensions of a wallet holo. Then I began to accost people in the street, flashing the blank paper while pumping Hairless' visage into their heads, and asking, "Do you know this man?"

It was broad daylight before I got my first "Yes." A bare-chested Zulu had said aloud, "Never seen 'im," while inwardly saying, "The sander at Bratsk's Bar."

Bratsk's Bar I knew. The Zulu took off as though impatient to report me to his boss, and I had a hunch I didn't have much time.

-Come on,- I told BB, who was hiding in an alley as instructed.

-Tired.- Grumpy, too. Our joint shield protected him from most thoughts, but the hostiles slipped through. He didn't like it; I'd had to restrain him several times. Now that the streets were filling, I'd have more trouble.

-Come on.-

-Grumble.- But he came, padding along on all fours. The passersby tended to press themselves flat against buildings—probably figuring it was a new style in holdups—but the majority radiated simple fear, and BB was used to that.

-Friend,- called Baby Bear, from somewhere behind me.

I turned. He was rubbing noses with a six-year-old whose crust of filth couldn't disguise his delight. The contrast with Kathie from the ho-com came unbidden. Even if Lomala shut down its TP program, even if she never learned to develop her talent, her community would make a place for her.

But the street waif playing with BB might have only the one chance. If his TP didn't become usable, he could easily spend the rest of his life in the Jungle.

I backtracked, and squatted. The kid eyed me incuriously, concentrating on BB. They were hugging and kissing in the territories of the mind.

"Hey, kid."

"Yeah?" Suspicious, he drew back a step, wiping snot from his nose.

"Got a guarpar?"

"No."

"You like my friend?"

"Yeah."

"Make you a deal."

"Whazzat?"

I fished in my wallet for a card, and extracted a bill to accompany it. The kid took both with a skeptical hand.

"Gimme a call at that number. I'm sort of busy right now, so call me . . . day after tomorrow. I might have a job for you."

"A job?" Sullenness descended over his pinched features. "Whadda want a job for?"

"The job'd be taking care of him." I nodded to BB. "Interested?"

"Him? You shit me." A typical attitude for the Jungle.

"Really."

"Awright, I call you."

"Good." I rose, then a thought hit me. "Kid."

"Yeah?"

"I might be done by then." I didn't know why I was talking that way—maybe I needed somebody to know the risks I was taking?—but he was more eager than he let on, and I didn't want him to lose the tenuous faith he had. "If I am, call—" I took back the card, and scrawled another number on it "—this number, and ask for Dr. Gastine. Tell him Ban sent you; tell him you've got TP. Can you remember that?"

He nodded impatiently, as though insulted by my question. He probably was. Kids down there are quick to remember survival tricks. "Whaffo?"

"Gastine might—just might—be able to get you a pet like him." I patted BB. "Would you like that?"

"Couldn't feed 'im," he pointed out with all seriousness.

"That's why I say call me first. Will you do it?"

"Day after tomorrow."

"Right."

"I call."

-Let's go,- I told BB.

He was reluctant, but the kid smoothed his fur and whispered into his ear. Then he grumbled, and followed. The kid watched us leave.

Bratsk's Bar was just around the corner. Small and cruddy, it had a reputation for encouraging brawlers and rolling drunks. It also offered 24-hour service. When BB and I pushed through the poorly-hung swinging doors, there were already five or six juicers drinking breakfast.

Two of the faces, familiar ones, filled with surprised recognition. Heads bent and conversations hissed. The black-haired bartender was new, though, and it was he whom I approached.

"No a-neemals," he growled. "Get tha' *oso* outta here."

"I'm leaving in just a minute, wanted to ask you, you

227

know where this guy lives?" I flashed the cardboard and listened closely.

-Upstairsa Luis,- he thought, saying aloud, "*Quien sabe?*"

"Then," I asked, still monitoring despite the pain, "tell me where Luis lives."

The address zipped through his mind—376 Lily—while he said, "*No hablo Ingles.*"

"You don't know Luis, either, huh?" I grinned at him, and pocketed the featureless photo. "Never mind, then. Thanks anyway."

He grunted a Spanish nastiness as I walked away.

"Janice?" There was a public phone outside 376 Lily; its survival astonished me. It even looked relatively new. Maybe Marianne was more successful at rebuilding the Jungle than I'd thought. It was possible—she did have a grim determination to achieve whatever goals she'd set for herself—and I was beginning to learn that I'd misjudged many of the people who'd streamed through my life. She could have been one of them. On the other hand, maybe the street toughs had reached a tacit agreement to leave public viphones alone. Even Zulus need them now and then.

"Ban, where are you?"

"At 376 Lily, where Hairless lives. I'm going in. I just wanted to let you know the address. Anything happens to me, pass it on to Marianne."

The taut lines of her face showed her upset, but her voice remained steady. "Hairless, you said?" She copied his address. "Ban—the army found the invoices. The supplies were delivered to Gallaghan's Warehouse three months ago. The signatures on the invoices are pretty illegible, but they could be Hairless."

"Oh, damn." I pinched the bridge of my nose as I tried to fit this new piece in with all the others. Hairless had killed Wheels, who had had a passport in the name of Ralph Tcazkuk, who'd been coughed after causing us to realize that there was a phony passport. Hmm. Hairless, who was presumably working for Catkiller, had also magicked paramilitary supplies meant for the Jungle's police force. Double hmm. An obvious solution, although one that called for more than a few guesses to fill in the blanks, was that Catkiller had rerouted the shipments to . . . where? For what? And how did Ralphie's passport fit in? But that would have to wait, till I'd talked to Hairless. "Jan, I don't have much time—I'll call you back later."

"All right." At once she became the efficient secretary. "I'll keep Marianne informed."

"You do that. Later." Pressing the off switch, I stepped into the hot sun.

BB, crouched at my side, was growling his dislike of the heat and the bright. I scratched his skull absently, and tried to figure a way to play it. Then I shrugged, and jiggled my rifle. No way to play it but straight.

I bumped into a man on the stairway, and did the photo trick on him. He wouldn't volunteer anything, but his subconscious surrendered the apartment number anyway.

For the second time that morning, I stepped into a vandalized room. A quick recon yielded two facts: Hairless, for all his ugliness, had had better taste than McCafferty. And his body was nowhere to be seen.

It took twenty more minutes to custom the place semithoroughly, and the best I found was a scrap of paper. It had been caught on the springs of a toppled chair. I was hoping as hard as I could that a breeze from the open window had wafted it there, because it bore the words, "Hairless to 577 Rose, #301."

The odds were that it was a trap. I crumpled it up and almost threw it away. Then, reconsidering, I smoothed it out and stared at it. Definitely a trap.

After brushing powdered porcelain off the viphone, I gave Janice a third call. She took down the address, and then relayed the information I'd been expecting. "Ban," she said briskly, not knowing the effect her words would have on me, "Hairless wasn't named in the autonomy agreement as an agent for the Jungle; he had to get special authorization to receive those shipments. I tracked that authorization down. It was signed by a man named Catkiller. Do you know him?"

"Yes," I said heavily, "yes, I do. I don't know where I can find him, though. He works for Big Unk—have you got his address?"

She consulted her computer. "A government ho-com off Interstate 90."

"Not in the Jungle?"

"No."

That baffled me. If Catkiller were pulling the swindle I suspected he was, I couldn't see him not keeping it under his eagle eye. "All right, thanks. I'll talk to you later."

As I hung up, I was thinking furiously. I wouldn't be

able to work through Marianne, because her staff was pro-Catkiller and not above doing me. Besides, her control of the Jungle was shaky, at best, and she could lose it all if she were known to be helping me. But I couldn't challenge Catkiller head-on, either: my arrival on the scene could provoke something I didn't really want to get into.

That meant, trap or no trap, I'd have to follow the one clue I had. If I went in quick . . . yeah, maybe I could do it. Might have to cough a few people, but I had to force some hard evidence out of Hairless before Catkiller scoped out what I was up to. I just hoped Hairless' captors weren't ready for me to come in hard and fast.

Frankly, I was scared. The strings I'd used to pull were all broken; the Zulus I'd used to command were either dead, or in someone else's army. Though it was hard to comprehend, I was now in enemy territory. The nominal ruler wasn't taking sides, but the true sovereign of the Jungle would call in his people to crush me if he could. And he'd had six years of virtually unchallenged supremacy in which to consolidate his authority. Christ. It was a wonder only my knees were shaking.

-Come on.-

BB took his nose out of the refrigerator. -Again?-

-Come on, come on.-

And off we went.

Whoever had ordered Hairless' abduction had clout. His building wasn't new, but the bullet scars had been filled in, and the soot stains sandblasted away. Every window on its three floors had glass; the top story even had screens. From the alley east of 577 Rose, I got only an acute-angled view of the lobby, but it looked clean and secure. Ominously, a hard-muscled teen-ager stood guard.

I had to reach the third floor without providing any warning to the inhabitants of #301. There was probably a back door to the building, but my guess was that the rear would be more heavily guarded than the front.

The kid with the softly gleaming rifle had to go first. A sniper shot would have lost him, but it was even money that it would also have been audible to the people upstairs. If they were alarmed, I was done.

A few moments of thought offered a solution. -Baby Bear, stay here.-

-Alone?-

-One minute, maybe two.-

-Grumble.- Back against the wall and head drooping, he was a two-ton statue of despair.

I hurried into the courtyard behind 577 Rose, where I took a right. A hundred meters west was Maple Street, which led back to Rose, but on the other side of my goal. I crossed Rose without a single glance towards the guard, passed 572, then thought, -BB, come here.-

His brown bulk filled the mouth of the alley. The few pedestrians in sight stopped, aghast. The glass door of the apartment building swung out. I pressed myself flat against the front wall and sidled towards it.

The guard emerged with his rifle at the ready. Every bit of his attention was concentrated on Baby Bear. A mistake could cost him dearly. Since there are no large, wild animals in the Jungle, the shambling beast had to belong to somebody. The kid had to answer two questions in a hurry: Was it friendly? and, Could its owner do him if he shot it anyway?

I was three meters away. His decision registered on BB's face. The great brown eyes glared; the curved fangs clashed. The kid brought his M-33 up in one smooth motion. His gentle finger squeeze had already started when the butt of my gun cracked his skull.

-Inside, quick!- While BB bustled past, I caught the kid under the armpits and dragged him into the lobby. I had to retrieve his gun, which couldn't be left on the sidewalk. Stray weapons made Jungle dwellers curious.

I arranged him in a corner that was more or less invisible from the street. -Come on.- I led the way inside, raising my eyebrows at the thick Turkish rug. Ritzy place. Carpets weren't used much, at least not by people who expected to find them the next morning. The guard was probably a 24-hour arrangement.

A functioning elevator for a three-story building confirmed my suspicions that powerful people lived in it. We took the stairs. The high and the mighty don't walk when they can ride; we were in less danger of being spotted on the barren, poorly lit staircase.

Four half-flights, taken at top speed, left us both dizzy. At the top I paused, for breath, for balance, and for last-minute reconsiderations. Finding no choice but invasion, I cracked open the fire door and peeked into the quiet hallway. It was heavily carpeted, and empty.

-Let's go.-

My air of caution impressed BB. When we were at the

right door, I said, -Do this,- and pantomimed kicking in the
door. -Then do this:- I mimicked the kicker jumping to
one side. -Can you?-

Hoisting his heavy foot, he stared at it, as if puzzled.
-Grumble.-

-All right.- I wiped my palms on the front of my shirt,
then gripped my rifle more tightly. I wished I had some
way of sending my mind in first; the odds were that an
M-33 was waiting on the other side. But I didn't have that
kind of power, so I'd have to be ready to fire before they
did. A huge, deep breath, then: -NOW!-

His incredible strength blew the door off its hinges. He
threw himself away from the wreckage. I was in place before the slab of wood hit the floor.

And there in front of me, stark naked on a black leather
sofa, was Shana. Slowly she raised her blue-green eyes. I
took a helpless step forward.

"It took you long enough, Bandy," boomed a smooth
and easy voice.

I spun, finger itching to flatten the trigger, but I re-
strained it. I wanted answers from the man, not blood.

Catkiller stood against the right wall, burly arms folded
on his chest, a broad smile on his tanned face. "Drop the
rifle, Bandy."

And I did.

Three long seconds elapsed before I realized that I
shouldn't have obeyed. I had no idea why I had. All I knew
was that the gun was on the floor, Catkiller's laugh hung
fetid in the air, and I was decidedly vulnerable.

"Leave it there," said Catkiller. "And don't use your telepathy on me."

I'd be damned if I put up with that kind of shit. I
cracked my shield and reached for his mind— . . . I
reached for his mind— . . . c'mon, dammit, REACH,
GET HIS MIND! But I was a paralytic trying to twitch
afflicted limbs.

Catkiller was amused by my obvious efforts to disobey.
"Tell your pet to stay right where it is. And Shana—" his
slate-gray eyes touched her lightly "—if it comes into the
room, cough it."

Shana fumbled in the cushions of the couch; her hand
came up with a nasty-looking automatic. She still knew
how to hold one with confidence.

232

-BB,- I said, -please, stay outside. Sit down and sleep. Sleep.-

A snore floated through the ruins of the doorway.

"Very nice, Bandy. How bad did you do the boy downstairs?"

"Just knocked him out." My eyes darted around the richly furnished room. Some of the paintings on display must have cost more than my house; two of them, I knew for sure, used to hang in T-23's museum. "How'd you know I was coming?"

"You're a real amateur, aren't you?" His scrutiny was puzzled, but condescending nonetheless. "Your viphone's been tapped since you got back."

"Oh, Christ." I could have kicked myself. I'd known Catkiller had federal connections—I should have . . . through my head streamed one of those useless "if only" schemes that so nag one in retrospect. "Where's Hairless?"

Catkiller checked the top button of his purple silk shirt before replying, "Who?"

"Hairless. He took delivery on the government shipments like you authorized him to. I want him."

"I've never heard of him, and I've never authorized anybody to receive any shipments." His voice sounded slightly different, as though the broken nose he'd suffered at Lomala had altered its pitch. I was pleased to see that the surgeons hadn't been able to restore it completely. "If there's a document purporting to confer such authorization, it must have been forged."

"Tell it to the judge," I muttered, still looking around.

"Judge? Are you suggesting I'm going to be iced for something?"

"Hey, kitty, I ain't suggesting, I'm *stating*."

His narrow face twisted at "kitty." "Think you're so smart, Bandy, let me tell you: it's gonna be *you* in the box, not me. Assuming you live until the frogs get here."

"Frogs? In the Jungle? You shit me."

"They'll come for the Catkiller, when I tell 'em I've subdued an armed robber." He grinned widely. "That's what my mistress and I will tell 'em you are—a gashead armed robber." Loosening his stance, in preparation for the fight that was to come, he tried to weaken me by igniting my temper. "Ol' Scarface *is* my mistress these days, Bandy. Not a good one, but better-disciplined than she used to be."

I almost fell for it. The white heat that shot through me

233

made me unwary. Then, catching myself, I decided to make his ploy boomerang. "That's right, you like shakers that don't talk back. Prolly comes from fucking corpses."

His eyes went very cold. He shook his head angrily; his thick brown hair fluffed like a cat's tail, then fell back. "At least I make life easy for her, Bandy—when she was with you, she had to *work*, take risks, worry about Leah. Now she's mine, and I'm good to her. All I ask— tell him what I ask, Shana."

Her voice was a zombie's, and that caused greater pain than anything else. "Catkiller asks very little, Bandy." He had *her* calling me that, too. "Just to take care of his prick, that's all. I keep it fat and happy and give it places to come in. Catkiller has the best cock I've ever seen, and as long as I worship it right, it's the only one I have to take care of."

Blood burned in my cheeks. Hatred roared in my eyes. Catkiller chuckled, softly, and added a final taunt: "When you get out of jail, Bandy, she'll be too old for me, so I'll let you have her back for a night. Won't cost but two bucks."

My fury erupted and I charged. Poised and ready, he hammered home a left and a right that knocked me to my knees. "Down so soon, Bandy?"

Up I heaved, and backwards. He was right on top of me, and landed three quick jabs. My nose crunched horribly. A tooth fell onto my tongue. Blood from both gushed over my mouth; I had to gasp for breath.

"I'm gonna kill you, Bandy."

And he would, if he could. I knew that. I had to position him so that I could finish him off before he damaged me too badly.

He could be suckered into throwing a long-armed blow that would leave him wide open, but not until I was on my last legs. Gritting my teeth, I let him batter my gut with a five-punch combination. The room lights seemed to dim. My punished solar plexus doubled me up. I retched onto the ivory rug.

His foot drew back. It was one of those moments when every sense operates at 100 percent. Out of the mirror polish of his steel-toed shoe shone my calculating eyes.

The shoe's backswing peaked. It hesitated for a heartbeat. Then, with a gentle shiver, it started forward, to make the bridge of my nose kiss the back of my skull.

My entire being shouted a single command. I found all

the blanks in his pattern, and recklessly stuffed myself into
them. His leg gained a thousand kilos. It lost all but a fraction of its speed. As astonishment bubbled out of his
mouth, my right arm lanced upwards. My fist slammed
into his balls. If he'd been firmly anchored, my clenched
fingers would have ripped right through his body.

He started to shriek, but the sudden, exploding pain
stunned his lungs. His torso wilted. His leg stirred up a
breeze that stroked my cheek as it passed. It kept on rising.
He couldn't have stopped it even if he could have thought
of stopping it. When it arched above his shoulder, its mo-
mentum tore him from the floor. He thudded onto his
back. Eyes bulging, mouth spasming, he curled himself into
a ball and begged for unconsciousness.

I could afford to catch up on breathing. My ribs were
broken. Blood dripping off my face splotched the deep carpet. Faintly, through a foggy red haze, I heard bare feet
brush wool.

"You fought dirty." Shana loomed above me. The gun in
her knowing hand neutralized her nudity more than clothes
could have.

"Yeah." My thoughts were too pain-scattered to explain
that rules of fair play pertain only to play; that when survival time arrives, you do what has to be done. "Yeah, I
did."

"I'm glad." She stepped away and almost negligently
aimed the gun. At Catkiller.

"Don't!"

"Why?" Her voice was as featureless as a misty landscape at night.

"I want the bastard alive." *Though I'm happier than hell
that you want him dead.* "I want answers."

"He'll never talk."

"He will when I get through with him." Kneeling on the
soiled rug, I marshalled my strength, and turned inwards.
There was my mind: not an Arkslsnaglian magnetic field,
but neater than a Terran radiator. Across it—under it—
around and through and in it—was a slimy cord, like a
rope left too long in water. I came out.

"Does he have some kind of mental power?" I asked her.

"Yes." She nodded like a windup doll. "He can force
people to obey him."

"Ah." Wonder how Lomala missed it . . . explains a
lot, though. Back in. Look at the rope. Sniff it. Yes. Catkill-

235

er's. Back off a pace; get angry at the way he commanded so effortlessly. Let the anger b-*u-i*-L-D to a sizzling boil and then! The restraint was gone. Only its odor lingered.

Now I could go for his mind. There—disconnect him from his nerves; agony ends and he stirs. His thoughts bite through me. He senses my closeness and wriggles. Disconnect him from his muscles before he can apply his power. Hah! Knowing his paralysis, he fears.

Now. Turn him slowly. Inspect him closely. Oh, what's this? Damn. That's *interesting*. Maybe valuable, too, so make a note of where they are. And that, over there. Could it be—prod it, hear the echoes reverberate. That's his power. Too bad, Catkiller.

He makes the noise flies would when small boys rip off their wings.

It's an appropriate noise.

And now to wad him up. Roll the vast snowflake of his mind into a ball. Hear him plead. Ignore him.

Take the ball . . . ah, yes, thank you, Obben. And you, Edgar Allan. Place it in a cranny and put a wall around it. -You're supposed to say, "For the love of God, Bander Snatch!"-

Silence.

So I finished the wall.

"He's done," I told Shana. "His power's destroyed."

"Then his orders should fade away . . . but they haven't. They're still inside me. I still have to obey." Her eyes were infested with despair. "C— I can't say it. He said I have to call you Bandy. Always."

I was tired, and hurting, and my muscles were so stiff they were practically frozen, but when she inserted the gun barrel into her mouth I found the strength to bat it away. "No," I said, pulling her to the floor.

She was an ice statue. "Don't, Ban—dy, don't. I'll have to defend myself. He told me I had to. Please."

"That's not what I want," I lied. "I'm just trying to tell you: wait. Be tough. I'll get you out of this eventually."

A fledgling smile parted her lips. "Even if it takes another six years?"

V

We were in Marianne's HQ the next morning. She invited us for a celebratory drink, but her real reason surfaced before the fizz had settled. She wanted the shipments.

"I know what happened to them," offered Shana, "but I've been bound to secrecy."

Marianne's eyes widened, then swiftly narrowed. Not understanding the situation, she was enraged. Her throat swelled. Her voice was harsh. Her obscenities were thought-provoking.

I couldn't blame her. She figured Shana was doing her—maybe to get me back in power—while she was hanging desperately to the sweep hand of the here-and-now. Few people who lost their grip on it landed safely, especially if they'd been Jungle Lords. Too many grudges were borne.

Her rifle pinned us in our seats and its safety clicked off. She was stammering an ultimatum when I eased the barrel to one side. "She'd like to tell you, Marianne, but Catkiller snarled her mind. Hold on. I'll see if I can't shake something loose."

I'd done a similar trick with Torikowski, but his mind had been forced into an unnatural pattern against his will. Remembered opposition had encouraged the resumption of its former shape.

With Shana it was different. Catkiller's talent was that he made you *want* to obey: you didn't argue when he told you snow was black, because you forgot all about white. So the subverted mind relished the shapes into which it contorted

237

itself . . . and hated with the fury of a blast furnace any-one who said, "Hey, you're upside down."

I wrapped us in my shield, and told Shana to recall every detail of the shipments. By the time I'd crawled through the brambles that barricaded her mind, one section of it was pulsing ruby red.

It was the Gordian knot all over, with the added stipulation that I had to leave behind an uncut rope, not a fluffy pile of chopped hemp.

I returned to awareness to tell Marianne that it would take a while—and tó finish my drink—then resubmerged. Crosslegged, I stared at the miserable tangle for eons.

At last I tugged on a loop. It fell free. I poked at another. A third. And so on. Perhaps the most irritating thing I'd ever done, it was also the most painstaking. I felt as clumsy as a double amputee threading a needle.

Nausea was a major hindrance. Every time I broke one of Catkiller's bonds, every time I moved a mind loop away from where he'd positioned it, I evoked his image. Her entire mind was impregnated with it. His voice echoed faintly; his face leered with Satanic delight. Not one to separate business and pleasure, he had delivered many of his instructions while riding my Shana.

When I emerged, Shana was looking at me curiously. Marianne was openly disgusted. "What the hell's the matter with you two?" she bitched. "We've been trying to wake you up for the last eight hours, and you didn't so much as fucking *blink*!"

"Sorry," I told her. "It was incredibly complex."

"Yeah," she snorted. "Got an answer for me?"

"Shana?"

"The shipments? Sure." She flashed a smile I knew was reserved for me. "Hairless moved them right through his warehouse onto freighters for Baja California. When they came back—skipping Customs because of the Jungle's autonomy—they were loaded with sand, heroin, and illegal aliens. Catkiller fed the pretty ones to his tumbler trainers. The others paid him a percentage of their salaries every week."

Marianne leaned back and toyed with the magazine of her rifle. The news had altered her picture of events—as Jungle Lord, she should have known all those details, but she hadn't—and she needed time to find a new perspective. At last, she sighed. The front legs of her chair thumped down. "And the crinkly he got?"

238

Shana shrugged. "He spent it all."

"On what?"

"Two nuclear bombs."

HQ was suddenly a deep-freeze. "What the hell for?" whispered Marianne.

"Blackmail—he was going to demand a billion dollars from Big Unk."

"Would that work?" she asked me.

"No doubt about it." I frowned. "With his talent, though, he could have gotten the Secretary of the Treasury to write him a check. . . . I don't know, maybe he wanted to give the politicians justification for passing it over."

"That was it," agreed Shana.

"Jee-zus." Marianne shook her head as if to break through cobwebs. "Where are the bombs now?"

Shana scratched the tip of her nose. "I don't know."

I broke in with, "Some of his people should. 'Course I'm going to uncork him tomorrow morning—Big Unk has a few questions for him—but if you could get his people to talk to you *first* . . ."

This time she smiled. A lupine hunger flitted across her face. Her square, rough hands caressed the stock of her rifle. "I think we can," she said softly. "I think a lot of people will kiss my ass for the chance to tell me." Abruptly, she slammed the full clip into the rifle, and levered a round into the chamber. "I'll bet they'll be dying to talk."

They were. Dozens of them. All former associates of Catkiller, some had been powerful inside the Jungle, others influential outside it. Now they were scared. They talked and they talked and they talked.

But none more than Catkiller himself.

He was in the hospital ward of the Ashtabula County Jail. There were too many people in the small room— Dourscheid, Gastine, Marianne, Shana, the FBI, Leah, myself—bumping shoulders, commenting on the noxious odor, adjusting the taping equipment, and wondering.

"Go ahead, Bander Snatch," said Dourscheid.

I looked at the vegetable on the water bed. He seemed shrunken, younger, and . . . somehow . . . innocent. "You sure you want him awake?"

"Got no choice," said Dourscheid. "So many people want him just like he is that we've *got* to wake him to find out what they've been doing."

"All right." Shana and Marianne held my arms. I opened my shield. Bright bitter thoughts from a thousand

239

directions spattered against me. I struck like lightning; hit the wall around his mind like a battering ram; retracted instantly. My knees collapsed, but the women kept me from falling. "He's open," I gasped. "Help yourselves."

The slate-gray eyes parted. Catkiller shook himself, stretched, appeared to fill out. With an easy motion, he sat up in bed. The old air of command clung to him, like the smell of smoke in a burned-out building. "Jail, huh?" His eyes fell on Dourscheid. "Nice to see you, Major. Get me my clothes and unlock that door."

"Neg that." The major laughed, and shook his head. "You're on ice."

"I said, GET ME MY—" And then it hit him. Looking from face to face, he realized that his power was gone. That he couldn't force anybody to obey him, not now, not ever. That whatever he'd had was gone, and that whatever he'd been, he'd never be again.

There was torment in his eyes. Then hatred. Then he went for me, but Marianne's rifle butt swatted him out of the air.

Huddled on the floor, he aged. The life went out of him. The charisma shriveled into dust and blew away.

"Please," he whispered. "Please?"

I left then. They told me later that once the questions started, he'd answered. And volunteered. And babbled.

Big Unk never did find the nukes, even though Leah, the FBI, the CIA, the DIA, the NRC, and eight other alphabet soups looked for them. Marianne couldn't find them, either. Nor could the Baja California separatists, who circulated around the fringes of the group. After about two months, each group grew convinced that one of the other groups had already located them, and was keeping quiet for reasons of its own. So then they started spying on each other, and on themselves, and on everybody connected with the whole business. The search tapered off because the seekers were tailing seekers who were themselves tailing seekers . . . it was almost like a comic opera, but they were all too involved to laugh.

I retreated to my house. BB welcomed me, and made friends with Shana immediately. Janice was haughty, and a bit possessive. It irked her to see me showering attention on Shana. For the first few days, sparks flew whenever they were in the same room. After a while, though, she began to realize that my love life wasn't impairing my performance as an ombudsman, which improved her attitude immensely. I still thought, however, that she'd have been happier if I had been celibate.

In the meantime, I arranged for little Kathie to have an interview at Lomala. And followed up on the Torikowski case. And fretted over a hundred other things as well.

"Your life's too complicated, Ban-*n*." Shana grimaced at the effort she'd needed to keep from saying, "Bandy." "You'd better get back in my head soon; there's a lot in there that needs fixing."

"I will, I will," I promised, "but it'll take time." Time? My God, Catkiller'd played with her for six years. Straightening out all the tangles would be like unweaving a medieval tapestry. But I'd do it. For sure I'd do it. Until then, I'd be sharing her attentions, and I do not believe in coexisting with ghosts.

"Well, you'd better get to it quickly."

"Why?"

"The afterglow is fading, Ban-*n,* and I want a brighter picture."

"Of what?" I asked.

"Of you!" She came over to me, and ruffled my hair. "It's really nice to know what you're like . . . it's good to have your, uh, your . . . your *soul* inside my head, where I can feel it whenever I'm lonely."

"My—" Catching on, I nodded. I don't know why, but it always comes as a shock to realize that I've left a print of myself behind. "Hey—listen there, Snow Tiger—once we've got the last of that mess cleaned up, you're gonna have me in your head all the time."

Her eyes clouded. "You think my TP—"

"Yeah." I didn't think, I knew. I'd felt it. "It's there, Snow Tiger—gagged, staked out hand and foot, buried under Catkiller's perversions—but it's there. It's alive. And when we scrape away the shit, you'll be able to use it again. You can join me any time you want."

"Even through your shield?"

"I'll give you a key. No matter where we are, no matter what we're doing, you'll be able to get in. It'll be like a . . . a passport, y'know?"

She smiled at the simile, and kissed me on the forehead. "Thanks."

"For what?"

"For the hope. That's what you do best, you know."

"Hope?"

"No." She shook her head gently. "You give other people a chance—a reason—to hope."

I waved off her flattery. My ego's big enough; it doesn't need a lather of bullshit to feel good. But Shana I pulled closer. *Her,* my ego needs.

So the good guy gets the girl in the end. It's nice when life parallels art—or at least, it looks nice in these crisp black letters. Maybe that's what art is all about: taking the fantastic elements of life, wiping the shit and the dried blood off them, and finding a neat, logical order in which to write out what's left.

Shame you can't live it that way.

But Shana's free. If I didn't reach the scene of the crime in time to save her honor, well, she didn't have much to start with . . . and besides, nobody else was willing and able to slay the dragon.

And St. George is now a nova antibureaucrat, charging into battle with his tape-slicing sword. I break up power centers whenever I can. Enough thrones have risen; enough men have tried to play despot. I'm doing my best to deflate them before they get too puffed on their own importance.

That makes me a well-hated man, in certain circles. That was inevitable from the start. As long as they come at me singly, though, it's okay. But if they ever get together, and start to convince Big Unk to strip me of my authority, well . . . it'll probably be time to tell them who found Catkiller's nukes.

Oh, yeah—the Jungle kid I gave my card to? He's out back, begging Baby Bear to give him a ride. BB has insisted that he take a bath, first.

I wonder who's gonna win.

ABOUT THE AUTHOR

KEVIN O'DONNELL, JR. was born in Cleveland, Ohio, in 1950 and studied at Yale University, where he majored in Chinese studies. He has lived in Korea, Taiwan and Hong Kong and traveled throughout the Orient. He began writing in 1972, and his short fiction has been published in almost every science fiction magazine, as well as some mystery magazines. A full-time writer, O'Donnell lives with his wife, Kim, in New Haven, Connecticut. This is his first novel.

OUT OF THIS WORLD!

That's the only way to describe Bantam's great series of science fiction classics. These space-age thrillers are filled with terror, fancy and adventure and written by America's most renowned writers of science fiction. Welcome to outer space and have a good trip!

☐	11392	**STAR TREK: THE NEW VOYAGES 2** by Culbreath & Marshak	$1.95
☐	13179	**THE MARTIAN CHRONICLES** by Ray Bradbury	$2.25
☐	12753	**STAR TREK: THE NEW VOYAGES** by Culbreath & Marshak	$1.95
☐	11502	**ALAS BABYLON** by Pat Frank	$1.95
☐	13006	**A CANTICLE FOR LEIBOWITZ** by Walter Miller, Jr.	$2.25
☐	12673	**HELLSTROM'S HIVE** by Frank Herbert	$1.95
☐	12454	**DEMON SEED** by Dean R. Koontz	$1.95
☐	12044	**DRAGONSONG** by Anne McCaffrey	$1.95
☐	11835	**DRAGONSINGER** by Anne McCaffrey	$1.95
☐	11599	**THE FARTHEST SHORE** by Ursula LeGuin	$1.95
☐	11600	**THE TOMBS OF ATUAN** by Ursula LeGuin	$1.95
☐	11609	**A WIZARD OF EARTHSEA** by Ursula LeGuin	$1.95
☐	12005	**20,000 LEAGUES UNDER THE SEA** by Jules Verne	$1.50
☐	11417	**STAR TREK XI** by James Blish	$1.50
☐	12655	**FANTASTIC VOYAGE** by Isaac Asimov	$1.95
☐	02517	**LOGAN'S RUN** by Nolan & Johnson	$1.75

Buy them at your local bookstore or use this handy coupon for ordering:

Bantam Books, Inc., Dept. SF, 414 East Golf Road, Des Plaines, Ill. 60016

Please send me the books I have checked above. I am enclosing $_____
(please add 75¢ to cover postage and handling). Send check or money order
—no cash or C.O.D.'s please.

Mr/Mrs/Miss_____

Address_____

City_____State/Zip_____

SF—8/79

Please allow four weeks for delivery. This offer expires 12/79.

FANTASY AND SCIENCE FICTION FAVORITES

Bantam brings you the recognized classics as well as the current favorites in fantasy and science fantasy. Here you will find the beloved Conan books along with recent titles by the most respected authors in the genre.

☐	10031	NOVA Samuel R. Delany	$1.75
☐	12680	TRITON Samuel R. Delany	$2.25
☐	11718	DHALGREN Samuel R. Delany	$2.25
☐	11950	ROGUE IN SPACE Frederic Brown	$1.75
☐	12018	CONAN THE SWORDSMAN #1 DeCamp & Carter	$1.95
☐	12706	CONAN THE LIBERATOR #2 DeCamp & Carter	$1.95
☐	12031	SKULLS IN THE STARS: Solomon Kane #1 Robert E. Howard	$1.95
☐	11139	THE MICRONAUTS Gordon Williams	$1.95
☐	11276	THE GOLDEN SWORD Janet Morris	$1.95
☐	11418	LOGAN'S WORLD William Nolan	$1.75
☐	11835	DRAGONSINGER Anne McCaffrey	$1.95
☐	12044	DRAGONSONG Anne McCaffrey	$1.95
☐	10879	JONAH KIT Ian Watson	$1.50
☐	12019	KULL Robert E. Howard	$1.95
☐	10779	MAN PLUS Frederik Pohl	$1.95
☐	12269	TIME STORM Gordon R. Dickson	$2.25

Buy them at your local bookstore or use this handy coupon for ordering:

Bantam Book Catalog

Here's your up-to-the-minute listing of over 1,400 titles by your favorite authors.

This illustrated, large format catalog gives a description of each title. For your convenience, it is divided into categories in fiction and non-fiction—gothics, science fiction, westerns, mysteries, cookbooks, mysticism and occult, biographies, history, family living, health, psychology, art.

So don't delay—take advantage of this special opportunity to increase your reading pleasure.

Just send us your name and address and 50¢ (to help defray postage and handling costs).